Finding My Olympia

A NOVEL

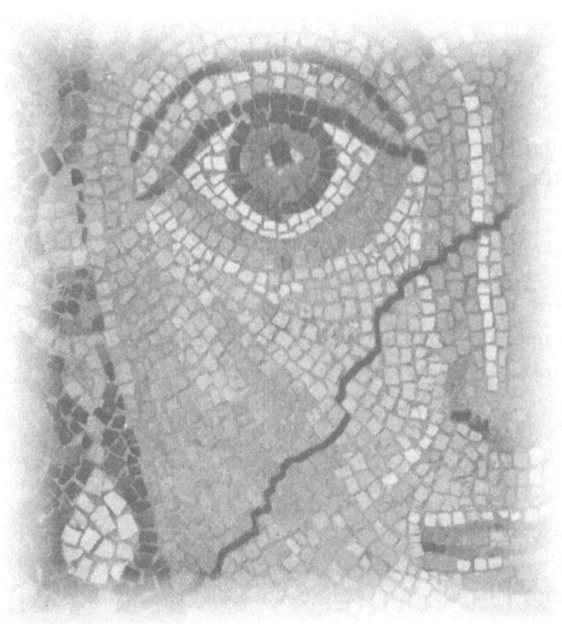

Nancy Econome

Published by Kafeneon Productions

Contact: nancyeconome.com

Finding My Olympia Paperback: ISBN 978-1-7344288-2-7
Finding My Olympia e-book ISBN: 978-1-7344288-3-4

Front cover: Original image via the Met Museum, New York
Fragment of a Floor Mosaic with a Personification of Ktisis; 500–550, with modern restoration. On view at The Met Fifth Avenue in Gallery 301.
The bejeweled woman, holding the measuring tool for the Roman foot, is identified by the restored Greek inscription as Ktisis, a figure personifying the act of generous donation or foundation.

Chapter Logo Original Art
Camera chapter logo original image credit:
© Kameraprojekt Graz 2015 / Wikimedia Commons / License: CC-BY-SA 4.0
Rolling Pin Whisk Chapter Logo Original Image: AdobeStock_349896483
Rosemary Chapter Logo Original Image: istock-1163580541
Credit: Alisa Pravotorova

Book Design: Happenstance Type-O-Rama
Cover Design: Nancy Econome
Additional cover graphics: Allyson Pirenian

www.nancyeconome.com

For my sister Janet,
with thanks for a lifetime of love, support,
determination and brilliance.

AUTHOR'S NOTE AND TRIGGER WARNING

This fictional story touches on themes of loss, grief, resilience and references to sexual assault. These topics may be sensitive for some readers.

ONE

Olympia's Diary

I'm alone and I have no idea where they've taken me. I'm a prisoner in a world that craves my beauty but couldn't care less about finding me. But why should they? I'm just an immigrant girl who dropped out of high school with the skills of a seamstress. I write my thoughts on these scraps of paper, hoping to quiet my fears.

I've been afraid before. Alone before. When I was thirteen, I was plucked from my Greek village, motherless, deposited in the small town of Woodland, California. I never blended in — although God knows I tried. My olive skin and long black hair kept me from the circles of respectable girls. Now I hardly feel Greek anymore. I am certainly not American.

I wish my family could help find me, but my Uncle Stavros only yearns to return to the simple village life in Greece. He's busy with his bakery and other not-so-legal business activities. And the other well-meaning Greek men who live with him. Well, they would be little use in finding me. They can hardly navigate daily American life.

My only hope is my sister Yianna. She is strong, younger and yes, much more American than I am. She charges ahead and doesn't fear shame like I was taught in Greece. I dream our bond as sisters will somehow draw her near. Or just maybe the power of our matching Evil Eye bracelets will pull her close and rescue me.

TWO

A week after Olympia's disappearance, Yianna had carefully washed and ironed her sister's apron, hopeful she would walk through the door any minute. After six months, the lifeless apron dangling in the bakery kitchen was a stinging reminder that her sister had not come home.

She tried to make sense of Olympia's absence, but chaos was the only word that floated into her mind. She had looked up the word in the high school library. To the ancient Greeks, Chaos was the emptiness, the abyss, the void before the world came into being. That was life now, a deep void where Olympia had been. To stop the aching, Yianna vowed she would search until she found her sister. No one else seemed to be doing the job. Especially the sheriff.

Just before Olympia vanished, Yianna remembered the two of them crowding around the Christmas dinner table surrounded by Uncle Stavros and the three old Greek men who rented rooms behind the bakery. Then, by the Monday after Christmas 1954, Olympia was gone. She simply vanished while walking home from work at Mira's Tailor Shop, at least that's what the sheriff wanted them to believe. His skimpy report said there were no solid leads, that Olympia had probably met a man and left with him. Yianna was sure Olympia did not seek a man's attention. Her sister would rather spend an afternoon digging in the garden, weaving on her loom or observing the movements of local birds than spending time with a man.

Ten years older than eighteen-year-old Yianna, Olympia filled the space their mother should have occupied. Now Olympia was erased from Yianna's life just like both her parents had been. One thing Yianna was certain of: her sister would never leave her. They had suffered too much together.

Olympia was decidedly Greek, down to her delicately accented English and her lowered eyes in the presence of men. Yianna, however, was American first and then Greek in that order.

By the time Yianna was a teenager, there was no older Greek woman in the family to teach her how to serve coffee when male visitors arrived or how to take the smallest piece of chicken on the platter. Yianna was the one who lugged around a camera and snapped photos everywhere she went.

Yianna had not sensed the coming danger to Olympia, not even a hint from the Evil Eye bracelets she and Olympia wore around their wrists. No warning from the thick coffee grounds slathered inside the cracked cup from which the local Greek lady told fortunes. No one seemed to know where Olympia was. Or no one was telling.

THREE

So, this is America in 1939? *Agh!*

Stavros lifted his feet from the sticky tiled floor in the murky Greyhound bus station and searched for a clean spot. Glancing about the terminal he was disappointed. This was no warmhearted welcome to America. Shouldn't this station be tidier than that grimy steamship on which he and his two nieces had just immigrated from Greece to New York? If Stavros had kept this lowly state of cleanliness in his own bakery in Argos, his customers would have never bought a loaf.

Not having a proper bath in more than a week was a problem for a man like him. He had always been a sweet-smelling gentleman in his village. Mustache trimmed just so. Stavros chaffed as he stepped down from the train that brought Olympia, Yianna and him across the country in five relentless days. He quietly congratulated himself on the success of providing meals, wiping noses and acting like the rock on which his thirteen and three-year-old nieces could depend, if only temporarily.

Stavros was at a loss only when little Yianna sobbed to convulsions, having left behind the rag doll handmade by her mother, his late sister-in-law. He took her hand silently, angry with his inability to quiet this willful child. What did Stavros know of dolls and mothers anyway? That was too much to ask of a bachelor. He finally spotted an ice cream vendor and bought the girl a melting ice cream bar to quiet her hysterics.

He couldn't really blame Yianna. Her mother Angeliki had been like a candle at their little St. Anthony Greek Orthodox church, one minute burning brightly, the next minute pinched to smoke and ash. She had suddenly died from typhoid fever only weeks before they were to board the steamship to America. After a miserable two-week quarantine, Stavros had no choice but to transport the two girls to his brother, Christos, their father, who lived in California. Now, after three weeks of traveling on a ship, a train and now a bus, he simply wanted this final leg of the journey to be over. *Amesos!* Now!

His original life's plan was to forever live in his small village home, to make joyful love to women and to bake perfect loaves with crusty tops and soft interiors. In Argos, Stavros had been a man of standing. A baker, an artist, revered for the texture and flavor of his bread. Friends and neighbors walked into his bakery hungry but waltzed out satisfied, their empty stomachs tamed by his fresh-baked treasures. Who could want for more? Stavros had crossed his fingers behind his back when he told his brother he would stay in America. He would do so — at least temporarily. It was a known fact in Argos that Stavros had a mind of his own.

Before the journey to America, he took great effort to learn important English words from his old friend Yorgos. They had played backgammon together nearly every evening in their village taverna, *O Chopánis*, The Shepherd, on the few nights when Stavros was not with a woman. But when his brother Christos finally sent money to buy steamship passage for his wife Angeliki, Olympia, Yianna and himself, Stavros began studying the phrases in earnest, small buoys that might help him navigate the sea of English he knew would soon overwhelm him.

Christos had decided the family would move to America, their safe, new home before another big war erupted in Greece. Christos had ears for everything political. Stavros depended on him for that since he himself rarely paid attention to politics. Stavros obeyed his brother because he owed Christos his life.

But now here in America, Stavros instantly felt like a stupid foreigner. He presented a note to the train porter which displayed the hand-printed sentence, "Need directions for bus to Woodland." Stavros could only hope the writer of the message, a fellow Greek train passenger, had scrawled it correctly.

"W-w-where?" Stavros sputtered to the porter, rolling his *r* and raising his eyebrows to act out the question. He also had learned to say: *how much*, *thank you*, *can I have* and *sorry*. Stavros mused he might need the *sorry* after a bar fight, considering his quick temper.

"Where?" He tried his best to avoid eye contact with this important man. The porter tilted back his cap in the blistering Sacramento midday sun and read the note. Dressed in his blue wool uniform, sweat beading on his forehead like bubbles, the porter scanned Stavros and the two children he dragged along. Stavros watched his eyes linger a little too long on his beat-up hat and the girls' worn, homemade shoes. Then, with a sigh, the porter simply pointed in a southerly direction.

"Than' you!" Stavros energetically headed toward the bus station, his nieces barely keeping pace with his steps. He was grateful Olympia was sufficiently knowledgeable in feminine ways to handle bathrooms and dressing situations with the electric Yianna. The sooner Stavros could deposit his nieces with Christos, the better.

His secret plan was to stay with Christos for a time, assist with setting up a household for Olympia and Yianna and then return to Argos. How could an impending war be as horrible as Christos imagined? As boys, both brothers had witnessed the brutal

Turkish annihilation of Smyrna, surviving by luck and, of course, because of Christos' cleverness. What war could be worse than that massacre?

Stavros owed his life to his brother but believed that Christos approached life too cautiously. His brother had married the beautiful Angeliki at a young age and refused to swig the jug or bet a *drachma* at their local taverna. Then Christos left for America to lock in a secure life for the Diamantopoulos family, always including Stavros.

Stavros grabbed the soft hand of his younger niece but her struggle to keep up convinced him he needed to carry her to make good time to the bus station. From there he would deliver the girls to a farmhouse in Knights Landing, near Woodland, about twenty miles northwest of Sacramento. A letter from Christos which Stavros kept secure in his jacket breast pocket listed the address and walking directions from the bus stop. He felt a little guilty, thinking about the girls like livestock. But little Yianna had jitters in her legs and his patience had been stretched to the limit attempting to keep her in sight.

Olympia was never a problem. She clung to her uncle as they passed groups of businessmen, their wrists weighed down with gold watches and their fingers heavy with pinky rings. Stavros watched her black eyes widen as she took in the young women who were unaccompanied by men right on the street, their hair loose, curls bouncing as they walked to work. Olympia self-consciously touched her rough brown scarf knotted under her chin and looked away from the young American women.

Stavros surveyed downtown Sacramento with a critical eye. He was unsure of his brother's assessment of this new world. He pulled the girls past the brick office buildings, a lonely tamale cart, an empty ice cream parlor with wire-back chairs waiting for customers. He passed restaurants with no outdoor arbor or backyard garden where minstrels could play their *rebetiko* songs. Sacramento held no special charm. But neither had Chicago or New York or any of the cities the train passed through. He might have been wrenched from the small village of Argos, but that did not mean he was devoid of elevated taste. Stavros knew he would forever be searching for a soft landscape with delicate, fragrant spring breezes, or a small cosmopolitan city center with charming restaurants, cafes and fountains. Like Rome, he mused, although he'd only seen a postcard.

But this responsibility, hauling two young girls halfway around the world, was something Stavros never asked for. This immense favor for his brother was thankfully coming to an end. And that suited Stavros just fine.

FOUR

"*Pou eímaste?* Where are we?"

Olympia had rarely strung together a sentence since they arrived in America. But now she was articulating the very question Stavros had been pondering. They had finished their bus journey only to walk half an hour to this place. Stavros, Olympia and an exhausted Yianna stood on the perimeter of a fierce green lawn that surrounded a small farmhouse drenched in dazzling aqua-blue paint.

Like a jewel, the well-kept wooden house was situated in a small grove of walnut trees which shaded the roof from the heat. Stavros could see it was jammed wall-to-wall with people. A few men who had spilled out into the garden were sipping beer from brown bottles. Stavros' energy had faded and he felt like a shirt left too long on the clothesline. The three travelers had consumed only a skimpy breakfast, a slice of hard tack bread and milk for the girls.

He crept closer, with his nieces following his footsteps, feeling uneasy in the midst of this crowd of men and women dressed in stiff black suits and dresses. The screened-in porch burst with faces, hands, plates of food and low chatter. The tempting aroma of *dolmadakia,* grape leaves tightly wrapping rice, sweet onions and herbs, filtered through the screen to the three travelers.

"*Miláneh elliniká!* They're speaking Greek!" Olympia impulsively ran toward the house, pulling Yianna by the hand as if starved for words that sounded like home. But Stavros drew forward slowly, warily. Why should the farmhouse his brother had leased for his family be crowded this time of day?

Inside the screen door, pushing through the bodies wedged together, he halted as if a guard had stopped him. He instantly understood. This was a *makaría*, a funeral luncheon, perhaps for one of the shepherds who worked with Christos. His brother had written about these older men who herded sheep with him in the Sacramento Valley.

From the open front door, Stavros could see Olympia and Yianna circling in the crowded kitchen. The girls slid several *paximathia*, Greek biscotti, from the stack of toasty cookies set on crystal platters and stuffed them in their mouths.

Olympia managed to balance two plates of white sheet cake squares along with two cups of grape juice and a plate of *mezedes*, a variety of Greek appetizers. She was guiding Yianna to a cushion so they could sit apart from the crowd and devour the treats without anyone bothering them. Watching the sisters, Stavros felt like an outsider. Olympia had completely taken charge of Yianna, filling the black void where Yianna's desire for her mother loomed. She wrapped Yianna in her arms, delighting her younger sister in small bites of *kouloura* ring bread and kasseri cheese. Stavros' eyes misted over to see how Olympia had naturally enveloped Yianna in her compassionate, maternal love, but he shifted his focus away from his nieces. He had to push on to find Christos.

A flock of gray-haired women fluttered through the room, offering the men small shot glasses filled with *Metaxá* brandy from silver trays to toast the dead. Stavros desperately searched for his brother's face. He knew Christos was smoking a hand-rolled cigarette grinning with his next big plan, and Stavros couldn't wait to hear it. He'd fly over to his brother and wrap him in a Greek man-hug, with Christos' familiar arms welcoming him to this new life. Still searching for him, Stavros inched nearer the table jammed with platters of fish, rice pilaf, feta cheese and *skourdalia*, the pungent garlic sauce that added a kick to the bland funeral foods.

Then Stavros' eyes dialed in on something. The noise in the room instantly diminished to a soft buzzing sound. Flattened in a black photo frame and surrounded by the stewed beans and a platter of fried fish, was Christos' familiar face. Stavros could not cry out. He could not breathe. He could only spin around and crash through the crowd, dashing down the porch stairs, out to the lawn in the afternoon heat, where he stood gasping for breath.

Christos was the honoree. His brother was the dead man.

Finding a corner in the garden, Stavros heaved again and again. Breathing heavily in the afternoon heat, he grasped a wooden fence post for support. A slim, young mother chased a small group of children in church clothes, warning of danger at every turn.

"Nikos!" Her little son ignored her as she shouted in Greek. "*Prosechseh!* Be careful! That is your good suit!"

Turning to see Stavros she offered a handkerchief hidden beneath her sleeve.

"Did you know Christos?" she asked sweetly. She tucked her dark curls behind her ear, a gesture that, on any other day, Stavros would have thought fetching. Her child was now only a speck on the dusty country road.

"*Neh*, yes!" He sucked in a deep breath. Slowly he exhaled words that seemed to beg help from this stranger.

"*O atherfos mou.* My brother."

The woman motioned toward the porch and instantly a crowd of people poured onto the grassy garden. Stavros was soon drowning in sympathy. Christos' soul should rise and go to heaven. May God rest his soul. May his memory be eternal. But Stavros abruptly peeled away from the crowd. His nieces should not see the photo of their father. Not like this.

Instantly Stavros had become their only living relative within six thousand miles. He must assure his nieces he'd hoist their problems on his back. He would carry their burdens and their lives could sweetly unfold like honey pouring from a jar. Just as Christos had promised him many years ago when they were boys.

But Stavros knew this was a lie. Could he, a bachelor, an artist in the kitchen and in the bedroom, become a father to these two young girls in America, a land so unfamiliar to them all? The weight of the years ahead, until his younger niece was grown and married, slapped him *stah moutra*, across his face.

Stavros was sure the Evil Eye had forced him, the younger, playful brother, only thirty years old, to pay his soul debt all in one swipe — and for decades to come. Or maybe it was a cosmic joke just to keep him in line.

He broke away to find his nieces and tell them.

Their father was dead.

FIVE

Three-year-old Yianna could not make sense of the crowd of women with squishy bosoms and hairnets decorated with tiny colored beads. They pressed too close, making it hard to breathe. They were sorry. So sorry. Did the sisters want to lie down? A handkerchief for tears? A cup of water? A quiet place to pray?

She had only wanted to fill her mouth with a hunk of fluffy white sheet cake and to be left alone. Why were these ladies smelling of lemon and garlic pushing her, breathing too close to her?

Suddenly, Uncle Stavros yanked the cake plate from her hands. She hurriedly stuffed a *paximathi* into her small mouth and locked her eyes onto her sister Olympia's long black hair swaying across her back. She would follow Olympia outside. Her sister would know what to do.

Yianna stood puzzled in the dirt driveway near the house, sun searing her back. Now Olympia was crying, saying they would never see Babá again — just like Mamá. Their mother had, for some reason, floated to heaven. Yianna remembered her sore backside from sitting on the hard wooden bench outside their tiny village church. Her mother's funeral service could not be held inside. No one was allowed inside to get sick like Mamá.

After staring at a lifeless mother lying in a box in front of the priest, Yianna couldn't look anymore. Where had her mother *really* gone? Holy incense smoke swirled all around her, clogging her throat. Three ancient women, every inch wrinkled, teeth just a memory, provided endless high-pitched wailing. The women brushed Yianna's cheek with their shriveled lips but Yianna kept her face stiff to avoid their touch. *How could her mother leave without her?* Her mother would never disappear without her *microula*, her precious younger daughter. Yianna was certain Mamá would come for her soon.

A few weeks after the funeral, Yianna remembered Olympia, tears in her eyes, folding her tiny clothes, placing them into a suitcase. She said they would travel to find their far-away father in a far-away place. Yianna thought of a scratchy beard and the smell of lavender. His photo, hung over the stone fireplace of their house, looked very serious, not like the gentle Babá she remembered. Was he the one who would save them? Or would it be Jesus whose icon hung in the church? With old men telling her what to do, how was she to know?

Yianna set aside her mother's inconvenient trip to heaven. She knew Mamá was really waiting around the corner. Looking almost exactly like Olympia, her mother's black hair would be wrapped in a neat bun atop her head with a tiny gold cross hung around her neck. Yianna knew her mother would scoop up her daughters in her magnificent hug and then walk her them home, swinging arms, chattering all the way. Once inside, standing on the well-swept dirt floor, she would concoct a *glykó portokalioú*, orange sweetwater, her signature maternal magic. She would dip a long-handled silver spoon into orange preserves and drop the sticky spoon into a tall glass of cool water. Yianna and Olympia would sip the sweet confection, lick the spoon and once again become calm in their mother's presence.

But now that Yianna's mother had been dispatched to heaven, she was no longer there to brush Yianna's long hair or make her favorite rice pudding with cinnamon on top. And now, at the farmhouse jammed with strange adults, several men announced that Yianna's father was missing too. Off to heaven where her mother had been harshly exiled. Yianna clutched two spare *paximathia* tight in her fist, wondering why her parents left behind their daughters like forgotten luggage on the curb.

Only Olympia remained. Someone she could count on staying put and not trotting off to heaven like their parents. Yianna loved her Olympia, who fetched figs and berries just to cheer her up. Olympia who, attempting to hide tears streaming down her own cheeks, played hand games with Yianna to keep her from sobbing for her mother.

Since her mother's funeral, Yianna walked behind Olympia every day holding the hem of her sister's skirt. Olympia's hair smelled like rosemary and lavender, just like their mother's. And Olympia sang the folk song their mother had always sung. The song told the story of sixty brave Greek women who, after the Ottomans invaded Greece, danced off a cliff, many with their children, leading them to death rather than risk being captured and made slaves – or worse.

The sorrowful tune haunted Yianna's memory. She could recognize any part of the song and instantly know her mother was nearby, waiting for her.

> *Farewell poor world,*
> *Farewell sweet life,*
> *and you, my wretched country,*
> *Farewell forever*
>
> *Farewell springs,*
> *Valleys, mountains and hills*
> *Farewell springs*
> *And you, women of Souli*

The fish cannot live on the land
Nor the flower on the sand
And the women of Souli
Cannot live without freedom
Farewell springs

The women of Souli
Have not only learnt how to survive
They also know how to die
Not to tolerate slavery
Farewell springs.

Before they left for America, Yianna watched Olympia's capable hands fashion a make-shift doll from old socks filled with sawdust to replace the lost doll her mother had created. Olympia was Yianna's mother now. Only Olympia, no one else, would do from that moment on.

SIX

Olympia's Diary

When I was twelve, my parents told me America would be "a better place" than our home in Greece. My sweet mother Angeliki had dreamed up joyful songs about America, trying to convince me of the happiness our family would find there. But I firmly believed our family did not need to wander to some unknown land like a flock of migrating geese.

My mother spoke with awe, as if our Babá was Alexander the Great, staking out a new territory of riches for our family. Just because we pulled our vegetables from the gravelly soil instead of a modern store shelf did not mean our family needed to be saved. We had afthonía, *an abundance, to eat and an overflow of cousins, aunts and uncles bursting from every village door.*

But I loved our Babá who was a tall, slim man with eyes like the black ink from the squid we cleaned for Sunday dinner. Each night Babá encircled Yianna and me with tight hugs and planted kisses on our cheeks. We were my father's perfect daughters who, he always said, would become brilliant women to help move civilization along. "We men need it!"

At that time, I was unsure what he meant. Now I understand.

SEVEN

Stavros sat on the stairs of the aqua-colored farmhouse for what seemed to be hours, his head in his hands. Mercifully, the last straggling mourners finally slammed the screen door and drove away in their dusty pickup truck. Stavros was alone with Olympia and Yianna who sat on orange metal chairs with rusted, scalloped edges. Yianna soon clomped across on the porch dragging her doll, insisting Olympia take her home. Stavros had to tell his young nieces that although their world had changed, he would be there to guide them.

With no idea how to proceed, Stavros turned to find three middle-aged Greek men standing nearby, dressed in out-of-style, threadbare versions of church clothes. Each wore a small glass vessel hanging on a leather string around his neck containing a tiny spoonful of Greek soil dug from his village garden. Many Greek immigrants wore such an amulet in case they perished before traveling back to the homeland. If they died in America, they could be buried under a bit of Greek dirt. Christos had rejected wearing one, forcefully declaring he would never return to a life of village poverty. He'd stick to his plan for a prosperous future. Stavros never hung Greek soil around his neck for the opposite reason, certain he would soon return to Argos.

The three men stood as if glued together, like choir boys, waiting for Stavros to respond. But he sat listlessly, distracted. Finally, he felt strong hands on his shoulders, rocking him, as if to wake him from this cruel dream.

"Stavros!"

The three men helped him stagger into the house and laid him on the worn sofa they must have found on the side of the road. The slim dark-haired man dressed in a thin white shirt bent over him, speaking loudly.

"*Keeta*! Look! I am Agamemnon. And he is Timoleon. And him—Panayotis, but we call him Lucky. And you will stay with us. All of you." Agamemnon seemed to be the leader. He tilted his head toward Olympia and Yianna. "We make room."

"We work the sheeps with Christos. Just north of here. May his memory be eternal." Timoleon made the sign of the cross with his three fingers flying across his body. His upper lip was as furry as a dead squirrel. Behind eyeglasses with unfashionable frames, his hound dog eyes were kind and sad at the same time. Next to Timoleon, barely five feet tall, Lucky filled a glass with water and silently handed it to Stavros. The three scraped the wooden floor with chairs as they pulled in close.

"Always room for fellow Greeks. And if you are Christos' brother, you will stay here like you are Christos himself." Agamemnon sat back in his chair.

Stavros peered through the screen door at his nieces outside. They looked even lonelier than he felt. Here they were in a world without language, without parents, without home.

Inside, the four men looked at each other wondering how to reassure the girls after their father's death. Stavros had no paternal instincts but braced himself like a Greek Evzone soldier ready to fight. Sucking in a breath, ready to approach Olympia, he felt the presence of the three Greek shepherds behind him.

"We go together," Agamemnon announced and Timoleon and Lucky bobbed their heads in silent agreement.

These men walked step by step with him. They had no wives or families and no experience comforting young girls about grave matters. But Stavros suddenly felt calm, as if they were herding him and his flock to a better place, a safer pasture.

Grappling for the right words to soothe his nieces, he reeled back to a day when he was only thirteen years old himself. The moment he was ripped away from his childhood and forced to accept the world as a spiteful place where adults could not be trusted to stay alive and raise their children.

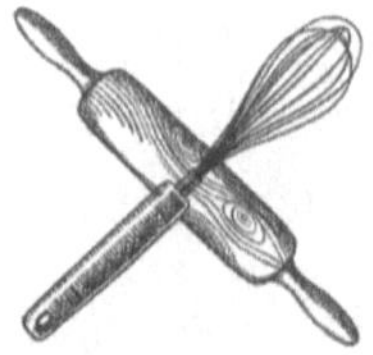

EIGHT

Christos and Stavros were born in Smyrna, an enchanting metropolis on a gulf perched on the western Aegean shore of what now is Turkey. In Smyrna 1922, people felt enriched by each other's culture—their food, their dress, their liquor, their music and especially their languages. The boys learned Greek, Turkish and French at their ancient wooden school desks and they could easily communicate with most of Smyrna's inhabitants.

The brothers loved roaming the narrow stone-paved streets, peeking in shop windows, walking under awnings and running near the docks busy with freighters and fishermen. The two boys raced on the shoreline crowded with women dressed in the latest fashions, many carrying extravagant parasols and handbags. They had memorized every family business, those that sold thick hand-tied carpets of crimson and blue, brass cooking vessels or rare spices and hand-picked herbs. Sometimes they simply walked arm in arm through the marketplace.

Vendors who knew their parents treated the boys to a crunchy *kadaifi* pastry dripping with syrup or a *pasteli*, a crispy sesame and honey treat. Around one corner they found Armenian flat bread with creamy, garlicky *babaganoush,* eggplant dip, to slather on top. Down another alley the brothers would indulge in Turkish Delight, the soft, chewy candy infused with lemon or orange. The Greeks practically owned the fruit market with its mounds of ripe pears, grapes, quince, lemons and figs. In Smyrna they lived in their own *cosmos* in the true ancient Greek meaning – a world in perfect order.

Stavros' family had owned a jewelry store in Smyrna for generations, *Olympos Kosmímata,* Jewels of Olympus. His brother Christos was, of course, expected to take over the business as the elder son. Theodoros Diamantopoulos, their father, was in the process of teaching him, and Stavros on occasion, how to measure the clarity of a stone, the techniques to spot fake jewels and how to calculate the price of gold.

Theodoros wanted to pass down to his sons how to pound gold into a luxurious work of art to be worn on a finger for a lifetime. Christos shared his father's agile fingers and discriminating eye for sculpting molds and setting stones. Theodoros often repeated their family's purpose was to make jewelry for the gods themselves and that's how the store was named.

Their jewelry store occupied a corner in the Greek section, not far from the Greek Orthodox Cathedral Church of Saint Photini with its lofty marble bell tower. The boys lived with the confidence that the future of the jewelry business was as bright as the diamonds their father polished.

A native of Smyrna, the boy's mother Dimitra could speak Persian, Armenian and Turkish as well as her native Greek. She instructed the boys on treating customers of all ethnic backgrounds with respect. She was the perfect hostess for the family shop. Dimitra would often model a string of pearls or a gold chain around her lovely neck surrounded by her dark, wavy hair so a young suitor could evaluate how his gift would look on his *nifi*, his future bride. Dimitra would take her leave of the shop in the late morning to roast a lamb or stuff tomatoes with rice, onions and spices for dinner upstairs in the family's apartment. The four Diamantopoulos family members circled their chairs around the sturdy, square wooden table and nourished themselves from the bounty that Smyrna markets offered. Young Stavros truly believed their family bond, the four together, was unbreakable. Theodoros, Dimitra, Christos and Stavros joined hands around the table and thanked God they were blessed.

No sweeter summer days were spent than those frittered away by the brothers riding one bicycle together, young Stavros balanced on the handlebars, Christos steering as they negotiated crowded streets. They were only three years apart in age, yet Stavros felt they were twins. Whatever game Christos enjoyed became Stavros' favorite. Whatever food appealed to Christos, Stavros sang its praises. Christos led and Stavros happily followed. Rarely a quarrel. Christos was everything good in the world.

"Stavros, we will make a plan and stick with it," Christos was known to say in his easy but serious manner. He had mapped the future for both of them. He would take over the family business. Stavros would become the traveling salesman, presenting Christos' handmade jewelry to mainland Greece, Turkey, Italy and beyond.

The city of Smyrna always seemed to be the center of a tug of war between Greece and Turkey, usually ending in terror or death for thousands. After World War I, decisions and treaties had granted Smyrna and the land near it to Greece. But the Turks were intent on removing the Greeks, Armenians and other Christians from their homes. In the forced-march genocide in 1915, they had already exterminated more than one and a half million Armenians from the Ottoman Empire. Then it was time to cleanse Smyrna for the purpose of establishing Islam as the only religion throughout Turkey.

Although their parents' business was bustling, the Turkish government was becoming inhospitable to Greeks because of their Christian faith. But the Diamantopoulos family's ancestors had lived in Smyrna for hundreds of years. This was their home, and of course, it would be for generations to come. Their friends were a loosely woven network of Armenian, Jewish, Italian, and Turkish families who also had established homes. But as days and weeks unspooled after World War I, small events chipped away at their safe cosmopolitan world.

Content in their peaceful but lively community, Stavros' parents had not paid attention. They could not perceive that Smyrna, the pearl of the Near East, could be crushed to dust and left to blow away in the wind. A crumbling began with a curfew. Then the government required a percentage of the profit from Jewels of Olympus over and above the taxes.

Christos usually protected his younger brother from the tougher boys in their Greek quarter. But one day fifteen-year-old Kosta, a hardened neighborhood delinquent, swaggered near Stavros with his broad shoulders and shifty, wandering eyes. Snatching Stavros' pocketknife, Kosta flipped the knife into his own hands and held it against Stavros' gut.

Kosta's neck was thick like a bull's. His tight lips barked his dare. "*Ella, deh!* C'mon stupid. I'm ready for you!"

Stavros held his breath, his eyes wide. His father had made the knife just for him, carving a beautiful handle and inlaying red and blue stones. Suddenly Christos leapt onto the bully's hulking back, pounding him between the shoulder blades like bread dough. Kosta yelped and dropped the knife into the sandy dirt, its handle glittering in the sun. Christos scooped up the knife and rushed to Stavros' side, ushering his brother away.

"We got him!" Stavros chirped as Christos pushed him into a jog, then a sprint to their home. Once inside, they locked the door behind them, catching their breath. They knew their home was their safe sanctuary with loving parents who would always protect them. This enemy had been defeated. But there was another set of tough guys over which the Diamantopoulos family had no power.

In August 1922, one of the best customers, Mr. Najarian, rushed into the store. Stavros' father looked up from rubbing a thick wedding band to a rich golden glow.

"You must leave immediately Mr. Diamantopoulos. Take your children!" A native from northern Armenia, Mr. Najarian had never appeared so deadly serious. "The Turkish army is almost here — only few miles away! Gather all your money and leave immediately. I know some people who can help you. But you must go now! My family and I are leaving today."

"*Pos?* How?" Theodoros scratched his thinning hair and looked around the store that had been in the family for four generations. "How do we take our shop with us? Where would we go? This is our home. And yours!"

"The Greek soldiers return from the war lands in the east." Mr. Najarian whispered hoarsely. "Starved, nearly dead from thirst or ready to die from their wounds. They have been defeated! Do you understand? Defeated! There is no protection for us! This will be Turkish land in a matter of days! Trouble is on its way, on horseback, with fez and guns!"

Theodoros blinked and solemnly thanked Mr. Najarian for the warning. And when the door closed behind his Armenian neighbor, Theodoros flew upstairs to the kitchen where Dimitra was slicing an eggplant to make *moussaka*, eggplant casserole.

"Najarian says we must leave! The Turks are coming and then who knows what?" Through the kitchen doorway, Stavros watched his mother search his father's face, reading his fear. Theodoros began to pace, with creased brow and pursed lips. He pressed his hand to his stomach as if a snake were coiled there, ready to strike.

In the streets, the boys had recently witnessed Greek soldiers stagger into town, bleeding, bedraggled from long days without food and water, their clothes filthy and torn. Soldiers carried the wounded in various directions with no medical attention for anyone.

Stavros had been certain their Turkish friends would do nothing to harm them, a Greek family. So how could such brutality be inflicted on Greek soldiers while his family lived in a world cradled with the rich pleasures in Smyrna? Stavros could not perceive that their community would allow their peaceful, precious city to crumble in an instant. It would not.

The destruction of their international community took less than two weeks.

On Saturday, September 9, 1922, a thousand Turkish troops rode into Smyrna. Stavros and Christos watched shutters, doors and windows slam shut. The boys peeked out from behind a fountain near their home. In minutes, Theodoros' hands pinched Stavros' shoulders and dragged both boys back to the shop.

In the upstairs apartment, Theodoros blocked the wooden doors with Dimitra's enormous mahogany hope chest, the family's only defense. At first Theodoros' every movement was purposeful but soon he melted into confusion. He mumbled aloud that the Turkish soldiers would certainly take the boys. Christos and Stavros were young men now, although slender and not yet tall. The Turks would see them as grown men. That night, Stavros' parents barely glanced at their sons although, later in the evening, Stavros could hear their quiet talk about what to do with the children. Could the boys run fast enough to slip away from the Turks? Could anyone?

For three and a half days the Diamantopoulos family padded quietly around the small living room. Each person nibbled bread in silence not wanting to draw attention to themselves by loud noises or cooking odors. But the waiting was suffocating. Stavros prayed to *Theotokos,* the Virgin Mary, that a cloak of invisibility would shield his family. Theodoros had silenced the extravagant clocks of all sizes and shapes in the jewelry store. Stavros missed the glorious chime, clang and bong that celebrated the breaking of a new hour. The minutes painfully ticked by in the upstairs living quarters as they waited without making a sound.

As the sun rays first cracked the horizon on Wednesday, September 13, Stavros was the first to hear it – a loud roar of voices down the street, approaching closer each second. He lightly touched his father who immediately jumped to his feet. Theodoros tiptoed down a ladder in the back of the house motioning the boys to follow. Once on the main floor, he pulled back a handmade rug to reveal a door to the cellar where Dimitra kept wreaths of garlic, sacks of potatoes, turnips, carrots and jars of peaches and cherries.

Theodoros slid a woven pouch into Christos' back pocket and then practically heaved his sons into the cellar. With one last backward glance, Stavros registered the terror in his father's deep brown eyes. Then Theodoros slammed the cellar door leaving the boys alone in the dark.

Stavros was stricken as if the blood had drained through his feet. Breathing hard, he began to puff, unable to pull air into his lungs. There was no way out. Stavros knew he and his family would die. At that moment, Stavros felt Christos' arm around him, pulling him tight. Christos' arm was quivering, but Stavros sensed his brother's strength. That one motion soothed Stavros' prickly nerves just enough to help him take his next breath. And then the next.

That night both Stavros and Christos were paralyzed with fear. They would not move from the secret place their father had secured for them. The boys had played in this space as small children and it was filled with the familiar smells of garlic, oregano, onion. After hours of waiting, Stavros nodded off to sleep dreaming this was simply one bad, uncomfortable night. Stavros wanted to believe that the next day, his life would return to its steady rhythm.

Then in the black hours of the early morning just before dawn, Stavros heard the front door to the jewelry store crash open. Heavy boots stomped on the wooden floor above them. Stavros clung tightly onto Christos and pressed his head against his brother's wildly beating heart. They heard the driving footfalls of a group men walking back outside the door. One gun shot and then a shrilling scream. Another shot. The sound of bodies dragged across the floor. And then nothing.

The boys did not cry. They did not breathe. Their heartbeats, it seemed, were arrested in their chests. For minutes, maybe hours they waited after the footsteps receded.

In the corner of the cellar, a crack in a skinny door allowed a finger of silver starlight to seep from the outside world and beckon them onward. Through the door, Stavros' mother had swept out the dirt and had flung away the invader mice she killed with her broom. The family had referred to it as the *pontiki-porta*, the mouse-door. An escape! At sixteen and thirteen years old, Christos and Stavros were thin enough to wiggle out through it.

Without a word, Christos shimmied through the gnome-sized door. Stavros followed his brother but was stopped short. As he slid his legs through the opening, his belt hooked on the door frame and suddenly Stavros was trapped at the waist. Christos immediately spotted the trouble and swiftly unhooked the belt with sure hands. He then pulled Stavros through the opening, feet first like a breech baby. Out on the street now, they heard footsteps rushing in their direction while gun shots reverberated off the plaster walls and screams erupted from windows and doors.

Perhaps because of a prayer their parents had murmured before they died, or because they were blessed with the luck of the young and innocent, they fell into the shadows. Or just maybe the Turks were too busy looting treasures from each home and shop they plundered.

The boys ran blindly in the early morning until they rounded a corner and skidded to a dead stop. A dozen bodies lay in bloody heaps, arms over legs, heads rolling free like bocce balls.

The morning's new light was soft and gray like a pigeon's color. Looking closer, Stavros could make out a familiar shape, blood spilling black ooze on the stony streets. He squinted to be positive. Stavros stared at this body's shoes, the shoes his father so carefully polished to present an impeccable image to customers. Then he spied his mother's small shoes beneath it. Eyes wide and his lips open to scream, Stavros felt a hand slide over his mouth and drag him around the corner. Fear froze Stavros. His turn had come.

The strong hand spun Stavros around and then shoved a forearm sideways in Stavros' mouth to silence him. Terrified, Stavros looked up. It was Christos! He thrust his face into Stavros' face, their sweaty foreheads touching. Silently drilling his eyes into Stavros, he seemed to scream: *Skase vlaka! Shut up, you fool!* He yanked Stavros by the collar and they darted away, hugging the buildings for cover.

After an hour of making themselves invisible, they reached the quay near the shoreline as did every other woman and child in Smyrna. Stavros and Christos silently snaked through the keening and crying on the shoreline without attracting much attention. If they did, they understood they would find themselves on a forced march by the Turks out of town with the rest of the men, a deadly end. The boys skulked low and hid themselves among the masses of agony and fear on the quay.

Thousands of people stood crammed together, their bodies forming the dividing line between the city and the black choppy waters. The mobs on the shoreline watched as their beautiful city was set aflame. First the Armenian district, then the Greek part of town and then the buildings near them blistered and burned like kindling. Angry orange and red flames raged. Thick gray smoke poured out of each structure, most of them wooden with a few brick buildings between.

Stavros attempted to block out the screams, the choking smoke, the sobbing and the horror of his skin turning white with ash. His lungs begged for a breath of clean air but were answered with billows of dark smoke rolling over the quay. Sharp explosions as each building was set afire were like bombs exploding while the two brothers waited in the shadows for God or a quick thinking adult to save them. Stavros did not want to believe that no one, no official, no government agent was coming to help. As the hours passed, the thick smoke shielded them from recognition by the Turks as young men who should be marched away or murdered. Weeping women sat in circles while children roamed everywhere, shrieking for their parents or frozen with fear, like statues.

Within hours the entire city was a searing fireball of blinding light. Some women carried their dead children while the injured were moved in every direction with no hope of a doctor. As their throats closed down, choking from the thick, noxious smoke, Christos laid his arm across Stavros' back. Their nostrils burned from the heat and ash. The brothers stood on the shoreline as their parents' bodies, their home, their city, their lives disappeared into smoke before their stinging eyes. Tears only made it worse.

Then Christos broke away and pushed to the water's edge which was now crowded with people attempting to swim to merchant ships in the harbor. Dead bodies floated like logs in the bay. Turning his eyes away, Christos ripped off a part of his shirt and wet it. He handed it to Stavros, showing his younger brother how to use it like a mask while he did without one.

His head twisting in every direction, Christos tried to find a spot for both boys to nestle away from the crowd, but solitude was impossible. They were shoved body-to-body with thousands of other human remnants the Turks deemed disposable. The flame of the childlike hope they kept alive in the cellar just hours ago was extinguished. The boys were merely two wretched waifs who fate had allowed to slip past the enemy. At that moment they were not sure if it was a vengeful fate that had spared them.

Out of habit, Stavros waited for an adult to tell him how to proceed. Instead, his brother pulled him up a few steps so they could peer over the crowd. The boys were merely a fleck in the mass of suffering that had exploded in few hours. Stavros could barely hear Christos' voice over the cries, the crush of bodies and the wind howling from the fire.

"Stavros, I will always take care of you," Christos promised solemnly, breathing hard. "Our family is just you and me now. I will always protect you. I promise this. Together we will make a plan and stick with it."

And Christos had kept his promise. He simply forgot to stay alive once Stavros' feet stepped onto American soil with his young nieces who were suddenly orphans, just as the brothers had become in their beloved Smyrna.

NINE

The strong winds blasting from the Sierra Nevada mountains, whistling through California's Central Valley, screamed that Yianna should be on guard. But of course, she was eighteen years old in 1955 and didn't listen. The chilling gusts that stirred the oak leaves outside Angel's Bakery in the afternoon became fierce in the evening when the stars were pressed against the blue-black sky, unusual for June in Woodland.

Dirt swirling from the sidewalk stung her ankles and the freezing air pierced her thin sweater like a set of claws. She desperately tried to keep her long black hair in place but soon admitted defeat as her wild strands lashed her face. Yianna should not have brought her camera, but it was too late.

Yianna climbed step by cement step to Porter's home. This place reminded her of the multi-layered wedding cakes they baked and decorated at Angel's Bakery. The grand house was painted in precious shades of gold and eggy cream with black handrails for dramatic effect. Before ringing the doorbell, Yianna examined the windows framed in crisp black paint and raised her Leica camera to take a photograph. She ached to turn around and run home to hide near the warm bakery ovens. But Porter had invited her, in a passionate and sweaty moment in the backseat of his car. Would Porter even remember his invitation?

At school he seemed to treat Yianna like a girlfriend. But she had no experience with boyfriends, and certainly not with boys who lived rich and easy. Yianna felt more at ease with Kenny and Frankie Chen, her trusted friends who lived on the next block from the bakery on Dead Cat Alley. Their family owned and operated the Good Day Laundry where the five Chen children helped their father and mother Vic and Vivian. They were like Olympia and Yianna, kids who usually rushed home from school to work with their parents in the family business. They were the reliable motor that helped propel their successful family enterprises.

Yianna usually walked through the streets lined with Victorian homes in Porter's neighborhood on her way home from school before her afternoon shift at Angel's Bakery. These homes, mansions really, were overdressed, wearing too much jewelry, showing their wealth on the street. Yianna was more comfortable a few blocks away at the bakery where she could hide in the tiny supply room where she had the privacy to worry about her future after high school graduation.

Yianna pressed the buzzer and ran her fingertips over the little diamonds and intricate geometric lines cut into the window glass above the polished doorknob. The frosted glass wasn't the lightweight type that Uncle Stavros and Agamemnon used to repair the windows at the bakery and boarding house. This was fine art to be someday admired by great-grandchildren. Yianna positioned her camera forward, framed the pattern of the ornate glass and snapped the shutter. She didn't know if she would have the opportunity to view it again.

Then the front door squeaked open a crack and Porter's eyebrows appeared — two chocolate-colored brushstrokes on his smooth forehead. The rest of his face, dark eyes and wide smile, popped out from behind the heavy door that swung open.

"Yianna! Glad you made it!"

Her throat felt tight and the air suddenly was sucked from her lungs. Yianna simply smiled and looked down at Olympia's shoes hoping Porter didn't notice paper stuffed in the toes, a size too large for her skinny feet.

Porter, with hands soft and oversized, like paws, pulled her inside. He was barely eighteen-years-old himself, but his face was cut into sharp, handsome angles which made him look older, always quietly confident. Porter had asked Yianna to "drop by his place" for his family's party. Drop by? At her uncle's bakery and boarding house, Yianna worked long hours when she was not at school. How casually Porter had asked, how nonchalantly he approached life, as if events would always unfold the way he wanted, the way he always planned. Porter would always sleep deeply, warm and reassured, tightly wrapped in the security of his powerful family and money in the bank.

Moving her camera to her side to appear less obtrusive, Yianna had no choice but to trail after Porter toward the crowded living room. They passed a small adjoining room from which a cloud of chocolate and butter aromas hung heavily over a giant dessert table. Yianna could not mention to Porter that all week she had helped Uncle Stavros prepare those double layer cakes, the macaroons dipped in rich, dark chocolate, tiny cheesecakes topped with raspberry gelée and handmade fudge. She couldn't bear to glance at her handiwork on the jammed dessert table as it was proof she was merely a servant to this upper class.

She stood with her arms wrapped across her chest like the cinnamon twist pastry the bakery offered that morning. She touched her camera hanging at her side and felt a little more comforted. This was an adult cocktail party, unlike the Greek *glendis*, the outdoor celebrations where juicy lamb roasted on a spit with cheap wine splashed everywhere. Yianna drew in a shaky breath, praying to become invisible, knowing she should not have walked past that threshold of unlimited wealth into the weighty atmosphere of old money. What was she doing here?

"Yianna," Porter breathed low and silky in her ear as he passed. "Maybe we can cut out early. Let's make an appearance for my mother and then we can leave through the kitchen. I'll get us some punch."

He gave her a slow wink, passed his hand across her shoulders and then lower to her behind, tracing her curves. Yianna was embarrassed there wasn't more for his hand to grab, but then she wasn't certain she liked his hands there anyway. Especially not in Porter's own home.

She flashed back to yesterday afternoon in the back seat of his parked car slanted off a road where the neat rows of tomato fields of Yolo County began. For Porter, it was the end of town, just a pack of weeds he barely noticed. But to Yianna, that was the spot where she made extra money each summer when she wasn't working at the bakery. Her job, in the dry, yellow heat of July, August and early September, was to weigh wooden crates loaded with ruddy, ripe tomatoes for the Hershel tomato processing plant.

Yianna hadn't put up much of a fight during their wrestling match in Porter's Chevrolet sedan. How should she position her arms and legs? When was the thrashing supposed to stop? Yianna had no one at home to ask, certainly not Olympia who had no experience dating boys. The cadre of old Greek men at the boarding house would close their ears to such talk.

Porter's hands seemed to already know the geography of her body. Yianna was sadly certain he'd had many girls in this car before her. A curtain of spring rain had secluded them behind the windshield and for a minute Yianna allowed his hands to go anywhere, everywhere. But suddenly she ripped herself away and breathlessly jumped out of the passenger side.

"I love you Yianna." Porter was standing next to her outside the Chevrolet, resting his head on her shoulder like a puppy. Yianna glanced at him, sifting truth from the passion. He wiped the rain from his face. Suddenly, Porter hugged her in a friendly way, like he was taking back the easy movements of his hands only seconds ago.

"Let's go home. We have time."

Yianna's head whirled in confusion. What did Porter really want? How was she supposed to react? She smoothed her skirt and took a long breath before she climbed back into the car with Porter, he on his side, she on hers. Porter had exhausted her body and certainly her mind. She kept to her side of the car as they rolled back into town.

Now, at his parents' party, Porter abruptly turned toward the punch table and Yianna looked past the men crowding the polished wooden bar and the women chatting in small circles. Expensive animal furs lay across the women's backs, a sign of their husbands' substantial bank accounts.

Yianna had made a special effort to look respectable: plaid skirt, knife pleats, starched white blouse, ironed it herself. That's as good as it got with her wardrobe. Porter was lucky she hadn't worn her bakery apron. She had slipped on Olympia's low black shoes with a small heel, reserved for special Greek church events. Yianna bit her lip to stop any tears that might blossom at the thought of her sister. Missing Olympia was now its own being—a strangling beast that poisoned most days and every night. Where was Olympia now? Was anyone protecting her? Was Olympia even alive? Yianna pushed away the possibility that Olympia might not be living.

Having nothing to do with her nervous hands, Yianna grabbed her camera. She snapped photos of the sparkling champagne trickling into tall crystal flutes, the giant roast beef ready for carving by men in chef's toques and the endless silver trays of canapés colorfully decorated with pimiento, red peppers and black olives.

Then the image through her viewfinder went black. She looked up to see a hand covering the lens. The hand was connected to Porter's father. He smiled over the camera while pushing it away.

"No photos tonight, dear. Not in my house. I oversee all photos taken for my campaign. Just put it away." Porter's father spoke as if Yianna were a small child.

"I'm sorry, Congressman." Yianna lowered her Leica. She had never met him in person but recognized his face from campaign posters and photos in *The Daily Democrat*. She blushed with shame. She had transgressed an unwritten law in this important man's home.

Where *was* Porter? She craned her neck to find him in the crowd. He could explain to his father she meant no harm. Porter knew how much she loved to take photos, that her curiosity was unlimited. He would defend her to his father.

"I won't shoot anymore." Yianna pushed the camera to her back to show the congressman her camera would be idle. But his attention was suddenly snagged by a group of ladies across the room. Walking away, he managed to mumble a meager "thanks" as he retreated. Another male face appeared to block Yianna's view of Porter, wherever he was.

"Hello, sweetie." Jack Reynolds, a city councilman in his thirties, projected a moist pudgy hand toward her. During this man's many visits to Angel's Bakery, Councilman Reynolds was always too attentive, his gaze clinging to her toothpick figure while slithering along Olympia's beautiful curves. Uncle Stavros kept a careful eye on him, stepping in to take his order when Reynold's eyes lingered where they shouldn't. Yianna even hated touching his money, his moisture leaking onto his cash. Worse yet, his shirt and pants never matched. Although Yianna owned no stylish clothes, she wondered how Reynolds was elected, looking like a clown.

"Good evening." She'd keep her answers short and perhaps the councilman would move on.

"What's new at the bakery? Just seeing you makes me think of something sweet!" The councilman swirled his drink. "Don't worry, I'll stop by tomorrow. Got to get a dozen of those Snowball cookies, you know!" As his eyes slid down Yianna's blouse, past her skirt to skim her legs, another face popped up, thankfully a familiar one. Principal Sullivan from Woodland High School. He greeted her with a big smile.

"Well, Yianna Diamantopoulos! Didn't expect to see you at a political gathering!"

Councilman Reynolds drifted away to the dessert table.

"I didn't know you liked politics." Principal Sullivan held a tall icy glass in one hand as he balanced a plate heaped with food in the other. He managed to sip from his glass without spilling, keeping his eyes on Yianna.

"I'm just, well, here for Porter." Yianna looked down at Olympia's shoes. "We're — friends."

"Of course!" Principal Sullivan moved closer and spoke in a quiet tone. "Any movement on finding your sister? Hasn't she been missing awhile? What does the sheriff say?"

Olympia's disappearance was old news. Why should the principal care about Olympia after she had been missing for six months and had left his school over a decade ago? Yianna could not speak. Luckily Principal Sullivan was swept away by a slap on the back from another guest and the two joined a crowd of men swarming to the bar. Yianna had a moment to take in a breath and blink back the tears. Perhaps Porter wouldn't notice when he returned. *Where was he? Why did he leave her alone?*

At that moment, a female figure materialized from nowhere. Her perfume too honeyed, gown too stiff.

"I'm Mrs. Trina Harrison, Porter's mother. Congressman Harrison's wife. So wonderful you could join us." With wine-colored lips Trina sucked the smoke from a long, filtered cigarette. "I hear you're spending time with my son."

Yianna's black eyes searched for Porter. He was across the room, charming a group of his parents' friends, no help to her.

"You're that bakery girl. With that camera everywhere you go." She did not ask questions or expect answers.

Not daring her voice to croak out an answer, Yianna nodded. She was in enemy territory. She cleared her throat, trying to breathe calmly, her anger beginning to bubble.

"That Greek baker's girl?" Trina's eyes flitted across the room. Her gown was a gold brocade, nothing like the clingy jersey dresses the Greek-American women wore to church parties. Olympia had described fitting a party gown tightly on Trina's slim body at Mira's Tailor Shop. "The rich women in town want expensive clothes to reveal their small waists and plushy bosoms."

"Niece. Not daughter." Yianna did not want to dole out more facts on which Porter's mother could pounce.

Slowly and dramatically, Trina placed her hands on her hips, her face close to Yianna's. Her dark green eyes striped with black liner stung like a wolf's glare in a dark forest.

"Don't get ideas, my dear." Trina's voice was quiet and chilling. "My Porter has a real future. First Stanford, management at the lumber mill. Then, of course, the legislature in Sacramento. Just like Cole, my husband. Congressman Harrison, to you."

Cocking her head, Trina smiled. Clearly Porter shared his mother's sharp, angular beauty. Now slowly circling around Yianna, as if lashing her to a tree, she spoke her words quietly.

"Look around. Take a good look. Do you really think you belong here?" Trina growled low and harsh. "Leave him alone."

Yianna was sweating, her eyes searchlights, hunting for Porter.

"All we need is for you to get yourself pregnant." She hissed the word. "That can't happen. Not in *this* family. After all, don't you have enough problems? With that sister of yours, Olivia? Olga? Olympia?"

Trina should never have spoken Olympia's name. Her sacred name. Olympia was smooth clear water while Trina was a treacherous murky undertow. Yianna's pain from Olympia's absence stung like a knife blade now. Yianna simply wanted her sister back and to get away from Porter's mother. Yianna stood on her tiptoes, chin forward as her eyes swept the room in a final search for a rescue.

Trina's pupils punctured Yianna with rage and disgust.

"You don't even know where she is, do you? Am I correct? No idea where she's gone?"

Yianna drew in a quick furious breath through her lips. Trina had landed the final gut punch about Olympia who Yianna cradled tenderly in her heart. All that remained of Olympia was a spirit, a love.

Yianna broke away, dashing to the monstrous oak front door, heaving it open. The borrowed shoes hardly touched the sidewalk as Yianna flew four blocks home, veering onto Main Street. Her camera thumped against her side until she clutched it close to her chest. Behind the building, behind the boarding house, behind the gambling room, next to the outhouse, Yianna found the latch open on the back fence. This was no mansion but at least Yianna belonged here, in a room with two twin beds, one perfectly made up, unused, waiting for the ghost Yianna hoped would someday come home to her.

TEN

The next morning, Stavros' boarding house was quiet. Only the spotted hens chortled in the tiny coop he had constructed in the alley behind the bakery. His eyes cracked open at the usual baker's hours of three in the morning despite his stinging hangover from last night's *raki* liquor. Timoleon would rise soon to operate his fruit stand and would need coffee to energize his tree stump seventy-year-old legs. Stavros didn't need the old shepherd asking questions about last night. At the end of their poker game, Stavros had excused himself and slid through his bedroom door where he entertained a young, delicate flower from Capay, a small town a few miles west on Road 16. Her skin had glowed with the evening stars of youth.

There were no secrets at Angel's Bakery. Agamemnon, Timoleon and Lucky knew everything about Stavros since the day he arrived. The first few years, the trio looked after Stavros. But being younger than the other men and supporting two nieces, Stavros needed to establish a secure income. He was certain he would bake for a living, as cooking was an honorable Greek man's profession. He was often told, "Where there is food, there is a Greek cooking it." And Stavros would live to prove it.

Over the years, their shared rooms, hot meals, wine, advice, the outhouse and card games had blended the men together to make a balanced and palatable brew, like the red wine Stavros fermented in his basement. Stavros supposed they were his family now, until he returned to Greece – after finding Olympia, of course.

Stavros' three shepherd "brothers" heard every creak in the uneven floor and they certainly sensed whose feet did the walking. Stavros' life was as open as the big recipe book he kept in the kitchen and just as dog-eared. The shepherds constantly teased him about the ghost women they never saw enter or exit.

Yes, the walls were thin, but cheap plaster was all Stavros could afford when he remodeled the place. When he added rooms for the boarders, he remembered his escape with Christos in Smyrna and installed an exit door from his own room. Any lady who slipped from Stavros' starched sheets was allowed an easy departure from his room to the outside world.

With a few moments to himself, before the onslaught of making a *proinó*, a breakfast of toast and coffee for Timoleon, his hands and feet slipped into the daily bakery routine, unfortunately without Olympia's help. Stavros attempted to ignore the hangover chiseling a layer of tissue from the lining of his skull.

Olympia had been the one to rise in the dark of early morning to silently knead the dough Stavros set out from the night before and start the Danish too. He missed Olympia and her quiet old-world ways. The two of them got along just fine, even when Stavros was forced to tell Olympia her mother had died. He remembered how she quietly absorbed the news and instantly began to hover over Yianna, the baby of the family. Barely a teenager, Olympia used the sleeve of her thick black sweater to soak up her tears so her little sister would not detect the wound of their mother's death.

From that day onward, Olympia held Yianna tight with her arms and her heart. Stavros sensed Olympia molding into her new role of mother. Didn't all Greek girls dream of marriage and a family? There was no question in his mind that Olympia would marry a boy marinated in old-world tradition. Although she attended Greek parties, Olympia hadn't even been on a chaperoned walk with a boy let alone eloped with some new man. Stavros reflected that perhaps he should have attempted to match her up with a qualified Greek suitor. But Olympia was too busy in her herb garden and concocting healing salves and lotions.

Olympia's beauty was mysterious, dark and luxurious, but she didn't seem to notice. Keeping her head down, she occupied her slim, experienced fingers at Mira's Tailor Shop. Olympia the healer. Olympia the seamstress. Olympia the weaver. Olympia the loving substitute mother. Olympia the good. She would never run off with a man without a year of introductions, family dinners and serious contemplation.

But now Stavros could not piece together Olympia's disappearance, no matter how he worked the puzzle. Had his reserved, proper Greek niece truly met a new man and left her family, as the sheriff had suggested? Stavros had immediately rejected the ridiculous idea that Olympia had willingly disappeared with a strange man. That dough did not rise to make bread. No, not his niece Olympia. Stavros truly wanted to find her but his English was only good enough to chit-chat with his customers. How could he express his thoughts with county officials? Stavros simply didn't know where to start. And he certainly didn't want the sheriff sniffing around his business — official and unofficial.

Looking at the big clock in the kitchen, Stavros realized he'd better move faster. Right on time, Timoleon shuffled from his room to the cafe tables Stavros had bought from a foreclosed ice cream parlor in Dixon, a small town about twenty miles from Woodland. The tables, comfortably seating two people, were of white marble with gray veins splashed across each disk. Heart shapes of thick, black wire supported the back of the chairs. Perfect for a bakery called "Angel's," although Stavros doubted he could personally live up to the name.

"You really hit it big last night."

Timoleon strolled past Stavros to the coffee urn, dribbled the strong American coffee into his cup, neutralizing it with an ocean of cream and three sugar cubes. He was the only bald man in the group. He took good care to oil his head every day and wear a cap to protect his crown while working at the fruit stand. A blue-eyed fair-skinned Greek, Timoleon's dimples pressed deeply into his smooth, round baby face. Dark oblong glasses weighed down the center of his head. Timoleon's ears were the size of eggplants and they snapped up tidbits of gossip like a frog's tongue snatched up insects. His middle was now a soft pillow and every day he wore a white shirt tucked into suntan pants from the military surplus store in Vallejo.

Timoleon had saved little so he continued to work, although Stavros would have let him stay at the boarding house for free. And the buzz of community news at his fruit stand gave meaning to his day. Besides, Timoleon's customers could not live without the jewel-like plums and nectarines in the summer and juicy oranges or tart lemons in the winter.

Timoleon collapsed his worn-out body onto a chair, ready to charge up his system for a long day with his customary three cups of coffee. He had hired a younger Greek man to drive the produce from the larger markets at five in the morning, yet he insisted on working six days a week from seven to seven, using his meager profits to pay rent and cover a few card games.

Stavros weighed the "big night" comment. *Aléthia*, in honesty, he could hardly remember the evening. Was Timoleon referring to his betting or choice of women? The boarders knew all his young women were well past eighteen since Stavros hardly needed police accusing him of illegal acts. They'd had enough trouble around the bakery lately.

"Hit it big? You think so?" Stavros laughed, buying time. Just then, Agamemnon burst into the kitchen, his bright flood of energy grating Stavros' hangover which required more coffee and two aspirin. Agamemnon took up where Timoleon left off.

"You lose a lot last night, *boufos*, dummy! How you expect to cover you' debt? That American, he only give you to next Monday to pay. I tell you, sometimes Greeks give a *patrioti*, a fellow countryman, a little more time. But these Americans—they always collect!"

Agamemnon poured a cup of coffee, sat at another table and fired up his morning cigar before taking a sip. His bushy salt-and-pepper eyebrows looked like caterpillars crawling across his forehead. Stavros always feared they'd catch fire when Agamemnon lit his cigar. He ran his fingers through his thick forest of gray hair until it nearly stood up, leaving one curl drooping over his forehead. Agamemnon must have been a showstopper in his youth, but years of herding sheep in the sun had cooked his skin to a leathery olive tan. He was still tall and lean with muscles hard from the outdoor work. Usually, his hazel eyes sagged with weariness, but today they flashed with energy.

Like one of his shepherd dogs with a meaty bone, Agamemnon would not let up about Stavros' debt. Stavros was certain Agamemnon would soon turn the conversation to him not helping find his missing niece. Stavros was silent. He could not admit to Agamemnon that since Olympia had disappeared that he had become untethered, less interested in keeping his gambling tables open, not so confident with women. Stavros was now uneasy when deciding who to trust.

"Where *you* gonna get the money to pay? You no worry? And that American gonna collect!" Agamemnon persisted.

He was right. Agamemnon was the brains of the bunch. He actually had earned a high school education in Greece. But when he first arrived in America, he was pushed deep into the silver mines of Utah to work more than twelve hours a day. After eight months a desperate Agamemnon walked off his mining job to live the life of a dock worker "just to breathe."

Next he worked as a farmhand and later a shepherd, inhabiting a series of trailers and bunk houses across the dry west, urging flocks of sheep to move from meadow to hills to mountain grass and back again. He thrived in the silence, the wind strumming its strings across the plains of northern California, his flock not asking more than he was willing to tell. Then he spent a few years in the United States Army and became a citizen. Stavros' boarding house was as close as Agamemnon, now in his sixties, had been to a family. He needed the company of these Greek men after years of loneliness with only a *baaaaa* to answer his questions late at night under a full moon and indigo sky.

"Why you drink when you bet?" Agamemnon took a swig of coffee, his eyebrows floating over the rim like fluffy question marks. "Why you never learn?"

He moved to Timoleon's table and the two began comparing notes on Stavros' losses. Like watercolors, last night's betting scene slowly began to seep into Stavros' consciousness. At the beginning of the evening he felt hopeful that this was his special night to win big. Then he would cash in the bakery and buy his ticket to Greece. But as the evening hours ground away, his bravado from the *raki* began to sag. Drowning in defeat, as usual, he allowed a young woman in his room to absorb his pain.

Stavros could not think about his debt now. His hands continued their work, automatically sprinkling flour on the large wooden pastry board, a simple pine plank he had purchased at the second-hand lumber outlet. Beginning with the pastry dough for the strudel, he worked his way to pie crust and finally rolled out dough for the Danish before the morning rush of customers. He shaped the dough for each Danish, twisting it into a figure eight and then spooning custard in one opening and strawberry jam in the other. Over and over his fingertips created four dozen perfect pastries. Those were his morning customers' favorites as they rushed to their government office jobs in downtown Woodland, the county seat.

Stavros had done his best to partition off the bakery with deep crimson velvet curtains from what he called the *sala*, the card room and dining room. He reserved that special area for his gambling comrades. From the front counter, customers would never guess four old Greek men and two young nieces made a home in the back of the building. At most, they might spot a stray poker chip on the floor or catch the scent of licorice from the used ouzo glasses.

At six o'clock sharp Stavros turned the worn brass bolt on the cranky oak front door. Olympia had hung lace curtains in the window to add a feminine touch to the place. In fact, she had starched and pressed the lace, another sign she had no plans to leave. The tiny metal bell on the front door began its one-note symphony announcing the morning rush of customers. Stavros believed that no one was in a bad mood in a bakery when selecting a fresh coffee cake or a rich apple strudel with crunchy sugar granules on top.

The bell tinkled. A mother and her children in search of breakfast. Stavros gave the kids free cups of milk. Tinkle Tinkle. County workers looking for Danish or doughnuts to dunk in coffee at their heavy metal desks in offices down the street. Tinkle Tinkle. Housewives calling for everyone's favorite: Snowball cookies. Stavros concocted that American name for his mother's specialty: Greek *Kourambyedes*. People liked the word "snow" in a town that rarely saw any slush or sleet. The small, creamy domes were butter cookies doused in a blizzard of powdered sugar and he served them in a cupcake holder, like all Greek *yiayiás*, grandmothers did. Only he used silver holders to add glamor to the Snowball theme. Stavros was fussy about that.

The rush was steady from six to nine in the morning. He remembered each customer's name and they loved it: Mrs. Wilson on her cane who always bought sugar cookies and a dozen Snowballs; Ralph, thirties, tall and skinny with the studious tortoise-shell glasses, who always ordered a single warm Danish. The slightly chubby but always cheerful Italian woman Anita, a secretary, who entered Angel's Bakery without fail, exactly ten minutes after Ralph. Stavros imagined they were secretly sleeping together but no one except himself, an experienced secret lover, knew it. And he'd never tell. If anyone met Stavros for fifteen minutes, they'd know he encouraged young love, actually, love at any age. Stavros followed his heart in all matters. Didn't the figures painted on ancient Greek plates and vases tell him that love was to be shared — no matter the sex combinations? He'd never criticize what he knew to be true. Love is love.

Timoleon already had slipped out the back door for another day of weighing peaches and helping customers select the sweetest honeydew melons. While Stavros hurried to serve his customers, he tried to calculate if his income from the brisk morning business might cover his losses. But he didn't have to wait long. Agamemnon had tallied last night's loss for Stavros on his small notepad.

Stavros made a note to himself to lay off the *raki* before playing cards. He needed to stay on top of things. But he quickly gave himself a pass on any guilt feelings. Why be guilty for a good time? Hadn't he paid enough by growing up with dead parents and raising his nieces? Was there only hard work in store for him? His soul wasn't built for casting his eyes downward, harnessed with work, with no time to dream or play. Stavros had learned to follow his *kardia*, his heart. He was still a young stallion bucking to reject a bridle when forced into labor. No one would stop him from gambling, drinking, playing, loving. His debt be damned!

"Seventy-six dollars." Agamemnon bounced his bushy eyebrows up and down. "You owe this. And by Friday."

Agamemnon slapped his worn notebook shut, shoving the pencil stub behind his ear and headed toward his room. "And no, my Social Security no come yet. Don't ask."

Then new trouble walked in the door.

"How the hell you keepin' yourself, Stavros?"

Marika's sweet, smokey voice rang out over the stack of Snowball cookies and the squares of chocolatey fudge Stavros had experimented with.

"Coffee and your best slice of cake – to go! I'm on the road again."

Everyone stopped to stare at Marika or to admire her. Stavros did both. She leaned on the door jamb, one hand on her hip for maximum drama. Stavros often sensed Marika had a secret desire for him warm in her bed. That their male and female *gnota*, their intimate animal breaths, would combine to be the perfect chemistry for Greek fire. Other times he felt like an undereducated fool, certain this acute businesswoman would never settle for a crumb like him. The minute or two with Marika would be the sweet, powdered sugar sprinkled on his day. And maybe a little chili powder too.

Marika had pulled out a few dollars from her purse and crinkled the crispy bills between her fingers, as if she were nervous. Stavros wanted to think she was anxious to talk with him.

"Throw in a Danish. I've gotta make it all the way to Oakland this morning. Six stops!"

"Anything for Marika," Stavros limply offered. In Woodland society, he was known for his repartee with women. But not with Marika. She was always a step ahead of him. He poured her a cup of coffee in a paper cup and dropped in her usual two sugar cubes.

Then he wrapped a slice of chocolate-fudge cake, slipping in a paper plate and an aluminum fork from the collection he saved just for her. He separately bagged her Danish, popping a lemon square into the bag that she could find later. His edible love note.

Lifting the glass dome covering the fudge, she popped a square into her beautifully lip sticked mouth. "I'm in a hurry but wanted to say *kali mera*, good morning to you and the boys."

Marika angled her face closer to Stavros and he could see the dusting of face powder across her nose and cheeks. She was a professional all the way. Her rouge was applied with an artist's hand and brush. Her teardrop gold earrings bobbled in the morning light and Marika's golden brown hair, like maple syrup, fell loose on her shoulders. Her skirt was just short enough to show off her legs but long enough to be respectable for a self-employed saleswoman. Marika's honeysuckle perfume mixed with the scent of Stavros' pastry was just enough to make him dizzy.

Stavros leaned closer and salivated just a little. Marika wanted him for something, he was sure. She would tell Stavros he was her man. Those young women who slipped in and out of his bedroom through the escape door were no match for her. Stavros leaned in closer. Waiting. Hopeful.

"So you hear news about Olympia?" Marika whispered, then took a sip of her coffee. "You keep the sheriff on his toes? He will do nothin' if you no apply the pressure. It up to you, Stavros. You know that. Everyone does."

His lungs deflated in disappointment. His shoulders drooped. She was chiding him for not helping in Olympia's search. No saucy half-smile. Just a critical reminder, which he did not need that morning. Stavros looked down into his own coffee cup that he nursed through the morning rush.

"Don't let up!" Marika laid out money, exactly the amount for her coffee, fudge, the cake, Danish and lemon square, as if telepathically aware he'd bump her the lemon pastry. As Marika dashed out the door, Stavros noticed an American man dressed in a suit waiting for her. Yes, he was jealous but had no right to be. His Marika should only be waiting for him. She could at least allow him that fantasy.

ELEVEN

Yianna waited behind the curtain peering into the bakery, watching her Uncle Stavros take Marika's order. He followed her every move like a dog baited with raw bacon. He drew close to catch Marika's electricity and absorb her effortless sexuality. Yianna watched as Marika left and stood near an American man, squeezing his arm, not revealing if he was a lover or just a friend.

One of the few Greek women Yianna knew who operated her own business, Marika was a buyer and seller of goods from Greece: olive oil, grape leaves in a jar, Kalamata olives, Greek feta, kasseri, kefalotyri and other cheeses made from sheep or goat. The suitcases she dragged from store to shop to home throughout California offered handmade gold and silver jewelry from Greece, and, of course, worry beads, some small and cheap for tourists. Others large and wooden for serious Greek men with serious Greek worries.

Marika owned her very own gleaming black Dodge sedan and maintained it in perfect condition. She drove her car from Sacramento to Redding and then south on sweltering Highway 99 all the way to the Greek specialty stores in the Los Angeles area. She had picked up the habit of wearing dark sunglasses which added glamor, although her excuse was that her eyes took a beating on the road. Having escaped Greece after World War II and the Greek civil war,

Marika had invented her business, somehow landed in Woodland and made the small town her home.

Marika ruled her own world and Yianna held her breath to watch her part crowds when she walked into a room. Yianna's eyes soaked up Marika's style like blotting paper, absorbing her independence, her charm, her brazen attitude. Marika had no reservation when speaking her mind. No older Greek women ever scolded Marika with a harsh *dropi sou!* shame on you! which younger girls suffered by the ladleful.

Before Olympia disappeared, the sisters would occasionally encounter Marika at a Greek dance in the church hall in Sacramento. Marika would usually give the two sisters a wink, the kind that said, "we women have to stick together." Once, Yianna and Olympia had burst into the bathroom, sweaty and laughing after dancing a lively, heart-pounding *hasapiko*. As the girls stood in front of the mirror, wiping their brows, Yianna thought she saw Marika dabbing tears from her eyes under the naked bulb. Surprised at the girls' intrusion, Marika looked up and immediately hid her handkerchief.

"Girls, remember whatever happens to you, don't take any *bool-sheet*." She croaked her words with a husky voice which proved she had indeed been crying. "God knows I've seen enough of it! Just don't take it! *Poteh!* Never!"

Yianna didn't want to believe that anyone or anything could wound Marika. She focused on this shooting star of a woman who drove herself up and down the state of California in the stinging heat, or across washed-out roads, always turned out in an appealing outfit. Marika earned her own money, paid her own rent, loved who she chose and rejected those not making the cut. And she was the only adult outside of Angel's Bakery to keep up barbed reminders to Stavros to find Olympia. Yianna felt as if she and Marika were the only ones desperate to locate her sister.

Yianna watched closely as Marika walked away from the American man. Then she gracefully pulled her legs into her car, revved the engine and took off toward Highway 80 and the little Greek church of Saints Constantine and Helen in Vallejo. Marika was very attuned to what Greek housewives wanted in their kitchens, the quality, the aromas, the textures. Some of the ladies in the area combined their lists to form a larger order so they didn't have to travel to San Francisco to buy their Kalamata olives and Greek mountain honey.

As Marika's car scooted out of sight, Yianna stepped behind the bakery counter to carry out her duties before dashing to school. She was late that morning but Uncle Stavros hardly noticed as he stood staring at the air Marika had occupied. Yianna had other worries on her mind. She would soon see Porter at school after she had run out on him the night before. Did Porter know his mother had harpooned her and that she was still bleeding from it?

Just then a miracle happened.

"Yianna, maybe you be late to school today? The customers, they no stop. I gotta get back to the kitchen. Cakes to decorate. Snowballs to bake."

Uncle Stavros had never asked Yianna to skip school to work. He kept a hard line between Yianna's bakery work and her schooling but today she was thrilled to fill in behind the counter for a few hours. Porter was only in Yianna's morning classes. Now she could easily avoid him. Yianna almost glowed with the simplicity of this plan.

"Yes, of course I'll help, Uncle Stavros. It's almost graduation anyway. I can go to school after the lunch break."

With any luck, Yianna could avoid Porter altogether today. Trina's message was a straight arrow to her heart: STAY AWAY! Balancing desire for Porter on one side of the scale and fear of Trina, the venom-spitting serpent, on the other, there was no question. Yianna had to be done with Porter.

She imagined Marika ripping Trina's head off her body, but Yianna could never muster that courage. If only her heart did not twinge a little when she thought of Porter. She would miss the daily coral-colored rose he brought her from his family's garden, the tiny red candied hearts, the sweet notes written in his tight scrawl, hoping her day was a good one. Yianna had temporarily lost a sister. Now she would lose a boyfriend who wasn't even officially her own.

"Than' you, *Ioanna.*"

The next customer in line was Councilman Reynolds.

"How's my beautiful girl today?"

Not now! Yianna did not want to endure his roving eyes scanning her body. Why did he have to come today? She had no time for this man. Yianna only wanted to serve the long line of customers, make an appearance at school and rush back to the safety of the bakery.

Uncle Stavros had vanished into the kitchen, but Lucky magically appeared and stood next to her at the counter. Yianna was thankful for the third Greek boarder, Lucky, a former shepherd and now the bakery dishwasher. Lucky silently raised a hand as if to say: "I'll take care of this one!"

Lucky bagged a dozen Snowball cookies, even offering the councilman a sample to taste, all in his usual silence. Yianna noted Lucky's trick: keep this man's mouth full of powdered sugar so he couldn't speak. Chomping his free cookie, the councilman gave Yianna a wink and then pointed to an empty paper coffee cup. Lucky filled it and the councilman swept out of the bakery with his bag of cookies.

Yianna gave him a thankful pat on the back and he beamed with pride. Although he spoke little, he had a natural wisdom to appear in the right place at the right time, always helping, never attracting attention. Most people did not appreciate the silent intelligence that Lucky demonstrated every day.

Fighting in World War I for the Americans was Lucky's path to citizenship. Two years of warfare in Belgium had left him what they used to call "shell shocked." Lucky was happy to be tucked away in the makeshift Greek family and to have a purpose in life, filling the jobs no one else wanted. Stavros demanded supreme cleanliness at the bakery and Lucky was instrumental in maintaining the white-glove standard.

Barely five feet tall and shaped like a bowling pin, Lucky rocked side to side as he walked. Because of his emotional war wound, he rarely spoke. He simply smiled and occasionally expelled a little grunt to show his pleasure or indicate a question. Lucky's fingers, like his body, were as chubby as sausages, but he worked them fast.

Agamemnon had told Yianna that in the Army during World War I, Lucky's job was feeding the belts of bullets into an automatic machine gun while a gunner named Jimmy did the shooting. Lucky was also assigned to keep a lookout for the enemy and he did just that, until the Germans overtook them. Lucky quickly turned the gun on them, but not quick enough to save his best friend Jimmy. Lucky mowed down a dozen Germans until he himself was gravely wounded.

After doctors cut out his spleen and rearranged several organs, Lucky would never again say more than a few words at a time. He was awarded a medal for bravery but kept it in a dusty box in his bottom drawer. He also tucked a photo of the beautiful raven-haired Jimmy in Army uniform on his dresser. Each night before bed, he made the sign of the cross in front of the mirror. Agamemnon said he never knew if Lucky was praying to God or to Jimmy.

But that morning, Lucky served as Yianna's assistant. She was his gunner as they worked together to serve the customers quickly and cheerfully. A customer would call out an order from across the glass bakery counter. Lucky would place it in its powder-pink cardboard box, tie it up with string and present it to the customer over the counter. Lucky never forgot the Angel's Bakery sticker which Agamemnon had designed to match the sign outside. That shiny sticker differentiated Angel's offerings from any old pink confection box.

Yianna collected the money and made change from the noisy brass cash register. No one ever short-changed Yianna with money. She had played poker with Greek men since she was five years old and no one separated her from her cash. Not a penny.

After the last morning customer sauntered away with two dozen cinnamon-sugar cookies in a crisp white bag, Lucky offered Yianna a handshake, his way of saying "Job well done!" Yianna smiled. Never could she find a better co-worker or co-uncle. All her Greek "uncles" attended her back-to-school nights and open house events. They wanted to ensure that Yianna and Olympia received the best education possible in Woodland. These men would never have children of their own, so Yianna and Olympia had grown to be their hope for the future. The two girls learned to play backgammon, to bet on a poker hand, to sing old village Greek songs and to choose the best fruit and never overpay for it.

Both Yianna and Olympia learned the bakery trade, but Olympia was more naturally suited to that work. Yianna's heart was already out the door.

TWELVE

Olympia's Diary

Thinking back to my tiny village school in Argos, Greece, I had earned the front desk reserved for the very best student. When my bosoms began to blossom, well, everything changed. A vague rumor buzzed among the parents that their daughters needed protection from any unsupervised male teacher, specifically the headmaster Makris.

When I was supposed to be asleep, I overheard my parents discuss that perhaps I should be pulled out of school. Hearing this, I laughed to myself at this absurdity. I could never leave! School was my place in the world. Although I was still a young girl, I knew I would become a doctor. Books were always my friends, my search for knowledge always present. Could I dare to dream of attending university in Athens? After a few weeks I heard nothing else about this preposterous idea of withdrawing from school. My education was safe.

At our small school, Makris kept a special library where his finest books were stored under lock and key. He allowed me to choose one book and then return it and select another. That small library smelled of ancient paper and felt like a gift just for me.

I was eager to devour every volume as best I could for my age. But the work that thrilled me most was The Alexiad, *written by princess* and scholar Anna Comnena who lived in the royal court in Constantinople. She was a trained doctor who managed a large hospital and orphanage. To think! A Greek woman wrote an account of her royal family, recording the specifics about their lives and their military and political history too. I wanted to soak up everything this princess-scholar knew. If only I could be like her!

One day in that library, I held The Alexiad in my hands. But I was cursed by the Evil Eye as wandering hands brushed across my body. A hand suddenly reached around my back to touch my breast which was the size of a small fig. I shivered and turned to see the blubber-bellied Makris track me with eyes lit by a strange fire. His stare locked on me. Slowly, Makris reached out to touch my hair. He leaned on my body and thrust a hand up my skirt. Infused with electric shock, I instantly pushed away both roving hands and darted like a minnow right past him. I ran from school, racing home without looking behind me, Princess Anna's book still in my hand. I slammed and locked the door the instant I got home.

I feared telling my parents about Makris and his disgusting hands. Would they claim it was somehow my fault? Why was I in a small, secluded space with a man? Or worse yet, I was terrified my parents would hold me out from school for a few weeks. I could not sleep that night or days after. Why did Makris have to live up to his soiled reputation?

A week later after church, my mother and father led me by the hand to our garden in the warm mid-day. I sat on a metal pail used for harvesting zucchini and tomatoes. Looking at my parents, I could see their eyes were flat as the dead marides, the small white bait fish we fried up for our afternoon meal. They told me the day Makris and I were in the library, a cleaning woman had been at the school to scrub the floors and desks. Neither Makris nor I had heard her footsteps, but she told my parents exactly what she observed.

"Keep your daughter away from Makris," she warned. "He is probably infertile at his age but you don't want to find out!"

And just that fast, my school days were over. I was cruelly torn from my books, mathematics and my dream of being a doctor. I cried every morning for the first month after I was barred from my beloved classroom. I missed my books, my small desk with initials carved in the soft wood, the slate and chalk, my classmates and the songs we sang. They were all gone.

As the weeks crawled by, I continued to wonder why I was punished instead of Makris. Would he do the same to the next girl? I later discovered that slimy rumors had followed Makris around for years. He was the fox that continually raided the henhouse. My anger built from kindling to a roaring fire but I had nowhere to put my feelings. My tears temporarily helped to put out the flames and my dreams for the future.

THIRTEEN

Yianna burst out the back door of the boarding house which opened onto the alley. Her important task lay ahead.

Running four blocks to the Yolo County Sheriff Department Yianna swung open the heavy front door. The rotund secretary at the front desk looked up and frowned at the nearly six-foot-tall teenage girl who showed up every week to ask for news about her sister. She followed Yianna with tired eyes while her hands pounded the typewriter keys as if they were playing an upright piano. Her steel-gray hair was pulled back into a stiff bun and small glasses hung around her neck like a cowbell. The secretary shuffled to the counter and reverently opened the visitor's ledger and printed Yianna's name on the first line.

Chewing a small wad of gum in her back teeth, she glared at Yianna with a wintery stare. "Diamond-tow-pooh-lace?" She pushed the ledger toward Yianna to sign.

"Close!" Yianna attempted a smile and signed the book. "Diamantopoulos," she whispered as if anyone cared how she pronounced her Greek last name. Yianna used her American accent when pronouncing her name for this secretary.

"This is about that sister of yours, right?" She moved her mouth to the side, still grinding her gum. "Again. The sheriff doesn't have time today. Nothing new, I can tell you that."

Her fingers flew through files hanging from a metal rack balanced on the massive oak desk. Fiddling with the chain to grasp her glasses, she finally rested them on the tip of her nose. The secretary smoothed out the page with a sweaty palm.

"This is what we call a cold case."

Cold? Yianna's breath quickened. There was nothing cold about her desire to find Olympia.

Did this secretary expect to brush Yianna off by offering no progress about Olympia's case? The same response as every other visit to the sheriff's department? Each night, while she lay in bed alone in their shared room, she sensed Olympia floating in dark space, waiting for her younger sister to catch her as she rotated in her orbit around the earth. Yianna needed to pull Olympia down to safety. To their home. Yianna sensed Olympia was still alive. She knew it.

"You'd better run along." The secretary slapped the file shut. "The sheriff can't see you today."

Yianna's face burned. To this woman, Olympia was simply an immigrant girl of no consequence. No face. No heart. Unpronounceable last name. Not worthy of official Sheriff Department effort.

The secretary twisted her portly frame as Sheriff Lewin strolled from his office. He stepped toward his deputy's small adjoining office and leaned inside, hanging playfully on the doorknob.

"Robbie? Ready?" He addressed the deputy. "It's eleven-thirty but my stomach says it's noon!" The sheriff smiled as if he did not solve crimes for a living.

Because Yianna had made it a habit to come to the sheriff's department every week, she was well aware that Sheriff Lewin usually vanished out the back door when she entered the front. But that day, Yianna had arrived before he left to fill his stomach at the Chicago Café, the place most workers frequented for lunch. She studied the olive-green uniform which he wore like a model in a magazine. No wrinkles, no sweat stains, starched crease in the pant legs, badge polished to a blinding gold. His buoyant blond hair surfed his head in waves. Broad shoulders, cowboy stance, thumbs tucked behind his belt buckle, cold blue eyes like marbles. To Yianna, he seemed too showy to be a sheriff. His ample shaving lotion stung her nostrils in the mid-morning heat. This youngish sheriff seemed to require a larger stage than his current cramped headquarters.

"Sheriff Lewin!" The guard-dog secretary flew from her chair to swing open the shallow wooden gate separating Yianna from the sanctified inner office. The secretary hobbled to a standing position as Yianna darted into the sheriff's space.

"You can't come in here! Get out!" The secretary stood with her fists shoved onto her battleship hips. "Stay out!" If she had a pole, she would have pushed Yianna away like a pig in a pen.

"I just need a minute!" Yianna smoothed her blouse and skirt which were crisp and modern. Hers was not an outfit of a poor immigrant. Her voice was clear.

"Do you have any news?" She and Olympia deserved his attention. "About Olympia Diamantopoulos? Anything at all?"

He slowly turned to face her, too calmly, too deliberately. She was nearly as tall as he was, her black eyes met his blue.

"Miss Diamantopoulos, I tell you this every week. We have no leads. This case is –"

"COLD! I already told her, Sheriff!" Mrs. Officious was dutifully performing her job for the boss. "I told her! A COLD case!" A strychnine smile pulled across the secretary's face as she chomped her gum, watching Yianna.

"We have very few facts to work with. We've conducted all the interviews. There are simply no leads. We're doing everything we can." He turned his golden head away from Yianna.

Subject closed. Flat out no information. Yianna was sure the sheriff thought his empty statement should be plenty for her, a high school girl who merely worked at her uncle's bakery. Not a member of his society. Not a member of any society. But she surprised herself.

"Six months! Six months she's been gone! When will you have more information?" She was yelling now, shouting for her sister. "We *need* to find Olympia! What are you doing to find her?"

"Listen, miss. There are lots of girls like your sister. Foreign, live under the radar and, well, just go missing. Sometimes they tempt boys. Then they take their consequences."

"My sister? Tempt boys?" Yianna's eyes flashed with fury and disbelief. "That's a lie! Take it back!"

The sheriff shot a quick glance at the secretary. Suddenly, the secretary leapt at Yianna and demonstrated the profound strength of her meaty limbs. Gripping Yianna by the elbow, the older woman pushed her through the little gate, across the polished floors and directly out the front door. The heavy wooden door slammed behind her.

Trembling with rage, Yianna's body crumpled and landed hard on the curb. Pulling her legs close to her body, she sunk her forehead onto her knees. She didn't care who on the street could hear her frustrated howling. Maybe it was time someone heard her cry. Maybe she should scream out loud and strong.

Then she heard the office door slowly squeak open and Sheriff Lewin began to speak. A spark of optimism kindled inside her. Maybe he would toss Yianna a morsel of hope — something she could keep close to her heart like the three shepherds with their teaspoon of Greek soil around their necks.

"Robbie, let's get over there before noon and beat the rush." They tramped past her toward the Chicago Café. The deputy matched the sheriff step-for-step but Yianna's sidewalk sobbing hooked his interest. Well-built like the sheriff, but with dark brown hair and chestnut eyes, Deputy Robbie swiveled his head at her weeping and looked back.

"Hey, I went to high school with Olympia! Nice girl." He touched the sheriff's arm. "Maybe we could just –"

Eyes straight ahead the sheriff pushed him away and the deputy followed him like a dog on a leash.

"Thinking about some Egg Fu Young and a plate of that Chow Mein!" he laughed.

The sheriff's words landed dead in Yianna's ears. She slowly wobbled to standing and dried her eyes with the back of her hand. It appeared the sheriff would do nothing to find Olympia. And Uncle Stavros was hardly helping. At that instant Yianna was stung with the realization her heart already knew to be true. She was on her own.

FOURTEEN

An hour later, standing on the sidewalk in front of Woodland High School, Yianna was at a loss as to which direction to walk. Her eyes were puffy, hair stringy from her tears. Although she had attended this school for years, today Yianna felt like a stranger stalled at the entrance of the bulky concrete building.

The lunch period was over and no students dawdled over sandwiches and soda. As a senior, Yianna knew kids often ditched school as a prank this time of year, something that would never be tolerated by Uncle Stavros. How well she knew every word of his somber lecture that a free education was a miracle. How as orphans, he and her father Christos would have treasured the luxury of a high school education instead of being forced to learn a skill like baking or tailoring.

Oak trees guarded the exterior of the school like soldiers. The hot air pressed in for what would be a scorching afternoon. Yianna climbed the dozen steps toward what seemed a lifeless mausoleum. She crept down the halls of inlaid white marble and carefully skirted the classroom where Porter would be studying trigonometry.

In a large arc, she walked around a home economics class where Mrs. Lawson was teaching a lesson about baking cinnamon rolls, something Yianna had accomplished in the fourth grade. Finding no hideout that suited her needs, Yianna could at least stay cool while hidden in the shadows before she walked home to stand behind the sweaty bakery counter, then cook a meal for the four old Greek men. In their younger years, the boarders had often helped with the cooking because they enjoyed mincing onions and garlic and the chatter that went along with it. But now Agamemnon, Timoleon and Lucky were too tired and mostly talked about the news of the world while Yianna cooked up dinner for six. No, only five, since Olympia had vanished.

A tall dark figure appeared at the end of the deserted hallway. Principal Sullivan often strolled the hallways but usually when students changed classes. Today he seemed to be aimlessly drifting like a ghost.

"Is that Yianna?" He squinted his eyes in the dim light of the hallway. "Yianna Diamantopoulos! Twice in one week—we meet again! What are you do roaming the hall?"

Yianna attempted a polite smile. "Had to fill in at the bakery this morning."

"Well, you're graduating next week!" The principal planted himself in front of her, stopping her progress. "What will you do with yourself after? Planning on staying at the bakery?"

"Uh, no. I'm, well—I'm taking my time. Figuring it out," she stammered, insulted that he automatically pegged her as a bakery cashier for her life's work.

"And how about that sister of yours? At the congressman's party you never did say if they've found anything." The principal looked up to the ceiling as if remembering Olympia. "Such a beautiful girl. So quiet. Stunning, really."

Yianna had to get away. Why was the principal fawning over her sister now when he had signed the papers allowing Olympia to drop out of school at sixteen? He must have read the single newspaper article about her disappearance months ago. The principal's interest made Yianna shiver in the summer heat.

"Nothing new in her case." She walked on, leaving the principal to himself in the darkened hallway.

Yianna knew of only one place in the school she might find a peaceful moment. Located at the end of a long hallway, the library pulled Yianna inside like a magnet. A carved sign hung outside the door, reading "Library" in old English script, as if Shakespeare himself whittled the guidepost to the volumes of his work trapped inside. Approaching the library doorway, Yianna noticed the librarian had fortified herself against the heat. Two large circular fans created a wind tunnel with the power to rip the thickest tomes off the sagging shelves.

This was her place to disappear, behind the shelves of dusty books no highschooler ever checked out. She walked from row to row breathing the stale smell of decomposing paper, not sure how to spend two hours until the final bell. Biography, Fiction, Science, History, Philosophy. Those sections were not welcoming, their book spines turned against her. With her camera on her back, Yianna began to think there was no temporary refuge here.

She bit her lip in frustration. She was so close to graduation, Olympia was missing with no trace, and she was far from deciding her life's work. But perhaps she could knit together her emotions and sort out her messy feelings in this quiet space.

Pacing up one aisle and then down another she spotted a single beacon luring her toward an island of safety. Walking toward the sign consisting of three letters spelling A-R-T, she felt protected there, as if A-R-T would somehow save her, shield her. She began to tremble, then shake as the giant fans whipped her hair and pasted her against the volumes of Matisse, Leonardo di Vinci, Rembrandt and Monet. As Yianna rested her back against a large volume about Michelangelo, she watched the librarian Mrs. Rose slide her bifocals up and down her nose like a trombone. She was staring at a book title, and then hunting down the space on the shelf the volume should rightfully occupy.

Yianna pulled her camera close to her body, preparing to hide in another section. Just then, Mrs. Rose wheeled her cart close to her.

"It's so stuffy where you're standing! Poor dear!" She whispered and rubbed a hand across her forehead pushing sweat from her eyes. "Have a seat over here, I'll get both of us some water." Her warm smile wrapped around Yianna and, like an exhausted child on the first day of school, Yianna did exactly as she was told.

Mrs. Rose returned with two paper cups of cool water and carefully placed one in front of Yianna. She sat close enough to speak quietly—it was a library after all. So close that Yianna felt her soft, friendly presence, like a favorite ginger tabby cat.

"You are Yianna Diamantopoulos!" Surprised, Yianna nodded but could not speak. "I've got an idea. Why don't I pick out a few books for you to start with and then you can explore! What do you think?"

Yianna dutifully sipped the water from her stiff paper cup. How did she know Yianna's name?

Mrs. Rose floated through the stacks cheerfully pulling books until her arms were loaded with hefty, mysterious volumes. Placing the books on the table, she pulled one from the stack and slid it in front of Yianna.

"I've watched you bring your camera to school every day. You must love to frame the world. My daughter in San Francisco, she's an artist. Loves these books. You might too."

Yianna curiously inspected the first title: *Classical Definition of Art—Plato and Aristotle.* She knew nothing about ancient Greece and its artistic contribution. She began to hungrily pore over the first page in the volume when Mrs. Rose placed other volumes in front of her: *Gardner's Art Through the Ages: A Global History; Great Works of Art Around the World.*

Well past the three o'clock final bell, Yianna remained fixed in her seat, her pointy elbows on the long, old-world library table. Yianna held her face close to the black type and large colorful photos and drawings. She noticed the books about art history were stamped with the word "reference" meaning they lived permanently in the library. With time running out, Yianna studied more intently. The books about art, especially Greek art, had grabbed her attention.

"Honey, it's time to go." Mrs. Rose tapped the library table near Yianna who was surrounded by books. "Just follow me to the checkout counter!"

Amazed how grounded she felt, Yianna trailed behind her. At the front desk, Mrs. Rose practically pulled the books from Yianna's arms. She took a step back and looked at Yianna and then the books.

"Well, I have another idea. These books are not used much and the term papers are finished for the year." The librarian looked up into the high ceilings where the heavy glass lamps glowed. "Why don't we just take these books off the 'reference' list?" She spoke to Yianna with quiet respect, as if they were fellow librarians. "You can return them before the end of the year. Before you graduate."

After the librarian officially stamped the reference books for checkout, Yianna crammed them into her bookbag. She could hardly stammer out thanks to Mrs. Rose who had instantly become her mother in this library. At the door, Yianna hesitated, readying herself for the strangling heat outside and looked over her shoulder. She smiled at Mrs. Rose.

"Say hello to your daughter."

FIFTEEN

Just for now, Yianna was peaceful walking home. The boulder of books on her back seemed to weigh nothing and her camera, her watchful eye, waited patiently to gaze at the beauty she encountered. Yianna hurried past the graceful mansions in Porter's neighborhood, skirting his block entirely.

When Yianna had wandered through this neighborhood last Sunday, before Porter's party, she had been fixed on the decoration of these ornate houses. She had snapped the shutter on the shiny brass, the cut glass front doors, the turrets, the crystal door knobs.

This time, Yianna focused her camera lens on the working gardeners behind the violet hydrangeas, the orange striped tiger lilies and the fragile pink roses twined around the iron fences. She studied the slim but muscular figures of the gardeners, skin browned by the sun and focused her lens. Yianna concentrated on their faces and calloused, experienced hands that worked the pruning clippers and the lawn mowers.

Hearing her camera shutter click, the Japanese and Mexican gardeners glanced up. She peered into their dark knowing eyes. These men quickly returned to their work, unnoticed by passersby as if in all seasons, nature presented itself in that flawless, manicured arrangement.

Yianna walked into the bakery after six-o'clock, knowing she had dawdled too long shooting photos. She was late in starting dinner for the men. The bakery was closed and surprisingly the Greek boarders were not warming up their poker hands at the card tables. For once, the hub of the bakery kitchen was as quiet as a Greek church on Monday.

On her way to deposit her overstuffed book bag in her room, she wandered past Agamemnon's room. Glancing through the crack in the door she watched Agamemnon drawing with charcoal pencils at a small table. He had propped up a piece of cedar in a slant to use as a table easel. Humming the old Greek folk tune *Samiotisa*, Agamemnon seemed lighter, younger, as he hovered over his drawing.

His eyebrows bobbed up when he seemed pleased with his work and he squinted his small hazel eyes when studying his next charcoal pencil stroke. Yianna's heart brimmed with admiration for this self-taught artist who never complained that his life's work had not involved creating art. He often said he drew and painted for pleasure and the beauty it might bring to the world.

Agamemnon pushed his chair back on the wooden floor to evaluate his work from a distance when Yianna caught his gaze. At that moment, Yianna wondered if all artistic muses were required to be female. The only muses familiar to her were Calliope, muse of music; Clio, muse of history; and Urania, muse of astronomy. She sighed. Always men inspired by women who had little to do with the actual making of art. But if males were allowed to assume that inspirational role, then Agamemnon was *her* muse, the person who inspired her to bravely pursue her art no matter who was looking.

His friendly glance seemed to give her permission to enter the room. Inside was only a well-made single bed, an art table, a small wooden dresser and a beat-up easy chair that had been Lucky's some time ago. But every inch of his four close walls teemed with his photos, paintings and drawings in charcoal or ink. Most were framed with cheap wood or had no frame at all. Agamemnon's photos captured Army life: cooks stirring pots in the mess kitchen, soldiers sitting shoulder to shoulder eating lunch, a platoon standing at attention, a close up of a soldier saluting with hand slanted over his eye.

On another wall, brilliantly shimmering Aegean blues dominated Agamemnon's watercolors of Greek fishing boats and beaches. Several offbeat collages of wool, leather, and hand-loomed fabric from his shepherd days lay tucked among his artwork. Like a personal treasure box, Agamemnon's room was a gallery displaying art reflecting his everyday life.

Agamemnon cracked a smile when his eyes lit on Yianna and turned his sketch toward her. He had drawn a mother and child caught in a lingering embrace in a village setting. His sketchy lines conveyed the affection between the pair as they stood on a dirt path near a primal water wheel with their empty wooden buckets stacked nearby.

"Well, what you think?" He tilted his head to one side, his eyes skimming the folds of the mother and daughter's dresses, the curve of their cheeks and the knots tying their scarves tight around their heads.

Agamemnon's drawing was like a knife slicing open a fresh wound for Yianna. For a quick moment, Yianna flickered on the memory of her mother, stretching to remember her kindness, her tender and sometimes playful love. But Yianna's memory had softened. She could only conjure faded brush strokes where a finished portrait of her mother once existed. She shook off her wispy memories and focused on his drawing.

"I love it! Who are they?"

"My mother and sister. We lose them in the second war. But here they live again." Taking his soft charcoal pencil and wetting it on his tongue, he deepened the shadows between the two figures, smudging the gray tones.

"You never be afraid of the dramatic shadows." Agamemnon observed his drawing with one eye. "Always the shadows tell the story."

Yianna secretly hoped he would offer her the drawing to hang in her room with the many others she had collected from Agamemnon's brushes or pencils. With so much of his artwork on her walls, she hardly had room for Marlon Brando leaning against his motorcycle on the poster from *The Wild One* movie. Instead, he removed his drawing from the slanted artboard on his desk and used a large brass thumbtack to stab it onto a tiny space on his clapboard wall.

"*Nah!* There! Now they are with me always, like I remember them!" Agamemnon spoke softly, like he did most of the time. "Now what have you been up to my daughter?"

He often referred to Yianna as his daughter and she loved to hear it. Uncle Stavros did not refer to her or Olympia as his daughters. She sometimes felt they were more like his obligation, although her uncle would never use that word. But she and Agamemnon were two spirits who loved fluid shapes, dusky shadows and soaring highlights in just the right places. They were born to look at the world with eager anticipation, to edit out the images they didn't want to see and allow entry to the beautiful parts they loved. In the everyday world of bakery labor, and a painful final semester of high school, Agamemnon lovingly held the door open to another world, and Yianna was ready to burst through it.

"The school librarian let me take home books about art history!" She rummaged through her bookbag. Yianna was certain Agamemnon would be interested.

"History good to learn!" Agamemnon turned the book spines toward him and noted each title. "You read them. Especially you read the Greek one." He stood and tugged on the glass knobs of his dresser drawer. He pulled out a single book, smaller than the encyclopedic volumes Yianna had lugged home. "This book for you, Yianna. The pictures, they made by a lady photographer."

Agamemnon presented to her a book with a paper jacket printed with the title: *An American Exodus — A Record of Human Erosion* by Dorothea Lange. An exodus? She was vaguely familiar with the Book of Exodus in the Bible. But since Uncle Stavros never sent them to Sunday school all the way in Sacramento, she knew nothing more.

An American exodus? She pulled the book close to her and flipped the pages. A *woman* had taken these photos? *A woman photographer*? A female's hands were in control of her camera? Her photos showed a forlorn woman staring at the camera, the woman's life told through the sense of weariness in her eyes. Yianna absolutely needed this book and was thirsty to learn everything about Dorothea Lange. Still knowing nothing of Dorothea herself or how she discovered her subjects, Yianna understood one thing: Dorothea's portraits captured real people doing important but ordinary tasks, or just simply living, as their surroundings told the rest of their story. Hers was the art of showing faces of pain, joy and the gritty character it took to survive their daily lives.

Then and there Yianna decided photography would be her life's work. And she would be a photographer like Dorothea Lange. She would try and capture the truth of people's lives and reveal their stories and spirits when she snapped the shutter. That moment of realization was like a flash of light, lasting only a few seconds but penetrating layers beneath her skin. She yearned for that feeling to last her lifetime. Yianna resolved she would not be some eccentric immigrant girl hauling a camera everywhere, using it as a frivolous toy. She was a serious observer and was ready to look, see and understand.

"Agamemnon, how did you know about ..." Yianna checked the photographer's name on the book, "Dorothea Lange?"

"I keep my big ears open." Agamemnon began shuffling about his tiny room, straightening photo frames and drawings on the wall, keeping his eyes on his art. "You know I work in photography department for the Army. Best job I have. There I learn to watch for people who do big things. Important things. And Dorothea, she make pictures of real peoples. The pain they suffer. The United States government hire her to take pictures during the hard times. You know, the Depression."

Agamemnon began to gather his pencils and place them in a tattered cigar box.

"I hear Dorothea Lange come to Woodland in 1942. They take away the Japanese families during the war. The government ship them to Sacramento and then to the concentration camps." Agamemnon stood behind Yianna looking at the photos in the book over her shoulder. "She stay at the Woodland Hotel. But she leave early, they say. She watch the Japanese peoples leave on the train and it make her sick. Very sick. So she have to leave."

That story was just another revelation that afternoon. Dorothea Lange, this woman was given the responsibility to record history. To bear witness for future generations. Yianna wanted to do work like this too. And Dorothea's work showed it could be done.

"*Efharistoh poli!* Thank you, Agamemnon!" She hugged Agamemnon powerfully, like the mother embracing the daughter in his drawing. She clasped the book to her heart when Agamemnon laid a gentle hand on her arm.

"One more thing I think about." He lowered himself into the overstuffed easy chair with worn arms and creaky cushion springs. "You need to know. I read about our Greek history and our Plato. He think about how we see things. Plato tell us how people look with their eyes!"

His words pulled Yianna back into the room as if she were reeled in.

"Plato say that all vision begin as small light particles in the eye. The particles they travel to what you look at, and then back to the eye. That is the method: from your human eye to your subject and back to your eye!" He lit up a cigar and puffed it quietly. "We Greeks, brilliant, no?"

"Doesn't the sun or light have some part in this?" Yianna asked, knowing full well that without some luminous source, vision was not possible. She wasn't a scholastic whiz, but she'd picked up that much in her elementary science classes.

"Oh, yes, that!" With a wave of his hand, Agamemnon washed away the pesky notion of science. "Yes, of course, the light. But how to know where to look, and when to look? It all come from the eye. *Your* eye! Plato know this! What you see, starts in your own eye."

He sat back setting his cigar down in an ashtray. "And another thing. Without that true vision, the *kako mati*, the Evil Eye, maybe come. And you know what Greeks think of that!" He laughed and did his Orthodox cross just in case the Evil Eye had been watching. Greeks could never be too careful.

Yianna fingered the Evil Eye charm on her bracelet that matched the one that hung from Olympia's slim wrist. She realized she had momentarily taken her focus away from the search for Olympia. And Yianna could not proceed with her life, her happiness, her camera, her viewing the world, without finding her sister. It occurred to her that to find Olympia, she just might have to use her vision the way Plato intended. Yianna needed to focus with her eyes, her brain and her heart on what she needed to see. And then go find it.

SIXTEEN

Olympia's Diary

After I was ripped from school, I missed my girlfriends but slowly, one by one, they also were forced to stay home and knead bread or sweep the dirt floors of their family homes. After six months of learning to sew, to darn, to measure, to serve, the brilliant colors of literature faded and my body began to step to the rhythm of Christos' Tailoring & Repair.

Babá's tailor shop was in the center of everything in Argos. In the morning the little bell on the door jingled and customers wandered in with their clothing needing repair or resizing. A new suit here, a torn skirt there. Our shop did it all. And I learned to work with my father and mother who knew every stitch ever performed by Greek hands. Every day I read a few paragraphs of Princess Anna's history and any other book I could borrow from adults with good reputations. I thought if I could keep my hopes of being a doctor alive, as if rubbing a magic lamp, they might come true.

I exercised my ankles as I rocked the black wrought-iron treadle of the Pfaff sewing machine for simple, evenly spaced seams. For the fine garments, Babá insisted on a skilled-hand stitch with a slim needle. He admired my needlework and declared my buttonholes were better than machine-made. Babá counted on me to tailor the men's suits although he handled the fittings. I served the tea and stayed in the background like a Greek woman-mouse.

We were a fine team until he got bitten with that nasty idea to travel far away to this land, America, which was supposed to be better. Was the work easier? The fruit truly sweeter? If we moved to America I would never again see my grandmother, cousins and girlfriends. How would I survive?

Babá said we would move because of some ghastly war that would soon level Greece to its knees. I had attended enough school to know that great wars had pummeled my country so many times in Greek history. This would be just another war for the history books.

After he left for America, my mother slipped into his space and efficiently ran the shop. My mother Angeliki's hair was long, black and glossy and she wore it caught in a net at work. I anticipated blooming into a cultured rose like my mother, to grow into her appearance, but I was frightened just the same. I observed how our male customers seemed polite to her face, yet their eyes twinkled a little too much when they paid her for tailoring services. Their gaze roamed over her dark smooth skin, the curve of her jet-black arched eyebrows and her midnight eyelashes that fringed her black eyes sprinkled with small flecks of gold. Just like mine.

Then, one day she folded over with stomach pain. Very soon she could not rise from bed and small red marks splotched her smooth skin. Ten days later she was buried in a box and for a week we could not re-enter our home for fear of contracting her illness — typhoid fever. How could my beautiful mother leave me with no warning — too weak during her final day to bid me a loving goodbye?

I decided I would shut down my dreams of a happy future. I would live only to help Yianna. If I were lost, where was the heart of a three-year-old? I vowed that if I were ever to become a parent, I would never abandon my child simply to visit a foreign land, no matter how much money it might bring. I would not break the bond.

Years earlier, before we left Argos, my maternal grandmother, my yiayiá, and I spent much time together, stitching quilts from scrap fabric, preserving apricots in glass jars, sweeping floors and singing old folk songs. She taught me about every herb and plant in her garden and their healing properties. And it was from my yiayiá *that I learned about the birds.* Yiayiá *called it Bird Lessons.*

Babá scoffed when my yiayiá taught me the art of predicting the future by watching the birds. Most people would. But we sat on a stone wall outside her home and looked out onto the open fields facing the hills.

Quietly we waited and watched as hawks or sparrows or geese or starlings suddenly took flight but changed directions to catch a favorable breeze. She told me that was good luck. A bird found dead indicated that one should leave a situation immediately. A noisy flock meant a confusing time was approaching. Birds jetting in from the east were always good luck, while birds migrating from a westerly direction were dangerous. And of course, when an eagle with prey in its beak circled but did not perch, that was a disaster.

The evening before we left our cherished patritha, *our homeland, I looked out the tiny window in our home while packing my clothes. An eagle carried a dark rodent only to drop it on the stone heap near our front door and continue to loop in the sky. I should have known. A catastrophe was waiting.*

SEVENTEEN

Six nights a week Stavros' card room was open to players who wanted to make money or just relax after a long day at their jobs. Often they hoped for both. The round tables, each with four chairs, squeezed nearly thirty men into the gambling room. Those were evenings when Italian, Portuguese, Greek, Chinese, Armenian and Mexican immigrants and a few Americans, stole two or three hours from their families and played together as men among men.

Hefty velvet curtains partitioned Angel's Bakery from the *sala*, blocking smoke from seeping into the kitchen. Stavros always sat directly across from the back door which he left open to dilute the sweat and cigar fumes. From there, he could also easily spot the authorities, should they choose to call.

To Stavros' right sat the short, lumpy Lucky. His shell shocked condition might have been a curse in his daily life but an asset when playing poker. Win or lose, Lucky's *prosopo,* his face, remained as passive as a Byzantine icon. He was known to lay down aces when Stavros was sure he harbored a losing hand. Then Lucky raked in big money—something Stavros rarely did.

Timoleon always sat to Stavros' left. A placid man who played only for amusement, betting little and folding early. Timoleon hid himself behind a handful of cards while harvesting gossip like the ripe, juicy cherries at his fruit stand.

He pulled a rumpled bandana from his pocket to wipe his naked head and poured himself more ouzo. Pushing his black-framed glasses higher on his nose, he folded his hand, grinning a jack-o-lantern smile. Timoleon's mood always bubbled with delight when surrounded by *parea*, friendly companionship.

Agamemnon's fluffy eyebrows dipped and rose over his cards but he rarely won. He might conceal his face behind his cards, but he could never keep his emotions from creeping across his face.

"You still keep a drinks tab?" With no hand to play, Timoleon stretched his contented lips to slurp his tiny glass of clear liquor. "Add this ouzo to my account. And another round for all of us. *Yamás!* To us!" He held his glass high in the air to toast.

"He'd *better* keep up his accounting!"

Agamemnon rose to find a tablet with the daily tally of alcohol tabs and bets owed to the house. Agamemnon's tall, sinewy body plunked back down in his seat to find the current page. His eyebrows arched at Stavros. "We need to keep this boarding house — *our home* — open. You owe the landlord for last month!"

"Why you tell me my business? Now you my big brother Christos?" Stavros blustered halfheartedly. Stavros often suffered *kakotychía*, bad luck or he simply blamed the Evil Eye for his empty wallet at the end of a long evening at his own tables.

To Stavros, Agamemnon's surly insistence on accurate bookkeeping was like a *griá*, an old Greek woman, poking at a leg of lamb in the roasting oven every few minutes. Agamemnon was the meddling wife Stavros never wanted, although Agamemnon was usually right in his accounting. Secretly, Stavros was relieved the old shepherd found importance in handling the finances.

"Stavros, you gotta take care of the daily cash. Or I gotta do it for you! You need pay attention! No drink so much!"

Stavros could not argue that point. Agamemnon moved close so that only Stavros could hear. "And you gotta ask these mens about Olympia. Maybe someone see something. That young American at the back table. He about Olympia's age."

Agamemnon moved his chair even closer toward Stavros.

"You gotta do something! You are the *theo*, the uncle, may your brother Christos rest in peace." He followed his short lecture with a speedy sign of the cross.

"I supposed to ask this American if he know Olympia? In a gambling room?" Stavros was sweating now. "He look kinda familiar, but I don't know him!" Stavros hissed.

Stavros got up to escape Agamemnon and make his rounds to the other tables for public relations sake. He roamed the room noting any unaccounted drinks to prove he was not a dilettante. In truth, Stavros hated the "business" part of his business. He would love his customers to drink for free, becoming slightly buzzed, engaging in friendly chatter. Stavros lived for interesting conversation, a spontaneous dance and a drink followed by tasty *mezedes*, appetizers. But Agamemnon was right. He had to keep his bakery and gambling den open for his nieces as well as his three boarders. As host, he ambled from table to table ramping up his energy, providing his *philotimo*, his Greek hospitality, to all his guests.

"Mr. Pearson, how you do? Your wife? She feel better?" Pearson puffed his thick cigar, the smoke seeping from his mouth in rings. The corners of his lips tilted up with contentment. Apron over his plaid shirt, he'd rushed from his job at the Nugget Market on Main Street to the card game, not wanting to miss a moment of camaraderie. Mr. Chen sat next to him pensively studying his cards. He had no need to advertise his business, as his laundry was the busiest in Woodland. The Chen family never lost a pair of socks or underwear, always impressing his customers.

Agamemnon followed Stavros as he checked if the other guests, welders, brick layers, construction workers and garbage men, were in good spirits. Agamemnon's short, fat pencil was his dousing stick, leading him to the extra whiskeys, glasses of wine and beers not yet paid for. Agamemnon told each man his debt for the evening and they quickly shelled out.

As they circled the room, Stavros remembered the week before Olympia's disappearance, after all the glasses were washed and the players had vacated their chairs, Olympia had quietly approached Stavros who was mildly drunk sitting alone at the back table.

"I've been thinking." Olympia's eyes held Stavros in place with an even stare. "I can do the nightly drinks accounting for the card games. I've watched you do it. I'm always here and I'm excellent at math."

Stavros looked up, surprised at Olympia's sudden self-assurance. Was his shy niece actually asking to collect for alcohol and betting tabs by herself? Working with gambling men at night?

"I would never interrupt the games." Olympia pulled a pencil from behind her ear like an experienced accountant. "But it seems that you are leaving money on the table. And we could use every penny."

She looked down at her figures while Stavros was stunned to silence.

"I contribute almost all my earnings to this household and we are usually behind on the bakery rent. But look here." Olympia pushed a sheet of paper in front of Stavros. "Every night that you don't collect, you lose about twenty dollars. That adds up!"

Stavros cleared his throat, preparing to answer that she, a beautiful woman, had no part to play in the evening gambling sessions. But Olympia's enthusiasm overflowed.

"And I can help with the bakery accounting! At Mira's I overheard a man talking about buying bakery supplies in bulk from a new warehouse in Sacramento. Cheap! And they deliver!" Stavros had never seen Olympia so focused. She waited for his response.

Stavros heart fell to his shoes. He had to kill this silly notion of his attractive, unmarried niece working at night with men.

"Collecting and keeping the books would fill my evenings." Olympia sat back, happy with the case she presented. "I don't drink, so I could keep a clear head. And it would not interfere with my job at the tailor shop."

Stavros absently scraped his shoes against the floor and looked up avoiding her eyes.

"Not such a good idea, Olympia." Stavros stammered his words. "The mens, they, uh—"

He poured himself another glass of Mavrodaphne and took a gulp.

"The mens they will give you excuses not to pay," he lied. "We gotta have a *man* collect from the *mens*. They take advantage of a woman."

"I think you are afraid to collect from your friends," Olympia boldly declared, sparks flashing from her eyes. "They expect to pay. You do not need to buy their friendship."

Olympia waited a second for him to say more. Her dark eyes locked on her uncle, then she lowered them and sighed. Laying aside the pencil she quietly ripped the sheet of paper into shreds. She carefully pulled her chair away from the table, walked swiftly to her room and closed the door, shutting out her uncle.

At that time Stavros told himself he had done the right thing. His duty was to protect his niece from the dogs who would hound her, sniffing her scent. Christos would want it that way. Yes, he had shielded her from men's advances.

But, looking back, Stavros realized he had not protected Olympia at all. He had flatly denied the willing and intelligent Olympia the opportunity to elevate his bakery and card room business, and herself. He should have allowed her the chance to use her *myalóh*, her mind. Every day since her disappearance, Stavros wondered if events would have been different if he had.

Stavros hadn't made his way to the last table when Yianna pushed her way through the curtains carrying plates of manouri and haloumi cheese and small slices of fresh baked French bread for the guests—on the house, of course. These few tidbits of food kept the men drinking more, playing longer, betting more, losing another hand. He didn't allow Yianna, only eighteen, to serve liquor. One never knew whose prying eyes would observe and inform the authorities. But he watched how the men slowly moved their eyes toward her, then, uninterested, focused on their cards. But when Olympia had passed, the men could not help but stare. Her even-ly-toned olive skin hypnotized most men with its silkiness, as if waiting to be touched.

In Stavros' opinion, Yianna was quite unaware of how a young Greek woman should conduct herself. She wore boys' blue jeans and a man's white shirt, the tails flopped out. As she set the plates down, the men looked up but did not stare. Yianna was not feminine the way Greek girls should be. Mostly hard edges. But what about her relentless inquisitive look? Couldn't she pretend to flirt a little? Perhaps a playful smile? Stavros feared she would not bloom into a marriageable woman.

As she set down the last plate at the back table, Yianna locked eyes with a young American man, dropping the plate with a clatter. Stavros jumped. Why was she so rude to a guest? He looked again but could not place the man. Yianna hurried to her room, the door rattling as she slammed it and jammed a towel under it to keep the smoke and voices from her room.

Stavros lowered his frame in a chair next to the three shepherds.

"How will I marry off that girl?" he sighed. "No one even look at her!"

Timoleon frowned, his glasses slipping down his nose. "What you talking? She a good girl. I never hear bad about her. And I would know! Yianna, she work hard. For you! For this family! What more you want?"

"But she eighteen. What she gonna do?" Stavros asked in all sincerity. What could this camera-toting niece possibly do with herself besides become an old maid? "And I supposed to carry her until she *someday* meet a man and marry? I never get to *patrida*, the homeland."

"You must leave the village behind, Stavros!" Agamemnon barked. "There is nothing left after the war. And compared to what you got here? How you no understand this?"

Stavros shook his head. With Olympia missing and Yianna's blurry future, his obligation seemed to stretch out long and limp.

Agamemnon folded his lousy pair of twos, a seven, a five and a queen.

"Look around, Stavros! The young womens in America—they want more than to sweep the floors and boil *horta,* wild greens, for dinner. They have their own ways now. The war change everything. This is America! And that one," Agamemnon pointed to Yianna's door, "she is different. She want more. Leave her to find it. She born in Argos but she American here." He thudded his fist over his heart. "Let her be!"

Ignoring his cards for a moment and folding his arms across his chest, Stavros' thoughts floated to the good, obedient side of Yianna. She never once shirked her duties at the bakery or the serving jobs in the card room. She had never pinched a dime or a quarter from the cash register. In fact, she often acted as Stavros' interpreter in business matters, translating documents and contracts from an early age.

But his thoughts stumbled when it came to her dogged American independence. To him, Yianna was like a bold sunflower positioned in a vase with the elegant pink hyacinth, delicate daffodils and reserved purple iris, all only whispering for attention. Yianna's energy was raw, straightforward—just too American. She no longer relied on her uncle for advice or money. He realized he was afraid of losing her as he had already lost Olympia.

Stavros poured another tumbler of his excellent red wine which softened the thought he wasn't the devoted uncle he should be. He drank it down nearly to the bottom of the glass where he saw Olympia's face. She seemed to ask why he couldn't rescue her from the dark corner to which she vanished. Rubbing his eyes, he realized this was another drunken apparition, the third this week.

In his collection of blurry memories, Stavros sifted out a moment when Agamemnon corrected him, that *philotimo* for Greeks was not just the presentation of supreme hospitality to guests. Agamemnon announced that *philotimo* also was a philosophy and it covered being a good person, doing the right thing. He said according to the ancient Greek sage Thales, "*Philotimo* to the Greeks is like breathing. A Greek is not a Greek without it." Olympia's image continued to undulate in the bottom of Stavros' glass like an exotic fish observed through the sloshing liquid. Was she now asking him to put aside his needs as Thales said, for the good, and help her?

Stavros looked around the room to survey his gambling colleagues and the American he did not recognize and, therefore, did not trust. Should he shove aside this cobbled-together, patchwork establishment he had created and nag the authorities to find his niece? They would certainly shut down the card game enterprise, his basement winery and perhaps toss Stavros in jail. Was he succumbing to the American way of life and placing too much importance on money and reputation?

These thoughts swirled in his head while he poured another tall tumbler of wine and headed for his room alone. Stavros would let

Agamemnon, Timoleon and Lucky close the card room. He was once again pulled apart by the person he was and the person he needed to become as Olympia's face faded from the bottom of his glass.

Stavros turned the handle of his bedroom door, when suddenly Timoleon's voice interrupted the desperate tug-of-war in his head.

"I know that American!" Timoleon was talking, almost shouting to Agamemnon. "He that sheriff's deputy. He come to my fruit stand at lunch time."

Fear gripped Stavros' heart. The sheriff's deputy? What was the deputy doing in the card room, playing endless rounds of poker, drinking his homemade wine? Why had Yianna dropped the plate when she saw him?

In Argos young males like Stavros worked together to keep the peace, protect the village women and defend the truth before things became violent or ugly. But here in America, failing to find Olympia had left him feeling hogtied, stymied, bewildered.

He had failed as a man.

Collapsing across his bed, guilt burned his body as if the sagging mattress was on fire. Stavros prayed he would immediately pass out. Perhaps tomorrow, when he rose to heat up the ovens once again, the early rays of dawn would erase this feeling of catastrophe that surrounded him, warning that his world had become horribly out of balance.

EIGHTEEN

Yianna savored the last of the cool morning air before the June heat sprang up to cook everyone indoors and out. She had hung her Leica, her constant companion, over her shoulder patiently waiting to be used.

Enjoying a quiet stroll down Dead Cat Alley, Yianna was picking up the newly starched and pressed aprons with the Angel's Bakery logo brightly embroidered on the pocket. She warmed to the opportunity to visit the Good Day Laundry and her friend Frankie Chen at his family business, a real family with a father, a mother—both alive. The oldest brother, Kenny, would visit Angel's Bakery to leave a few herbs for Olympia when he grew something special in his garden. He was studying botany at the university in Berkeley, usually referred to as "Cal." Kenny had earned a full scholarship to Cal, adding more status to the Chen family.

The little laundry was a predictable quiet hum of washers and steam irons. Everyone, including the children, occupied their Saturday workstations.

"Your order you pick up?" A smiling Mr. Chen met Yianna at the door. She pulled her camera to her side, making room for the laundry.

She handed two dollars to Mr. Chen. He returned two quarters and five spotless aprons, neatly folded, wrapped with crisp blue paper and tied with string. Yianna's eyes searched behind the counter.

"Go!" Mr. Chen's hand whisked her to the back rooms of the house. "You know where everybody work!" Mr. Chen winked. Yianna crossed to the kitchen where Mrs. Chen, small and spider-like, scrubbed stubborn ink stains from a man's white shirt with a pumice stone. Her open-toed blue sandals slapped the tile floor as she turned to her six-burner gas stove and opened the oven door.

"You want?" She pulled out a platter of warm *bao*, pork buns. Yianna smiled at Mrs. Chen's bright eyes, endless wells of hospitality and motherly care. Delighted, Yianna snatched a pork bun and allowed her teeth to bite through the sweet sticky bun to the spicy pork hiding inside.

"Thank you, delicious as always! Frankie home?" Mrs. Chen smiled and pointed to the next room. Frankie looked up from yanking shirts, underwear and uniforms from a clothesline. In this room, the boys slept on hardwood bed frames, constructed by Mr. Chen, which were topped with thin cotton mattresses. Thick cord strung across the room weighed heavily with shirts, pants, underwear and cotton towels drying in the early morning air. Frankie's job was to fold them or separate each piece for ironing which took place in his sisters' small room next door.

"Yianna! How you doing?" Frankie was taller than most boys in her school and his smile had always welcomed her since their days together in kindergarten. Because Angel's Bakery was located near the Good Day Laundry, Yianna and Frankie had walked to school and home together nearly every day of their elementary years. But in high school, Frankie's baseball practice had separated them from their daily walks and exchange of news. Yianna had not seen Frankie in several weeks.

"Did you hear? Got my Cal baseball scholarship a couple of days ago. I'm going, Yianna!" Frankie laughed, his face beaming. "I'm going to Cal! Just like Kenny!"

Yianna swallowed her bite of pork bun. "Just what you wanted! That's the best news I've heard all week, Frankie." Yianna's mind skipped back to Frankie as a young boy, practicing past sunset with anyone who'd play catch or toss pitches over home plate. Many times, it was Yianna who pitched.

"I'll be practicing all summer." Frankie glanced at his baseball glove hanging on the wall beneath a signed photo of Willie Mays in his New York Giants uniform.

"But you never told me, Yianna. What will you be doing?"

Yianna stuffed the rest of the puffy bun in her mouth and smiled.

"Not sure," she mumbled. Frankie knew her better than anyone and she hoped he wouldn't notice her eyes were glued to the floor.

"Well, you should come visit me in Berkeley. Kenny takes the bus back and forth all the time. You could go with him." Frankie's hands expertly folded a pile of men's underwear into neat stacks. "Don't forget about graduation practice at noon. Only a week to go and we're free!"

Yianna was uncertain how to respond as her future seemed a haze, like the gloomy tule fog that settled in the Sacramento Valley after a winter rain. She needed a place to hide, a shield. Yianna pulled her Leica over her face. Frankie posed as if he were up at bat, ready to swing for the fences as she snapped.

"Yianna!"

At that moment, the oldest Chen sister Ellie buzzed into the room pulling several men's white dress shirts off the line. The cotton shirts fell over her arm as she pulled Yianna to the corner of the tiny room.

"Look at the promise ring Lloyd gave me last night!" Ellie had always treated Yianna like a little sister. She was a whirlwind of laughter and high spirits in a slim body. Her wide face was not delicate and always flushed with color.

"He's two years older than me." She looked toward the door. "Shhhh don't tell my parents. He's Caucasian, you know." Beaming, Ellie held her hand away from her body, fingers close together. With a dreamy smile, she studied her small silver band with a tiny diamond chip nestled in the center. Yianna stood in awe at Ellie's determination to do exactly what she wanted, no matter what this union might mean to her parents.

Just then, Kenny wandered into the room, breaking off Ellie's tale of romance. His eyes were soft and inquiring and his long fingers always seem to move when he spoke. Kenny was taller than his brother and as graceful as a dancer.

"Yianna!" Kenny clapped her on her shoulder, happy to see her. "Hear anything about Olympia? Anything at all?" He spoke directly to Yianna, as if his siblings were invisible.

Ellie scampered to the ironing room, her room, across the beaten wooden floors of the small clapboard house.

Yianna met his concerned dark eyes. "A standstill. And no one is helping us. Still."

Yianna lowered her eyes, ashamed to deliver the empty reality of no sister and slapped her hands to her sides in a gesture of surrender. Admitting to Kenny she had no clues, Yianna felt as if she had personally failed Olympia.

The lines between Kenny's dark feathered eyebrows deepened with worry.

"Exactly what happened when my auntie in San Francisco vanished. They said she must have left town 'with a man.' They called it 'Another Chinatown Mystery.' She was a cook in a Chinese restaurant on Washington Street. The police hardly looked and never found her." He shook his head and stared at his black canvas shoes.

Kenny began to stuff his duffle bag with serious intensity. "I gotta get back." He scribbled his number on a scrap of paper and pressed it in Yianna's hand. "You let me know if anything turns up. And if there is something I can do. We need to find her." Kenny's eyes blazed a hole into Yianna's. "You know how I feel about Olympia."

Yianna was stunned. She had *absolutely no idea* what Olympia meant to Kenny. Olympia with whom she shared every secret, the sister to whom she trusted her heart, had told her nothing. Olympia had kept this landmine from her.

Yianna stood in quiet amazement. He flickered a sad smile and disappeared out the front door, duffle bag over his shoulder. Yianna lifted her camera and snapped the backwards lettering of the Good Day Laundry on the window while Kenny, small in the frame, gracefully loped down the street toward the Greyhound bus stop.

The starched aprons under her arm, Yianna approached the bakery munching on another pork *bao* Mrs. Chen had shoved into her hands. How many other secrets had Olympia kept from her? And exactly when would she stumble across the next one?

NINETEEN

Walking past the orange and blue Rexall Drug store sign on the corner of First and Main, Yianna thought about the Chen family. They were a tight clan and each member was directed at furthering the family's laundry enterprise. Their hard work had earned the Good Day Laundry a golden reputation. As Yianna remembered back to when she first met them, the Chen boys had always protected Olympia and Yianna.

One sweltering April afternoon when Yianna was in grammar school, the neighborhood boys began their haranguing. In those days, her classmates continually asked if her sister Olympia, with her dark good looks and sculpted cheekbones glowing with Asian charm, was "oriental." "*Did you have the same father?*" "*Yianna must be adopted,*" they cracked. "*Ioanna — Ya Wanna?*" they taunted with their tongues hanging out, panting after the petrified Yianna. Or "*Sister Ophelia — I wanna feel ya!*" Cackling with laughter they'd run ahead to taunt her again.

One day, Yianna had enough. She threw down her bundle of books, found a few small stones and began flinging them at her tormentors. Working herself into a sweaty fury, Yianna heaved rocks, tin cans or anything she could find at the older boys who screamed insults her way. But the boys on the fence only jeered more, delighted she was agitated. Then, a figure materialized next to her, hurling rocks at her enemies, hitting their mark every time. It was Frankie, using his best baseball skills. One by one, the group thinned as Frankie's rocks hit arms and legs, stinging the coyotes who ridiculed Yianna.

"Well, that ought to shut them up!" He dusted his hands and laid a kind arm around Yianna. She wiped her tears with soiled hands and began to gather her books that had tumbled into the dust.

"Thank you, Frankie." She straightened the collar of her plaid cotton shirt and adjusted her skirt. Her face was hot from her humiliation. "I hate them!"

"They're just stupid. Some of 'em are on my baseball team anyway. I'll talk to them." Frankie bent to help with her books. "They won't do it again." He smiled. "Guaranteed."

Frankie walked with Yianna toward Dead Cat Alley and even bought a strawberry ice cream cone for each of them for a dime, a tip from his laundry work. They each wandered home, their friendship cemented. The bullying boys never taunted Yianna again.

Yianna was painfully aware when she wore Olympia's resized hand-me-down clothes, she broadcasted the image of a poor immigrant girl. She was simply the girl to pity, not to befriend. Quietly unpopular, Yianna owned no fashionable outfits or even a charm bracelet, aside from the Evil Eye charm on her wrist. She loved to play baseball with Frankie's friends in the neighborhood and wore shorts under her dresses so she did not worry about sliding into second base. Frankie was in her class every year which made her feel safe. His desk was always nearby: C for Chen, D for Diamantopoulos. Yianna often studied Frankie's quick smile, his easy manner with boys or girls. Everyone in school wanted to buzz around Frankie and be his friend.

But what exactly did Kenny mean to Olympia besides a friend? Yianna knew Kenny protected Olympia when she had first arrived from Greece, understanding no English. Kenny had not come calling for Olympia as a boyfriend, had he? In the past, Kenny had come to trade his knowledge of Chinese herbs with her ancestral knowledge about Greek medicinal herbs. Yianna loved the bundles of brown and green herbs and grasses tied with kitchen string that adorned Olympia's workspace, the bakery kitchen. She had watched her sister write in the Greek alphabet on tiny paper bags the name of her favorites: Wild Malotira, Sideritis or Fliskouni. Then she dabbed small pieces of tape to seal each bag.

Almost at the bakery Yianna smashed directly into someone's sturdy body. Porter! Standing on the corner outside the bakery door, his arms were folded tightly across his crisp button-down shirt.

"Yianna, what happened? Why did you run away from the party?" Arms outstretched for a hug, he took a step toward Yianna. She instantly drew back.

Didn't he know? Was he unaware that his mother had attacked her?

"You know what happened." She tried rebalancing the freshly laundered aprons under her arm, her voice flat. "I'm leaving you alone. That's what I'm supposed to do!"

"Well, I don't –" He stumbled on his words. "I don't understand you, Yianna. What about you and me?"

She held the glass door to the bakery ajar before stepping through. Her camera clattered against it.

"Just go away." Yianna's eyes narrowed, her face drawn in pain. But her voice was strong. "Your mother says I'm not good for you."

She let the door close behind her. The little bell on the door, which usually tinkled cheer to customers, now irritated Yianna's ears. Feeling the instant cocoon of protection from the old Greek men, the bakery door separated Yianna from the painful threat of the privileged wealthy class whose rules she did not understand.

The sweet smell of Uncle Stavros' cinnamon rolls welcomed Yianna. At the counter three giggling girls dug deep into their pockets to buy sugar cookies with sprinkles. Lucky busily waited on the customers, serving up a gentle grin with every order.

For a moment she sensed Angel's Bakery from the customer's point of view: the rich aromas of vanilla, butter and sugar; the rhythm of customers anticipating the purchase of a special layer cake, cookies or strawberry-filled Danish; the satisfaction of nourishing people, this haven for good spirits. Could a person truly feel distraught in a bakery? Over her shoulder Yianna watched Porter slowly turn away from his post at the corner. Maybe Porter had never been lashed by his mother's scathing tongue. Quickly donning an apron, Yianna took her place behind the counter and passed Lucky a clean one from the stack under her arm. She vowed to put Porter out of her mind.

"Good morning!" Two older women counted their change before ordering. Yianna stood behind the freshly baked pies and forced a smile. "What would you like today?"

Festooned with a crown of a golden braided crust and coarse sugar sprinkles, each pie waited behind the glass case, begging to be taken home. The older woman pointed a crooked finger at the apple pie. She smiled contentedly as Yianna gently boxed it and slid it to Lucky who made change. Helping her next customer, Yianna relaxed a bit, allowing the divine aromas to curl around her and soothe her confusion.

At that moment, Agamemnon rushed behind her, pulling the ties of her apron and spinning her around. "*Prosecseh!* Beware! He's coming!"

Yianna whipped around to face him.

"Who?"

"Your future husband!"

TWENTY

Yianna finished waiting on customers as the morning rush trickled to a drip, then walked slowly to the kitchen and washed her hands in the deep stainless-steel sink. Had Uncle Stavros blindsided her by inviting some strange man seeking a sweet Greek girl for his bride?

She was aware that many Greek girls her age were offered suitors. After an initial meeting, and several Sunday dinners with the family, the young woman would tell her parents if she consented to marriage. Then a lavish Greek Orthodox ceremony and wedding feast and the newlyweds would manufacture children as soon as possible. Preferably boys.

Yianna wanted no suitors. No husband. No lacy veil. No golden wedding band or children playing about her feet. Her indignation was at a frothy boil and ready to spill over.

She looked about the *sala* in search of Uncle Stavros but the chairs stood empty. Pushing open the door to his room without knocking she saw him struggling over accounting ledgers, a look of confusion on his rough, handsome face. He worked his eraser on the page, then finally planted his head between his hands. Yianna softened for a moment but steeled herself. No husband. No way.

"Agamemnon said my future husband will be coming for dinner tonight." She stood behind him, her voice loud, edgy. Ready to attack, she did not have enough nerve to truly punish her uncle who she knew tried his best to raise her and Olympia without much complaint.

"A suitor? For me? *Really*, Uncle Stavros?"

He slowly turned to her, shoving aside his gnawed pencil.

"No' what you think, Yianna." He wiped his eyes with his handkerchief, his voice shaking. "*Neh*, yes, this man is open to marriage. But after what happens with Olympia, I think maybe, with a husband you safe. I no protect Olympia. I fail for her."

Uncle Stavros unexpectedly collapsed around Yianna's shoulders hugging her tight.

"Thanasi a nice man." He sniffed. "You come to dinner. You see. I make *yemistes domates*, tomatoes stuffed with rice and lamb, your favorite. Just come meet him. Please!"

Yianna frowned. Should she scream at her armful of wilted, weeping uncle or humor him a little? He was always a mixing bowl of raw emotions.

"Because I love the way you cook, I'll come. But, Uncle Stavros, tell him I'm not marrying anyone."

He nodded compliantly and Yianna broke away. She stormed into her own small room, flopping onto her bed. She glanced at the empty, perfectly made twin bed across from her own.

"Now he'll lose us both, Oly."

Yianna had always allowed guilt to taint her heart because of her uncle's sacrifice for her and Olympia. But she also had listened to Agamemnon as she read letters from relatives describing the atrocities of the Nazi occupation of Greece and the civil war that followed. Those events prevented Stavros from packing up the girls and hauling them back to what had been his simple quiet village. The bad news from Greece reported that many villagers and city dwellers had been starved to death, women raped and men and boys had vanished to defend Greece, leaving empty homes and unproductive fields. During the war and the following years of scarcity and sorrow, Stavros understood the United States to be a safe land of plenty in comparison, just as his brother Christos had predicted. Still, Yianna knew Stavros dreamt of his old home, his memory of his Argos more perfect with every sip of *raki*.

She looked up to the mirror. Black hair, black eyes, smooth olive skin — just like Olympia. But she was a shadow of her sister's beauty. Taller, skinnier, more angles, hair flying, no soft waves like Olympia's that naturally rippled around her face. No curvy figure to hold a man's attention.

With a heavy sigh, she turned away from her mirror and stared at the large black and white poster of Marlon Brando seductively leaning onto the handlebars of his Triumph Thunderbird 6T motorcycle from the movie *The Wild One.* His beautifully sculpted features gazed upward — all male, all adventurer, plenty of swagger. Yianna wanted to be transported into Marlon Brando's renegade hell-bent life in that movie. Sloe-eyed, full lipped and cap tilted low over his forehead, Brando was poised for danger as he draped himself over his vehicle ready to escape the suffocating society in which he did not fit.

As Yianna studied his eyes she fell into a daydream. Suddenly she was no longer in Woodland but somewhere far into her future, an adult, an adventurer too. A wild one. She leaned forward to pull Agamemnon's book of Dorothea Lange photos from the small wooden table serving as a bedside nightstand. She leafed through Lange's dramatic black and white photos. These were people whose faces whispered the pain they suffered beneath their skin.

Breathing hard, Yianna pulled her thick dark hair forward and reached for a sharp pair of Olympia's sewing scissors. With one gleaming snip of the shears, Yianna slashed off her heavy length of hair, a maiden's burden, and allowed it to drop onto the floor. Energized now, she squinted at her image in the mirror as if it were a pool of water. With choppy snaps, she evened out the first major cut. What emerged was a dark, edgy hairdo that suddenly appeared modern and somehow flattering to her long thin face.

Yianna tossed the scissors onto the bed and dashed to the alley. She nearly tripped on the unofficial lost and found box which lay rotting with card players' forgotten jackets and empty wallets inside. Digging down to the bottom of the weather-stained cardboard box, she pulled out a thick worn black-leather jacket made for a man twice her size. She slipped into the heavy jacket, snapping it shut in front.

Not satisfied, Yianna dove back into the box to find a pair of men's straight black cotton pants, probably cast offs from one of the uncles. Pulling them on, she cinched a thick black belt with a weighty buckle tight around her hips to hold them up. In her imagination she was a young photographer-artist and she craved a distinctive stylish touch, something Marlon Brando would approve of. Racing back into her bedroom, she dug into Olympia's shallow top drawer and found a long silky scarf, the color of champagne, with the small delicate Greek key Olympia had embroidered near the rolled edge. Perfect — a little Greek drama felt just right. She stared at herself in the mirror. Now she was almost ready for her prospective groom.

Shrouded in her black tough-guy ensemble, Yianna swiped a few dark lines around her lashes with the eyeliner she had used for school plays. Her black outfit matched her mood — angry, defensive. A little bit dangerous. Suddenly she remembered her high school graduation practice was over and she had missed it. She laughed out loud. Wild ones did not practice.

Yianna glided from her bedroom to the card room where she nonchalantly began setting the table for the usual crowd plus one more. She straightened the utensils from the army-navy surplus store on the table, humming to herself.

Agamemnon wandered in and looked up. His eyes lit on the new version of Yianna. He said nothing, but a tiny smirk worked one corner of his mouth beneath his mustache. Then Timoleon walked into the *sala* clutching a crinkled brown bag spilling with aromatic apricots and cherries. Lucky was close behind.

"Look! The best apricots! And cherries they ripe too! Just come in today!"

As a Greek, the ripeness of fruit was the most important subject of the moment. Neither Timoleon nor Lucky glanced at Yianna's new look. Keeping their eyes lowered they would not venture into the unknown jungle of a young woman's choice of clothes or hairstyle. Much safer to stick to fruit.

Stavros walked in from the kitchen with his tray of *mezedes*, appetizers. His eyes registered a shadowy form in black attire. He blinked to see Yianna's face attached to it.

"Yianna?" He dropped the tray on the table. "Yianna, that is you? What happens with you?" He sat down to study her in great detail—her agitated hair, her oversized leather jacket, the heavy black leather boots she wore when she worked in the tomato fields during summer break. Rubbing his eyes and sliding his hands over his unshaven face, Stavros sat stunned.

"This is the way I look now, Uncle Stavros." Yianna tossed her short hair, her black eyes hooded with eyeliner. "I am an artist. Your friend Thanasi might as well know it."

She zipped up the jacket although the warm evening called for her to remove it.

"Maybe you wear dress for dinner?" Stavros' voice was desperate. "Thanasi come soon."

Yianna was determined to break out of her chrysalis and beat her new wings until they were dry and beautiful. "This is me. He can like it or not."

Timoleon pushed Lucky with his fingertips as they scuttled away. "We go to basement and get *krasi*, wine."

"*Férte poli!* Get plenty!" Agamemnon studied the drawdown between the newly minted beat artist and old Greek cook. "We gonna need it!"

TWENTY-ONE

An hour later in the *sala*, the middle-aged Thanasi seemed uncomfortable, shifting in his chair and gulping glasses of cool water. He was tall but round everywhere, certainly not a young woman's dream. His watery brown eyes were cast downward while he nervously picked at his cuticles, waiting for the meal to begin. Yianna sat across from him in her black leather jacket, short hair wild and her camera lovingly cradled on her lap.

Agamemnon, Timoleon and Lucky had scrubbed their nails clean, to show the prospective groom they were a civilized bunch, but each man seemed nervous. Timoleon's thin voice filled the air, prattling about trivialities. Lucky tapped his foot incessantly under the round table but was silent. Yianna occasionally lifted her Leica to snap a photo of each person: Thanasi's blank look, Stavros' beads of sweat under his forehead curls, Lucky and Timoleon quietly sipping their wine. Amazingly, Thanasi did not react to Yianna's photography, keeping his focus on his plate.

Only Agamemnon shot dark arrows with his eyes to Stavros for this stupid match up.

"Eighteen-year-old girl and thirty-five-year-old man?" Agamemnon hissed in a quiet tone at Stavros who sat close to him. "You think you doing good with this match? This is your niece! Your Yianna! What would your brother Christos say?" Agamemnon raised his voice a notch. "You feed her to this lion?" He looked at Thanasi slowly munching his *tiropita*, a toasty triangle dripping with cheese. "Or maybe the lamb."

Timoleon cleared his throat and changed the subject.

"Stavros, this year's wine – the best yet! You get your grapes from the Bianchi family again?"

"Yes, always! I drive to Kenwood every September, the day after Labor Day, with my truck." Stavros rose to fill the wine decanter from a larger jug in the kitchen. He had bathed and shaved carefully for the special guest. "No place else I get good grapes! My secret: buy good grapes or grow them yourself!"

Yianna downed her short fat glass of wine and switched her empty with Lucky's full glass. Although under legal drinking age, Yianna was no stranger to sipping wine with old men. If she ever needed a glass of wine, it was now.

Yianna avoided looking at Thanasi. He was a walrus whose heavy cheeks melted into his sweater vest. Now his swollen eyes were fixed on Yianna. She felt like the prized sheep he was sizing up for his herd.

"Please, Thanasi, try my delicious *kouloura* bread. Just baked today." Stavros offered a plate stacked with his fluffy bread. "Yianna help me in the bakery. She know how to cook good!"

Agamemnon rolled his eyes.

"And she take pictures too. With that camera." Agamemnon pointed to the Leica on her lap. "Our Yianna is artist! *Yassou!*" Agamemnon raised his glass in a toast.

Yianna in her dark leather jacket and very male pants shifted uncomfortably in her chair.

"And when do you graduate, if I might ask?" Thanasi was nervous, tentative.

"High school. I'm graduating *high school*." Yianna's voice was flat and cold. Had Thanasi never talked to a young woman in his adult life? "I'm only eighteen. Maybe my uncle forgot to tell you."

Thanasi's thin lips pulled back into a tight smile but Yianna couldn't hate him. It was her Uncle Stavros who had set up this dinner meeting. Thanasi probably assumed she was ready and willing to marry.

As the men dug into their meal, silverware clicked on the thick white ceramic plates but Yianna could not touch a bite. She reached for her camera and memorialized the dinner with a portrait of Uncle Stavros sipping wine, Agamemnon appearing solemn and suspicious and the pleasant Thanasi who blandly reached for a second helping of stuffed tomatoes.

She set her camera on her lap again, her pet, her inner vision. The simple action of taking the photos calmed her roiling temper. She would not be the object of anyone's desire. A twinge of longing for Porter sprang up, someone her own age, someone whose face lit up when she entered the classroom. Someone she had trusted. Yianna watched as Thanasi's excellent table manners navigated his knife and fork with precision, capturing each grain of rice with the tines of his fork.

"So, you own a grocery in Ukiah?" Uncle Stavros already knew the answer. Anything to change the direction this dinner had taken.

"Yes, downtown Ukiah. It is my family's business. But my parents are older now, so I manage it. Well, except for my mother who always wants to do the books! Can't keep her out of the store. Or my life!" He chuckled and Yianna watched his belly jiggle over his belt.

Well, go marry your mother! she thought to herself.

"Beware the *petherá*, mother-in-law." Agamemnon, sitting next to Yianna, rumbled in his lowest register. "Catastrophe." He chugged a long drink of wine and shook his head.

"We have wooden floors in our store but soon, we will expand into the space next door and lay tile." Thanasi's doleful gaze drooped back onto Yianna. "If I have the right partner, we could make it a success for the next generation. For our kids!"

All heads turned as Yianna tossed her silverware on her plate with a jarring clank and shot to a standing position.

"No! Don't think of me that way! Don't think of me at all!" Stealthy like a cat, ready to pounce, she circled the table. "Maybe Uncle Stavros did not tell *you*, Thanasi! I am not going to marry anyone. And definitely not someone I just met. I am not for sale!"

Dramatically swirling her long scarf across her shoulder, she turned back.

"Another thing my Uncle Stavros did not tell you. My sister — *his* older niece — has been missing for over six months. The men in this family don't know how to find her. So I don't ask myself who I will marry. I ask how I will find my sister. And why aren't all of you looking for Olympia too?"

Sweating and flushed, she tramped away in her heavy boots from the promise of a Greek Orthodox wedding and a life of sweeping the floors of her mother-in-law's grocery store. She did not look back. Yianna slammed the door to her room, the door that separated her history as a Greek immigrant from this new person — perhaps an artist. But first she desperately needed to make good on her promise to find Olympia, for her sister's sake as well as her own.

TWENTY-TWO

The gravel road crunched under Yianna's worn black boots as she trudged towards Mira's Tailor Shop, which was located in a lonely free-standing building along the less populated Road 113. Despo, the owner of Mira's, had renovated the Flying A gas station into a cozy storefront. Here she and her younger twin sisters stitched, fitted and hemmed dresses, trousers and blouses and even whipped up wedding gowns for same-day nuptials, no questions asked.

Despo, fifty-five years old and head of her family, was round as a small barrel. Her uniform was always a jersey dress, usually black, honoring dozens of dead relatives in Greece. A narrow matching belt tied her in half with a bulge on top and a soft lump on the bottom.

Despo rarely smiled. Her thick dark eyebrows were heavy above her eyes. Living an immigrant life in America, Despo had promised her father in Greece she would watch over her twin sisters Alethea and Tasia if something should happen to him. After he perished in World War II, Despo brought the twins to California to work at her established business. Greek women knew they could always scratch out a living with needle and thread, but Despo had bigger plans. The trio established themselves as the most capable alterations group in the area and their business thrived. Few people had met the twins outside the tailor shop as Despo kept them tamed inside.

Despo had accepted the lifelong mission of keeping her sisters pure and untouched by male hands. The forty-five-year old twins Tasia and Alethea were like kittens, endearing and domestic, two lives contained in their small safe sewing box of thread, needles and pins. The twins rarely spoke but when they did, they both adjusted their glasses at the same time and breathed in unison, then smiled no matter the subject. When Tasia began to speak, Alethea finished her sentence. Both twins were taller and slimmer than Despo. Their kindness was their charm. And because their older sister had provided for their passage to California and given them a life, they rarely questioned her rule.

In the quiet of their bedroom, Olympia had once secretly revealed to Yianna that Tasia, the younger twin, had been proposed marriage by an Irish Catholic man, a bricklayer. Tasia salivated over having a loving husband, the command of her own kitchen and, God willing, a healthy child or two. That proposal was immediately vetoed by Despo, taking on the mantle of her dead father who allowed only Greek Orthodox unions. If Tasia married outside the church, she would have no job, no sisters. Despo said her family's reputation would be ruined. Understanding the landslide of pain she would cause, Tasia begrudgingly crawled back to her position as third-ranked female in their small all-woman world. She donned the lifetime cloak of the Greek spinster, although her fingers guided a needle through fabric instead of spinning wool into yarn.

Tasia's twin Alethea attempted to make up for the sorrow in Tasia's heart. Alethea soothed Tasia's brow when she wept for her bygone lover and gently sidestepped Despo's criticism. Alethea was the rope between two boats sailing on the choppy waves, the peace treaty between Despo and Tasia. Alethea, the quietest of the three, took her middle-sister duties seriously and prided herself on holding her family together.

Alethea certainly had not forgotten the painful gut twist of hunger when the Germans starved her village during the war. At Mira's Tailor Shop, she was desperately grateful for all she had: three meals a day, a job, enough money for the church tithings and more than an ounce of respect from customers. It was no wonder the tailor shop was named "Mira," the Greek word for the three sisters of fate. One sister spinning, one measuring, one cutting.

Yianna was aware the sheriff had officially visited Mira's Tailor Shop soon after Olympia had vanished. Yianna visited the shop at least once a month searching for a morsel of information that could lead to her sister. After all, these sisters were the last to see Olympia. But Despo always was guarded, repelled questions and seemed uneasy with Yianna's presence. As Yianna was not a professional investigator, Despo had no obligation to give Yianna information.

But now, in Yianna's mind, she was initiating the search for her sister once more with a clean slate. She was determined to cut through Despo's barbed wire and discover why she wasn't welcoming the search for an overlooked clue.

A warm wind cut through the flat Sacramento Valley and pushed Yianna forward, her Leica bouncing on its leather strap. It would be another scorching summer day. Yianna could almost hear the small green tomato plants pushing through the rich dark soil in nearby fields and could smell the wildness of earth tilled in perfect rows, tall weeds encroaching on the edges. She realized her steps were probably retracing the path on which Olympia walked the last day she was seen. Just outside of Mira's front door, she stopped and shot a photo of the carefully repainted gas station and its wooden sign in the shape of a spool of thread with needle piercing through.

Yianna had found a black sleeveless shirt in her bottom drawer and had draped her leather jacket over her shoulder in the morning heat. Bracing herself for the critical gaze of older Greek women who worked with fashionable clothes every day, Yianna breathed deeply then stepped inside the shop.

Hundreds of horizontal bolts of fabrics lined the walls. Slashes of wool, cotton, jersey, percale, velvet, flannel, gabardine and chambray were arranged in a circus of colors. The air was heavy with the musty smell of old fabric. The clunk of Yianna's boots on the wooden floor was muffled by the wall of fabric which absorbed the sound like a giant sponge.

"*Kali mera*, good day!" Yianna called out cheerfully. All three sisters rushed from different entrances to the main room. Yianna smiled to think that Mira's Tailor Shop was much like Stavros' bakery with its attached male boarding house. But this was a harbor for energetic Greek women who worked just as hard and created their own world to survive.

"Yianna!" Despo's smile disappeared. "What you wearing?" Her eyes moved from Yianna's short, chopped hair to her thick leather jacket, to her boots with worn heels.

"Just a costume, Despo." Yianna dropped her jacket onto a green upholstered chair which husbands often occupied while waiting for their wives. The twin sisters Alethea and Tasia rushed to her side and Yianna breathed a sigh of relief.

"So, you graduating tomorrow?" Alethea encircled Yianna with her graceful arms, her scent earthy like Greek mountain tea and fresh cut lemons. "All the girls getting their dresses ready!"

"Yes, tomorrow." Yianna struggled to pretend her graduation was important. In fact, she'd hidden the official school announcement from her uncle and the three shepherds. The new vision of herself did not include crossing a stage wearing a meaningless medieval black gown.

Tasia propped her elbows on the glass counter which displayed rhinestone buttons and silver buckles in a lighted case. She whimsically set her head on her clenched fists like a schoolgirl admiring a new boy in class.

"So then, where you go? What you do?" Tasia smiled waiting for Yianna's answer.

"After you graduate?" Alethea finished her sister's sentence.

"Yes, well, that's why I'm here." Yianna cleared her throat, hoping to sound more official.

"I wanted to ask a few questions, again. About Olympia's last day here."

Losing steam, her voice trailed off. She needed to practice her presentation if she were to find Olympia. She must transform into an adult investigator, not a wobbly teenager groping for words. Instead of forcing a speech, she pulled a notebook and pencil from her pocket. She would soften her approach.

"Maybe you can remember." She smiled at Despo. "What happened the day Olympia disappeared, the Monday after Christmas. Can you please tell me again, Despo?"

Fetching a broom, Despo began to violently sweep the floor, eyes downward, brushing away the question. Alethea and Tasia took their cue and gently backed away. Yianna found herself standing alone next to a mannequin decked out in a fluffy white bridal gown with applique flowers, the mirror opposite to Yianna's black, rugged outfit.

Remembering the nickname in the Greek community, Despo the Despot, Yianna decided to ignore the sweeping.

An icy wall slammed down around Despo as she swept away from Yianna. Her black eyebrows pushed downward, her face a stone. She shoved the broom into a corner and retreated behind the counter to sort pins and needles.

"Why *you* ask us this again?" Despo's voice was sharp as a long stainless steel pin. "The sheriff ask after she missing. We tell him everything we know. You think we don't?"

Despo eyed Yianna suspiciously and suddenly slammed her hand on the glass case. The silver buttons jumped on their velvet pads.

"Enough! Nothing happen here to Olympia! She come to work, she do her sewing and she walk home. Like she always do." Despo let her words out in one breath. "We run honest business. No bad girls work here. Only good girls. And your sister is good. My best customers, they always ask for her!"

Despo pushed up her sleeves signaling a finish to the conversation and then vanished into the back room.

What did she mean "only good girls work here?" Yianna wondered.

Pushing forward, Alethea and Tasia guided Yianna to the chair and gently pushed her shoulders down to sit. Alethea scurried to bring teacups and saucers while Tasia poured chamomile tea into iridescent cups. Tasia drew close to Yianna and both lifted their teacups in unison. Together they looked like twin owls at midnight, blinking their wide eyes behind their cat's-eye glasses.

"Forgive our Despo." Alethea smoothed her navy blue and white print swing-skirt, more fashionable than Despo's widow-black. "We cry too much for our Olympia. She is like daughter for us. We no talk about it here no more." She fanned herself with a McCall's pattern cover.

"Your sister, may she be found soon." Tasia made the sign of the cross and then pushed a few wild strands of hair away from Yianna's face, attempting to soothe her.

Yianna sipped her tea, confused. Did Despo think Yianna implied she ran a slipshod establishment where girls went missing? Or that she'd failed to watch over her favorite and youngest employee? In Greek society, shame was a powerful hammer. Wicked tongues could pound away at fresh gossip and a reputation would soon crumble. And Yianna knew reputation was everything to Despo.

Fingers of unrest crept up Yianna's spine. Did Despo hold Olympia responsible *for her own* disappearance? And was she now a bad girl because she went missing? That thought translated to nausea and Yianna gulped her tea to wash it down. She breathed deeply, calming her bristling temper. She needed facts, not blame. Yianna turned to Tasia, the most talkative of the tailoring trio. She had to keep trying.

"Did Olympia come to work on time? What happened that day?" Yianna's words were sharp, attempting to uncover scraps of information that may casually lay unnoticed or were purposefully buried beneath the floorboards.

"We check our calendar book," Alethea quickly responded, "but the sheriff, he already look there."

Tasia shuffled behind her in low heels that matched her emerald green dress and costume jewelry. Olympia had said the twins always dressed up for work, attempting to upgrade Despo's older-woman outfits. They had eyes for fashion, not just tailoring, and dressed well even though they lived in a small Central Valley town.

Alethea looked over her shoulder to be sure Despo was out of sight. She flipped the large black leather-bound appointment book to Monday, December 27, 1954, and pushed it toward Yianna.

"See here. Everyone good customer. And the sheriff take the full list of all our customers. We know them all for years. Good people they are."

Yianna ran her finger down the list of alteration appointments written in Despo's scratchy handwriting — all customers with sterling reputations in Woodland:

Madeline Fong — alteration, suit and jacket

Councilman Reynolds — alteration, two suits

Trina Harrison — alteration, evening gown and skirt

Carol Baily –dress hem for Rainbow Girls formal

Deputy Robbie Sanders — alteration, two uniforms

Suzie Randolph — pick up graduation dress, paid

Yianna looked up with a little gasp. The twins nervously adjusted their glasses.

"What you see, Yianna?" They hovered behind Yianna but most people knew Alethea and Tasia could not read.

"Not too much." Yianna swung her camera around and snapped the shutter, photographing the list of customers. "A photo so I can remember the names."

Deputy Robbie Sanders was on the list. Hadn't he said he knew Olympia in high school? And wasn't he in Uncle Stavros' gambling room only a week ago? And Councilman Reynolds, the man with roving eyes and sweaty hands. Had he lingered after hours, then taken away her beautiful sister? But why would anyone take Olympia? Yianna winced at Trina Harrison's name on the list. That woman was everywhere.

Yianna could run to the sheriff and ask if he had interviewed those customers but he would insist he had.

Suddenly the room was stifling. She scooped up her weighty jacket, so unseasonable for the sizzling morning.

"Thank you, Alethea, Tasia." Yianna hugged them both, kissing each twin on both cheeks, then slung her camera on her back. She stepped outside into a wall of Central Valley heat and began her one-mile march back to the bakery for her shift behind the counter.

Suddenly she heard the light click of heels, like crickets, beating the pavement behind her. It was Tasia, in her emerald-green glory, knife pleats stretching like accordion wings in the wind, necklace clanking, hurrying toward her. Panting, she fearfully glanced towards the shop.

"Despo, she is busy sewing wedding gown for mayor's daughter now." Tasia grabbed Yianna's wrist and shoved a scrap of brown paper into her palm. "I find this and keep it."

Yianna turned the crumpled strip over.

325 Eddy Street S.F.

Tasia took a few steps toward Mira's Tailor Shop, then twisted her slender body back around.

"*Toh vrika!* I found it — in her coat!" Her voice was a hoarse whisper. "In Olympia's coat. She leave it behind. The camel wool." Tasia's eyes were wide and a band of light sweat shone on her forehead.

"Why she leave her coat behind, but it so cold that day. I find that little paper before Despo give the coat to the poor." Her intense stare locked onto Yianna. "You no tell no one! No tell Despo I find this and give to you!"

With that diamond of a clue in her hand, Yianna watched Tasia hurry toward Mira's Taylor Shop and slip back in the front door to fit into the sardine can of her life.

Yianna tucked the scrap of paper into her pocket but immediately retrieved it. She laid it on the pavement holding it in place with a stone. She pulled her camera forward and snapped a photograph. Now the address would live someplace else, just in case she became separated by the same forces that swept away her sister.

TWENTY-THREE

As the first rays of light pierced the lacy curtains of the bakery, Stavros lugged three cartons of bottles filled with homemade wine up the stairs from the basement. No labels. No identification. Simply red wine in thirty-six green bottles sitting upright in cardboard boxes.

Wearing a small hat shaped like an ice cream vendor's, Agamemnon hurried to the deep fryer to survey the donuts bobbing in hot oil. He moved the fried dough about with a slotted spoon, one eye locked on Stavros and the unidentified wine.

In the months since Olympia had disappeared, Agamemnon had taken a larger role as Stavros' early morning baker. He didn't come to baking naturally but had worked in many kitchens after his sheep-herding days. He savored creeping out of his room in the dark morning hours and secretly tuning up his instruments of mixing bowls, deep fryer, tongs and cooling racks. Donut-making suited his artistic nature. He was determined to create the next donut more perfect than the last.

Stavros' pride kept him from asking Agamemnon to work every day, but Agamemnon gently suggested he try out for the role in exchange for paying lower rent. Within a week, the two Greeks worked together as comrades, or, as Agamemnon said, just as a bouzouki and guitar wove harmoniously together in *rebetiko* music, the Greek folk tunes.

"Who buy this wine?" Agamemnon's voice was tinged with suspicion. Usually, Stavros sold only a few bottles at a time from the back door of the alley and only to the families he had known for years. Agamemnon's look reminded Stavros he was breaking his own rules.

Tentatively, Agamemnon circled the wine cartons as if they would either bite him or beg to be carried back to the cellar.

Stavros fastened the top flaps of the cartons with masking tape. "My *spiti krasi*, homemade wine, make good money. Help pay the rent for 'dis place." He avoided the glaring fact that if he were a more diligent business man in the bakery and the card room, he might not have to sweat the rent every month.

After a minute Agamemnon turned back to his work. "You no tell me who buy this wine." Agamemnon pulled a dozen donuts out of the deep fryer to cool and began to dip a previous batch in maple frosting. He suspiciously eyed the three cases again.

"The man who play at the middle table yesterday." Stavros stared at the carton. "Young man. Always wear black suit. Black tie. Insurance business, he say. Name is Johnny. He come every few weeks. He like my wine and want more."

Stavros finished taping the cartons, stacked them and pushed them aside on the counter.

"I sell him wine for more than a year now. No worry for this."

Stavros began to feel as if his friend was prying too much into his business. Stavros was well aware of the legalities of selling homemade wine to the public without the proper licenses. But so far he had kept under the official radar of the newly established California State Department of Alcoholic Beverage Control in Sacramento.

"For over a year, you sell a stranger your wine?" Agamemnon was incredulous.

"He no cheat me!" Stavros' voice was gruffer than he intended. "And he always want more. I make good money on him."

Agamemnon raised his nose in the air disgustedly. "Stavros, you risk all of us!" Scowling, he turned away.

Stavros changed his tone to a lower, softer voice. "He say if I keep selling to him, he no say nothing to nobody."

Agamemnon raised an eyebrow but remained silent.

The little bell on the door tinkled a new arrival. Both men looked up to see Marika had come uncharacteristically early for her road trip sustenance.

"*Yassas*, boys!" Marika called out in her low, liquid voice. "I'm early but not too early for a bakery. Fill me up for a long trip! Today I drive to Nevada, then Utah. Not back for two weeks. I need new territory. Too much competition in L.A. Too many Greeks like me selling."

Stavros gazed at Marika with admiration. A single woman with drive, ambition and a standard of income she expected of herself. She would accept no less. Secretly he wished he had the same ambitious spirit. He might have owned three or four bakeries by now, even a café or two. And look how her silk blouse softly rested across her breasts. Was her skirt just a little shorter today? Seeing more of her legs was just fine with Stavros.

Emboldened by the spell Marika always cast over him, Stavros smoothed his mustache and stepped around the counter, untying the strings of his apron and whipping it off. At that moment, his body wanted all of Marika and he would have taken her to his room on the spot. But his brain blared warning signs. To cross the line could cost his friendship with Marika. Stavros' instincts told him to hold back, pull in his reins. His pursuit would be slow, Marika would not be easy to catch. Plus he wasn't a wealthy businessman. Perhaps her opinion of him was not as good as he hoped.

"Marika, you look very beautiful today." Stavros made a small bow. "I am thinking when you return, we go to Petros Kazanis' name day celebration?"

Marika raised her eyebrows but Stavros bravely rolled on.

"We go together." He straightened up proudly in front of her, unaware of a smidge of flour on his forehead or the masking tape stuck to his hand.

Marika's face broke into a well-lipsticked grin. "Yes. I think yes, we go."

She accepted the full bag of hot donuts that Agamemnon presented over the counter and turned to leave. Then Marika pulled Stavros by the collar. She brought his face close and he could feel her soft breath and smell her luscious perfume.

"One thing you gotta know, Stavros." He inhaled her sexuality, her slender but hypnotic shape, her amber voice, her self-confidence that no other woman possessed.

Marika pulled him closer, their lips nearly touching.

"I do the driving. You drink too much."

With that, Stavros watched Marika spin around, donut bag in hand and slowly saunter out the front door. The yellow-and-black print silk scarf tied to her purse fluttered in the breeze as she walked away, a fanfare trailing behind her. Stavros did not blink so he could imprint her essence, her energy on his mind. They were a perfect match, Stavros was sure. Both strong, both over forty, both having lived lives that made them independent with no one to rely on.

He felt Agamemnon close to him as they watched Marika begin the lonely drive east.

"Be kind to that one." Agamemnon spoke softly. "You only know the flame of the match. Our Marika is bonfire but her heart is golden."

Tying on his apron once more, Stavros returned to his wine cartons.

"You hear me?" Agamemnon rarely raised his voice. He added a sharp edge to his message. "You no break her heart. Not this one."

TWENTY-FOUR

Walking towards the high school that day, Yianna's pace was slow and deliberate. The last day of school. The senior class had the day off because of the evening's graduation ceremony. With her camera over her shoulder, Yianna carried the art books Mrs. Rose had lent her. She was melancholy about her task as she hated to part with the books. Yianna did not want to be separated from Michelangelo, DaVinci and El Greco, let alone the sculptors Phidias and Praxiteles.

And then there was graduation. She still had ample time to rush to school and sign up for her cap and gown but that task seemed meaningless, or maybe just overwhelming. Better to ignore a painful, abrupt ending before she was spit out into a life she hadn't yet pieced together.

Yesterday when Tasia had given her the small paper with an unknown address, Yianna felt energized and brave, at least for a moment. Yesterday she'd found a place to start her search. Now she took a full breath down to the bottom of her lungs. Chest forward, she climbed the stairs of Woodland High School for the last time and hurried to the library at the end of the main corridor.

Opening the door, Yianna found no students slumped over books at the long oak desks. No bodies lurked in the stacks, not even an amorous couple kissing in the back. After a few long minutes, Yianna heard a shuffling. Mrs. Rose, her back to Yianna, was boxing up books and stacking them in a closet behind the long, wooden counter that separated them. Yianna cleared her throat to announce her arrival.

Mrs. Rose turned and took in Yianna and her new all-black, all-boy appearance.

"Yianna! Good to see you! And on the last day." Mrs. Rose spoke as if Yianna were her daughter who had been gone for years.

"I wanted to return these before you closed for the year." She lowered her head respectfully. "Thank you, Mrs. Rose. I love these books."

"Perfect timing Yianna!" Mrs. Rose shuffled to a drawer and whipped out a pamphlet and slid it across the counter. It was a booklet advertising the California School of Fine Arts in San Francisco.

Then she went about her business of opening books, stamping them, piling them into a tall tower that appeared ready to tumble. "My daughter just started at that school a few months ago. She is a painter but they teach photography too." The librarian nodded at Yianna's camera dangling off her shoulder. "Something to think about." Mrs. Rose gave her a subtle wink from across the counter. "Could be exciting!"

Yianna grasped the pamphlet with both hands, as if she was worried it might fly away and become lost to her. Opening the slim front cover, Yianna ran her finger down the list of faculty and midway down was a name Yianna did not expect to see—Dorothea Lange. Looking up to the librarian with her eyes glowing, as if she had been transported into the world of the possible, Yianna could hardly yammer her thanks.

"Mrs. Rose." Yianna's small tear caught in the corner of her eye. "Thank you." Her deep gratitude was served up in those two words.

"My daughter could still be there by the time you arrive. Just let me know how you fare out." Mrs. Rose smiled, hands folded on the counter, beaming as if Yianna had already been accepted and somehow had generated funds for tuition and a rented room in San Francisco. "You'll be fine. Just keep going forward."

The librarian smoothed her hands over the three books Yianna had returned and slid *Art Through the Ages* back at Yianna.

"I think that book was ready to retire." Mrs. Rose took Yianna's hand and squeezed it. "May your art take you around the world. Good luck, my dear."

Yianna clutched the book to her heart, floated out of the library and down the steps of her former high school. She felt as if her opaque vision of the future had cracked and a pinhole of sunlight poured in through the tiny space. Yes, that night's high school graduation was an ending but she had just been given the ticket to her future, or at least a pass through the first hallway toward a definable direction. But first, she needed to find her only true family member, her would-be mother, her sister, her Olympia.

TWENTY-FIVE

The cigar smoke was thick that evening in Stavros' *sala,* every table occupied by ardent gamblers. With not much else to do on a June evening in Woodland, they had settled in for a long night of playing cards, smoking, betting and drinking Stavros' homemade wine. These days, as Stavros circulated, Agamemnon followed with his small tablet, scribbling names and the drink tabs the gamblers would owe at the end of the evening.

Lucky and Yianna ferried small trays of Parmesan cheese cubes and homemade bread from the kitchen to keep the customers thirsty and ordering more drinks. Suddenly, Yianna, in her black garb, put aside her tray and slid onto an empty chair at a table where Timoleon was the dealer. He spun her a handful of cards.

Stavros rushed over.

"What you do, Yianna? You play the cards tonight?" Yianna was underage, as if it counted for anything in an illegal card room. Stavros worried she could be swindled by the card sharks. In the past, he'd allowed her to play poker for pennies, but only with the three shepherds who would never cheat her. Didn't she know the Friday night crowd would make no allowances for a young female player if they had the chance to win?

Yianna looked up at Stavros.

"If I'm going to find Olympia, I need money to get to San Francisco. I'll begin there. After that, who knows where I'll need to go?"

Ignoring Stavros who was breathing hard, Yianna focused on her cards. She gave Timoleon a little nod. He launched her a single card. Not looking up again at her uncle, Yianna's face was blank while organizing her cards as if casually arranging flowers. Stavros fell silent, helpless. The sting of being a less-than-first-rate provider set in. He possessed no savings account, no stocks, no retirement pension to draw from. And now his teenage niece was doing the heavy lifting.

Stavros marched back to the kitchen dragging Agamemnon to conference with him.

"Why Yianna do this? What the mens gonna think if a girl play?"

Looking out through the heavy curtain, Agamemnon could see the card room humming along. With her dark masculine outfit and short hair, Yianna easily blended into the smoke and mass of card players. Not one player seemed ruffled by her presence. In the back corner, a small cheer went up by a winner of a big hand just like any other Friday night.

Too nerve-wracked to walk through his card room again, Stavros sheltered in the kitchen busying himself with tasks for the morning, setting out utensils and measuring flour.

Agamemnon, however, kept an eye on Yianna. He glided behind her, gazing over her hand while taking drink orders from the players at her table. Yianna got a lucky hand with a full house. The players at her table threw down their cards, grumbling and pushing their bills and towers of coins toward her, unphased by her youth. Yianna pulled in the stack of cash with both hands and fanned the bills to count them, her face an expressionless mask.

A little smile spread across Agamemnon's face. Moments later he burst into the kitchen causing Stavros to turn and sprinkle flour onto the floor like falling snow.

"She winning!" Agamemnon giggled in glee. "We teach her good, no, Stavros? Our girl—she make money!"

Stavros could not share his friend's joy. He could not appreciate that his niece was playing poker for cash when he could not provide funds to help find Olympia. Wanting his young niece out of the den of males, Stavros wrapped one hand around a full bottle of wine and reached for a glass with the other. But before pulling the cork, he tried to calm himself. He wanted to shut down Yianna's play but not break her spirit. She was attempting to do something positive for their family. Just let her move on to something else, he prayed. Something that fit her age and sex.

Together the men peered out from behind the curtain. After another hand, Yianna's impassive, stony face broke with a smile. They watched her quickly roll up her bills, sweep the coins into her hand and shove the money deep into her leather jacket pocket. With a simple, "I'm out!" she left the table and walked out the front door. A winner.

Legs spindly and feeble, Stavros skulked to his room, shutting the door. He was so incapable that Yianna, a girl just graduated from high school, had pulled the reins from his grip and taken the lead. Yianna had shifted into the man's role.

The roller shade of reality snapped up revealing Stavros to be naked and weak. His had failed by not preventing Olympia's disappearance in December and again, immediately after, when he could not muster a rescue plan. Yianna could see he was half-hearted in business, a bad provider, hardly a man. Stavros was deeply ashamed but had no idea what to do about it.

Wearily stretching out on his unmade bed, Stavros felt himself drowning in dark waves of insecurity. Before Olympia vanished, he was cemented in his path of keeping the bakery running, the card room humming and the wine production flowing until the girls were married off to good providers. He would then return to Greece to enjoy the comfort of his village, his rituals, his history, his Greece.

Stavros knew the three shepherds did not share his personal vision for their future, nor did Yianna, nor the hard driving Marika for that matter. His shepherds continually reasoned: why go back to Greece when you could turn a reliable dollar in America? Why make a home in a country torn by war for nearly a decade?

Stavros' anger sparked like the pilot light in his bakery oven. Who were these people to say he couldn't find peace for his ravaged brain and aching soul? Who were they to say his ears could not hear bouzouki music every night in the taverna? Why shouldn't he eat vegetables that were lovingly grown in his garden and plucked out by his own hands? Stavros' desire for a long afternoon nap every day, the fragrance of freshly cut oregano, the tantalizing scent of fish sizzling on a grill were sirens for his return to Hellenic soil. These modest pleasures provided by his homeland had spread like a root from his brain pushing stubbornly through his heart and settling deep in his gut. And that root needed more than a teaspoon of Greek soil to flourish.

He knew some assumed Stavros was simple and stupid, merely a lover of women and accomplished baker. Few looked deeper to see that he thought himself to be an imposter. He posed as the brave uncle securing a world for his nieces when he, in fact, was the timid younger brother who had endured an early life of heartache and terror, always waiting for Christos to save him. He knew he was inadequate, needy.

And now Yianna knew it too.

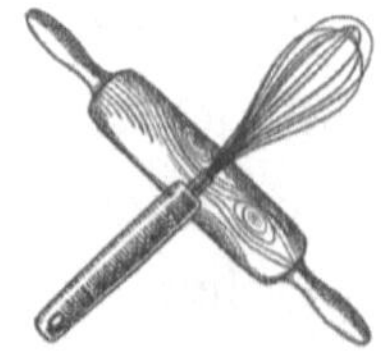

TWENTY-SIX

Stavros' mind spun back to the endless week when he and Christos waited for a rescue on the quay in Smyrna as the flames raged like a bonfire from hell. He remembered how Christos had been his guide, his father, his family.

The days and nights blurred into a week of anguish for the citizens of Smyrna who fled their homes, awaiting their fate which lay limp in the cruel hands of the Turks. That week Christos and Stavros moved as one, the younger brother a shadow of the older. As the brothers and thousands of refugees crowded on the shore begging for any kind of lifeline, a few French and Italian ships took on passengers. Large American and British ships floated in the harbor merely observing the misery, doing nothing to help. Their orders were not to anger the Turks with whom their countries desired future oil trade. By refusing Christian refugees, they would keep on friendly terms.

Desperate bodies dove into the bay, swam to the ships, climbed the rope ladders, hoping for sanctuary. But many of those strong swimmers were rewarded with a push back into the ocean for their heroic efforts, only to become swollen corpses floating in the harbor. The large British and American ships would not allow refugees to board until the Turkish leader Mustafa Kemal agreed. It took five days of human suffering for him do so.

Just because the brothers had escaped their parents' fate did not mean they were safe. The Diamantopoulos brothers, small for their age, were forced to hide among the women and children, hoping no one would reveal their secret of peach fuzz and testicles. The boys watched as men, young and old, were force-marched to the eastern countryside to be shot or worked to death. Christos and Stavros did not exchange words. They knew their fate if discovered.

After nightfall, Christos picked off scarves and flowing clothing from corpses lying in the street while Stavros cowered in the shadows. Christos stepped over endless rows of dead bodies, men, children, pregnant mothers, mouths gaped open. Flies swarmed in the September heat celebrating the genocide.

During the day, the brothers had made themselves invisible, crouching with the old women, scarves over their heads, shawls around their bodies, hiding their identity. The boys held their breath, heads down when Turkish soldiers on horseback pushed through the crowd.

Stavros remembered the hysterical screams of girls and women at midnight, always at midnight. He dreaded that hour as the shrieking and yelling could only mean Turkish soldiers were brutalizing desperate females who waited for any transport from the quay. To keep the peace, the British war ships beamed a massive searchlight on the screeching crowd. The women then suffered molestation in silence.

After nearly a week of causing death, rape, starvation and fear, Mustafa Kemal became convinced it was in his best interest to remove the thousands of Christians by transporting them away from Turkish soil. With scarves hooded over their adolescent faces, the Diamantopoulos brothers boarded a merchant Greek ship that was permitted to take away the Christian leftovers.

Stavros never again spoke of the chaotic refugee camps into which they were herded in Piraeus and then Athens. He never again mentioned the cold, nameless orphanage into which the brothers were enrolled. Never again would Stavros express his apprehension about the employment arranged by the orphanage in Athens. But Stavros never questioned Christos' promise of enduring protection.

The orphanage arranged that Stavros would live and work in Kyrios Vlachos' bakery in exchange for room and board. Christos was sent to the home of a tailor several districts away. Each learned his new trade and worked diligently. After all, they had no other place to go.

But now Stavros was alone, an unexpected provider, a reluctant leader. The sham head of his family, apparent to all.

During the long years after Christos' death, Stavros simply pretended his wounds did not exist. He shoved them deep in a small dark corner of his heart and carried on. Still, after draining a bottle of wine, he never became completely numb. He would always be an orphan, always at a loss. Worse yet, Yianna, also an orphan, had demonstrated initiative and would soon dive head first into the search for Olympia, leaving him behind.

Stavros could only dribble wine in his glass and toss it back. He prayed his homemade wine would flow through his body, soothe his pain and diminish the fear of the weeks to come.

TWENTY-SEVEN

With no idea of how long she would be gone in search of Olympia, Yianna collected a fresh shirt, underwear, socks and a toothbrush and shoved them into a tattered green knapsack she'd found in Uncle Stavros' cellar. Having graduated, even without the formal ceremony, she lacked an imposed school schedule as a meter for how she spent her days. She found luxury in mapping out her own afternoons, always beginning the day with a morning shift at the bakery.

Embarking on a journey with an unknown destination was the ultimate schedule without limits. Realizing she was on her last roll of film, Yianna resolved to buy more. She knew her camera needed feeding and care. Giving her great comfort when resting over her shoulder, her Leica grounded her, gave her purpose.

The morning was cool and breezy and clouds churned in the sky promising a summer storm. On her way to the corner drug store, Yianna planned her departure for San Francisco. After buying film, she would purchase a Greyhound bus ticket. She had sewn small pouches holding waterproof containers on her camera strap to hold the film rolls. Agamemnon said that "Frisco" had an Eddy Street, the same street scribbled on the scrap of paper Tasia had slipped to her. She'd only been to San Francisco for two funerals and one wedding at the Greek Orthodox cathedral. How was she supposed to find Eddy Street? She made a mental note to buy a map of San Francisco.

Ready to push open the thick glass doors to the pharmacy, Yianna looked up to meet the watery-blue eyes of Porter's father, Congressman Harrison.

"Uh, hello." Yianna's voice was low, her eyes lower.

Porter's father spread his politician smile across his face and offered a rigorous campaign handshake.

"Yianna! So nice to see you!" He pumped her hand while his shiny teeth gleamed in a hundred-watt smile. "You must have just graduated like Porter!"

Yianna sucked in her breath. Didn't this man have a meeting to attend? Vital legislation to pass? She began to sweat despite the cool breeze that pulled the door as she held it.

"Yes. Graduated!" Yianna cleared her throat. "Like Porter."

"My boy will be off to Stanford in the fall. We're so proud of him." He looked up into the sky, imagining the future.

"Porter wants to stay in town and help me with the November election. But you don't get a second chance at Stanford. That's my alma mater too, you know." Yianna nodded.

Pulling a long cigar from his pocket, he rummaged for matches and lit up. Yianna wanted to melt into the sidewalk, but the dreaded question came anyway.

"And you?" The congressman's thin lips encircled the cigar. He drew his breath and let out little puffs of smoke. "Your big plans?"

"I'm going to art school." Yianna blurted. "As soon as I can."

The congressman patted her camera. "Yes, I'm sure you will, honey."

Yianna plastered on her best smile. "Well, goodbye, Congressman Harrison." She stepped one foot inside the pharmacy but his next words froze her.

"One more thing, Yianna."

She swung her body back outside, her camera clacking against the glass door.

"I'm sorry about your missing sister. It must be troubling for your family. But I'm sure the sheriff is doing everything in his power." Another puff on his cigar. "Just wanted to remind you, Porter's mother said you need to stay away from our son. It's a good idea to listen to my wife. Just stay in your neighborhood. And let Porter stay in his."

Reaching out, Congressman Harrison gently patted Yianna's hand with his fingertip as if he was sending a secret message.

"We don't want anything ruining Porter's future. Good day, dear." He tipped his soft felt fedora toward her. "Best of luck to you."

The politician hurried away in his expensive hard leather shoes giving her no opportunity to say she was finished with Porter. How dare he tell her to stay away when Trina had already delivered that message like a jackhammer? Sadness welled up as she remembered the fistful of wild lilacs Porter brought to school one spring day. Yianna steadied herself and marched into the pharmacy. Porter's parents had tainted the few memories of a first love that she might have treasured. All that was over now.

Yianna wandered across the green tile floor of the pharmacy to the photo department. She nearly collided with a life-size cardboard cutout of a bouncy young woman in a short yellow skirt caressing a box of Kodak film. What did this leggy cardboard woman have to do with photography? She twirled a metal rack stacked with yellow boxes, red logos stamped on the side and located her 35 mm film. She'd resolved to be judicious before pressing the shutter during her journey to San Francisco, and to give great consideration to each shot, just like Dorothea Lange would do.

After her purchase, Yianna had the afternoon off. No more droning teachers' lectures, no gym class, no more football games. Drifting through the downtown, counting the hours before her late afternoon shift at the bakery, Yianna soon found herself on the edge of town. She turned a corner to see Timoleon's fruit stand, actually a medium-sized produce market, buzzing with business. Timoleon had made connections with local growers who gave him first pick: the meaty walnuts and juicy pears from Lake County, ripe yellow corn from Dixon and Vacaville, luscious Bing cherries from orchards up the road in Cherry Lagoon and the orange blossom and clover honey from beekeepers in Fairfield. His seasonal offerings drew crowds of locals and passing motorists.

Yianna stopped to inhale the perfume of the dewy, ripe melons still chilled from the early morning harvest.

"Yianna!" Timoleon was somewhere behind a stack of shiny green bell peppers. Adjusting his black framed glasses, he ambled around the wooden stalls to greet her.

"Agamemnon tell me you leave soon to find our Olympia."

"On my way. Tomorrow."

Timoleon turned to pick a long bean from a crate and chewed the end of it.

"You safe where you go?"

Yianna shrugged. She had been more worried about money than safety.

"Sure, I'll be fine." Yianna tried to smile reassuringly, more for herself than Timoleon.

"I want us find Olympia." Timoleon munched his green bean. "But I don't know what to do. I just know the fruits and the vegetables." He lowered his voice. "Besides, I got no papers."

Timoleon had talked about his lack of citizenship many times before but only at the bakery.

"But Uncle Stavros can do more. A lot more! He just worries about his gambling room and selling his wine. What about Olympia? She's out there alone somewhere!"

Timoleon turned to the Coke machine that stood like a round-shouldered soldier on the side of the wooden building and pushed a dime into the slot. Pulling the lever, he yanked a bottle of Coke from the window, popped off the bottlecap and offered it to Yianna. Then he bought one for himself.

"Your father Christos was the man of action. Your uncle, he watches. Stavros no like decisions. And if the police find his wine or his card room, they throw him in jail. If he get caught then who gonna help *him*?"

Frowning, Yianna sipped her Coke. She was not ready to hear excuses for her uncle.

"Yianna, you more like your father than Stavros." Timoleon mused. "You know what you want. You fight for it. And one other thing."

She looked up sharply, expecting him to invent another excuse for her uncle.

"Agamemnon, Lucky and me, we help Stavros after your father Christos dies. Your uncle, he is good man. When he make bakery, he take us with him. He make place for all of us living like one family. So we are safe. He never forget his friends. Just like he try for you and Olympia."

Yianna paused and shook her head.

"But now Olympia is missing. And I'm the only one looking. It's his obligation to help!"

Timoleon's eyes misted behind his dark eyelashes, head nodding in agreement.

He walked to the cash register and punched the No Sale key. The wooden drawer sprang open and the register clanged. Timoleon reached in and pushed ten dollars into Yianna's palm. Opening a brown paper bag, he dropped in a sack of peanuts, homemade beef jerky and a large chunk of hard cheese from the cold box.

"You no go hungry."

Yianna hugged Timoleon. How could she haul that weight in her small knapsack?

"Now you detective, just like Humphrey Bogart in the movies. You go find Olympia." Timoleon folded his hands across his green apron as if the matter was settled. "Your Uncle Stavros, he depend for you, Yianna. All of us do. You gotta find our Olympia and bring her home.

He turned to ring up a sale for a pound of cherries and a sack of thin purple eggplants for an elderly customer. Sipping her Coke, Yianna envisioned her sister somewhere in the universe with arms outstretched, waiting for a sign from a relative or a friend. A sign keeping her alive one day at a time.

A tidal wave of responsibility crashed upon her and Yianna hurried away from the fruit stand. She would leave the next day. Finding her Olympia was not a frivolous challenge or adventure. Her sister's life, if Olympia was indeed still alive, was in her hands.

TWENTY-EIGHT

Sitting on the curb outside of Angel's Bakery later that afternoon, Yianna arranged and rearranged her knapsack. Finished with his baking duties, Agamemnon walked out to join her, wiping his hands on his crumpled white apron. Dropping down next to her on the curb, he watched her juggle the block of cheese, peanuts and rolls of film, attempting to fit them in her knapsack.

"Always make room for the film!" Agamemnon smiled.

Yianna grinned. Of course, an artist would give her that advice.

"This come for you today in the mail." Agamemnon passed a folded form letter to her.

"I didn't send for anything." Yianna waved it away as if it were the electric bill.

"You look, Yianna. It the application to your art school. For your photography." Agamemnon stretched out his body, elbows propping him from the back. Yianna grabbed the application, unsure if she should leap for joy or shove it back into Agamemnon's hands.

"What am I supposed to do with it?" Her voice cut with a bitter edge. "I won a little money at the poker game but I need every penny for this trip. I have no time for art school, Agamemnon. No money. No future. No nothing."

"You got no time now." Agamemnon patted her knee with a fatherly tenderness. "But you will. I find your paper for the art school and then I send for this application. You can keep it in here." He pointed to his head. "And here." His heart.

Yianna rested her eyes kindly on Agamemnon. This old man would have loved to attend art school anywhere. Instead, he created art when he could, making the perfect donut or when an angle of light in nature inspired him. He would never be famous or even a footnote in a small gallery. His artistic spirit came from his personal Plato-vision. It then pulsed through his fingers, to his brushes and onto paper or canvas. Agamemnon had told her he had to create, otherwise *tha spasi tin kardia mou*, his heart would burst.

"You keep the application for me." Yianna gently pushed it back to Agamemnon's hands. "Maybe later."

"Yes," he gave her hand a squeeze. "When Olympia is home and our family is happy again." Yianna tried to smile back. If only she was as certain of a happy future as Agamemnon seemed now.

At that moment, Yianna and Agamemnon noticed two black canvas shoes walk into their view. They looked up to see a tall figure in the sunlight. Loaded down with parcels, Kenny seemed nervous and looked everywhere but down at them.

"I came to return some of Olympia's things."

They both popped up from their curbside seats.

"Kenny!" Yianna burst out with surprise. "What things?" Yianna held out her arms for the bundles he offered.

"I gotta be quick. I don't want anyone from that sheriff's department to see me. I've had enough questions from them lately." Kenny dusted his hands. "She left these with me that night. The night before she disappeared. I can't keep them anymore. The sheriff will see them as some kind of evidence. I knew you'd want them back."

Yianna examined what Kenny had unloaded into her arms: Six thick oblong books, like old-fashioned ledgers from a hotel. They were Olympia's notebooks cataloging the herbs she grew, their medicinal properties and her experience with each. Olympia had called them her herbal bibles. Yianna had witnessed her sister and Kenny talking head-to-head, late into the night about oregano, *Niu Zhi,* for fever, colds and lung infections; Barberry, *Fu Niu* to cleanse the spleen and gallbladder; Dendrobium, *Shi Hu* to boost longevity and sexual health, and many others. They sipped tea in small cups and chatted happily about their discoveries. But why had Olympia unloaded her treasured history of herbal medicine, her life's work, with Kenny?

Suddenly Kenny stepped to the corner, peering down the street.

"Uh, one more thing," Kenny stammered, turning to her. "Christmas night. We were standing near her garden. That Italian lady next door, Mrs. Parisi. She watched everything we did. It was raining like hell and, uh, I asked Olympia to marry me. I tried to give her my grandmother's jade ring. The night before she went missing."

Marriage? Olympia and Kenny? A ring? Yianna was jolted by the revelation but more so from her own blindness to their love. How had she not realized their deep connection?

"At first, she argued and would not tell me why she said no. I was so angry! I yelled at her because I couldn't understand. But the worst thing was Olympia couldn't stop crying — sobbing. She was hysterical. And so was I!" Kenny began to sweat, breathing hard, reliving that night.

"Then she just shoved all these books into my arms. I was so mad, so hurt when she wouldn't tell me anything. Then she ran inside the bakery. I never saw her again. That next night she was gone."

Agamemnon silently made the sign of the cross.

"Why give these to me, Kenny? She obviously wanted you to have them." Yianna shifted the bulky bundles from arm to arm. Kenny shot her a desperate look.

"You don't get it. That sheriff and deputy keep coming around when I'm home here in Woodland. And they tracked me down at Berkeley. Twice! The sheriff calls me China Boy and hangs around like I'm going to make a confession or something. They keep saying I was the last man to see her and that we argued. And that damn deputy just stands there and takes notes while the sheriff berates me. They said they don't have any other suspects and they need one. They want to think I'm responsible for her disappearance — and maybe more."

"But you are friend to Olympia." Agamemnon scooped up half the books from Yianna to lessen her load.

"The sheriff doesn't think so. Mrs. Parisi apparently told the sheriff she heard us arguing. That I shook Olympia. But I was only pleading for her to marry me. And she couldn't stop sobbing. We were down that alley near her garden." Kenny pointed toward the alley, then shoved his hands in his pockets. "I was frustrated that Olympia couldn't say why she wouldn't marry me. Still am." Kenny's voice was tight, agitated. "She wouldn't even look at the ring. I thought she loved me. But now she's missing and I'm their main suspect. I wish that night never happened."

Yianna remembered that Olympia had never discussed the subject of men and boys in the privacy of their bedroom. And she had never spoken about her feelings for Kenny. But now Yianna instantly realized Olympia and Kenny should have always been lovers. Always together.

"I will find Olympia and bring her home. I'm leaving tomorrow." Yianna knew she was bold making this statement but all along felt a spark of hope her sister was alive. She would nurture that ember and fan the flame.

Yianna looked up but Kenny was gone, vanished before the long arms of the sheriff's department could reach out and detain him again. For being male. A close friend to Olympia. And for being Chinese-American.

TWENTY-NINE

Olympia's Diary

*Back in Argos, my yiayia instructed me on how to heal her village
neighbors and educated me about the natural world. My grandmother
was a Greek medicine woman. After my parents forced me to quit
school, I had time to work with her.*

*Tending to sick people and finding the proper lotion, tincture,
tea or salve was the best use of my talents. Oil from the primrose
plant — good for eczema and irritations. Calendula oil (the common
marigold flower!) for skin irritations, horehound tea for colds, wild
yam tea for menstrual cramps. And a strong cup of chamomile tea for
almost everything else.*

*In our village, my grandmother and I set simple broken bones but
sent people to Napleon or even Athens (for those who could afford it)
when we detected serious illnesses. We treated most common ailments
like gout toe (drink the juice of cherries), eliminated fungus on nails
(a little tea tree oil did the trick) and headaches (feverfew tea and an
icy towel across the forehead was the cure). We kept a pharmacy of
home grown herbs in glass jars, from ceiling to floor, and we stockpiled
the rest in the cellar. If my parents had not ripped me from school and
molded me into a tailor, I would have found my place in the medical*

world with my grandmother. But my dream of working as a doctor had passed me by.

Looking back at that time, my mother and I were cursed to be born with large black eyes and defined exotic features that men found appealing. Dark eyes? Slender waist? Large breasts? You can keep them! What good did they do me? In America, the boys at school whistled every time I walked by. They pulsated their hips and groins in despicable gestures. I can't count the many times I was flattened against my locker by a boy who pushed his hot breath into my face and tried to violently kiss my mouth. I don't care if they called me "beauti-ful" or "date material." I hated the boys and avoided most men. Except for Kenny. But as always, I kept silent. Perhaps those high school boys sensed I was afraid of them—that I would not fight back. Who would want to stay in school while living in fear of recess or being alone in a hallway?

After a boy shoved his hand up my dress on the way home from high school, I did what any girl would do. I dropped out—away from the world of these cruel young men.

After I left school, my best defense was to become invisible behind the bakery counter. By my twentieth birthday, I gave up hoping for a miracle that might lead me into an interesting life, a future to be proud of. Finally, when Despo convinced me to work at Mira's Tailor Shop, I buried myself among older women who used needles and thread as a shield, women who believed I was a master of my craft. I had a place to land and I dove into stacks of suits and dresses. There I became invisible again. Only Kenny saw who I really was.

THIRTY

Hot and grimy air assaulted Yianna's face as she sat on a wooden plank waiting for the Greyhound bus to San Francisco. Two large buses expelled exhaust while idling fat and lazy beneath a low overhang. Signs on each windshield indicated one bus would head to Eureka, the other to Redding, no help to Yianna.

Dressed in black jeans from the thrift store and a black shirt with sleeves rolled for summer weather, Yianna worried she would return from this trip with no more information than when she began. No closer to Olympia. Then she wondered if she would return from this trip at all.

Yianna had a half hour before her bus would lumber into the station and take on passengers. Besides her knapsack, her camera was her only cargo. Stretching out her long thin legs and stuffing her hands in her pants pocket, she touched the slip of paper with the Eddy Street address, her ridiculously singular clue. In her other pocket rested a small zipper purse stuffed with the roll of bills she had won at her successful poker game. Yianna's stomach began to churn with nervousness. It was easy enough to be fierce in a familiar setting, but it was much harder to toss oneself into the unknown, keeping chin high and hopes higher. Bravery was relative, in her opinion, and completely overrated.

A Greyhound employee in a worn blue-gray uniform strolled past the bench where Yianna and three others waited.

"Bus to San Francisco. The Number 6. Broke down on the Bay Bridge. Gonna be another hour. At least." He ambled toward his tiny shack-for-an-office, wiping his brow with a grimy bandana from his back pocket.

Minutes slowly ticked by, but Yianna had no desire to return to Angel's Bakery to wait. She settled on the bench next to a woman in her early twenties. She was everything Yianna was not and she packed that everything into a tight cotton sundress. Her unnaturally white-blond hair cascaded in a sulky wave over one eye and continued to luxuriate onto her shoulders. The low, square-cut neckline of her dress framed deep cleavage, lusting to break out. Little beaded tassels swung from her ears and bobbed as she shimmied on her seat, uncomfortable as the heat notched past eighty-five degrees. Her feet were pushed into black sling-backs with worn-out heels. Dragging her purse onto her lap, the woman snapped open the clasp, fished out a tube of Revlon's *Love That Red!* lipstick and applied another layer. Next, she blotted her mouth with a crumpled Kleenex. A high society princess on a drug store budget.

Yianna felt like a dark shriveled prune in comparison to a pineapple. Not so many years older, this woman was open and luscious, no shame in her sexuality. Knowing they might share the hard wooden bench together for another hour, Yianna slowly moved her camera to her lap. She opened the back cover, loaded her roll of film and advanced to the first frame. As she closed the film door, she could feel her bench companion watching her. Yianna decided to be bold.

"Do you mind if I take your picture?" Yianna asked politely.

"You some kinda photographer?" The voice was a little shrill but not unfriendly.

"Working on it. I was just looking for people to photograph. I need practice." Immediately, Yianna swung her camera between her subject and herself, her position of safety, and concentrated on the composition. She already knew that framing a subject forced the eye of the viewer to examine, to understand. The audience could interpret the image later. But the photographer decided what was important in the first place.

"Let's start with a full-length photo." Yianna needed to engage this woman and build trust from behind the lens.

As her subject crossed her legs showing the maximum amount of skin, Yianna snapped a wide shot. How did this woman know to do this? Slowly Yianna moved in to focus on the woman's face and white-blond waves. Click. The woman then flipped open her small compact so her nose and mouth were concealed from the camera, revealing only her eyes. Click. She applied face powder to her temples, masking the moisture rising from the heat. Click. Yianna hunted for another shot. Two lonely charms dangled from the thick braided silver bracelet: a four-leaf clover and a dollar sign. Why only two? Had she run out of money? Had a boyfriend stopped giving? Or were two charms enough? While her subject applied an expert eyeliner touch-up, Yianna pressed the shutter. Luck and money. Was that the axis of this woman's world?

Yianna set the camera back on her lap just as the bus to San Francisco suddenly rolled in early. It stopped under the giant overhang and wheezed to a stop.

"Guess that's us!" The blond stood, straightening her dress. "I guess you know me now. Wanna sit together?"

Yianna had revealed nothing about herself yet this woman sought her out as a friend. Her Leica had done the work, extending a handshake, silent conversation and connection. It seemed this young woman had felt she'd been seen for her truth and was valued for all she was, two charms and all.

Did Dorothea Lange have experiences like this? Marveling at the unexpected frontiers a camera could open, Yianna smiled. She was the flipside to this woman's sensual presence, yet the woman wanted to connect as friends, as confidantes, one in front of the camera, the other behind.

"Yes! Let's pick a good seat." Yianna smiled and quietly followed her to board the bus.

As they rode out of Woodland, Yianna relaxed next to her new blond friend, realizing her camera could open a dialogue, even if she herself did not have the right words.

THIRTY-ONE

The afternoon was lazy. Only a few customers dribbled into Angel's Bakery. Outside was hot and steamy, as if the San Francisco Bay were on a low boil pressing moisture into the Sacramento Valley and to Woodland in particular. After his usual afternoon catnap, Stavros stood alone in the kitchen while Lucky kept watch for an occasional sale at the front counter. With a large metal spatula, Stavros moved the golden buttery mounds of Snowball cookies from the hot baking sheet to cooling racks. He would wait a few hours for the cookies to cool, then dust each with a halo of sifted powdered sugar.

Smiling to himself, Stavros remembered the many men who had cooked in his village. Not cookies or pastries—that was women's work. Men made real food, roasted meats, stews, soups, food to stave off hunger after a long work day or a stint at the taverna. But in America, customers clamored for the crumbly almond-kissed butter cookies with powdered sugar on top. Woman's work or not, he would continue to crank out dozens of them until the day he shut down the bakery. This was his number-one seller, his signature cookie. Baking them was an artform, and if people referred to his work as "just bread" or "only cookies," Stavros was silently insulted. For him, baking was serious work, his personal gift to humankind.

The little bell chimed as three girls rushed in, heading straight to the small refrigerator stocked with cool sodas. They were somewhere between young women and their former childlike selves. Pulling out orange sodas, they turned to the cookie case and pointed out their favorites through the glass. Stavros smiled. At that age, Olympia and Yianna also had selected sugar cookies and Snowballs. Twittering among themselves the girls moved to the café tables to divide up their purchase.

Councilman Reynolds was next in line.

"Good afternoon, Councilman," Stavros announced walking from the kitchen.

Most customers, when deciding which luscious pie or cake to order, glued their eyes to the glass case. Not the councilman. His gaze lingered too long on the young females in the room. He'd had this habit for years, whether it was Stavros' nieces or other customers. This time was no different. Stavros watched the councilman stare at the girls fussing over their treats.

"I am happy to serve you!"

Stavros admitted to himself that when entering a room, he might survey the beautiful women but never stare. He never allowed his eyes to linger and never gawked at the young ones. That thought brought shivers up his spine.

"What you want today?"

Councilman Reynolds pointed to the Snowball cookies.

"A dozen of those beauties!" The girls who fixed his attention were probably younger than fifteen years old. Stavros remembered that Councilman Reynolds had looked at Olympia like that too. He always held his breath until Reynold's order was filled and he disappeared.

Stavros rushed to place the Snowball cookies into a pink box and efficiently move the Councilman out the door. His heart pounding, he exhaled and walked back to the kitchen to finish his work. Until

Olympia disappeared, he had dismissed Reynold's shameless gaze at women as "what boys do." But now his world had turned. He was relieved when a few housewives filed in to buy his freshly-baked bread and coffee cake.

A few minutes later Marika squeaked open the front door and snuck inside. In a tight-fitting black suit with brass buttons shimmering on the jacket and sleeves, she somehow looked elegant and cool despite the heat of the day. Her gold bracelets jingled as she raised her hand to wave at Lucky. She smiled and called out to Stavros.

"Hey cook!" She walked to the entrance of the kitchen. "*Pooh eeseh, tembelis?* Where are you, lazy-boy?"

Brightening, Stavros set down his spatula and baking tray. He pulled off his giant brown oven mitts and puffed out his chest, attempting to look his most fetching for Marika. Would she ever notice what a fine male specimen he was? Marika always tossed out a flirty tease but then hurried off to her next activity. Today Stavros would be more direct. He would express his interest in Marika, respectfully, of course. But Stavros bit his lip with worry about the reaction he might receive.

"I just come from Mira's! I have news! About Olympia!"

Hurrying from the kitchen, Stavros stripped off his apron and tossed it aside. He smelled of vanilla and almond extract but what could be done about that now? Stavros smoothed his hair and mustache the best he could. Flying to the front of the bakery, Stavros poured a cup of coffee and set it on the table in front of Marika. The ceramic cup meant she would stay to chat. If he poured coffee into a paper cup she might scamper away.

"The news! What about Olympia?"

"Lita Hernandez came to see Olympia the day she disappeared!" Marika grabbed the coffee and took a sip. "Maybe Lita, she know something!"

He sliced her favorite coffee cake with cinnamon crumbles on top and placed it in front of her with a fork.

"Why no one say this before?" Stavros sank into a chair across from her. His eyebrows squeezed to a point between his eyes. "How the sheriff not know this? How you find out?"

Marika rolled her eyes.

"The twins, at Mira's Tailor Shop, of course! They scared of the sheriff. They scared of Despo too. They don't say anything when she around. But this morning Despo leave. And Alethea, she tell me everything!"

Stavros leaned in closer. Reeled in by her low raspy voice, honeysuckle perfume and her milky skin, Stavros struggled to keep his mind on Olympia.

"Tell it from the beginning." He kept his eyes hungrily glued to hers.

"I go there to pick up my jacket they mend. No Despo. She go to post office to mail orders. The twins say they talk together last night and remember something. The day Olympia disappear, her friend Lita, she come to visit at lunch time. She bring soup and they sit in backyard to eat. It very cold, but they sit outside to be alone. Olympia usually she take no lunch, they say. But that day, she and Lita, they talk for long time."

Marika stared intently at Stavros. Eyes of a lioness, Stavros mused to himself, but he quickly shook off that thought.

"We must go see Lita and ask her," Marika spoke rapidly, announcing her plan. "It is you and me, Stavros. We go ask Lita. We need to know!"

Bursting with emotion, Stavros grasped Marika's hands across the table. This strong, capable woman, who truly needed no man, had joined him in the quest to find his niece. Now they had new information and Marika seemed to consider him an equal. Stavros was propelled forward with such good fortune.

Marika gripped his large hand tightly. Was she just excited to move on this information? Or was she expressing affection for Stavros? His mind was spinning.

"We can't let Yianna be the only one to carry the weight. God knows where she is! We no need two girls missing. Together we do this, Stavros!"

Marika's compassion melted Stavros' heart, as if together they were parents to his nieces. This was the woman he wanted, needed. His heart, drenched in comfort and excitement, was finally at home.

Stavros would not bring up his desire for her now. That would have to wait. Olympia was more important. Stavros tried to make his voice deeper, endeavoring to wrap a hug around Marika that she would remember later as she lay in bed.

"Lita, her father, he come here to play poker some days." Stavros hoped Marika's hands would never move. "I know him. A good man. We go tonight to visit. You come back tonight. We go together?"

Marika pulled her hands away.

"Of course, Stavros. Of course, I come back. Anything for Olympia." Her face softened as she looked at Stavros. "You know I come back. I feel Olympia here." Marika placed her hand over her heart. "She like my family too."

In a flurry of commotion, she collected her things to leave. Stavros hurriedly wrapped her untouched cake and poured coffee in a paper cup. Stavros wondered if Marika realized he was a man who would take loving care of her as she traversed the western states. But maybe she did not want a man fawning over her. His mind was buzzing like a beehive as he attempted to sort out her feelings for him, if there were any at all.

Shaking off his confusion, Stavros' instincts told him to be bold, straightforward, the way Marika presented herself to the world. He had always felt confident and daring with younger women who revolved through his bedroom door. But he had little experience with a woman like Marika. She was fully developed in every dimension. His desire had never been stronger.

"Marika," Stavros spoke in a low tone, no pretenses. "You meet me here at seven o'clock. We go to the Hernandez house. Talk to her family. We no tell the sheriff. Yianna is right. The sheriff, he no care. He do nothing. It is you and me. We do this together. Then I fix you something to eat back here."

Marika quickly turned around in her shuffle to leave. Her eyes locked with Stavros'.

"I am here at seven. We go." Marika adjusted her jacket and reached into her purse to locate her keys. "Yes, you can fix me dinner." She sighed like an overtaxed working woman. "That would be wonderful, Stavros."

Marika snatched the paper-wrapped cake and coffee cup from Stavros and raised an eyebrow.

"Be sure to make it spicy!"

Stavros watched every step as her heels click-clacked away from Angel's Bakery.

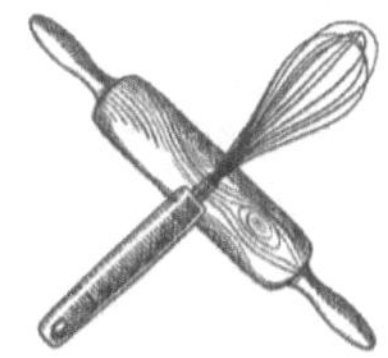

THIRTY-TWO

Stavros had not felt this optimistic about finding Olympia since he had driven his battered, cream-colored 1940s Ford delivery truck several months ago down the same road towards Sacramento. That day, with no one's knowledge, he had chugged his truck through downtown Sacramento, to J Street to be exact. His destination had been near the Sacramento Southern & Pacific train station that once had received him and his young nieces as immigrant newcomers to California.

But on that particular dark, drizzly spring morning, Stavros had parked the truck on the street and walked two blocks to the DeWitt Private Detective Agency on the third floor. Unlike detective offices in the movies, DeWitt's office offered no waiting room with an alluring receptionist, no window blinds casting mysterious shadows on the wall. Instead, Stavros trudged up three flights of wooden stairs and opened the door to a tiny office probably not refurbished since 1925. A single desk, a naked bulb overhead and a metal trash can were the only décor.

Mr. Richard DeWitt, Private Investigator, lifted his lanky body from the chair to meet Stavros. Tall, thin, sixtyish, DeWitt presented himself in shades of gray — suit, hair and complexion. His thinning waves were combed back to reveal a gray scalp and his gray wool suit pants rode high over his waist. Stavros immediately detected a scent of booze on his breath.

"Good morning Mr. Diamond, Diamond, uh eh –"

"Diamantopoulos." Stavros rolled it off his tongue, irritated a professional had to be corrected.

"Wonderful to meet you." DeWitt looked down at a yellow tablet. He'd written Stavros' full name with a blue fountain pen.

"You are an immigrant, Mr. Diamantopoulos?"

Stavros' temper immediately flashed. This was his first question? Why should it matter? Wasn't the cash in his pocket as green as the next man's?

DeWitt had been recommended by a Greek lawyer who had stopped to buy ripe oranges at Timoleon's fruit stand. He said DeWitt was a cheap but efficient investigator.

"Yes, my niece, she gone. She disappear." Stavros quickly related Olympia's story. His face expressionless, DeWitt scribbled down Olympia's first name and the last date her family had seen her.

"One day at home, the next day never coming home from work."

"And how will you be paying, Mr. Diamond-pulis?" Stavros did not correct him.

"Cash, of course." Stavros patted the wad of bills he'd secured with a thick red rubber band. His rent at the bakery could wait a few days.

To Stavros, DeWitt was as dry as an overcooked biscuit. He should be asking about the facts, not angling for cash. Stavros shifted in his seat, ready to jump up and sprint for the door. His instincts screamed that this man was only interested in his money. That he will never find –

"Mr. Diamond? Are you listening?" Stavros' attention snapped back to the small stuffy room. Surely a professional, recommended by another Greek, who worked in the capital city of Sacramento, could locate Olympia. At least he might dredge up a few avenues

Stavros himself could pursue. To keep steady, Stavros clasped his hands together. He felt himself walking across a swinging bridge, more hopeful than confident he would reach the other side.

"I've heard many of your people, your young women, disappear overnight."

These words instantly chilled Stavros' heart like an unexpected winter frost.

"You are saying that many Greek girls disappear like Olympia? How this possible?"

"Not just Greeks, Mr. Diamond. Mexican girls. Indian. Italian. Negro. They are too tempting. Or they simply make themselves too available. Men being men, of course."

Stavros fluffy eyebrows crashed together with worry. Not his Olympia.

"Mr. DeWitt. Olympia she is good girl."

"I'm sure she is. Most families think their loved one has no faults." A tight smile stretched across DeWitt's face. "Well, give me a couple of weeks. I think I can find her for your family. See what I can do." DeWitt placed his long fingers on a piece of cream stationery and turned it around to face Stavros. Sign here. The first installment is two hundred dollars."

Stavros was gut punched. Two hundred? When he telephoned, DeWitt said one hundred seventy-five dollars to start. Stavros felt the hair on his neck stand up.

Sensing hesitation, DeWitt smiled warmly revealing smoked-stained teeth. "Let's do this for Olympia."

Beating back his finely developed instinct for sniffing out liars and thieves, Stavros signed. For Olympia.

He slid a hand into his front pocket and pulled out his tight roll of cash. Paying in twenties, Stavros laid the green bills across the desk in a neat row. Spotting a gleam in DeWitt's eye, he slowed his counting.

"That's fine, Mr... well, may I call you Stavros? Easier for me."

Not answering, Stavros rose to leave, feeling more unsettled than when he arrived. Not bothering to shake hands with DeWitt, he only glanced back at the money on the desk, calculating how many Snowball cookies he must sell to make up for it. He walked out of the office into the gray drizzle, knowing he had rolled the dice with this private investigator. Pulling his lapels toward his face for warmth, Stavros wanted to bask in the comfort that he, the head of the family, was doing something to find his niece. He hoped it was enough.

That meeting with DeWitt had been a bust. DeWitt never returned a call or followed up with information. In fact, he had left Sacramento for parts unknown. Luckily, Stavros had not revealed to anyone that he'd engaged DeWitt in the first place. His three shepherds assumed that Stavros' bad mood was simply melancholy due to another hangover. And Stavros was sure Yianna believed her uncle had again drunk away most of another month's rent. DeWitt was his personal secret disaster and Stavros only hoped his bad luck had run out.

The calendar pages had now flipped to the last week of June and Stavros was again driving toward Sacramento but this time to a different destination. He stopped a mile from the State Capitol building that resembled the United States capitol in Washington D.C. The architecture always reminded Stavros of an ice cream scoop waiting to melt on the capitol mall.

Stepping out of his truck, Stavros looked down the wide street littered with cheap motels, dingy bars and family restaurants. He walked straight toward the flashing neon sign reading "Madame Fortuna • LOVE • MONEY • LUCK."

Stavros had been told by another Greek that Madame Fortuna was an accurate contact to the psychic world. As Stavros planted his feet on Madame Fortuna's welcome mat his mind flickered back to his days in Smyrna when he and Christos visited a gypsy fortune teller who read the boys' fortune for a single drachma. The brothers apprehensively asked one simple question: would the brothers be together most of their lives? They were delighted when the fortune teller, declared "they would be one." They gleefully left the gypsy to play their boyhood games, knowing they could expect a future enjoying their brotherly bond. Years later, after Christos' death, Stavros soberly remembered that prophecy. The gypsy meant one brother would be left standing alone. She had omitted the other brother would be dead and buried.

Walking into this fortune teller's den, pangs of dread lodged into Stavros' gut. He attempted to relax, telling himself the fee was only five dollars for a reading. The name Madame Fortuna sounded exotic, but when Stavros opened the squeaky door to the parlor, his nerves instantly calmed with the familiar aroma of roasted chicken with lemon and oregano.

A small woman waddled from the back in cloth slippers, bunion pushing through the fabric, nylon stockings tied in knots beneath knobby knees.

"C'mon! C'mon!" she chortled as she escorted him inside.

Not exotic at all, Madame Fortuna was about seventy-five and hardly taller than his shoulder. Her body was round everywhere and her bosoms sagged with weight and age. Her graying waves caught in a hairnet, Madame Fortuna did not dress in a costume, nor was her small house decorated to add mystery of the occult. Instead, she had placed lacy doilies on the headrest of the chenille sofa, just like any Greek *yiayiá*, grandmother. In a faded pink cotton apron, she appeared ready to baste her roasting chicken.

She looked him up and down, before sitting behind a small table. "You Greek?"

Stavros nodded.

"*Parakaló*, please, what do we have today?"

With youthful energy and a kindly face, she spread her hands over the tools of her trade. A small crystal ball, a demitasse coffee cup, Tarot cards, a deck of playing cards and a dark purple sack lay neatly in front of her. She floated her hands over the items, seeming to attract their vibrations. Next, Madame Fortuna presented her hand to Stavros, palm up inviting him to offer his. She took hold of his calloused hand and closed her eyes for a few seconds. Stavros waited for the predictable: *Money will soon be yours, You will soon meet your true love, You will have excellent luck in business.* Then her eyes popped open and her hands gravitated directly to the purple velvet sack.

He was aware that Greeks had been reading coffee grounds and throwing divination bones for centuries. To Stavros, fortune telling was merely harmless hocus pocus. But now that Olympia's disappearance had dragged on for more than six months, he had depleted his options. Maybe, just maybe, Madame Fortuna might give him a sign, a clue, a morsel he could pursue.

Madame Fortuna pulled back the draw strings on the purple sack, then spread out a cloth of midnight-blue velvet with two large concentric gold circles painted on it. She spilled the contents of the bag into the middle of the circles.

"The bones tell me information is in plain sight." She spoke calmly, flatly as if her vibrations had already drifted out in the universe attracting spiritual advice. Staring at the velvet fabric, he saw the bones were actually the remains of small animals. Were those ankle bones of a fox? A rabbit's small skull? Parts of a hoof? He stared at the middle of the cloth noting other familiar symbols: a thimble, a wooden coin, an eagle feather.

Determined not to give away personal information, Stavros waited for Madame Fortuna to dazzle him with psychic talent.

"The thimble is empty." Her eyes were closed as she held the thimble between her palms. "Has been dry for quite a while."

Madame Fortuna shifted her weight in the chair. She breathed deeply as if she had connected with the helpful spirits in the universe.

"He is missing. No! Two of them. The two boys must be found." The corners of her tiny mouth curved downward. "Evil take them. Get them back. You must do this soon. Don't wait!"

Stavros pulled his chair closer to stare at the bones more intently. Would they rise from the table and explain themselves?

Madame Fortuna picked up the bone that appeared to be a paw of an animal. "This is a symbol of strength. But not your strength. Two important ones to follow and find. Yes! I see two boys gone. One older and one younger."

TWO GIRLS, Stavros' mind screamed. *You got it wrong! TWO GIRLS, you misguided woman!* Couldn't she divine anything helpful?

"I have two nieces and one is missing." He spouted out that single clue hoping it would redirect Madame Fortuna in locating a solid clue in her sea of meaningless warnings.

"Important and dangerous. Near, yet far." Her hands slid to a moonstone that had tumbled to the center of the velvet cloth. She held it in her right palm as if weighing it.

"Never accept defeat. The dear ones, they await your strength. Your persistence. The moonstone tells us to never give up!"

Madame Fortuna's eyes opened and stared at Stavros.

"That will be five dollars. Cash, please."

Stavros angrily tossed his tattered five-dollar bill on the table. Two boys? He laughed bitterly to himself. The flicker of hope from Madame Fortuna was smashed to the ground. Olympia was no closer than before.

Stavros stomped out the front door and cursed himself for wanting to believe in magic and spirits. He promised himself from that moment on, he would depend only on himself. As the head of household, as a replacement for his honored brother Christos, he willed himself to play an important part in finding his niece, his card room and winemaking be damned. With Yianna traveling on her own to find Olympia, Stavros knew he must uphold his end or forever feel himself a worthless uncle and male guardian. Perhaps the meeting Marika arranged with Lita would move the search forward.

On the drive homeward, the truck began to spit steam from under the hood. For months, Stavros had been aware he needed a new radiator. Pulling to a dusty side road a few blocks from the bakery, Stavros slowly lowered his forehead on the steering wheel. Aside from Madame Fortuna's epic failure, he was profoundly struck by a painful absence, a lack. He realized he ached for both nieces.

And now they were gone.

When Christos died, Stavros was in shock. But as the years passed, he secretly looked forward to Olympia and Yianna's presence at the dinner table, chattering away about their adventures at school. He relied on the girls' help reading documents in English and, of course, he depended on them to tirelessly help in the bakery. With tears in his eyes, staring at his hissing radiator through the dirty windshield, Stavros realized he deeply loved Olympia and Yianna and longed for their happy youthful presence. He wondered if all parents felt, as he did, the mix of belonging, pride and astonishment at the intelligent and complete beings the two girls had become.

The dull realization that he hadn't expressed his affection to either Olympia or Yianna seeped into his mind. Did his nieces know he loved them? He had been so fixed on returning to Greece, he hardly realized it himself.

Then Marika flickered to mind. Yes! Marika! Maybe with her help, her strength, he could finally succeed. He would follow her lead.

An hour later, Stavros pushed the truck down Main Street in Woodland and allowed it to roll to a stop near the bakery. Wiping the sweat from his forehead with a rumpled sleeve, it occurred to him that a broken-down truck and an ill-informed psychic were not an auspicious beginning to his campaign to find Olympia. He certainly did not need divine help to interpret this symbol. But then again, he remembered the message of the moonstone: never give up.

THIRTY-THREE

Market Street in San Francisco was nothing like Main Street in her hometown. Yianna had been in the city before but not without her uncle and certainly not on a mission to find a missing sister. She felt distinctly out of rhythm with this hectic city where everyone seemed to have a purpose: businessmen hurrying with ties flapping in the wind, secretaries in low heels and wide skirts smoking together on a break; men hoisting boxes of fresh fruit and vegetables to restaurant back doors. The pavement vibrated as streetcars inched closer under a tangle of electric cables that looked like a web created by a confused spider, bells clanging at jaywalkers.

Yianna's mannish black jeans and heavy boots were not as conspicuous here seventy miles and eleven bus stops from home. Her Greyhound had rolled through the Sacramento Valley milk stops of Davis, Dixon, Vacaville, Fairfield, Suisun, and then stopped in the Bay Area burgs of Vallejo, Crockett, Pinole, Richmond, Oakland and finally this big city.

The salty ocean air against her cheeks was a relief from the dry Central Valley summer heat. It relaxed her limbs, slowed her breathing.

Hoisting her knapsack and camera on her back, Yianna wanted more than anything to fit in with the passersby. San Francisco rivaled Paris and New York, at least that's what she was told. If these people live here, they must be cultured and knowledgeable about ballet, opera, painting, photography! But for the moment, she pushed such thoughts out of her mind. She needed to hurry and locate the address written on Tasia's slip of paper. She had not bought a map at the drug store as she had intended.

Yianna pulled the scrap from her pocket and approached a grandmotherly-looking woman wearing a pillbox hat, cotton gloves and proper black leather purse.

"Can you tell me how to get to 325 Eddy Street?" She prayed the older woman wouldn't assume she was a runaway from the bus station.

The woman stared at the address. Twisting her short solid midriff in the opposite direction, she pointed toward the Ferry Building tower just sounding five o'clock with deep resonate chimes.

"Down Market Street and left at Taylor. Left on Eddy." The old woman looked back at her. "Honey, you going alone? It's not such a nice part of town. Where's your father, anyway?"

With a forced smile, Yianna nodded her thanks. She hoped to find the address before dark. She had no place to stay for the night and was hungry, having ditched the block of Timoleon's cheese on the bus because of its weight and nose-wrinkling odor. But Yianna began to regret ignoring the old Greek wisdom of bringing plenty of food on a journey. At least her Leica had made it safely this far. If daylight held out she would allow herself the luxury of shooting a few frames of film. She was always at home behind the viewfinder.

After knocking on the dark walnut door at 325 Eddy Street, Yianna waited. She glanced toward the sidewalk, past the tall set of black wooden stairs, then back again at the unanswered door. What type of building was this? Residence? Business? Next door a corner grocery store sold fresh produce from bins on the sidewalk. On the other side, two elderly men sat on a stoop drinking from small flasks in crumpled brown bags. No stranger to old men drinking, Yianna shrugged and knocked again harder, louder, begging someone to answer.

The heavy door was slowly opened by a short, square woman with skin the color of blanched almonds and the expression of a bulldog. A white linen cloth tucked behind the ears covered her hair. Was she a maid? A nurse? Hovering behind her stood a tall, thin young woman with sandy blond hair pulled into a bun. Her unstylish dress had seen too much laundering.

"You need something?" The older woman's voice was a low soft growl. Her neck was thick and sunk into her shoulders.

Yianna cleared her throat. "I'm looking for someone. A girl who might have been here."

"Ain't they all." The woman with the white headscarf crossed her arms in front of her ample chest. "And who are you?"

"Her sister—of the girl that might have come here. You may have seen her about six months back. Your address was found in her coat pocket. Olympia Diamantopoulos, she's missing. Maybe you know something about her?"

The faces of the women showed no reaction. Were they even breathing?

"This is her." From her knapsack, Yianna pulled a small black-and-white photo of Olympia from a cardboard envelope. This was one of the few shots Olympia had allowed Yianna to snap over a year ago. Olympia's eyes stared evenly into the lens, confident but dark and mysterious, as always. Nested in the graceful hollow of her neck was her delicate copper cross.

Suddenly the young woman stepped in front of the older.

"The pretty one! Didn't we see her, Mama? A while ago?" The young woman sounded almost jubilant with the recognition. Her mother seemed more skeptical and measured.

Yianna's heart nearly beat out of her chest. Did these ladies see Olympia? This was the first connection anyone had made to her missing sister. What did they know?

"C'mon in, sweetie." The mother's face relaxed and welcomed Yianna into a long hallway leading to a small living room. Stiff-backed wooden chairs with needlepoint seats were placed as if the area were a waiting room. Next to a desk were two other chairs as if conferences were a daily occurrence. The nervous clenching in Yianna's stomach overcame any hunger pangs. Although the women seemed welcoming, Yianna sensed something unusual took place here.

"Sit, dear. So, you're looking for your sister, not needing the same services?" Was there an Irish brogue in this woman's speech?

Yianna slowly sat on the overstuffed pink corduroy sofa, holding tightly onto her knapsack. "Services? What services are you talking about? Tell me, please."

The women exchanged glances.

"Well, sometimes a girl is in trouble and she needs someone to help her."

The daughter stood nervously before sitting as if her mother made all the decisions in the household. The mother pulled her to sit down and patted her daughter's small hands which held a ledger book. "We've helped many girls in our home. We don't talk in the neighborhood about it. We're just wantin' to help 'em."

Yianna gasped so loudly both women stared at her in surprise.

"You mean –"

"Actually, *he* said she be wantin' help, the man who brought her. Your sister, she didn't have much to say. Mostly looked at the floor, she did."

"Did you help her?" Yianna hated using code. "What actually happened?"

"The man left with strict orders for us to lend our services to your sister." The mother looked at the floor, tugging at her head scarf, her voice weary. "But she be silent while that man was here."

"She didn't like him much." The sweet voice of the daughter chimed in. "Neither did I." She clasped her hand over her mouth as if she had revealed too much.

The mother nodded. "When he left, your sister would not go to our examination room. Or move from where you are sitting now. She refused our services completely. She would only say, 'Leave me be. It's mine.'"

Yianna's mind reeled. Olympia must have been, or still might be, pregnant. Her Olympia. Her sister who had little to do with men. Her sister who wove on her loom most Saturday nights. The sister to whom Yianna could never ask questions about Porter because she assumed Olympia had no experience with boys.

"What happened then? Was she safe? Who was the man?"

The two women exchanged glances.

"We don't ask questions like that, sorry." The younger searched through the ledger book. "Only reserve appointments in our book. Most people use false names for the reservation anyway."

Pulling out reading glasses from her pocket, the mother balanced them on her nose to examine the ledger more closely. She flipped the pages backward.

"Let me see here. That's it, here it is. Monday, December 27. Eight in the evening. Joe Johnson. That's the name he used. Of course, we didn't know your sister's name until you told us. We don't ask that. Why give a girl more trouble than she's already got?"

"A younger man came right back the next day. He thought we was done with it." The daughter nodded.

"And land sakes, when he found out we did not do the procedure, he was upset, confused. Made clear the older man told him the services should happen. Seemed the older man would be unhappy." The mother's raspy voice droned on but Yianna absorbed every word.

"That first man, the older one, left her alone for the night. He wanted us to convince your sister to do the right thing. We were supposed to do the procedure early in the morning. But we never force our services on any girl. It's always the mother's choice. No matter what any man says. Of course, the poor thing stayed with us the night. She was terrified. Cried all night long."

The daughter moved closer to her mother on the pink love seat. "We gave her tea and cinnamon toast. Then we tried Mama's soup, but she'd touch none of it."

"Do you remember anything about the older or younger man?" Yianna leaned forward.

"They both had dark hair. Dark suit. Hat. Overcoat. Not light skin, but not dark. Even features." The mother spoke for them both. "Like all the other men walking around San Francisco. Definitely not tradesmen."

"The older one paid cash before he left." The daughter glanced at the register. "But –"

The mother finished her daughter's thought. "But when the younger one came to get her the next day, we gave it back. No services, no charge. Besides, she was already gone. Snuck out before we woke!"

Yianna felt like a truckload of stones had been dumped on her. Now her burden was to sort them out. Olympia had been pregnant, that was undeniable. But where did the trail end? The man had not taken her. Instead she had run away. And the men they described could be almost anyone in San Francisco.

"Don't worry, dear. Your sister will turn up." The mother patted Yianna's hand and began counting on her fingers. "Four, five, six, seven, eight, nine. She could, you know, be holding a baby in her arms by now. Both of them probably just fine."

Unconvinced, Yianna rose from her chair, slipped her knapsack onto her back and tossed the strap of her Leica over her shoulder. The mother eyed the camera apprehensively.

"Please don't take pictures of our place, will you honey? We don't advertise our services. Never will. We do this for the troubled girls. To give them a safe, clean place. To avoid them butchers in the alleys. We don't need the police around here."

Snapping photos in that house was the last thing on Yianna's mind.

"Of course, no photos." Yianna turned to leave. "Could I see where she stayed that night? Before I go?"

The daughter led her down the hallway into a small, cozy room with a single bed covered with a handmade patchwork quilt. A small night table held a kerosene lamp like an old west movie. Yianna sat on the bed attempting to feel Olympia through the mattress springs. Looking up to the mother and daughter who had not forced Olympia to act, a flood of gratitude swept over her.

"Thank you for helping my sister. Where do you think she went from here? Did she say anything at all?"

The mother and daughter looked at each other and sighed, shrugging their shoulders.

"We could hear her praying," the daughter finally spouted. "In a foreign language, I think."

That was Olympia. Her sister would pray at a time of deep trouble. Again, thanking the two women and slowly making her way down the steep stairs, Yianna was halted by the mother's voice.

"One more thing, dear." The stout woman gingerly made her way down the black stairs and stood next to Yianna who towered over her.

"Please don't think badly of your sister." Her lips were a tight line while formulating her next thoughts. "Some people call them bad girls. Girls who have sinned. But each one I've helped was truly good.

Usually, some man or boy just made it difficult for them. Hurting them. I'm sure your sister is a good woman. When you find her, be gentle."

Yianna's mind was overflowing. An hour ago, it had not occurred to her that Olympia might be pregnant. Yianna fiercely rejected that Olympia could earn the label "bad." But something bad had happened to her. With this new information Yianna rambled through the Tenderloin district as if in a dream.

In the west, the sun began to slip behind the Golden Gate Bridge and a chilling fog bled through the streets. Yianna desperately wished she had brought her thick jacket and began to lament the loss of Timoleon's cheese.

On Turk Street a sign read: Manny's Rooms for Rent • Nights • Weeks • Months. She could afford two dollars on a night's lodging. This rough part of town was good enough for the night. She checked in and left her knapsack in her room but kept her camera over her shoulder. Yianna crept back onto the nearby streets of Turk, Golden Gate and McAllister. Had Olympia, pregnant and alone, traveled the same streets she now walked? Yianna sensed the terror Olympia probably felt alone in a strange city, running from a man wanting to control her.

Unlike Olympia, Yianna refused to pray. She needed time to piece things together and some luck. Perhaps someone in that neighborhood had seen her sister with a stranger. A cold wind pushed Yianna through the smudged glass doors of the Civic Center Diner on Market Street a few minutes before six o'clock. From the back of the open kitchen, over the clanging of pans and the scrape of a spatula across a hot grill, came the sweet sound of a miracle: Greek was spoken here.

THIRTY-FOUR

Yianna slipped onto a stool and surveyed the diner. Not much on décor, stainless steel was the basic theme in the small restaurant. She sat at the shiny white countertop, worn areas in front of each stool. She left a space between her and the only other customer.

Perched on her seat, Yianna was relaxed for the first time today. Her ears delighted with the familiar sound of her first language. With the single customer at the counter, the cooks behind the grill continued their exchange in rapid Greek. One tall waiter looked up and slightly raised his chin in the Greek tradition of recognizing a newcomer. His inky black hair was slicked back with a matching mustache.

"You wanna order?"

Yianna plucked the menu from the stainless-steel holder and scanned it.

"Two eggs and toast." She dared to speak in fluent Greek. "And a chocolate milk shake." Yianna watched the cook move toward her, wiping his hand on a dishtowel.

"*Apo poo eeseh?* Where are you from?"

Yianna smiled. "Woodland, near Sacramento."

"*Keh steen Elátha?* And in Greece?" Greeks always wanted to know where a person's Greek village was located, not their American home.

"Argos. Peloponnesus." He nodded and walked back to his station. Yianna grinned hearing the gentle sizzle of eggs hitting the hot griddle.

In an instant, a platter of sausage links, three eggs, hash browns, buttery toast and a frosty milkshake topped with whipped cream appeared in front of Yianna. Her stomach flipflopped with excitement at the plate of hot food and she lifted her fork to dig in. At that moment a voice from down the counter offered its opinion.

"Next time you should really try the grilled cheese and coffee. Best thing on the menu."

Yianna looked up to see a man no older than twenty-five with round spectacles framing his greenish-gray eyes. His corduroy coat and casual slacks said he wasn't a laborer, but he was not a businessman either. He took a giant bite of his sandwich and turned to face Yianna with a warm smile.

"And a side of tomato soup! That's my dinner nearly every night." Munching, he pointed out the window. "I work in that direction. The *Examiner*. The *San Francisco Examiner*, that is."

He gestured to the camera cradled on her lap.

"Nice camera. An older Leica." He turned back to his sandwich and took another hungry bite. "What do you do? Photographer?"

"Yes, well, trying to be. But right now, I'm looking for someone." Yianna hesitated but pushed ahead. "Not sure how I'll find her. I just need more leads." Yianna looked up from her over-easy eggs. "So, you're a –"

"Reporter. Trying to be. Will Stafford." He extended his hand for a friendly shake. "My beat is the South Bay. But I live up the street in a little room for rent. Cheap place until I know they'll keep me on staff. I've only worked there for six months. They've had layoffs before so you never can tell."

They both returned to their meals. Yianna shifted in her chair. Should she continue talking to a strange man?

"Need leads, huh? Well, I've finished work for the day. Maybe I can help. Just gonna type up notes on my current story later tonight, anyway." Will took out a sharpened pencil from a canvas satchel and held it against his notebook as if he were interviewing Goodwin Knight, the governor of California.

"So who are you looking for?"

"My sister."

"Name?"

"Olympia Diamantopoulos."

"Why?"

"She's been missing for over six months."

"Where last seen?"

"We saw her when she left for work in the morning. They saw her at work. The police say she ran away with a man. But that's their easy out."

Yianna sped through the lethargic police investigation and the Eddy Street address keeping the information vague about the "procedure."

"So that's where I am now. A sister born in Greece, a seamstress, a good girl, woman. Not many outside interests. Grew herbs and wove on her loom. One night she just did not come home from work. Period."

"She speak Greek like you?" Will continued scribbling in his book. His frameless glasses fogged up from his excitement of a story. He wiped them clean with his napkin.

"We were both born there. I was three, Oly was thirteen when we came over. Our parents died when I was very young. She was more like my mother than my sister. She was mine," she added quietly.

The black-haired waiter wiped down the counter with circular motions. Closer now, he refilled Will's coffee cup.

"Any idea where you'll go next?" Will sipped his coffee waiting for Yianna's reply.

The waiter interrupted in broken English.

"You look for you' sister, here in 'Frisco?"

Yianna nodded, surprised. The rest of the kitchen crew dressed in stained white uniforms were busy clattering glassware and ceramic cups as they prepared to close for the night.

"Excuse me, I am Aleco. I hear you look for Greek girl here in this town?" The waiter had worked his way down to the end of the counter and spoke to them from a few feet away. "Why you no go to church? The Greek church! Everybody go there. Someone gotta know something." He smiled. "And the women they talk, talk, talk. And the mens talk too!"

"Of course! The church!" Yianna had the urge to reach over the counter to hug him. "Yes, Aleco! Thank you! I am *Ioanna!* Yianna! *Efharistoh*, thank you!"

Will raised his eyebrows and jotted something on his reporter's pad. "I know exactly where that is. Valencia Street. And tomorrow is Sunday—perfect!"

Yianna wiped her plate clean, sucking the last of her milkshake through the red and white striped straw. She waited for the check, counting money she had pulled from her pocket.

"I'm not doing anything tomorrow, it being Sunday and all. Sure, I accept your invitation to walk with you to the church." Will took the last sip of coffee and smiled. "If you want, that is."

Yianna was reserved, not knowing if she wanted the help of a man who seemed harmless enough. Maybe those were the same thoughts Olympia had about a stranger close to her before she disappeared. But the thought of help was appealing.

"Let's meet here tomorrow morning." Yianna did not look at him directly. "We can walk there together. I could use someone who knows the direction. But that's all."

Ready to leave, Will popped his fedora onto his head. To Yianna he looked like the earnest young reporters in the movies. He slipped his notebook into his satchel and tipped his hat in an old-fashioned manner.

"Tomorrow, say, ten o'clock?"

Yianna nodded.

"I'll go home and practice my Greek." Will looked up from under his hat and Yianna searched his face to detect a warning, a flash of maliciousness. But her eyes lit only on a soft, friendly, intelligent face. Will spun around looking over his shoulder. "G'night!"

Watching Will confidently saunter out the door, Yianna hoped she had not made a mistake. She looked for a check to pay.

"No charge for a Greek girl." The cook waived his hands back and forth. "You go find you' sister. Come back and tell us when you do."

With that, Yianna had made a little home in the San Francisco world of Greek men, not so unlike her home at Angel's Bakery. And she had taken another step on the path to finding her Olympia.

THIRTY-FIVE

The gloomy San Francisco fog held fast and low on every part of the city. Only a few cars cruised down Market Street, dodging the occasional streetcar running on a Sunday schedule. The workaday men and women who usually buzzed along the main thoroughfare were safely tucked in their homes or churches.

Yianna had been standing near the entrance to the Civic Center Diner since nine-thirty. Pulling her thin jacket close to her body, Yianna was watchful of every person, man or woman, who passed her as she waited. She did not want to look anxious or desperate to the reporter she had met last night. With her camera strap across her body and her knapsack held tightly to her shoulder, Yianna would take no chances after her disastrous trek back to her rented room the night before.

After accepting Will's offer to help her locate the Greek Orthodox church in the Mission District, Yianna heard the cook lock the door behind her and she began her walk back to Manny's Rooms for Rent. Although not looking forward to sitting alone in the tiny room, Yianna increased her speed as the dank cold air wrapped itself around corners and gusted in her face. *So, this is June in San Francisco?* Only a few hours ago she welcomed the air conditioning of the San Francisco Bay. Now, wishing she had brought her thick leather jacket, Yianna recounted the pleasure of a sleeveless summer night in Woodland.

Walking swiftly back to her rented room, a pair of hands appeared in the night. They yanked the camera away from her grasp and began to pull the strap from her arm. Yianna instantly wrenched it back and a tug of war began. A short, stocky man would not release the camera from his clutch. Pursing her lips together, Yianna, taller and leaner than the trespasser, swung her boot and kicked him hard in the stomach. He let go of the camera and fell backward. Yianna jumped on his body and jerked her Leica out of his sinewy hands.

"It's mine!" she hissed, beyond anger, knowing in her gut she could never afford a new one.

The camera clenched in front of her, Yianna ran the remaining block, boots slamming the sidewalk, until she reached her room-for-rent. She ducked into the lobby, ran to her tiny room and bolted the door, secure for the time being.

"Ready to go?"

Will's greeting broke Yianna's awful recollection of the camera-snatching scene from the night before. Smiling, Will had hung his reporter's satchel over his shoulder, appearing ready to lead her to the Greek church. She took a deep breath and swung her camera up and snapped his photo as he waited patiently for her.

Without another word, she fell in step beside him. He was becoming less of a stranger by the minute. He had agreed to help her and at least he didn't jump her for the camera.

They passed corner stores operated by Italian, Irish or Mexican families and storefront bakeries selling coffee cakes and Danish pastries. Newsboys on corners called out to sell the thick *San Francisco Chronicle* or *Examiner* Sunday editions for twenty cents. After arriving at the church, Yianna and Will finally settled in the last pew in the Greek church outside downtown San Francisco.

Yianna kept a distance from Will as she didn't want to risk the wagging tongues of Greek gossip somehow reaching her uncle to report she was with an American man. That would only worry him and Yianna knew he would beg her to quickly return. Better he knew nothing.

As the incense-filled liturgy came to the last prayer, the men and women donated quarters or dollars into the large brass plate passed from person to person. The small woman seated next to her shot Yianna an evil-eye stare. Dressed in printed jersey with a pink hat and matching gloves, the woman tsked her disapproval at Yianna's outfit. Glaring at Yianna's hair she lowered her gaze to the black pants and boots and turned away with a sniff. Yianna felt as if she were disobeying the ancient rules by merely occupying space in the last pew of the church. Although she had little religious training, she wondered if Jesus would think her outfit so horrible.

Yianna turned her head toward Will who had been patiently observing the church service. The congregation finally rose to be dismissed and receive their *antidoron*, the blessed cube of bread handed out by the priest at the end of the service. Lingering at the back of the church, Will gave her a discreet wink as she walked back up the red carpet. The priest had just begun to close the doors leading to the altar.

"Father! May I speak to you?"

The church was now deserted. Her words bounced off the large icons painted in deep blues and reds which depicted Christ's life on the church walls. The tableau began with the annunciation to the Virgin Mary and circled the church to end with Christ's ascension to heaven. Over the priest's head an imposing crystal chandelier with layers of dazzling sparkles illuminated the church.

Looking over to the boys working at the sides of the altar, the priest motioned them to continue with their work. He turned to Yianna.

"Yes? I am Father Demas. How can I help you?"

His accent was thick and Yianna wished he'd simply speak in Greek. About fifty-five years old, his graying beard and oblong spectacles softened his face. Golden vestments draped over his egg-shaped body. This priest did not seem to care about her male-looking outfit.

Unsure how to approach a priest she had never met, Yianna made a slight bowing gesture. She stood at the bottom of the two stairs leading to the altar but stopped on the lower level. She was never exactly sure where the line of demarcation lay—the line women and girls were not permitted to cross.

"I'm looking for my sister. Perhaps you've seen her." Yianna's words rushed from her mouth. "Olympia Diamantopoulos?"

She pulled out the black-and-white photo of Olympia with the copper cross at her throat. "Would have been five or six months ago. Have you seen her?"

Yianna's voice was too impassioned, too troubled, too loud for this space. At almost six feet tall, dressed in black, she suddenly felt like a negative presence in this heavenly world of incense and gold leaf.

As if he were ready to dive into prayer, the priest calmly clasped his hands in front of his chest. Then he slowly reached out to hold the photo closer to his glasses.

"This woman? She come to my church? When you say?"

"Maybe five or six months back. Perhaps after Christmas?" Yianna held her breath, waiting for information to dribble out.

Slowly he shook his head. "I no remember this." Then switching to Greek, his words ran together. "I don't recall this woman. I do not think I can help you. I wish I could." He shrugged his shoulders.

Dejected, Yianna ran her hand over her face and sank down onto the steps in front of the altar. No words would come as she gulped her frustration. The priest continued to hold the photo.

"*Esos*, perhaps..."

Yianna sprang upright to face the priest.

"Boys! *Ella ethoh, parakalo!* Come here please! *Tora!* Now!"

The young altar boys, in various states of shedding their golden uniforms filed out from the changing room with expectant looks.

"Can you remember this girl? Did we see her sometime after Christmas?" he asked.

The oldest, about sixteen, snatched the photo from the priest's hands.

"The one who waited in the alley for us to open for Sunday service? Last winter?" His voice was lower than a grown man's baritone.

A second altar boy, younger than the first, stared carefully at the photo. "Of course, it's that girl! I'd remember her anywhere. A real looker—uh, I mean, very pretty. But not like *that* picture. Her hair was messy and her clothes all wrinkled."

"Sad." The youngest of the four boys chimed in with a high, clear voice. "You could tell. Like she had no place to go."

Yianna remained silent, not interrupting the flow of information the boys poured out.

"She needed money." The oldest boy suddenly remembered. "That's all she said."

"Ah, yes, I remember now. Thank you boys!" The priest pulled Olympia's photo back toward his face. "No, she did not look like this. I ask what her problem was, what she need, but she no say. So I give her five dollars." He looked sheepish. "Then I give her five more. That's all I have in my wallet. Most of my pay for the week."

The air was thick with Yianna's expectation for more information—any small detail.

"Then she walked away. Fast," the older boy recalled. "Like someone was on her tail. Then she was gone."

The priest paused a moment and then looked up at Yianna. "I suppose that is all we know." He held his hands up with nothing more to add. The boys disappeared to change into their street clothes.

Glancing toward Will, the priest whispered, "Are you in danger too, my daughter? Where are you staying? What are you eating?" Just the questions Uncle Stavros would ask. And most Greek mothers.

"I'm OK." Yianna stared down at her boots. "I'm at a place called Manny's Rooms for Rent on Turk Street. I eat at the Civic Center Diner."

"*Mia stigmi, parakalo.* Just a minute, please." The priest hurried into the sanctuary of the church and was back in a flash.

"Here is five dollars for you too." He handed her a matchbook reading *The Apollo Hotel* decorated with the Parthenon stamped in gold foil. "You move to this place. Nice Greek lady, Thalia, she runs it. Say Father Demas send you. She look out for you."

He shoved the money into her hand.

"Take, my child. Be safe." He made the sign of the cross over her head. "And may you find your Olympia."

After thanking the priest, Yianna turned to walk down the red carpeted aisle to the exit, but she turned back.

"Did you send my sister to The Apollo Hotel too?"

The priest looked perplexed, his memory seemingly muddled.

His eyes rolled upward toward the large painting of Christ looking down from the ceiling dome.

"I no remember so good. I give Apollo Hotel matchbook to people who maybe need help. They no always go."

With that answer, Yianna nodded and walked to exit the church. She turned for one last view of Father Demas, who, with his back to her, made a sign of the cross in the air, softly repeating Olympia's name in his prayer.

THIRTY-SIX

The sun cracked the gray morning haze as Yianna and Will slowly ambled from the church on Valencia Street back to Market Street.

Will examined the destination signs on the streetcars.

"Where now, Miss Yianna?"

"Before we go to the Apollo Hotel, we need more facts. Any clue or mention about a woman, a girl, a baby or some kind of accident."

"Well, I'm your man." Will folded his arms. "I live for facts."

"I need to search all of the San Francisco newspapers. Every issue after Christmas until now. I guess it's the library?" Yianna's words trailed off into a question.

"Closed on Sunday. Like everything else in this town." Will stopped his loping gait. "Newspaper you say? I've got keys! Let's get some facts! Then, the Apollo Hotel."

A half hour later, they sat side by side in a study room outside the *Examiner* archives, both hidden behind newspapers. The editions from the last six months were stacked on the closest shelves, awaiting reporters, historians or investigators.

Seated at a polished library-style wooden table, Yianna gathered a stack of newspapers printed just after Christmas. Hours ticked by as they diligently scanned each page. Soon the dazzling afternoon sun beamed through the pie-shaped window pressing heat into the compact room. By evening, they were drowsy from breathing the stale air but found nothing that might point to Olympia's disappearance.

Will stacked the last of the papers with the current Sunday edition on top.

"That does it, Yianna. No breadcrumbs here."

Yianna rubbed her temples, exhausted. "But now what? All we know is the priest gave her money. That's where it ends."

"Let's take a minute and think about it." Will picked up Yianna's knapsack and jacket and tossed them to her. Looking around the room, Yianna was fascinated by the mountains of newspapers—a perfect still life in black and white. Sweeping up her Leica, she shot several frames from high and low angles.

Back outside, Will began walking quickly and motioned for Yianna to hurry and catch up.

"We're officially taking a break!" He smiled walking in the direction of Market Street.

"I have to keep searching, Will. I'll run out of money soon and I have to go back to Woodland with some news, a lead." Yianna redistributed the weight of her knapsack and camera as she hurried to catch up. She didn't want to grumble after the work Will had done that day.

"I know you're desperate to find your sister." He stopped and turned to her. She was aware her face was close to his. "But it's Sunday and everything is closed. We can at least have some dinner. An empty stomach makes a bad detective."

Yianna remembered Uncle Stavros saying it was the Greek way to work hard and eat well. Besides, her stomach twisted from hunger as she had only eaten the *antidoron* all day. A half hour later, they stood in front of a colorful cafe on Columbus Street in North Beach. The outdoor murals of Vesuvio Café and Bar welcomed them with whimsical scenes painted in orange, yellow, green and blue. A small, wooden sign with hand-painted lettering announcing "Vesuvio" was decorated with a caricature of a chubby, tattooed naked lady sitting on a low stool and beckoning customers. The color, the whimsy, the human touch of the exterior, welcomed everyone to come inside. Yianna began shooting photos from every angle but after several minutes, Will pulled her inside.

"Time for a drink." He and Yianna climbed on stools at the long bar, placing their elbows on the rich maple wood. Inside Yianna soaked up the chaotic artwork decorating the walls, framed vintage prints, magazine covers, handwritten letters from the 1800s. Crystal chandeliers and Tiffany lamps added to the artistic unruliness. The U-shaped second story was crowded with charming, odd artifacts and customers huddled around small tables sipping drinks.

"Two Kahlua and creams?" Will waited for her approval of his order for both. She shook her head.

"I.W. Harper and soda back," Yianna announced to the bartender.

"Think I've got an expert on my hands." Will smiled at the bartender who seemed to overlook Yianna's youthful appearance. He produced the drinks in a flash and wandered away.

In her world of Greek men, Yianna always had been "old enough" to drink. As was tradition in Greece, Uncle Stavros had watered down the small glasses of wine she and Olympia sipped as children. As she became a young woman, she'd been allowed to sip the basics: wine, whiskey and maybe a little *raki*. And I.W. Harper, Uncle Stavros' favorite, was always on hand.

Delighted with the complex charm of Vesuvio, Yianna turned to Will and was caught completely off guard. As if he came into focus through her camera lens, she caught her breath while glancing at his profile. His reporter's hat pushed back, he sipped his drink unaware a tiny bit of cream clung to his upper lip. Yianna sensed Will's spirit: smooth and easy like a stream flowing over pebbles, always ready to follow a story. In their few hours together, Will had become the teacher, although he hadn't lorded it over her. Curious and reliable, he had unknowingly opened a door showing Yianna an escape from a small-town existence. Will had brought her to this neighborhood of artists, as if knowing she hungered for a place like this. Yianna wondered if he needed these places too.

At that moment, a saxophone began to play in the corner of the upstairs level. Sipping her whiskey, Yianna relaxed as the warmth of the liquor slowly seeped through her body.

"This place is wonderful. Do you and your friends come here?"

"Don't have many here. Most of my friends are up north, where I was raised. A tiny town on the coast. Point Arena." Will took another sip. "I love this neighborhood. Artists, thinkers, and the best *gnocchi* this side of Rome, not that I've actually been there. Once I'm full-time with the paper, I'll move here to North Beach. They say rent is cheap, exactly what I need."

He looked around the café and smiled. "Nope, nothing like where I'm from."

Will's honest admission that he was still learning and vulnerable cracked open Yianna's heart. Maybe they could learn together. Yianna quickly pulled back that thought. *No romance! Find your sister!* She reined back the part of her that would impulsively reach out and kiss Will, partly for his easy charm and partly because he was the link to this new artistic world she desperately wanted to join.

Yianna realized she was staring at Will and his eyes were locked with hers. His greenish-gray eyes sparkled with tawny specks. He opened a menu.

"Let's order." Will finished off his drink. "We gotta eat something because we have another stop to make."

Before Yianna could protest, Will pushed his rimless glasses up on his nose. "Don't worry. You can't do much more to find Olympia today. There are places you need to know in San Francisco. I've just discovered them myself. Remember, I'm a small-town guy too."

Yianna knocked back her whiskey, wiping her hand across her mouth like Uncle Stavros always did. She needed to switch gears, shake off her attraction to Will and keep her mind on finding her Olympia.

After inhaling a large plate of spaghetti and meatballs, Yianna grabbed her camera and took a few last shots of Vesuvio.

"Let's see the recommendations of a San Francisco reporter!"

Will gently took her wrist and led her along the street. They crossed narrow Adler Alley to a small bookstore cluttered with paperback books, new and used.

City Lights Pocket Book Shop facing Columbus Street was open and the people who browsed the shelves and tables of paperbacks represented a cross section of the neighborhood. Older men stood leafing through books and groups of young women and men in twos and threes, many dressed in all-black jeans and sweatshirts, circled around the small shop quietly searching the piles of books.

Yianna tried to hide her enthusiasm and appear nonchalant, as if she belonged in City Lights. But her eyes were wide as she hungrily took in this scene. Woodland had no local bookstore. Yianna had only visited the eclectic Beer's Bookstore on J Street in Sacramento where she and Olympia sometime accompanied Agamemnon on his hunt for used art books. Of course, Agamemnon took them for ice cream before they took the dusty but reliable bus back to Woodland.

At City Lights, Yianna slipped through the maze of shelves offering poetry, non-fiction and modern fiction. To Yianna, each book seemed to represent an island of knowledge. How could a person decide on one book when there was so much to learn?

Her heart beat faster while deciding which books to investigate and which she would save for later. A bearded man in a plaid shirt and jeans behind the counter did not seem antsy for customers to hurry and purchase. The other bookstore personnel seemed equally accustomed to people searching for literary treasures, with no time limits imposed.

After a half-hour of blissful browsing Will bought a paperback, *East of Eden* by John Steinbeck.

"It's been out for a couple of years." Will shrugged his shoulders. "And I have lots of evenings to myself these days."

Yianna's hands were magnets for art books like the ones Agamemnon collected. Soon her arms became heavy with volumes on the theory of photography, classic European paintings and graphic design.

At the register, Will plunked down his book and removed his wallet to pay. "I'll get you a couple of those, if you want."

Yianna looked up in terror. She could not allow an almost-stranger to buy her expensive books. What would he expect in return? Was this the way Olympia had disappeared? One moment she accepted a favor — the next minute she was missing?

Yianna immediately returned the books to the shelves. "I'm OK, thanks. Too much to carry."

Yianna watched for Will's reaction but he simply paid for his book and placed the Steinbeck novel under his arm. "Good books go well with good coffee. Let's get some!"

Yianna watched Will walk out of the book shop and, through the window, she could see him waiting on the street. She hurried to join him.

Sitting over an espresso Will had ordered at the Savoy Tivoli Bar and Café, Yianna's face was drawn as the meal and coffee had spent the last of her energy after the long day.

"I'm almost too tired to make plans for tomorrow. But I can't stay in San Francisco more than another day. I've got to watch my money. Don't know how long I'll be on the road."

She took a sip of the delicious dark brew from her tiny cup. "And I'm not sure what our — uh — my next step is. I mean, where to go tomorrow."

"Let's go over exactly what Father Demas said." Having drained the cup, Will pushed his coffee away, pulling out his reporter's notebook while pressing money into a passing waiter's hand.

She thought back to the priest and altar boys' recollection of the Sunday morning when Olympia appeared. Her hands reached into her knapsack and plucked out the Apollo Hotel matchbook.

"This is what Father Demas gave me." Yianna opened her hand to show Will. "He told me to rent a room here. But maybe he sent Olympia there too. If the Greek manager would look out for me, why wouldn't she look out for Oly too?"

Yianna stared at the address: 200 Van Ness Avenue. Looking to Will to gage walking distance to the Apollo Hotel, Yianna realized she relied on him to navigate the city instead of struggling on her own. She chided herself for not being more independent. She could not succumb to Olympia's fate. Reporter or no, she had to keep up her guard.

Outside, Yianna fell in step with Will as he hurried through streets illuminated by the lights of the bars and outdoor cafes. As they rode the streetcar down Market street, an enormous sense of belonging swept over her. Yianna realized she and Will fit and that she desperately wanted to live in his world.

But the dark specter of Olympia's absence hung on her like a weighty cloak. Finding Olympia, had to be her priority. Yianna sighed and continued trekking with Will to the Apollo Hotel. She had no idea what information she might uncover there. As she creaked the door open to the tiny, worn hotel, Yianna prayed that perhaps Apollo or any other benevolent Greek god might reveal the next scrap of information.

THIRTY-SEVEN

When Yianna and Will stepped into the hotel their toes were nearly vacuumed off by a tall, middle-aged woman pushing her Hoover with short, powerful strokes. With the heel of her black pumps, she clicked the off-button to stare at them.

"And what I can do for you tonight?" The woman's generously accented English was mostly understandable. She examined Will from his soft gray hat, now a little crumpled, to the slightly worn-down heels of his shoes. Switching to Yianna, her eyes squinted as she surveyed the crazy angles Yianna's hair had taken since she'd attempted to arrange it hours ago. One hand was planted on her hip while the other held up the vacuum. She seemed to pass no judgment but simply observed the details of the two newcomers.

Yianna plunged into fluent Greek.

"Do you have any rooms left for the evening?" Yianna's voice projected a hint of pleading.

"*Ellinitha, eeseh?* You are Greek girl?" The woman walked slowly behind the counter to rummage through the registration cards in a small box. Looking up she raised an eyebrow at Will while taking a drag on her cigarette.

"*Mono enah?* Just one?" She gave Will a stare that would make the ancient Greek dramatists proud. "Or for two?"

"Just one, please." Yianna would not fall into the trap of being judged by an older Greek woman. Clearly her disheveled appearance was already suspect and not proper for a young Greek lady.

"*Neh*, yes!" The woman continued in rapid Greek. "I got one small room left."

Yianna produced the matchbook.

"Father Demas sent me and—"

She was still speaking while the woman rushed around the counter and squeezed Yianna tightly, then gave her a good long look. She switched to her broken English.

"What else you need? You hungry? You need to make phone call?" Her motherly instincts blossomed with the mention of the priest's name. "I am Thalia. I manage Apollo. *San to spiti sou!* Make yourself welcome as if was your home! I've got some *hilopites*, noodles, cooking in back." Thalia pointed toward her apartment in the rear of the hotel.

Wearing a close-fitting black dress with a slightly revealing neckline, Thalia showed feminine curves on her athletic frame. Her hair was black as crow feathers but softened by a few silver streaks. Her vibrant dark eyes and fringy lashes needed no make-up and she walked in a cloud of Chanel No. 5 perfume.

"Thank you, I've got everything I need. But first, I must ask you, have you seen this woman? My sister?" Yianna handed her the photograph of Olympia. "Last winter? After Christmas?"

Thalia pinched the photo between her fingers with one hand and took a drag from her cigarette with the other. She exhaled and studied Olympia's face through the smoke. "So many girls come here. Some girls Father Demas send to me, some just walk in. When you say?"

"About six months ago. Her name is Olympia Diamantopoulos." Yianna looked to Will who remained glued to the front door reassuring Thalia that Yianna was single, unencumbered by a man. Thalia had shut her eyes tight, lips pursed as if she were conjuring up Olympia's image. Yianna held her breath.

"*Malistah!* Yes! I always remember the Greek girls! Your sister — beautiful — she stay with me. One night!" Thalia flipped backwards through a giant registry book. "This you' sister name, no?"

Yianna stared at Olympia's loopy, old-world handwriting. *Olympia Diamantopoulos.* She pressed her fingers over her sister's signature, hoping to somehow feel her whereabouts.

"Thalia remember everything. Always do!" She stood behind the counter and reeled off her recollections. "Your sister, she come here without anyone. But in the morning — *amesos*, quickly — a man is there to find her."

Yianna opened her mouth to speak but Thalia cut her short.

"I see everything. He tall and young. Dark hair. Not fat. Raincoat, *akrivo*, expensive. I think he American. It rain hard that morning. They walk fast away from here. I hear a car start up the street but I no see. Yes, a young man. They go together."

Proud of her steel-trap memory, Thalia crossed her arms in front of her body. Then circling back around the counter she handed a key to Yianna.

"Exactly the room she stay. My single room for girls. Room 238. I bring her tea at night. She looked pale. Later I hear her, uh, be sick with her stomach."

Leaning closely toward Yianna, Thalia whispered harshly. "She no look happy. I ask, can I help. She say no. She cry." Thalia's own dark eyes became glassy with tears of sympathy remembering Olympia. "Her sorrow she no can hide. But away she goes with that young man in the morning. She no look at me when she leaves."

Nodding, Yianna quietly slipped the key from Thalia's fingers. She smiled a good night to Will, who seemed to understand it was time for a man to leave and not whip up gossip.

"See you early tomorrow morning, Yianna? At the Civic Center Diner?" He turned to leave, tipping his hat. "Night, ladies."

Yianna signed the guest ledger and walked up the stairs to the end of the hallway. Room 238 was small and simple. Thalia had arranged sprigs of lavender in a pitcher to cleanse the air. A rusted enamel sink stood in the corner with a mirror hung over it. Across the room a nightstand held a small ceramic lamp painted with pink roses, topped with a fluffy lampshade. A dark purple cotton bedspread covered a twin bed crowned with a laminated wood headboard.

Slowly circling around the modest room, Yianna imagined Olympia walking that same space, tormented with the worry of carrying a baby. Whose baby? Then Yianna stretched out on the unfamiliar bed, her hands behind her head, staring at the ceiling. Grateful she was closer to Olympia than she had been in six months, she was also a world away. Yianna knew she had to keep pushing, but her own next step was unclear, as she imagined Olympia's had been months ago.

THIRTY-EIGHT

Pacing in front of the Civic Center Diner before dawn the next morning, Yianna shivered. She had silently slipped out the front door of the Apollo Hotel before Thalia took her place of command at the front desk. The rich aroma of Greek coffee and Thalia's singing in the far corner of her apartment had alerted Yianna that the manager was nearly ready for business. Not wanting to explain about Olympia or Will, Yianna thought it best to leave early that morning.

She imagined the glorious warmth of a large cup of hot chocolate as the waiter Aleco jangled the keys to open the door from the inside exactly at six o'clock. Stepping into the diner, Yianna melted into the Greek world that nourished customers each day, just like Angel's Bakery.

Behind her, a small crew of working men and women pushed their way into the diner, settling in seats they probably inhabited every day. Orders of toast and coffee, waffles, bacon and eggs over-easy popped up from every table and seat at the counter. Aleco immediately sailed out from the kitchen with coffees and plates stacked with hot buttered toast. The pancake batter splashing on the griddle and the steamy warmth of the ovens were comforting to Yianna, reminding her that Uncle Stavros was gearing up for another week at the bakery. How were they handling the morning rush without her? She considered calling them later in the afternoon. But she only had minimal progress to report and did not want to divulge just yet that Olympia had been pregnant. Or maybe still was.

Yianna took a seat at the counter and soon was sipping a hot chocolate with a mountain of whipped cream. She nervously opened and closed the Apollo Hotel matchbook wishing she could be like the brave, bold goddess Athena for whom the ancients built that marble temple. Athena had represented wisdom and warfare and Yianna felt she could use a generous dose of both.

"This seat taken?"

Looking as if he might have slept in his clothes, Will popped onto the stool next to her. He tossed the morning *San Francisco Chronicle* on the counter and looked at Yianna. His glasses had fogged up from the outdoor chill and the indoor heat.

"Where to today, boss? I've got some work to do but maybe I can squeeze in some fact-finding." Will smiled and ordered eggs, bacon, waffles, toast and coffee. Aleco disappeared into the kitchen only to instantly reappear with coffee, working double-time that morning.

"I ordered too much. Maybe we can share." Snapping open the newspaper, Will scanned the headlines as if he were seated at his own breakfast table. Minutes later, Aleco hauled out the steaming platters that Will had ordered and an extra plate. Yianna smiled her thanks.

Will turned to Yianna. "You decided where to look today?" He pushed half his breakfast onto the spare plate and set it in front of her.

Yianna continued to flip the matchbook cover open and closed. "I slept in Olympia's room last night. Will, my sister might be pregnant and she's not married. I know how it sounds. Olympia isn't a bad girl — but something bad happened to her. I need to find out who that man is that Thalia saw her with. Was it the father of her child? Where was she going?" Yianna rubbed her forehead attempting to concentrate. "And where is she now?"

Suddenly a hurricane rolled into the restaurant. It was Thalia, wearing a full-length red coat held together by oversized black buttons. A silk scarf was tied under her chin peasant-style. Flat shoes carried her in a jog.

"*Perimeneh!* Wait!" She ran to Yianna and hovered over her shoulder. "I remember!" She stopped to catch her breath.

"I know everything that happen at the Apollo Hotel!" Panting now she spilled her story. "The man with your sister say he need to find the lost coat! Yes! That is what he say!"

Rocking back on her heels, proud of her contribution, Thalia held her purse with both hands, waiting for praise.

"Lost coat?" Yianna spun around on her stool to face the confident Thalia. "Are you sure that's what he said?"

"He find your sister as she leave in the morning. At the door of the Apollo. He tell her 'We gotta find the lost coat. You must come with me!' Your sister, she look very sad. She walk with him away, slow. Then I hear a car start up the street. She never come to the Apollo again." Thalia stood proudly facing Yianna. "I would remember this. Jus' like I remember this man say to meet you here for breakfast." Thalia pointed to Will. "Thalia never forget!"

Thalia excused herself to hurry back to the Apollo. In the same flurry she had arrived, Thalia whooshed out of the Civic Center Diner.

"What a woman!" Will sipped coffee blinking after the trail of energy Thalia left behind.

"Yes, she remembered everything." Yianna swiveled her seat around to finish her breakfast but could not take another bite. "But really, a lost coat? A lost sister and now a lost coat?" She sipped her chocolate and sighed at another dead-end.

Next to her Will slurped his coffee and popped the last piece of toast in his mouth.

"Lost coat. Can't figure that. But during my lunch break we can go to the police station to see if they've heard anything." He dropped a few dollars onto the counter for the meal and hurried toward the door. Yianna popped off her seat to leave with him.

"And if they don't know anything?" Yianna swung her knapsack over her shoulder draping her Leica over the other. "I just don't get it. A lost coat? Who would possibly care about that?"

Market Street was humming with Monday morning activity. They walked nearly a mile in silence, each sorting out Thalia's recollection. Then, just before they turned to cross toward Mission Street, Will stopped and turned to face her.

"Wait, Yianna."

A large cluster of people pushed past them hurrying to cross the street.

"I was just thinking. Maybe I'm getting used to Greek accents. But to me, she wasn't saying *lost coat,* exactly. I think she might have said *Lost Coast.* That's a place — the Lost Coast. North of Point Arena where I grew up. The Lost Coast of California."

Yianna slowed to a stop considering the Lost Coast was an actual location. A pedestrian pushed her from behind and she stumbled forward but regained her balance. Without transportation, no additional information and not much money, Yianna believed her only hope was to follow this meager clue.

"I'm not sure where that is but the Lost Coast will be my next stop!"

After walking a few steps she stopped and looked up to Will.

"And how far is that?"

"Up U.S. 101 from San Francisco. About five hours by car."

Now, two simple words, Lost Coast, were the only links to Olympia that Yianna could track to this hidden part of California.

THIRTY-NINE

The sweet taste of Marika's lips from the night before teased the edges of Stavros' mind like fragments of a dream. Expecting an evening of ecstasy and dazzling passion, Stavros was not disappointed. But at five o'clock in the morning, alone in the bakery kitchen, Stavros' step was weighed down by the realization that Marika was more than an attractive, wildly sensual woman. True, she was independent, had many male suitors, controlled her own money and ran her own business. But to Stavros, Marika's true fascination was her optimism, her unshakable drive to accomplish and that she never took no for an answer.

But last night, what he had learned rocked him to the core. Marika had revealed a vulnerability he had never suspected. Reviewing the events of the last twenty-four hours, he attempted to make sense of the situation as his hands twisted, kneaded and pulled dough for the loaves he would bake.

After she'd called on her last account, Marika had shown up at Angel's Bakery. Removing her jacket for the evening ahead, her silk blouse appeared more wilted than usual. Stavros could tell she had brushed her hair and reapplied lipstick, determined to present her best, even after hours. They drove together to the Hernandez home,

Marika in the driver's seat of her Dodge sedan. Stavros directed her over the railroad tracks to a street near Tafoya's Market where Manuel Hernandez had built a small home for his family. Marika knocked on the screen door and stepped back near Stavros.

"Hello Manuel. We come to talk with Lita for a moment. About Olympia," Stavros announced quietly when Lita's father answered. "If you allow."

Manuel opened the screen and shook hands with Stavros. Manuel's wife jumped from the family dinner table, wiping her hands on her apron. A small energetic woman, she had a welcoming smile. The oldest, Lita, two teenage boys and a girl about ten sat crowded around large platters of carnitas, roasted ears of corn and sliced tomatoes.

Manuel pulled out a chair for Marika. She politely shook her head and remained near Stavros. Manuel pulled Stavros aside.

"What you want with my daughter?"

Aware of his intrusion on Manuel's family, Stavros spoke in a soft voice, kneading his hat if he were still working in the bakery.

"As you know, we are missing our Olympia. She gone for six months now. Maybe your Lita help us." Stavros gave a respectful nod to the young woman at the table. "Lita and Olympia good friends. Maybe she know something. Olympia maybe she say something."

Her thick dark hair loose down her back, Lita was dressed in a sleeveless white blouse and blue capri pants for the summer heat. Stavros knew Lita to be about Olympia's age although her petite stature gave her a youthful look. She looked up from her plate with a shy smile.

"I really don't know anything. I miss Olympia too." Dabbing her mouth with a napkin Lita ducked into the small kitchen.

Stavros felt unsure of the next step. They had already interrupted the Hernandez family dinner. But Marika slipped away from his side with a gracious smile.

"May I?" She pointed to the kitchen and Mrs. Hernandez nodded her permission.

Stavros could see Marika quietly put her arm around Lita as tears rolled down the girl's face. Then Lita clasped Marika with strong arms and burst into full sobs.

A half hour later Stavros and Marika rode back to the bakery. Marika broke the silence.

"Lita, she know a lot." Marika steered the car into the parking space outside of the bakery. "But Stavros, she afraid to speak. And I don't know why. *Who* make her afraid? Something is not right. But she tell me nothing. She just cry. That don't help us."

At the bakery Stavros jumped too late to open the car door for Marika who'd already popped out of the driver's side. Had she forgotten their late dinner? He hurried to unlock the front door of the bakery.

Marika continued to hammer on Lita's connection with Olympia.

"You say they are friends since Olympia come to United States." She frowned. "Lita she know what happens, I am sure."

Stavros held the front door open as he spoke. "But we cannot force her. She is young and afraid. Maybe we go back to her in a few days. You think?"

Marika nodded and followed him inside. Stavros quickly arranged the food for their dinner before she could change her mind. "Everything almost ready. You just sit at a table in front and relax."

He reached for the red wine he had aged in the basement. His best batch in years. Stavros poured his ruby-red Zinfandel in a short tumbler he had polished to sparkling that morning.

Stavros watched as Marika planted herself in one of the café chairs. Tossing back half her wine, she let out a giant sigh from deep within her body. Stavros wanted to interpret it as a sign of loneliness, perhaps a hankering for close contact, but he thought the better of reading too much into her every move.

Sliding the thick marinated lamb chops under the broiler, Stavros presented to Marika a Greek tomato and cucumber salad, lemon-drenched roasted potatoes and *yaprákia*, grape leaves stuffed with rice, loads of onions and lemon. He was brandishing his prelude to love, perhaps even more important than the lovemaking itself. Maybe this working woman needed a real man to take care of her.

After sharing the food and two and a half bottles of his homemade wine, she insisted they move on to her apartment away from the observing eyes and ears of Agamemnon, Timoleon and Lucky. Several hours later, Stavros found himself wide awake and still breathless in Marika's bed as she rested next to him.

At two o'clock in the morning, Stavros lay awake, not because of the uninhibited sparks when he and Marika touched. He had expected they would instinctively know the steps to each other's dance. Well aware their connection would be sweet and spicy, Stavros was amazed that Marika had no prim or proper idea of baring her body to him. She was not shy and challenged him in a way no other lover had. Without saying a word, Marika placed his hands where she wanted them, expecting her full satisfaction. And Stavros was only happy to comply. After he had pleased her in every way he could imagine, the wine and his experience guiding him, Stavros felt his restless sexuality had finally found a home. He was content. He only hoped he was man enough for Marika.

The dark velvet Zinfandel had loosened her tongue and heart. Her skin appeared to glow from the streetlight beaming through the high transom window. Certain he wanted to be close to her forever, Stavros absorbed her essence but stopped himself from speaking. He did not want to appear a moonstruck fool, although he longed to curl up in Marika's lap.

"I gotta tell you something." Marika rolled over in the sheets. Her gravelly tones suggested too much wine and too little sleep. "About me. You don't know this. No one does."

Sucked out of his reverie from making love to the finest woman he had known, Stavros braced for rejection. He rolled toward her, propping up his head on his hand and stared at what he desperately hoped was his woman.

After the last hours of fiery lovemaking, what could she reveal that was so crucial? Did she have another man on standby? Was she moving for her work? Maybe she hadn't enjoyed his version of love. Perhaps he had been too rough or not romantic enough. He dreaded her next words waiting for his dismissal.

"I have a child." Marika turned on her back, staring at the ceiling. "Yes, a boy. He lives somewhere I don't know. In Greece, in Albania." She turned to Stavros. "I lost him. My son."

Stavros struggled to make sense of the words falling from Marika's lips.

"Costas, my boy, my baby, they take him away." Suddenly Marika was not in bed with Stavros, but far away in her village. "We live in the mountains after the war, the *communistes* come. They worse than the damn Germans. They invade our village and take away the children to I don't know where."

"In 1948, Costas is three years and I hold him in my arms. Then they take him. The *communistes* they steal Costas and other children and put them on a train."

Marika could barely catch her breath to finish her tale. She choked on her tears, her mascara smeared and her lipstick worn away. Stavros waited for her next words.

"I cry for weeks. Don't know what to do. The old village men who were not killed, they tell me run away. No use to look for Costas, they say. I should find him later. So that is what I do. I come here to United States. I work hard to make money and make a home for Costas. But where to start looking for him? My heart always with my boy."

Stavros was silent but stunned with sympathy. He wanted to wrap Marika in his arms and make love again to wipe out her pain.

But Stavros' brain told him that's what *he* wanted, not Marika. The air hung heavy between them as he sensed her profound pain. He calculated that if Marika was around forty now, she would have been in her early thirties when Costas was stolen. He desperately wanted to rage against the *communistes* who had long been defeated. But instead he slid his muscular arm under her back and held her tight.

"*Toh lipameh poli.* I am so sorry, Marika."

With that simple tenderness, Marika flooded the bedroom with the rest of her story.

"I was living in Florina with my grandmother. The rest of my family killed in the war. Most of them killed by the Germans. My father and brother killed in the mountains of Albania. But a soldier pass through our village, a young Greek. We make love in a world of war. I loved him but we only have three weeks before my Greek soldier, he leave. He never know about our baby. I name my baby Costantinos, like my father."

Marika sat up in bed now, her breasts bare and the sheets pushed aside so that the soft curves of her body swamped his brain.

"Nobody care I have no husband. At first anyway. The Germans take everything and leave us nothing. Not enough to eat, we even eat grass. But I make enough milk for my boy. I only care about my boy."

Stavros was frozen on his side of the bed, listening to her story, not sure when to break in and offer sympathy or horror. Marika, it seemed, had kept her painful memories in her private book, like Olympia's pressed plant samples. She told her story in bits and pieces, fragmented, as if told in full detail, the pain would be unbearable.

"Then the *communistes* come to our village. They always accusing people of things they did not do. We never find out what happen to our men. They just never come home. My grandmother help me raise Costas. We keep to ourselves and stay out of village politics. We have enough pain from the Germans."

Stavros absorbed this information and silently thanked his brother Christos for anticipating the war and forcing him to immigrate to the United States. He mentally made the sign of the cross for his own dead brother.

Marika should not be naked when telling this story. Stavros sat up beside her and gently set a turquoise silk robe on her shoulders. Her mind still back in 1948, Marika hardly noticed as the silk touched her skin. Stavros pulled a sheet over his lap while Marika's story unfolded.

"First there are only a few *communistes* in the village, then many more. Finally, they take the children. They say to feed them and give them school. Better for the children they say." Marika stared through Stavros and he imagined she was staring down a communist whose hands lay on her young child. "I feed Costas, every day. Every meal. I go without, but my boy he always eat. No one need to take him."

Standing up now and wrapping the drawstring around the robe to cover her body, Marika whirled around and faced Stavros.

"Then they pull him from my arms. They say they kill him if I move. They say it for the good of the children." A single tear trickled down Marika's cheek as she blushed with anger and pain. "They rip him from me. He cry. He scream. I want to help my baby but they have the guns. They take him away on a cart to the train station with the other children. And then the village children, Costas' age and much older, they all gone. To where their mothers never know."

Before the Germans arrived, Marika revealed, her grandmother had hidden gold jewelry in a tin box deep in a hole she had dug under a fig tree. With Costas kidnapped, her grandmother gave the stash to Marika, instructing her to sell it, find relatives in the United States and leave. Her grandmother stayed behind just in case Costas came home.

"Be smart, she tell me. Learn English. Make money and bring Costas to America." Marika smiled, attempting to pull a blanket of hope over her wounds. "So this is what I do. Every day. I work for Costas."

She collapsed onto the bed, placing Stavros' hands between her breasts, onto her heart.

"You understand what I'm telling you, Stavros?"

Stavros nodded, not exactly sure what she wanted. Should he acknowledge her agony? Her loss? Her strength? The barbaric kidnapping that the communists committed?

"Yes, I do." If anything, Stavros understood the pain of great loss, when nothing could undo it. Perhaps this understanding could help Marika if she indeed chose him.

Marika unexpectedly pulled him down on the bed next to her and pressed his bare chest next to her bosom wrapped in her silk robe. Stavros would allow this woman to do whatever she wanted with his body.

"I knew you understand, Stavros. The thing I want you to know. I am always a mother first."

Stavros was surprised at this definition Marika offered of herself. This outspoken female, this energetic businessperson, this honest woman and banquet of lovemaking did not define herself as any of those things. Marika was, and always would be, first and foremost a mother.

Stavros pulled Marika closer so there was no space left between them. They remained bonded until a chorus of sparrows chirped their sharp wake up call. At four-thirty in the morning, Stavros hauled himself from the warm bed to the cool kitchen of Angel's Bakery to begin his day, two hours late.

Eyes red and blurry, Stavros felt ragged, weary. His feet were slow but his hands began to automatically perform their duties. Stavros felt as if he had been through a lifetime of losses but the day had just begun.

FORTY

As the sweltering July afternoon rolled on, Agamemnon worked the counter, allowing Stavros time to untangle his thoughts. A brutal hangover splitting his brain remained after the passionate evening with Marika, the wine and her confession. Somehow he had to become Marika's reliable rock, possibly her *andras*, her man. And maybe, over time, he could help her slip from under her great sorrow.

With emotions swirling between his brain and his heart, Stavros profoundly missed his nieces and vowed he would put more effort into finding Olympia. When the girls were nearby, he could pretend his family had not truly left the earth. Now, as he worked in a den of old Greek men, Stavros could not recall why he wanted to marry off the girls in the first place.

The heat of shame crawled up his neck and burned his cheeks. He had taken the gift of his nieces for granted and had forsaken the memory of Christos. Now, one niece had been missing for over six months and the other was thrashing about California using a camera for a sword. He had failed both with no guarantee they would return.

On the oversized calendar in the bakery kitchen, Stavros had slashed the days Yianna had been gone to find Olympia. Over a week so far. Yianna was doing the job for the entire family, a man's job, his job. He worried that she had not telephoned to give an update and vowed that if his two nieces returned healthy and whole he would ensure they lived the rest of their lives without judgment.

The sharp jingle of the little bell pierced Stavros' brain and jolted him from his muddled daydream. Agamemnon flew to the back of the kitchen to find Stavros.

"She need to talk with you!" Shuffling backward, Agamemnon was clearly uneasy. He swiftly vanished to the front counter.

Stavros' eyebrows raised in expectation. Had Marika come to declare she was in love with him?

Whipping off his apron, Stavros hurried to the front ready to greet his love. But instead of shapely Marika, it was Trina Harrison, the congressman's wife. He took in a long breath, praying he didn't reek of last night's wine.

"I'm hosting another fundraiser. I want all your best pastries, like last time!" Trina blurted her order without a proper greeting. She paced arrogantly in front of the glass case waiting for Stavros' attention.

Stavros assessed Trina. She wore a cool aqua-colored linen dress, belted tightly at the waist. Her slim figure wore the clingy dress well. Her hair was beautifully sculpted and had not wilted in the heat like the housewives who had shopped at the bakery earlier that afternoon. Did rich women everywhere present themselves with such perfection? Stavros reached for his order pad and pencil. Usually, one of Trina's kitchen staff brought in the order for her large society gatherings. Stavros wondered why Trina herself came to his bakery.

Stavros poised his pencil for the order and politely waited. Trina looked away, as if lost in thought. Just as quickly, she snapped to consciousness and barked out orders.

"Remember my bakery order for the congressman's re-election campaign at my home? Do you still have a record of it? I want it just like last time! But no fudge—too hot. And I want an extra three-dozen Snowball cookies. Those are excellent!" Trina exhaled having bleated her orders all in one breath.

Stavros copied her order on his pad and did not need this woman to remind him that his Snowball cookies were excellent. He held his hand over his order pad so Trina could not see he wrote in Greek, not English.

"Yes, ma'am." Stavros knew to be subservient to this woman who owned the town. "When you need delivery?"

"Next Thursday. The fundraiser starts at five. So deliver between three and four. We did so well with the first one. Raised a boatload."

Trina had not offered one *please* or *thank you* in the few minutes she stood in front of his bakery case. Stavros' skin prickled. Keeping his head down to polish the glass counter, Agamemnon silently avoided Trina's hailstorm of orders.

"You can pay when I deliver. Like always." With a flourishing slash mark on his pad, Stavros signaled he was finished taking Trina's order and she could now leave his bakery.

Stavros laid his hands on the counter and patiently waited as long seconds ticked by.

"Anything else I do for you, Mrs. Harrison?" Stavros pasted a flat smile on his face.

"Yes, there is one more thing." Trina regained her sharp edge and she leaned closer to Stavros.

"You make sure that niece of yours has nothing to do with this order, the delivery, my house. Or my son."

Stavros attempted to make sense of her words.

"You mean Olympia?" Stavros blinked. "She is missing for months. We look and — "

"For heaven sakes, man! The other one! The girl who just graduated high school with my son Porter. Isn't she your niece?"

"You mean Yianna? She help me deliver orders to your house many times and — "

"Just make sure she stays away from my place." Trina was a statue, arms folded, speech delivered. "I don't need her kind of girl around our home, especially before the election!"

Exactly what were these accusations against Yianna? Stavros ransacked his memory to recollect why Trina bared her fangs in Yianna's direction. His voice caught in his throat and a fiery rage began to kindle in his gut. No stranger to insults or street fights, Stavros tried to control his anger. Couldn't this woman just leave his bakery?

Trina lightly touch her hair, confident it was in place then slowly strolled out the front door, eyes forward, no goodbye.

Stavros turned to Agamemnon. They both searched for words as Stavros stared at the order written on the pad. The thought of tearing up the order to punish this woman floated through his mind. But that order was worth hundreds of dollars, easily the rent for the month and part of the next.

Immediately the little bell clanged as the front door opened again. Stavros eyed Sheriff Lewin and Deputy Robbie's shiny metal badges and his heart pounded hard behind his apron. After his evening with Marika, how could his luck run out so fast? That sweet memory was immediately washed away by two olive-green uniforms standing in front of the glass counter. These were two large men with badges, men with whom Stavros did not want to exchange information or anything else. He mentally scanned the card room hoping the gambling chips and cards had been safely hidden away after the last gathering.

"Sheriff! Deputy! Good afternoon. What I get for you today?" Hoping to move the officials quickly out of the bakery, Stavros struggled to keep the tension from his voice. Next to him, Agamemnon plucked a wax tissue from a box, ready to reach into the case and fulfill their order.

"We didn't come to eat. We came because that niece of yours says we aren't doing our job." Sheriff Lewin's voice was sharp and his eyes darted to all corners of the bakery. He raised his chin to look across the counter toward the back room. "Your *girl* is telling us how we should work this case. So we came to ask questions. Might as well start at the missing girl's home. Or whatever this place is."

"Olympia." Deputy Robbie added in a quiet voice, producing a notepad from his back pocket. "This missing girl. Her name is Olympia."

"Just a few questions for you and the old men who live here." Sheriff Lewin's eyes searched the bakery for the other boarders.

The old men who live here. Stavros' world gave way and forced him to firmly grasp the glass counter. He got the message: Yianna had accused Sheriff Lewin of not doing enough to find Olympia. So Lewin would turn the investigation on Agamemnon, Timoleon, Lucky and himself, four males living near Olympia. A wave of nausea crept up Stavros' stomach. He wanted to run to the bathroom and be sick.

"Won't take too long." Sheriff Lewin pushed behind the counter toward the card room. Glancing over his shoulder, Stavros was relieved to see Agamemnon had neatly arranged the wooden tables and chairs from the last game. No cards, no chips and no tally sheets were visible to hang Stavros out to dry.

"Start with me."

Stavros spun around to the clear, loud voice of Agamemnon, his trusted friend. He always knew what to say. He had found the courage to speak to these law men.

"Start with me!" Agamemnon repeated his words, moving to a small café table. He plunked down in a wire-backed chair and displayed a friendly grin as if he welcomed friends to his table.

"Have some coffee. And a pastry or two." Stavros poured two cups and set them down at the table where Agamemnon awaited the officers. He made his voice as welcoming as he could muster. "On the house!"

Hurrying back to the pastry case, Stavros produced two plates of warm apricot Danish pastries for the men. His heart flooded with gratitude for Agamemnon's quick thinking to distract them from the gambling room.

Four cups of coffee, two apricot pastries, a few donuts and an hour later, Deputy Robbie slapped his notepad closed. "That does it for us."

Dusting crumbs from his uniform and draining his cup, Sheriff Lewin rose from the café table. "This man knows nothing. Wonder how he gets along in life at all." He leveled a steely look at Stavros. "But we're coming back for the others. Tell me again. I can never get them foreign names."

They were exactly the same height. Stavros locked his soft brown eyes on the sheriff's crystal blues and would not blink. He spat out the names as if he were a double agent, caught by an enemy. "Agamemnon you speak to now. Also there is Timoleon and Panayotis, we call him Lucky. And I am Stavros."

Slightly befuddled by the Greek names, Sheriff Lewin hesitated, turned to his deputy who again was writing in his notebook. "Got that? Let's go."

Then Sheriff Lewin inched so close Stavros could smell his acidic shaving lotion and his sweat. He spoke low and gravelly.

"Next time I come back for you too, and that god damn gambling room of yours. I know what's going on. *They* all come here. The ones from the field, the ones working at the tomato plant." He sniffed, placing his hands on his belt. "And tell that girl of yours I'm doing my job. She can keep her nose out."

As the two law men strode out the door, Deputy Robbie turned back to shoot Stavros a helpless look of concern. Then he hurried back inside the bakery to drop a dime on the table as a tip. The little bell tinkled his exit.

At the plate glass window, Stavros watched the sheriff and deputy shrink to insignificance.

"The final insult." He held the dime between his two fingers. "He leave us servants a tip."

Stavros tossed the coin to Agamemnon who caught it mid-air and examined the coin as if it was minted by alien hands. He looked up and smiled at Stavros. "We use it at the game tonight!"

Both men broke out into laughter knowing their amusement might be short lived. If Sheriff Lewin was on to them, their poker enterprise was on life support. And without that income, they had only the bakery which barely broke even most months.

With no customers, Stavros poured two more coffees for Agamemnon and himself. He never rested in the café area where the public could see him relax in his work clothes. But the heat had kept customers away and he needed time to think. His head spun from Marika's revelation, his worries about Olympia and now the sheriff meddling into his gambling business. And what were these accusations about Yianna from the Congressman's wife?

He shot an appreciative glance at Agamemnon who had faithfully played his part that day. In his book, Agamemnon's bravery was the definition of a real man. Sheriff Lewin was a fool by thinking less of him.

Stavros rose to his feet and fetched a small flask of whisky, pouring a shot in each of their coffees. Lifting his cup to his lips, Stavros attempted to steady his shaking hand. He would do his best to appear he was in command, the man in charge. Agamemnon could never suspect his world had officially spun off its axis and he had no plan to regain control.

FORTY-ONE

With Thalia serving as vigilant watchman, Yianna spent another anxious night alone in her room at the Apollo Hotel. Early the next morning, she scuffled along Market Street, with a touch of hope, a new direction, flimsy as it was. The two words: *Lost Coast*.

Will had volunteered to drive her to a town with the strange name of Petaluma on the way to his next assignment. Then, Yianna would catch a bus traveling further North on U.S. 101 towards other unfamiliar towns: Willits, Laytonville and Garberville.

With no idea how to locate her sister after she stepped off the bus, Yianna planned to show Olympia's photo to everyone she encountered and maybe catch a break. A stranger as beautiful as Olympia must have made an impression on someone in the area. And she only needed one someone to help.

Until Will was off work, Yianna was free to ramble about San Francisco. Thalia had offered her a standing invitation for tea and *koulourakia* cookies in her small apartment at the hotel, but Yianna was bursting to explore the city. Now, following a tourist's map, her first destination was Chestnut Street, home to the California School of Fine Arts. With the librarian's brochure in hand, she walked nearly two miles up and down the inclines of Jones Street.

Signs advertised *Mixed Cocktails, Sandwiches — Cheap*; *Imperial Art Foods*; *Central Liquor and Tea*; *Quality Shoeshines — A Quarter*;

Check Cashing 24-Hours. The clutter of neon lights and plate-glass windows soon melted into apartment buildings painted in muted golds, greens and browns with fire escapes zig-zagging geometric patterns. The Padre Hotel, the King Hotel, the Williams Hotel appeared like magnificent castles as their large regal canopies hung over the sidewalk welcoming visitors. As her uphill walking increased to a mountaineering effort, Yianna's eyes were entertained by the expert parking skills of many San Franciscans, slanting their cars sideways on the street, defying gravity.

With every step, Yianna felt the excitement of a street photographer. Having loaded film before leaving the hotel, she slid the viewfinder to her eye and found interesting stories to capture wherever she pointed her Leica. Young couples dressed in wool coats for the foggy summer walked to work passing mom-and-pop corner stores, bars and flower stalls. Trucks double parked in the street clogging traffic as vendors lugged boxes of vegetables to small markets. Passersby of all ages contorted their bodies in their attempt to hike up the unforgiving San Francisco hills.

By nine o'clock in the morning she had climbed to the top of Russian Hill. The sun poked holes through the thick blanket of morning fog as it slowly dissolved. As Yianna reached the top of the hill, the sharp gray waters of San Francisco Bay dazzled her eyes. This is where she would make her future, a city like this. Just as Dorothea Lange had. She was ready. But first, Olympia.

Inhaling a deep breath of sharp ocean air, she turned onto Chestnut Street and reached a fillagree wrought iron gate, worn yet inviting. The California School of Fine Arts. Yianna touched the curves of the iron as if it were the entrance to paradise, the home to all artistic knowledge, the palace where Dorothea Lange and other important artists imparted their wisdom.

At that moment, a young man carrying an oversized folder and a canvas bag walked up behind her.

He slid past her and entered the gate with no hesitation. He belonged here at this school of fine arts. Yianna watched his every movement. She stepped back in reverence but at the same time felt he was her mirror image. His black hair was slicked back and he wore a slouching black leather jacket, camera over his shoulder. Behind him a woman wearing tan slacks and a reddish-brown bouffant hairdo with a cream-colored headband hurried through the gate. She carried a large portfolio with a plastic handle.

"Coming in?" The young woman held open the gate and cocked her head, waiting for Yianna to step forward. "Well, you coming?"

Yianna hesitated. For a moment she stared at this young woman who had swung open the entrance to the world of life-changing art. She peered into the tiled courtyard where a large square fountain in the center gracefully spouted water, like an Italian piazza.

"Yes, I'm coming! I most certainly am!"

The art student smiled and hurried away. Long corridors of whitewashed archways surrounded the square courtyard. Yianna gobbled up this European atmosphere and her heart swelled with enthusiasm.

Moments later, more students peppered the courtyard on their way to classes. Some carried supplies in cloth bags, some hauled stretched painted canvases to class and others, like Yianna, carried cameras. Sitting at the base of the fountain, Yianna watched the student artists whom, she hoped, would someday be her fellow students. She imagined exchanging ideas as they walked together to class. When, she wondered, did a student become a full-fledged artist? Could she ever make the grade?

The students slowly thinned out and Yianna marshalled her courage to find the admissions office. Swinging open the heavy door, she dug down deep to speak to the woman behind a desk.

"Is Dorothea Lange teaching today?"

The woman with warm brown eyes and easy smile turned in her chair and pointed down the hallway.

"Well yes. That was her just now. I believe she's walking to class."

Thanking her, Yianna ran to the doorway to glimpse a small woman walking down the hallway with a slight limp. Wearing a mid-length beige raincoat over gray wool pants, she turned a corner out of sight.

Staring at the empty hallway, Yianna sensed the power Dorothea Lange left behind in her wake. She considered running behind her and standing in the back of the class, simply absorbing any speck of knowledge. Thinking the better of intruding, Yianna vowed she would attend this school — but exactly when was the question.

FORTY-TWO

Will's repainted mint-green Plymouth coupe rolled northward across the Golden Gate Bridge. From the passenger seat Yianna looked over to see him driving relaxed, one hand on the wheel, the other planted outside the window in touch with the cold, foggy air. The Plymouth ground away with an occasional jerk which Will mentioned was "just a little timing chain thing." Yianna hoped his car had enough power to reach Petaluma, which was the farthest point north Will could take her.

The sticky fog shrouded both laddered towers of the Golden Gate Bridge. Driving across, Yianna felt she was traveling to a new world, as she had never set foot in any town on U.S. 101 north of San Francisco. In fact, she still lamented never laying eyes on the Golden Gate Bridge, as gray clouds made it invisible on this trip.

As the Plymouth rolled northward, Yianna peeled off her jacket in the radical temperature shift. She began to unwind as the breezes blew a gust of warmth and the thermometer inched up with every mile. Twenty minutes north of the bridge, Will turned off U.S. 101 into the little town of San Rafael and drove down Fourth Street.

"A detour will make you feel more at home." Will guided the car slowly down the street. "A drug store, a couple of bars, a little grocery, a laundry—just like Woodland, I'll bet."

"Don't miss it much." Yianna was agitated remembering her dusty Central Valley town. "I'm certainly not thinking about Woodland now. Wait, can you stop here?"

Will had scarcely braked to a stop when Yianna jumped out, hands on her Leica. She'd never seen anything like the Mission de San Rafael chapel with its lofty bell tower with smaller towers on either side, a graceful nod to Spanish colonial architecture. She framed the scene through her viewfinder while working men and women strolled by the century-old churchyard as if the mission were part of their everyday lives.

Yianna realized she'd taken so many shots she'd already used up a roll of film. Not knowing where film would be available on the Lost Coast, Yianna dashed to a nearby drug store. She shut her eyes tight as the store register rang up five dollars for a roll of thirty-six exposures. Grabbing the box of film, she sprinted back to the mission. Soon she had slipped back into the Plymouth, satisfied with her exploration and they continued northward toward Petaluma.

FORTY-THREE

Since the Gold Rush days, the Washoe House anchored the corner of Stony Point and Roblar roads on the outskirts of Petaluma. Inside, the men at the card tables were mostly farmers in dusty jeans or overalls. Every head was topped with a western hat, every pair of jeans belted with a bulky metal buckle. The long wooden bar took up most of the real estate and round tables crammed with chairs were crowded with men playing cards.

Yianna's poker hand was not a good one—a two, three, seven, nine and a jack—but she projected confidence as she fanned her cards in front of her. She had learned tricks from the old Greek men: tilt your head to one side to appear thoughtfully considering the hand; crack a small smile and then immediately appear concerned; use a single, heavy breath or quick head scratch to appear slightly uncomfortable with the cards in your hand. Keep all emotions under the radar, nothing overboard. These men probably did not know what to expect from a young woman dressed in black like a boy.

Two hours earlier, when Will drove through Petaluma, Yianna was uncertain as to exactly where he should drop her off. They drove past the small terra cotta train station with mission-style arches and then turned down Washington Street to the small but vibrant downtown.

"You can just drop me anywhere. Know you have to get back." Yianna knew Will needed to research a story several miles south but had driven her north anyway. She shifted in her seat as she would soon burst into a new world with no direction, friend or even acquaintance. She tried to appear calm and self-reliant. Will had helped her navigate life outside Woodland and she hoped her dependence on him didn't show.

"I'm not dropping you just anywhere. Let's find a place you can get a good meal and a room. I can go a little farther and still get my work done. Let's keep driving."

"I've heard of this place, the Washoe House." After driving ten more miles, Will pulled up in front of the establishment on the corner of two well-traveled roads. The large porch extended to each side of the building. Mostly men, but a few women, sat outside enjoying the warm afternoon sun.

"This will be good for photos if nothing else." He smiled as he pulled open the car door and jumped out. "You ready?"

Yianna was more than ready. She was actually tired, scared and desperately wanting to get to the Lost Coast. She prayed this journey was not a time waster or another dead end. Will reached into his jacket pocket and pulled out a slip of paper.

"Before we left San Francisco, I picked up a bus schedule for these parts. Let's see." Will ran his finger down a list of pickup times for Petaluma. "A bus should come by at eight fifteen tonight. Or you can catch one tomorrow early afternoon. Maybe take the day bus. Safer."

"I'll take the bus tonight!" Yianna jumped at the chance to move on. "Then I won't even have to rent a room." Yianna swiftly examined the schedule. "Looks like the bus takes me to Garberville, wherever that is. I should be fine." Yianna added the last words with too much enthusiasm, attempting to convince herself.

Yianna pulled her knapsack on her shoulder with her camera around her neck. She caught herself stalling as she prepared to say goodbye to Will, probably for the last time. Her stomach tightened and again she cursed her inexperience with men. What was she to say? How could they keep in touch? Did Will even want to remember a tall girl, thin as spaghetti, wearing no makeup and the same black clothes every day? At that moment, she did what any photographer would do.

Yianna grabbed her Leica and focused her lens on Will, small round glasses reflecting his eyes, hands in pockets, smiling as if he expected her to do just that.

"With that I'm off!" Will walked to the car leaving behind the trace of his smile and quiet charm. Yianna hoped he would have revealed more emotion toward her, but if he had, would she have known how to respond? She only mustered a wave of her hand and a smile towards Will's car.

"See you soon!" she blurted out as Will jumped in his car to head south. Yianna admonished herself for her stupid sign off: *See you soon!* When would she see him? They had not exchanged personal information aside from her working at Angel's Bakery in Woodland. She kicked herself for her inept social skills. Would she ever develop them? But more immediate matters were at hand.

Making her way through the front door of the Washoe House and into a pack of strangers, Yianna pretended to be nonchalant, as if she were a local. She attempted to add swagger to her walk but immediately gave it up as she reached the bar. If Vesuvio Café in San Francisco was a crazy castle of artistic memorabilia, then the Washoe House was its western cousin. Every shape and size of antique mirror clung to the walls and large, colorful stained-glass lamps hung low over the bar.

Taking a deep breath, Yianna inhaled the heavy smell of beer, disinfectant and a rich stew cooking in a kitchen. She looked above her head to see hundreds of American dollar bills tacked to the ceiling, a quilt fluttering overhead. Yianna considered money from heaven a symbol of good luck. She was determined to make money and replenish the funds she had spent on film. Her time on the road was open ended. She simply needed more cash.

At the bar, she ordered a Coke, then took her time sidling between the round wooden tables where men picked through their cards nursing whiskey and beer. An open window brought a warm breeze and the smell of sweat hung heavy over the card tables.

She surveyed the playing field and tried to judge where to slip in. Betting at cards with a bunch of old men was nothing new and she imagined Agamemnon, Timoleon, Lucky and Uncle Stavros in place of these men. Looking for the most grandfatherly bunch, she decided a table with the oldest men might accept a young female player. She took a long look at four men crowded around a dark wooden table.

"Mind if I sit in?" She slid her long leg over the chair, keeping her knapsack on her back and pushing her camera, still hanging around her neck, to the side and out of view.

None of the old timers looked up or seemed to care who was playing. Under his accountant's eyeshade, the dealer of the group roughed out a few words.

"Ante up three bucks."

Yianna produced her money. The dealer was ready to start the next round when suddenly the tallest man of the group rose for beers. His head nearly scraped the dollar bills on the ceiling. He soon returned with five beers. One for Yianna.

She was in.

"You new around here, gal?" The giant man slid a beer her way.

"Just passing through." Yianna took a sip to seem grateful. "Thank you."

The dealer flung the next round of cards with the precision of a magician, the cards spinning into place in front of each player. He gave Yianna a good look. "Of course, you're twenty-one, right?"

"Sure thing." Yianna pulled her beer close and sipped again.

"Ya gotta know something about this place before we play." He had finished dealing and offered Yianna the cards to cut.

"The Washoe House was here before the Civil War. But after Lincoln was killed, these parts were still divided because Santa Rosa up north leaned for the Confederates and in Petaluma, we, of course, were with the Union. Well, words were spilt in the Santa Rosa newspaper insulting the memory of our murdered president. Everyone was hot under the collar."

The tall man who had fetched the beers finished the story.

"Us Petalumans were so angry, we sent a group north to fight them damn Santa Rosans in the name of Lincoln, hell, right in their own town. But riding was hard that day and they pulled over here, at the Washoe House, for beer. It was a stagecoach stop in those times. Well, one thing led to another and after a few more beers, they cooled down. They decided to forget their campaign altogether and hoisted a few more. So ended the Battle of Washoe House."

"So as we play our cards, we are in the midst of history." The dealer looked at Yianna. "And by the way, *we* were on the right side of history. Don't know where you stand on that." He raised his eyebrows.

"The Union, definitely." Yianna nodded to a new card. If these men were still caught up in the politics of the Civil War, she would play along. Maybe her boyish appearance was working in her favor as she slowly melted into this world of men. She looked at her new card. *Damn, a seven.*

Two hours later, Yianna was sweating a river. She did not want to appear desperate as the early evening air pressed down on her. Although she lost most hands, Yianna won a few small pots to stay in the game and reserved enough to bet big should an opportunity come along. She mentally whipped herself for spending extra money on film, although it had seemed like a good idea at the time.

But now, down to the bottom of her stash, she needed to win it all or go broke trying. She'd have to make this round count to earn her bus fare to travel north. Losing meant coming home empty handed and hitching a ride back to Woodland which Uncle Stavros had always warned against. Yianna shut her eyes tight to invoke a winning hand like Lucky usually did at the end of the evening.

Looking down at her cards, she held three queens, a three and a four. Hope pulsed behind her temples, but her face revealed nothing. The betting was lively as the other players around the table pushed in their money, mostly fives, tens and some silver dollars. Yianna was able to match the bets, as did the tall man who was last to play.

Keeping her three queens safe, she discarded two cards and then held her breath. Looking up to the ceiling covered in dollar bills, she prayed for luck—just a little. She opened her eyes hoping to see her bus ticket to Garberville.

As if Olympia herself had sent a card from a place beyond the ceiling of money, Yianna's eyes rested on an ace and another queen—making four queens! The Queen of Hearts! Four of a kind! A Ladies Run! But she kept her face long, unsatisfied, discouraged. The betting players before her did not like their draw and folded despite the substantial pot. When her turn came, she pushed in all the money she had.

But the tall man was still left to play his cards. Having drawn only one new card, he appeared confident. Yianna's heart hammered like Will's Plymouth with its bad timing chain. Appearing to show sympathy for a girl on her last dollar, he met the bet but did not raise it.

Then he quickly laid down his hand. A full house. Good—but not good enough.

Instantly, Yianna knew she had won and calmly set out her cards on the table. How would winning the giant pot sit with these old men?

"Looks like the ladies win it today," the tall man chirped a little too enthusiastically. She felt the air change around her, from a warm welcome to a cool breeze. She moved to collect her money, wait for the bus and leave the Washoe House. Time to disappear.

Like a ballerina, Yianna placed her arms in a circle and swept the bills and coins into her knapsack to sort later. She quietly rose from the table scraping the chair across the wooden floor.

"I'm out. And thanks for the beer. Beers." Yianna remembered the tall player had refilled her beer glass several times.

She wished Will were waiting for her outside to dash her someplace safe where she could catch her breath and count the money. But the Washoe House was an island unto itself in the country. Few vehicles passed at that time of evening. She would wait on the porch until the bus arrived, just like the stagecoach long ago.

As the darkness skulked in from the countryside, Yianna huddled in a chair on the porch, again surprised by a cold wind blowing, yearning for the heavy leather jacket she had left at home.

A long thin shadow sat down next to her in the only rocking chair on the porch. A pipe lit up the darkness and in that spark, Yianna recognized the tall gambler who had bought the beers.

"Evenin' ma'am." The old-fashioned greeting surprised her. *I am probably his daughter's age*, she thought to herself.

"Yes, nice evening."

"You staying here for the night young lady?"

"Just waiting."

"For the bus? Where to?"

Why should I tell him? she thought to herself. But she supposed other travelers often waited on the porch for the bus.

"Live around here?" She changed the subject.

"Used to, but now I'm up north. Got me a lot of driving to do tonight."

In the silence the hum of early mosquitos hung in the air.

Towering over her as he rose from the rocking chair, the skyscraper of a man vanished and the chair rocked oddly in his absence. Within moments, he returned with a paper plate of small salami sandwiches, thick with mayonnaise on fresh, French bread. He placed the plate between them and offered Yianna a napkin. An unctuous waft of the home-baked bread and fatty salami reached her nose and her stomach wriggled with hunger. After only a few beers that day, Yianna helped herself.

"We've both got a long road ahead. Might as well stock up." He spoke quietly into the night. When she looked over, he wore a fatherly expression, content that she was eating. He picked up a sandwich for himself and sunk his teeth through the crispy crust. "Make 'em good around here."

His name was Harry. He said he recently lost his wife and was trying to keep busy. Formerly from Petaluma, he lived in Mendocino County now and came to the Washoe House often "for a little brotherly friendship and a nip or two."

With an hour before the bus was to arrive, Harry re-lit his pipe and puffed the scents of leather, lavender and spices, like the men at the bakery card room. Yianna relaxed, as if the Greek old men's club was nearby, taking care of her.

"How far you say you're goin' on that bus?"

"I didn't. But I'm going to Garberville tonight." No harm in telling a new friend her destination.

"Garberville!" Harry turned his body toward her. "Well, that bus will take all night! I don't know if you gonna be safe on that thing. You better come with me!"

He pointed to a shiny dark green pickup truck parked on the side road. "That's me. Over there. I can get you there in half the time. No stops, no sitting next to strange people. It's dark out there, after all. A gal like you needs to stay safe."

Harry fetched two ice cream sandwiches from the kitchen. "How 'bout one for the road?" His smile was genuine, somehow familiar.

Yianna heartily bit into the creamy vanilla bar topped with a chocolate wafer. She thought about repaying Harry for the snacks but didn't want to open her knapsack and risk her winnings flying out in all directions.

"Well, gal. Let's get going! Let's test out my radio on the drive. The top forty is on tonight!" Harry winked at her in a grandfatherly way. His energy was infectious and Yianna was thankful she wouldn't be on a dark bus filled with strangers.

FORTY-FOUR

With a stomach full of sandwiches and half an ice cream sandwich lodged in her mouth, Yianna trailed after Harry who helped her into the Ford pickup with its large wide running boards and roomy seats. Yianna settled in, her backpack between her knees. She swung her camera away from Harry, too tired to talk about photography.

They rode peacefully in the dark silence and Yianna began to unwind while Harry reached for the radio and snapped on the top hits: *Cherry Pink and Apple Blossom White* followed by Bill Haley's *Rock Around the Clock* and *Learnin' the Blues* by Frank Sinatra. Yianna's eyes squinted for highway signs to estimate how long they would be on the road to Garberville. She realized by taking Harry's quicker transportation instead of the Greyhound bus, she would arrive in Garberville in the dead of night with no lodgings in a tiny town.

The truck reliably hummed north along on U.S. 101. They flew through Geyserville, Cloverdale, Hopland, all unfamiliar towns, and Yianna was happy to tick them off in the rearview mirror. As Hopland whipped passed her window, Yianna noticed Harry brought a brown paper bag to his lips and a sharp scent of whiskey cut the air.

"Just a little medicine to keep me awake!" Harry smiled his reassuring grin. But his hand continued to locate the crumpled paper bag and pour liquor down his throat as if he'd been parched for days.

"Hey, Harry, maybe you should lay off a little?" She tried to make her voice sweet and conversational, like a daughter. "We've still got a way to go." To comfort herself, Yianna considered that Harry probably knew the road well and driving drunk was nothing new.

"We'll be fine. Gotta keep my mind on the road." Harry jagged the steering wheel unevenly to the right and then left to bank for curves in the road. She knew how Uncle Stavros drove when he was tipsy. But he was never drunk like this. Yianna had to keep Harry awake enough for him to guide the truck into Garberville. But Harry was mute, floating in his black silence of alcohol. Yianna chattered about nothing for what seemed like an hour, her eyes locked onto the road as if to steer them both to safety.

"So, where you learn to play poker *like that*, anyways?" Harry's voice took on a sarcastic, cruel edge. His whiskey breath filled the truck cab like poison.

"Uh, my uncle taught me when I was little." Yianna answered quietly, hoping she could diffuse the subject of her win and Harry's loss. "You know how luck goes. Some time you have it —"

"Well, I'm gettin' some tonight!"

Harry stomped on the gas pedal. The truck was a splash in the night as it leaped ahead, taking up the highway like a sprinter.

"Harry, slow down!" Yianna screamed with no attempt to mask her fear. "Take it easy! Stop! You're gonna kill us!"

"Shut up and gimme what you got! You robbed me! Imma' get everything you owe me!" The truck screeched to the right toward the forest, then swung madly to the left near the highway's edge. Harry slugged back another gulp and reached for Yianna's breast under her shirt, catching a handful but losing his grip on the wheel.

"I know what you come here for!" Harry barked.

Yianna's unblinking eyes stared straight ahead, nails dug into the leather seats, all her systems shut down. *If I stay quiet, maybe he will forget me —*

But Harry's long arms forgot nothing. His claw-like grip clamped the back of her neck and pushed her head down to his crotch, forcing her face against his bulging jeans. His physical power shocked Yianna to silence. Her body was now horizontally splayed across the front seat, pinned against him.

Yianna could hardly draw a breath and the stench of Harry's acidic breath covered the truck interior like a blanket.

"You owe me, you shill! Gimme what's mine!"

Harry's words ricocheted off her ears. She felt nothing, as if her spirit lifted from her body. Yianna was hogtied in her own nightmare as Harry's muscular arm trapped her tight against him. She could only battle with her fists against his bull-strong sinewy arms, but his strength was too much. This mad driver, so fatherly only an hour ago, mashed her face down hard on his jeans and increased his speed careening around the highway curves. Heart beating like a jackhammer, Yianna's brain flashed only one message. *Get out! Get out now!*

But as a captive in a truck weaving wildly on a forlorn freeway, she was frozen, no way to break free. Jammed in place by Harry's grip, her entire body reverberated and her limbs were paralyzed with fear. Yianna could not move, could not utter a word. Only one thought, one feeling enveloped her mind: FIGHT! She had to strike back with every ounce of strength — and the time was now.

Harry used his drinking hand to unzip his jeans and the combat in the front seat continued at a fever pitch. Yianna's arms beat on Harry's legs but to no use. She kicked the passenger door hard with her boots attempting to push away from the filth of this horrible beast. Her long legs were her only defense and she slammed her boots again and again, rocking the truck with all her might. But the passenger door remained closed, mocking her attempts to free herself.

After long minutes of kicking and muffled screams, Yianna felt her energy slowly drip away. She summoned her last bit of strength for one final attack. Yianna's mind flashed on Olympia's photo, adorned with the cross around her throat, watching, waiting for her to escape.

Using the parts of her body she had control over, Yianna slammed both feet again and again against the heavy passenger door but it barely creaked open, weighed by the gravity of the uphill climb in the road. She flailed her arms but Harry's immense hand was now around her throat, cutting off her wind as she gasped to inhale, sucking in oxygen like an injured dog. The truck twisted around the next curve and she used her last weapon. Yianna drilled sharp teeth into Harry's crotch, locking her jaws around some kind of flesh. *This is for Olympia! I will wound you, bastard!*

A shrill, hawklike scream pierced the cab. For just an instant Harry loosened his grip on Yianna's neck. One more explosive kick and the heavy door swung open as the truck banked a downhill curve. Yianna projected sideways out of the open door, landing hard onto the asphalt. She felt the fall in every bone in her body. Pain shot through her spine and limbs, air pushed from her lungs. Her leather camera strap was a noose strangling her neck as she rolled head over legs like a tumbleweed into the brush and down a long sharp embankment. Finally, after flailing like a ragdoll, her roll slowed and was finally stopped by something stiff and solid. Yianna heard a *clunk* as her head took the hit. Her body was motionless. In an instant, the forest was quiet again, waiting for her next move.

FORTY-FIVE

A light rain sprinkled her face as Yianna lay on her back in a dazed heap. She stirred. Cracking one eye open, Yianna tried to sit up but sank deeper into the clotted mud and fallen limbs from the trees above. Numbness tingled her shaky arms and her legs did not respond when her brain commanded movement. The black velvet forest that received her from Harry's violent truck ride now allowed Yianna the comfort of slipping into unconsciousness.

Hours or minutes later, Yianna awoke once more to no light, no direction and no protection. She slowly moved to unwind the camera strap from around her collarbone, but even her hands ached with every movement. Attempting to judge the damage done to her body, she forced her hands to slowly maneuver up and down her torso, feeling for breakage and wounds. A bloody gash from her forehead slowly dripped and Yianna tasted blood on her lips. Blindly feeling the ground around her body for her knapsack, Yianna realized most of her belongings and her money had vanished around the curve with Harry. She vaguely remembered her film, used and unused, was secure in the pockets she had sewn onto her camera strap. She was truly alone in the wilderness with only her camera for protection.

The drizzling rain cracked open to torrents of water so loud that Yianna covered her ears. Soon the ravine where she lay began to fill with rainwater and her reclining body was soaked to the bone in a giant puddle of forest sludge. Yianna pulled her gangly limbs tight against her body to wait, for what, she did not know.

She thought of Uncle Stavros working alone in his kitchen during the magic hours before dawn. His ovens were probably hot and his sourdough loaves already crispy brown. She remembered his strong, wide hands kneading dough on the large cedar board, the rhythmic motion comforting. Those hands would have pulled me to safety tonight, she thought. He would have protected me.

But the slashing rain continued and Yianna began to imagine the end to her story. In myths she had read, lost characters were always saved by magic doors or spirit guides. But this black forest offered nothing enchanting and certainly no safety, only the absence of light with no guideposts and rainy misery. Panic exploded like fireworks in her chest.

Her shoulders began to shudder from the cold rain which cascaded in sheets down her soggy shirt and pants and one boot, having lost the other in the downward fall. Summoning strength from every part of her body, Yianna desperately willed herself to rise. *Keep moving. Get your blood circulating. You can do it. Start moving. Do it for Olympia.*

Wobbling on her two feet but sinking deeply into the soft brushy forest floor, Yianna winced from a sharp ankle pain in her bootless left foot. She tucked her camera under her arm for protection. Wringing out the rainwater in her sopping hair, Yianna knew she would have to keep walking, no matter how slowly. She yearned for a soft light in the darkness to guide her through the forest. But her logical mind knew that would never happen. Hoping to avoid becoming raw meat for a mountain lion, Yianna decided her next goal was to see morning light. She could only wait out the hours until the sun rose and shot its rays through the trees.

With anticipation for daybreak, Yianna placed her one good foot in front of the other painful one. At that moment she felt closer than ever to Olympia. They were both lost in the darkness with hope dwindling. Uncertain of her sister's exact circumstance, Yianna realized only her grit and unbroken resolve would enable her to survive and just possibly find her sister.

FORTY-SIX

A few days after her plunge into the forested ravine, Yianna sounded as miserable as she felt. She coughed a deep rattle that reverberated in her chest like a tambourine. With no food and only rainwater to drink during her famished days and bone-chilling nights, Yianna thought she spied a small path in the thick of the woods. Not trusting her blurry vision, she assumed the path was just another mirage. Her hungry eyes had invented images she believed were paths to a town, a ranch, a farm, only to find leafy shadows instead. She sighed and passed off this path as another delirious wish unfulfilled.

The mid-day sun shone from high above into the blue-green trees and Yianna took advantage of the warmth. She dropped to sit near a fallen redwood tree where shoots of new growth sprouted up reaching for the sky. Long, elegant sword ferns grew near the log and, if not for her desolation and hunger, she would have admired the natural beauty of this setting.

Yianna rubbed the stinging sole of her shoeless foot and noticed blisters bubbled over the cuts and bruises from walking the forest floor. Her thick cotton sock had worn out and her foot was slashed to bleeding. Some of the cuts had become red and promised infection but Yianna was numb to the unrelenting pain. Having no extra clothing to wrap around her injured foot, she took a moment to rest.

With her long arms tight around her legs and head on her knees, she dreamt of Uncle Stavros' delectable roasted lamb hot from the oven.

Soaking up the sun like a cat on a window ledge in winter, Yianna rested. Although the warm afternoon seemed to offer protection from the forest, Yianna's wits stood guard, listening for a rustle which might signal an attack from an animal or, even more dangerous, a human.

The previous day, just before dusk, Yianna had located the hollow of a tree trunk and crawled inside. She rolled herself into a human ball and waited, having become accustomed to the soft cheerful chirp of the American robin at sunset. As evening crept in, owls provided their part in the forest musical theater with low, soothing hoots. Recognizing the gentle call sounding like "poor will" from the Common Poorwill, Yianna silently gave thanks to Olympia for her endless chatter about the birds of Greece and America. Those birdcalls which could have sounded like predators in the night were now invisible friends to Yianna and she imagined they chirped encouragement to her, urging her to carry on, to survive.

But the bitterly cold nights tortured her with every growl or piercing animal cry. Some calls were feral and catlike which signaled a mountain lion's presence. She rested with eyes open, guarding against a pair of glowing eyes tracking her in the darkness. For defense, she held a thick tree branch like a baseball bat across her chest as if it would somehow protect her.

With a last lingering moment of sun on her back, Yianna pushed herself to continue walking a short distance further. If she stepped lightly on the edge of her injured, shoeless foot, she could move slowly ahead. Her energy had dipped past empty but she pushed up from her sitting position to walk a half mile, maybe more. Then she would quit to again find a makeshift shelter for the night.

At that moment, Yianna's eyes lit on the narrow footpath she had earlier judged to be imaginary. That path could have been worn down by deer or other animals, but it was more than that. Her eyes narrowed to focus and her pulse quickened. Was it a foot path humans might have tramped? Could it possibly lead to help? Wheezing from the bottom of her lungs, she pushed herself to take a few more steps toward the trail she hoped would not end as quickly as it appeared.

For two hours, Yianna slowly hobbled along the ambiguous path in the thick of the forest. Her soles were bloody and her ankle screamed with pain. When the trail diminished and seemed overgrown, she diligently retraced her steps to locate it again and then continued slowly, tracking the trail with every step. Soon the late afternoon began to swallow the sun and the darkness rolled in with the evening mist.

Once more, Yianna needed to find some semblance of shelter, a natural ledge in the forest, a group of rocks or an inviting thicket of trees. Her hopes of finding the end of the trail had evaporated and she collapsed on the ground, camera bouncing against her body. Another day lost. She anticipated another evening of dread dissolving into a night of fear where sleep was nonexistent. She burst into a coughing jag which left her weaker and lying down in exhaustion.

Yianna again wished she had Olympia's knowledge about the outdoor world. Which plants were edible? Which would kill her with their poison? Yianna would take no chances and only ventured to drink water collected on leaves. Without tools to ignite a fire in the wet forest or to capture small game, Yianna mentally switched off her hunger and concentrated on situating herself for the night. She sat up and found a nook between two redwood trees where her back would not be exposed to the elements or predators. As she'd done the other nights, she would use the leaves and needles from the forest floor as her bed clothes and a mossy log for a pillow. Now accustomed to spiders and field mice crawling over her at night, she hoped to avoid larger, hungrier mammals.

Sitting back, she waited for darkness to creep around her like a soft, reliable quilt. Resting against the welcoming giant redwood, she rubbed her back against the fragrant bark. Yawning, she hoped to catch a quick nap before the frigid temperatures set in chilling her bones and stiffening her ankle.

Suddenly, Yianna thought she heard a note floating in the air. Where was Olympia to identify that lilting bird? Her ears, like detectives, searched the atmosphere for clues. Then a syllable, a word floated to her and immediately her heart soared with hope.

> *– fish cannot live –*
> *– flower – the sand –*

Yianna jumped up on her injured foot but did not feel it. Was that a human voice? Picking out low resonate tones, Yianna's memory strained to recognize the song. Had hunger sent her into vague hallucinations? Had the days of silence in the forest tricked her ears?

> *– the women –*
> *– cannot live without freedom –*

Yes! She knew that song! The song Yianna's mother sang when stirring soup over the hearth or pulling vegetables from her garden. The one Olympia sang to her when they first learned of their father's death in America!

Yianna limped in the direction of the song. Struggling for breath, she followed the path leading to a clearing. From an elevated place in the forest, as the darkness descended, Yianna silently observed a woman pulling shirts and aprons from a backyard clothesline. Her back to Yianna, the woman sang her song in a low, rough voice.

> *Farewell poor world,*
> *Farewell sweet life,*
> *and you, my wretched country,*
> *Farewell forever*

Yianna stood in disbelief. She attempted to weave together tattered memories to retrieve the song from her childhood in Greece. The plaintive folk tune, about the valiant Greek women who leapt off a cliff to avoid capture, sank into her heart. Peering into the clearing, Yianna could see the clothesline was near a small cabin perched on the outskirts of a group of rough-hewn buildings. Silently she thanked her mother's spirit for orchestrating the song to save her—and just maybe Olympia too.

FORTY-SEVEN

After hearing nothing from Yianna for three weeks, Stavros began to sweat although the dark hours after midnight were chilly in the bakery. Both nieces were now officially missing and the weight of their absence was squarely on his shoulders.

As the man of the family, he needed to summon the courage of the Greek god Ares, find his girls and bring them home to safety. Then Stavros remembered that Ares also was known to be moody and unreliable, so maybe best not to wish for his powers. Reconsidering, Stavros yearned to be blessed with Marika's brains and Yianna's bold impetuousness. He then chided himself for wanting the qualities of women. What would his male village friends in Argos think of him now? He shook off those thoughts in hope of constructing a plan to find Olympia and Yianna. He needed to focus on his nieces and not his reputation.

In his brown, elbow-length oven mitts, he pulled loaves of whole-wheat bread from the oven, then mixed dough for Snowball cookies. At exactly three o'clock, Agamemnon silently appeared at his side. Tying his apron and moving to the large calendar on the wall, he pulled a thick graphite art pencil from his back pocket and scratched a diagonal slash through the day before. Another day without Yianna. Over the slash he wrote the number two hundred ten, the total days Olympia had been missing. Next he washed his hands, scrubbed his nails with a short-bristled brush and took his place behind the kitchen worktable. He took a spoonful of Snowball cookie dough and begin to delicately roll a perfect sphere between his palms with the hands of an artist.

In no mood to talk, Stavros worked with Agamemnon in silence. After several minutes, the two men heard a shuffle of slippers from the bedrooms in the back of the building. Timoleon appeared, tying a thick knot on the belt of his worn-out blue chenille bathrobe.

"*Kali mera?* Good morning?"

Why was Timoleon awake so early? Stavros frowned. His friend never rose before six o'clock, never enjoyed his toast and coffee before seven and always exited the bakery exactly at seven-thirty to open his fruit stand by eight. Timoleon was a reliable morning metronome. Stavros set the dough back in the bowl and stepped closer to Timoleon searching his face for a fever, a cold sweat, an illness.

"What bothers you, Timoleon?" Stavros walked around the worktable and examined Timoleon's eyes. "You sleepwalking?" His friend stood looking down at his slippers, now fully awake and trembling.

"I am at my fruit stand yesterday afternoon, in the back. I pick out the bad apples from the good." Timoleon looked up to meet Stavros' stare. "Then I hear two girls talk out front. They are standing near the Coke machine. They talk and talk. They tell about what boy loves what girl in town. Then I hear the name Olympia! Yes, our Olympia!"

Wiping his brow with a handkerchief from his pocket, Timoleon was sweating unusually for the early morning. "They say Deputy Robbie like her and meet with her after work. The girl say Robbie think no one beautiful like Olympia. That he like her in high school and still does."

Stavros quickly walked to Timoleon and gently led him into a chair in the café area. Agamemnon poured coffee and pushed a cup in front of his friend. Both Stavros and Agamemnon sat down at the café table waiting for Timoleon's next words. Stavros allowed his friend complete silence so his memory of the conversation did not dissolve into dust.

"They say a month before she disappear, they together at Corkwood Diner! The one in the bowling alley! *Together!* Our Olympia!" Timoleon gulped half of his coffee and sat back in his chair, exhausted. He clearly had not slept that night. "One girl is waitress there, she know for sure!"

Stavros' heart skipped a beat, a look of confusion on his face. "*Our* Olympia? You sure?"

"Yes! How many Olympias in this town?" Planting his elbows on the café table, Timoleon lodged his head between his fists in contemplation. "The deputy say she most beautiful in the world. Like Aphrodite. That is Olympia."

Stavros dropped into a chair sorting out Timoleon's story. Why would Robbie talk about Olympia? Stavros had heard tales that Sheriff Lewin was a womanizer but heard nothing about Deputy Robbie. Did Sheriff Lewin know when conducting the investigation? Why hadn't he revealed this when Yianna asked for information at the sheriff's office?

Observing his friend, Stavros was truly concerned for his health. Timoleon's hands shook as he raised his coffee cup and soon he laid his head on his arms, spent.

Rushing to the kitchen, Stavros pulled a large skillet from the rack overhead and began scrambling eggs. A good meal was always his answer to anxiety, sorrow or any difficult state of affairs. Without Stavros saying a word, Agamemnon understood. He sliced a freshly-baked loaf for toast.

Pacing up and down the narrow kitchen, Stavros pulled out his copper *briki* and began making strong Greek coffee. He shook the copper pot forward and back on the burner in contemplation. A few minutes later, Stavros placed a platter of warm fluffy eggs in front of Timoleon while Agamemnon added a plate of toast stacked high. Soon the men comfortably munched breakfast and Stavros watched as Timoleon's strength began to pulse through his body. The hot breakfast worked its healing magic and Timoleon slowly revived, reaching for another piece of toast.

When it was time to go back to work Timoleon followed Stavros and Agamemnon into the kitchen, refilling his cup with coffee.

"We go visit the sheriff." Agamemnon planted the last Snowball cookie dough on the baking tray and slid it into the hot oven. "What else we do? Finally, we have new information!"

Stavros took a quick swig of his coffee. They certainly would have to follow up on these new facts, but should they go to the sheriff? Stavros, a man familiar with romance and its fallout, knew the deputy would not have told his boss of his connection with Olympia. Otherwise, Yianna would have heard about it at her weekly visits to the sheriff's department. He shook his head.

"*Lepón*, well then, something else." Timoleon took one last gulp of coffee before raising his hound dog eyes to his friends. "That girl say the Deputy Robbie ask Olympia to marry him."

The bakery floor lost its gravity and Stavros held onto the worktable for balance. Agamemnon dropped his spatula with a clatter. Stavros could not imagine this coupling. Had Olympia lived a secret life? Had their little family known her at all? How long had they been seeing each other? When? Where? Why?

Stavros walked away from the kitchen and pushed open the front door to breathe fresh air. He glanced up at the Angel's Bakery sign. A small halo surrounded the point of the capital A on the sign. Olympia's story had taken a dark turn and her seemingly angelic past was now in question. As dawn painted the sky turquoise blue, Stavros realized a new day had indeed dawned on all the members of Angel's Bakery.

The crew worked silently most of the morning. Stavros finished cake orders while Agamemnon and Lucky manned the counter.

About nine o'clock Marika hurried in, checking her watch, pacing as other customers ordered their donuts and bear claws.

"Two corn muffins, raspberry Danish and a cinnamon roll. All to go." Marika reached for her wallet to pay. "I no be home for three days."

Hearing her low velvet voice, Stavros darted from the kitchen and pulled her to the side of the café area.

"At the fruit stand, Timoleon hear that Deputy Robbie love Olympia." Stavros sucked in his breath and exhaled a blast of air. "And the gossip say he want to marry her. Our Olympia!"

Marika's eyes narrowed and she placed her hands on her hips. "Well, then, we go now, Stavros." Impatiently she shifted her purse from one hand to the other watching Stavros who was frozen in place. "We go to the sheriff now."

"When Yianna go there, they no help." Stavros grumbled. "And that young deputy, he play cards *here* at our gambling tables. If we go to the sheriff, we ask for trouble." Stavros shook his head to dismiss the thought. "And we risk everything."

Marika's eyes were swords piercing Stavros' body and striking his core.

"Stavros! We go! Now!"

He yanked off his apron and tossed it behind the counter. Nodding to Agamemnon and Lucky, he hurried to the broom closet for his hat. With Marika's hands gripping the wheel of her Dodge, they peeled away from the bakery hoping to find one shred of truth in their search for Olympia.

FORTY-EIGHT

Pulling up to the sheriff's department, Marika squealed the brakes to a stop. She leaped out of the car while Stavros took longer to move in the direction of Sheriff Lewin. After experiencing the Turks in Smyrna, he always hesitated to voluntarily visit law enforcers of any kind. Today was no different. Stavros sensed trouble lurking nearby and he was sure it wore a badge.

The late July morning was already sizzling. He watched Marika slide sunglasses over her eyes and stride into the sheriff's department like a movie star. Stavros had no choice but to follow her. It was too late now.

"Good afternoon." Marika flashed a charming smile at the secretary sitting at the front desk. "May we see the sheriff?"

"Sheriff Lewin is in a meeting now." Eyeing Marika's sunglasses, the guard-dog secretary coolly defended her domain. With large sweat stains under the sleeves of her uniform blouse, she slowly stood from her creaky office chair. "What seems to be the –"

"You need to understand." Marika gracefully swung open the low gate separating visitors from the office personnel. She lowered her sunglasses and smiled over the rims. "This is emergency."

Hands planted on her hips ready for confrontation, the secretary huffed like a train engine when Sheriff Lewin strutted from his office.

The secretary's face dropped with embarrassment. "I told them you were in a –"

The sheriff's eyes traveled over Marika's body, from her soft brown waves to her curvaceous legs held up by high-heeled sandals.

"And what can I do for you?" As the sheriff tipped his hat with a courtly flourish, Stavros had to stop himself from rolling his eyes. He watched Marika rest her purse on the secretary's desk as if she were planning to stay.

"Thank you for seeing us, Sheriff. We come to talk about Olympia Diamantopoulos." She looked around the office. "We need to know the facts. We need to learn all the people you speak to and exactly what they say. And your deputy has more information. We are certain of this."

Darting out of his office, Deputy Robbie came to an abrupt halt behind the sheriff. His dark brown eyes were alert, watching, waiting for direction. At that moment everyone's attention was briefly diverted. Outside the open front door Congressman Harrison and his wife Trina had drawn a crowd while tacking up posters for the congressman's re-election campaign. They noisily discussed where to place the placards, clearly enjoying the crowd and attention.

"The Diamantopoulos case?" The sheriff stalked to a metal file rack on the secretary's precisely organized desk. His fingers tip-toed along the tops of the files. Pulling out a worn manilla folder he leafed through the file, then tossed it on the desk. Stavros could see Olympia's name handwritten on the folder in large letters.

"Nothing new here. Like I've told that other girl, her sister. We got no new leads." The sheriff shrugged his shoulders and planting one muscular thigh sideways on the secretary's desk, he casually leaned toward Marika.

"With these missing girls, the family doesn't know they have a boyfriend. Then the girl runs away with him while no one is looking.

Simple as that." He stood again and put his hand on the gate, ready to escort them out.

Marika gently but firmly folded her arms in front of her body.

"Your deputy here. He know more about this case. We know this to be true."

Stavros clutched his hat and looked down at his shoes, waiting for the fallout. But the chatter of the congressman, his wife and their admirers again distracted Sheriff Lewin. He slowly walked to the front door, rested his hand on the doorknob, then turned back to face them.

"Why can't you people understand? Is it a language problem?" He tapped his foot with impatience and pulled a sheet of paper from the file.

"We have a list of Mira's customers we interviewed right here. We have no witnesses of her actual abduction. We collected the statements from those old ladies at Mira's Tailor Shop. They said Olympia came to work and stayed late for a female customer. We talked with that customer and she had a solid alibi. Then we learned Olympia closed up the shop that night. The door was locked up tight in the morning. My deputy has no more information than I do. I'm telling you, she's out there somewhere with a man. She just doesn't want anyone to know. Right Robbie?"

Stavros glanced at Deputy Robbie. His face was dripping with sweat which had leached down his shirt, soaking the front of his uniform. Usually smooth and tan, his face was now ruddy with color.

"Uh, that's what we know." The deputy avoided Marika's gaze.

As the congressman, his wife and their entourage moved across the street to hang more signs the sheriff closed the front door and strolled to the desk. He waved the list of interviewees at Stavros and Marika. "This is all we got. We have nothing else to go on."

"We hear you and Olympia –" Marika began.

The deputy's eyes seemed to plead with Stavros to stop her.

"I knew Olympia in high school. Same class. I've told the sheriff she was, is, a very nice girl."

"Our Olympia is an angel." Marika's eyes burned with fire. "All these months, you no find her body nowhere in the countryside. That means Olympia is out there. Somewhere. Alive. She suffer while you do nothing."

Robbie could not meet Marika's eyes. His voice dropped to a whisper. "We have no more information for you, ma'am."

Marika's voice was muted, gritty. "Then we must do your job for you."

With that she plucked the list of interviewees from the folder, grabbed her purse, and marched out the front door.

Eyes wide with astonishment, Stavros followed her to the car. He slid next to the woman he wanted more than all others. He looked back to see the sheriff at the window, intensely writing something, probably Marika's license plate number. What would the fallout be from their visit? And exactly who would be hit with the deadly shrapnel?

FORTY-NINE

On the road back from the sheriff's department, Marika said little and Stavros had absorbed her dark, pensive mood. Now, stepping inside the bakery, Stavros found Agamemnon and Lucky buzzing behind the counter, bagging orders for the late morning customers. Still in his chair, Timoleon, who had never opened the fruit stand a minute past eight o'clock, sipped what Stavros estimated to be his fifth cup of coffee.

"You no work today, Timoleon?" Stavros began wiping down the tables preparing for the lunch trade. "Nothing you can do here."

"I need to know! What say the sheriff?" Timoleon sat forward anxiously awaiting a tidbit of news.

"The sheriff is a *gaídaros*, a jackass. Like always he think Olympia run away with a man. But that deputy. He more quiet than before. We at the same place as we start."

Agamemnon broke the silence. "So what we do for Olympia now? We all just go back to work like nothing happen?" He poured himself a cup of coffee and joined the group.

Stavros' conscience weighed heavy with that same question as he wiped down the café tables. He had no answers. For months Marika had nagged Stavros to do more to find his niece and had pushed him to see the sheriff that day. As Timoleon walked out the door for work at the fruit stand, Stavros realized he had rubbed the same tabletop three times with his polishing rag. He threw it down. He knew what to do.

FIFTY

Later that day, the summer sun was still high in the sky but the big kitchen clock had struck six. After locking the bakery front door, Stavros rushed to his room, combed his thick salt-and-pepper waves and slid into a clean shirt. No immigrant bakery odors for the man-to-man conversation he had in mind.

Minutes later, Stavros opened the door to the Chicago Café, the favorite eatery for the sheriff's department and everyone else in Woodland. Sitting alone at the counter, hovering over a plate of Chow Mein, Deputy Robbie hungrily shoveled food into his mouth. His close-cropped dark hair bore the marks of his official felt hat which sat next to his plate on the counter. Still wearing his olive-green uniform, he motioned to the waitress to refresh his iced tea. Sipping from a straw, he looked more teenager than adult law enforcer.

Stavros quietly slipped onto the next stool. A waiter in white shirt and black pants stopped in front of him.

"Coffee, please. Black."

Stavros looked to see if the deputy recognized his voice but he did not twitch, blink or look to his right. A cup of coffee magically appeared and the waiter silently vanished. It was Stavros' show now. His approach would be gentleman-to-gentleman. One man wanting to understand the other. No attack. Just a smooth press for information.

Stavros stirred his coffee with a tinkling sound. "I watch you at the sheriff's office." Deputy Robbie briefly glanced at Stavros then looked straight ahead again.

"It's you." His voice was quiet, flat.

"Yes. I am Olympia's uncle. Stavros Diamantopoulos." Stavros held out his hand for a manly shake. "Her father was my brother."

"I already know that." The deputy gazed at his empty plate. Stavros lowered his unshaken hand and dove right in.

"Again, Mr. Deputy, how you know Olympia?"

"From high school. A long time ago. I told you and that woman who came in today. I'm not hiding anything."

Reclining against the seat back, Stavros attempted to appear relaxed but his mind was whirling.

"The talk in the town say before she disappear you see her. You meet her at a restaurant. That's what people say." Stavros hoped his voice sounded indifferent, chatty.

Deputy Robbie gasped when Stavros mentioned the restaurant.

The deputy began to look to his left, anywhere but toward Stavros. "Why didn't you mention this in front of the sheriff? This is a set up. What do you want?"

"I think you good man," Stavros hesitated. "Not like your boss, who no listen to nothing."

"I don't know what you mean. Sheriff Lewin is doing everything he —"

"He do nothing." Stavros' voice took on a harder edge, his dislike of the sheriff bleeding through. He immediately softened his tone. "But I come here to ask, why you come to our card game at Angel's Bakery? What goes on with you and my niece?" Stavros dared to touch the deputy's chair turning him so they were face to face. "You close to Olympia? Tell me."

Like a child, Deputy Robbie rubbed both hands up and down his face as if washing away any involvement.

"Everyone knows Olympia and I were in high school together, but that was over ten years ago. I felt sorry for her. A beautiful girl, but lonely, I think. And smart too. Beat me in algebra every test. But nothing for her at school except torture. In high school she was almost a woman. And that's what drove the boys nuts. I saw it. Every day. Every minute. That's why she dropped out, Mr. Diamond-two-polis."

The deputy mispronounced his name but Stavros remained silent.

"I told that to the sheriff. He knows her—our—background."

The deputy nervously chugged the entire glass of iced tea.

"And what about you together at a restaurant?"

"That he doesn't know about." Deputy Robbie's voice dropped again, slightly above a whisper. "Nothing went on. We ate dinner."

Stavros' head pounded but he kept his voice low. "But peoples, they see you together! Many times!"

"OKAY!" The deputy nearly shouted but continued to stare ahead. He nodded for yet another refill of his iced tea and continued in a strained monotone.

"I'd see her walking home from work every day on my patrol. A far distance for a young woman to walk alone. Especially in winter in the dark. I'd give her a ride from time to time. Sometimes she'd let me take her for something to eat before she cooked at the boarding house."

Stavros' guilt for asking Olympia to cook after a full day of work surged through his chest. But he remained silent, hoping the deputy would continue.

"I always liked Olympia. I'd drive her home in the squad car but leave her off around the corner from the bakery. That's the way she wanted it." The deputy sighed, relaxing just a little. "Such a lovely woman."

"So, you give her rides home? What happen at this restaurant?" Stavros quietly pressed.

"One evening while she walked home, I saw she was crying. Seemed like she was in pain. I stopped to ask if she was hurt. Did she need to go to the hospital? She only cried harder. Sobbing, really."

The deputy's eyes seemed to look through Stavros. "I took her to a restaurant for a good meal. She had to get home but I convinced her we could eat real fast. She hardly touched her food. Mr. Diamond-two-polis, she was nearly hysterical. Even in pain, she was so beautiful. I wanted to protect her. Take her home and keep her forever."

Stavros jerked in his seat at the word "keep."

"Not like that. I wanted to protect her from her agony. I asked her to marry me. But when I asked, she just cried harder and shook her head no. Olympia couldn't even speak that night at the restaurant. I meant it. I loved her. Did your gossips tell you that too?"

Stavros ignored this. "And you no tell your sheriff?"

"He would think I was somehow involved with her disappearance. I just wanted to help Olympia. I never touched her. Never would. And now I suppose you and that woman are going to tell Lewin everything. Then I'm done for."

The deputy rubbed his face again.

"I just was looking out for her, I swear. Then she disappeared. Maybe I should have said something but I just got this job last year!"

Stavros crossed his arms over his wildly thumping heart. This was the most information about Olympia he had received since her disappearance.

"So why you come to our game at the bakery?"

"Olympia's sister comes to our department nearly every week for updates about the case. I wanted to check out the games, maybe scope out someone who might have been involved in Olympia's disappearance. But I think your card room is a dead end. Penny ante stuff. Just a bunch of old men gambling."

Stavros rubbed his hands over his face attempting to calculate the deputy's guilt or innocence, truth and falsehoods. After a moment, Stavros drained his cup to conclude the meeting.

"Now I know about you and Olympia. And you know about our card games." Stavros swiveled around and planted his feet on the floor and stood looming over the deputy like a stern father. He left change on the counter for the coffee. "I guess we both keep quiet. For now."

Nodding a goodbye, Stavros walked out of the diner into the heavy air of early evening. He pursed his lips, his mind racing. Was Deputy Robbie just good at covering up grisly facts? Should he have pressed the deputy for more? He imagined Marika would have come away absolutely certain of the deputy's guilt or innocence. But Stavros had needed to play it man-to-man, give the deputy his respect, keeping the door open for future exchanges.

As Stavros shuffled down Main Street, he was unsure of his next move. Timoleon, Agamemnon and Lucky expected progress from him in the search for Olympia. But on his way to their expectant ears, Stavros faltered. He was a bit more informed than when he'd left—and even more confused.

FIFTY-ONE

Standing on the incline behind the cluster of outdoor buildings, Yianna watched the woman slowly pull laundry off the line and drop it into a woven basket. Her voice was low and a little off tune as she sang the folk song about the heroic Greek women. Yes! That was her mother's song, the tune Olympia sang during their early years in America.

To Yianna, that song was home. Her battered feet were stiff but she limped down the rugged hillside, hoping the singer would not retreat. The last few yards of the hill were steeper than Yianna anticipated and her injured foot caught a thicket. She was instantly airborne and landed in a heap, sliding down the remaining slope. With arms and legs thrashing in attempt to break her fall, she finally landed with a thud at the feet of the woman near the clothesline. Looking up from the ground, Yianna opened her eyes to see the woman's black cotton dress and thin black stockings covering her short but sturdy legs. Her laundry basket was fixed on her hip.

The woman, about fifty years old, gray strands fading her auburn hair, stared down at the dirty, broken mess at her feet that was Yianna. Squinting her eyes, she bent over, closely examining Yianna's torn clothes, missing shoe, blood-drenched sock, matted hair and camera with the strap tangled around her neck. For a moment she seemed pensive, then suddenly blurted out her words.

"Come! You come to my house, down there." She pointed to the nearby cabin with smoke curling from the chimney. Looking over Yianna again, her eyes lingered on her bloody and blistered foot.

"You need help." Her words were heavily accented. "Come!"

She put down her basket to take Yianna's arm. Limping beside this woman in a daze, Yianna wondered if she dreamed the folk tune her mother and Olympia had sung. Or had her yawning hunger overtaken her brain? Knowing she could hardly survive another night in the wild, Yianna allowed herself to be led along by this woman in the wilderness.

As Yianna dragged her injured foot down the path, she found her voice. "*Melateh Ellinikà?* Do you speak Greek?"

The woman shrugged and kept her eyes forward. "*Fysikà!* Naturally!"

Two hours later Yianna was sunk in a bathtub up to her neck in hot water. The woman squeaked open the door, handing Yianna a large white rectangle of soap. Lowering her eyes in modesty, she wiped her hands on her smock-like apron.

"*Ella, tha fameh tora!* C'mon, we eat soon. And your name?"

"Yianna. *Ioanna.* Thank you very much." Yianna accepted the soap, still in awe that she should run into a family, a Greek family at that, in this wilderness.

An hour earlier when Yianna had followed the woman to the cabin, she noticed a small red neon sign reading *Garberville Café* on a building which seemed to share a wall with the cabin. A restaurant owner in this wilderness? Uncle Stavros' well-worn axiom echoed in Yianna's mind: "Where there is food, there is a Greek cooking it." Appreciating her good fortune as much as the hot bath, she dunked her head below the surface and allowed the warmth of the water to penetrate every pore.

Minutes later, wrapped in a clean quilted bathrobe designed for a matron, Yianna limped out to the small living room. The woman and two other family members scurried around a table, preparing a meal that to Yianna seemed like a Thanksgiving feast. She was astonished that a small table could hold so many platters of food: tomato and cucumber salad, two golden roasted chickens, fluffy rice pilaf and feta cheese cut into small rectangles. On a side table, a two-tiered china stand proudly displayed baklava heavy with honey and walnuts.

Yianna lifted her eyes to see a fiftyish man and a shriveled ancient woman dressed in black who had prepared the meal with the woman who found her. The older woman's hawk nose was the prominent feature on her small face but she welcomed Yianna with kind eyes and a generous smile.

"This my husband Pete, and his mama Eleni. And I am Lula." Looking at Yianna, Lula beamed a smile. "We can't believe we find a Greek girl out in the forest! Like a nymph!" She hugged Yianna tightly, pinching her cheek with worn fingers. "*Fáge!* You eat now!" Lula spooned a mountain of pilaf onto Yianna's plate and a meaty chicken breast to accompany it.

The man whose eyebrows were as thick as the Mendocino forest sat down at the head of the table. His steel-gray hair was brushed into a crew cut. He pushed up the sleeves of his handknit sweater with patched elbows. He motioned for everyone to be seated and Yianna obeyed. She would not miss this meal. The man made the sign of the cross and the older woman silently mouthed prayers over her empty plate.

"My mother here, she no talk, but she cook good!" Pete patted his bulging stomach and smiled. "Welcome to our home. Lula and I work the diner here in Garberville. Right next door!"

Yianna looked up from her plate which had been the center of her attention. "You mean you have a restaurant? This is Garberville?"

"Yes!" Pete nodded. "I bring my wife and my mother here to America after the war. The diner was my brother Yorgos's place but he move to San Francisco. So now it is mine." Pete munched away on his tomato and cucumber salad. "This place too cold for Yorgos but we like it here. And Mama no have to talk here. She just can rest and walk outside."

Pete leaned close to Yianna speaking in hurried English. "The war. She see too much. After she no talk."

Eleni tilted her head toward Yianna, eyebrows raised.

"She wanna know why you here. You a girl, alone in the forest." Lula spooned more pilaf on her plate.

Yianna swallowed a forkful of tender chicken and she sighed in satisfaction of food settling in her stomach. Wanting to inhale her plate of food she realized her exhausted limbs could hardly move. She took a breath and in rapid Greek, summarized her story.

"My ride left me off in the wrong place." Yianna skipped to the end. "Then I got lost. And spent nights in the forest. Don't' know how many. Then I saw Lula!"

"Well, you here now, *Ioanna*." He used her formal name. "You want we should call your family? We take you home?" He reached for an unlabeled bottle, poured himself a small glass and sipped the cherry-colored wine.

Yianna shook her head no. "Not yet. I have to find my sister."

The aromas from the dinner table intoxicated Yianna to drowsiness as she nearly fell asleep over her plate. The last thing she remembered was Lula and Eleni leading her to a small wooden bed, its fresh sheets smelling heavy with starch. Yianna slept deeply through the night until the afternoon, wrapped in the safety of her people.

The next day, Yianna found her freshly-laundered black pants laid out on a chair in her room. Next to it was a soft cream-colored blouse, a woman's tweed blazer and various worn men's flannel shirts and jackets. Because the diner was closed on Sunday the trio had time to assemble multiple pairs of used boots and shoes lined up like a shoe store window. The women's clothes were too small for Yianna and even the sleeves on Pete's jacket were short on her arms.

After a few minutes, Yianna emerged from the tiny bedroom dressed in male clothing and modeled her outfit to the waiting family. She happily walked on the thin rug in Pete's old workboots. Yianna's heart brimmed with love for this little family, a home far away from her Woodland home. Yianna instantly understood these clothes were worn every day and were not leftovers. They had given the best they could.

"Thank you for taking me in, for these clothes, the food!" Yianna knew her words were inadequate compared to the gratitude she felt. Thank you!"

"You look good in my clothes!" Pete laughed and lit up his pipe while Eleni signaled Yianna to come and sit next to her. Dragging out a small metal tub of warm water, she motioned for Yianna to take off her shoes and socks. Eleni then plunged Yianna's feet into the tub tossing in Epsom salts. After about a half hour, she tended to Yianna's cuts and blisters with salve, then wrapped clean bandages around her feet. Then the old lady sat back and stared admiringly at Yianna. A tear ran down her weathered face, but Eleni said nothing. Kissing the gold cross on the chain around her neck, she sat close to Yianna, eyes shut, laying her head on Yianna's shoulder.

"Her daughter Antigoni, she tall and strong. Like you," Lula spoke quietly. "She is remembering her. The Germans, they take her, they violate her, God rest her soul. Then they shoot Antigoni while Eleni watches. She no talk again."

Yianna took Eleni's hand, knowing it would never be enough for this old woman and the sorrow she endured. As Yianna relaxed, Pete continued his conversation.

"So how we help you?"

"Like I said, I have to find my sister. My Olympia." Yianna studied the warm, comfortable cabin knowing she would soon have to leave.

"My sister. I think she is pregnant." Before the family could pass judgment, Yianna blurted out. "But she is a good girl, smart, works hard. I don't know what happened. But before I learned she was pregnant, she had been missing for six months. Gone! Since after Christmas last year. And now it's the end of July."

"And you want to go to the Lost Coast, you say?" Pete lit his pipe again.

"I heard a man might have driven her there." Exhausted, Yianna finally burst out with her question.

"If a girl was in trouble like that, why would she be taken to the Lost Coast? Why the Lost Coast?"

Pete and Lula looked at each other and Pete set down his pipe.

"There is only one place." His voice was stern. Lula moved to Yianna giving her a firm hug.

"You be ready tomorrow." Lula's voice was low, serious. "Yes, only one place. Pete, he work our café tomorrow. But I drive you there. Maybe find your sister. Your Olympia."

FIFTY-TWO

Any given Friday night, Angel's Bakery was usually bristling with energy and optimism as the weekly players took their places, hoping the cards would fall lucky. The shuffle of cards, the clink of whiskey glasses, the strike of matches lighting cigars and the low hum of male voices were a symphony tuning up for the evening concert ready to begin.

But tonight, Stavros sat alone in the dark bakery sipping black coffee. Since Deputy Robbie admitted his meetings with Olympia and his knowledge of gambling at the bakery, Stavros had cancelled the games, his last connection to Greek village life. Now he forced himself to stay vigilant, allowing Sheriff Lewin no reason to come snooping.

Stavros knew that if the sheriff decided to arrest him for running a gambling outfit, then Olympia would be labeled as "bad" or "loose," the corrupt reputation of illegal gambling reflecting on her. It was clear that his every move could be observed by government men. He did not trust Sheriff Lewin and was unsure of Deputy Robbie. He could take no chances now.

With no card game, Agamemnon, Timoleon and Lucky left earlier for an evening stroll which inevitably became a visit to The Stag Bar on Main Street for a shot and a beer back. Stavros felt more at home in his bakery all alone. He sat in the early evening darkness, aimless in his solitude. Then the little bell tinkled as the door creaked open.

Marika walked into the bakery on tired feet with no trace of her usual spirited pace. Her hair was softly curled but her shoulders slumped as she threw her purse on the chair next to Stavros. Then she planted herself across from him.

"I can't do this anymore, Stavros." Throwing her back against the chair she kicked off her black pumps, which seemed more work-a-day without her electric spirit. "Too many Greeks open shops in their own towns. Not many want to order from me. And I need new tires every year."

Stavros instantly jumped up, pulled a bottle of homemade red from the lower shelf behind the counter and poured Marika a full glass.

"I'm tired, Stavros." She poised the glass at her lips and splashed a gulp down her throat. "I work on a new plan."

She drained the glass and gently shoved it toward him. Automatically he poured her another, then rummaged in the bakery refrigerator to offer a plate of cheese, olives and a soft, fresh hunk of bread. He sat close to her, filling his own glass. He cautiously slipped his arm around Marika as a husband might do for an ailing wife. They had made blissful love a few weeks ago, but an ocean still separated their bedroom passion from their daily exchanges in the bakery.

For an hour they sat together in the dark bakery sipping wine. Stavros' mind manufactured scenes of how his life together with Marika could play out. Could he earn enough so she would not have to work? Would such a firecracker want to stay home? Would she bake baklava and crochet like other women? Stavros shook off that thought. No chance of that happening. What was her new plan? Did Stavros have a place in it? Marika always knew what she wanted and, better yet, what she didn't want. He would make sure she wanted him.

Gazing at her red fingernail polish and the gold bracelets jingling on her wrist, Stavros then and there dedicated himself to be her man, marriage or not. And he would start immediately.

Grabbing her jacket he gently laid it around her shoulders.

"We go." Stavros guided her out the door but she stopped abruptly.

"No matter what," Marika fished in her purse for the car key. "I drive."

Stavros smirked, knowing that Marika had not completely abandoned her spirit. She slipped into the driver's seat and, gripping the wheel, turned to look deep into his eyes.

"So, Stavros. Where we go? How we get there?"

If only he could reveal a roadmap for their future together. But first, he had to invent it.

At that moment, Stavros realized they had drunk too much and helped her out of the car. Together they strolled the downtown streets of Woodland.

The rest of the evening, Stavros' only thought was to cheer Marika and weave an enchanting web around her. In his heart, he knew there would be no relationship if Marika didn't desire it too. So his plan became simple. He would create a world where she wanted a life only with him. He would be indispensable, a rock of support and lover beyond compare.

Their first stop was a small Italian restaurant off Main Street. At a tiny back table, they each polished off a plate of creamy fettuccini alfredo and another bottle of wine. Outside again, Stavros gently took Marika's hand and walked with her like a teenager drunk on first love. Glancing at her, he wasn't sure if she was tipsy or if she felt the same. Remembering a house party nearby, Stavros led Marika a few blocks to seek the warmth and familiarity of an old-fashioned Greek *glendi*, celebrating a saint's feast day. They could hear faint music in the distance and walked a few blocks toward it.

The *glendi* was in celebration of St. Salome, one of the women who, with Mary, had attended Jesus' body after his death. The *glendi* celebrated all others named Salome as well. The house was crowded with so many Greeks that men and women had spilled onto the patio. Tables were filled with *pastitso*, Greek lasagna; *dolma*, stuffed grape leaves; roasted lamb and chicken, four types of cheese, roasted eggplant and thick slices of ring bread topped with sesame seeds. A separate table offered three kinds of Greek pastry and Stavros recognized the Snowball cookies he baked yesterday. The women wore party dresses and most men sported clean white shirts tucked into their suit pants. On the patio sipping a glass of red, Stavros realized the wine, too, was his own work. He had sold a case from his basement to the host last week.

Lights strung around the patio added a soft glow to Marika's cheeks while three musicians sat on a riser and burst into a lively *hasapiko*, the butchers' dance. The bouzouki, guitar and lilting clarinet were all Stavros needed to pull Marika into the circle of dancers. Stavros danced light-footed and nimbly and Marika smoothly followed his lead, her arms strong across the back of his shoulders.

A few more tunes and the crowd thinned. Then the clarinet player slowly stood and began a haunting *Zeibekiko* tune, an improvisational song. Usually only one man would dance to this music, showing the world his pain and suffering through his dance. No exact beat, no planned steps and certainly no one would dare to interrupt a man dancing his sorrow in front of a crowd.

But that night the men moved to the food table loading their plates. Suddenly, Stavros saw Marika step out of her pumps and stride forth, all alone, arms up, head down. She began dancing her grief, moving and twisting with anguish and regret. Swaying right and left with torment and sadness, she reached for the floor and swept her hand up and then turned around to begin her solo dance again. Stavros could not keep his eyes from her athletic, graceful body as it twisted, revolved, spun and circled. Marika's movements sang her life's sadness and sent a cry to the universe while the rest of the party guests rushed to refill their drinks. Few people noticed the solo female dancer but Stavros' eyes were fixed on Marika who told more from her dance than she had revealed to Stavros in her bedroom. Her well of sorrow, the black, deep hole Marika masked every day, was plain for all to see.

As the three-piece band finished the tune with one sustained clarinet high-note, Marika returned to Stavros, pulled on her shoes and headed for the bar. She tossed an impish smile to him over her shoulder, the pain seemingly drained temporarily away. He was now fully aware of the infinite sadness Marika had trapped inside her. Rushing to the bar he spun her around amidst the packed throng of party-goers. He needed to become her shield from pain and harsh memories to help heal her soul. Stavros wrapped her in his arms and kissed her deeply. With his heart and every molecule in his body, he would find a way to revive the best part of the woman he knew to be Marika.

FIFTY-THREE

Yianna sat sandwiched tightly between Lula and Eleni in the front seat of a late 1930s Chevy pickup with a battered front grill. The black truck sported shabby wooden rails framing the truck bed and the springs squeaked when the tires hit potholes. They rattled north along rugged U.S. 101 near the Avenue of the Giants, the most ancient redwoods in California's north country. Camera in hand, Yianna attempted to snap a photo of the colossal trees which were much grander than those in the forest where she struggled only a few days ago.

Snugly crunched next to Eleni in the front passenger seat, Yianna closely observed the two women as the truck hammered along. Lula, intent on her driving, used her muscular arms to wrestle the leather steering wheel into submission. A heavy wool jacket covered her flowered cotton dress and her worn black loafer stomped on the gas pedal to keep the truck moving. On the passenger side, Eleni's small, rough hands clutched both of Yianna's. The sky quickly darkened as the redwoods became dense and blocked the sunlight outside the foggy truck windows.

"We go to the religious ladies. Catholic. They live by themselves near the Lost Coast. They do everything. Grow garden, make food, build houses. They choose a hard life in the *exohi*, wild nature." Lula turned briefly to Yianna. "People say they take in girls who need help. Pregnant, out in the forest."

Yianna tried to picture these religious women, hoping they indeed had sheltered and protected Olympia. Her only experience with Catholic nuns was watching them from afar as they walked single file down Main Street in Woodland toward the Holy Rosary Catholic Church. How could women dressed in stiff headdresses and full-length black habits survive in the wild? Yianna shrugged and decided to reserve judgment. She simply hoped they provided a safe path for her sister if she stayed with them.

"We meet them together." Lula's energetic voice shook her from her thoughts. "Only hour and a half to go!"

From a basket at her feet, Eleni pulled out a hard-boiled egg, a hunk of feta cheese and a few twisty, toasty Greek cookies. Nodding to Yianna to eat, the old woman sat back contentedly, having accomplished her job of nourishing the youngest in the group.

Suddenly Lula began to sing a plaintive folk song in her low slightly off-tune voice.

> *Toh yelakaki, pooh forees, to eho ego rameno, meh pikres keh meh vassanah —*
> *The little vest that you wear, it is I who have sewn it with troubles —*

Yianna found herself humming along while mentally knitting together memories of this folk song Olympia had sung years ago. Then she joined in with the words she recalled and Eleni nodded her head in rhythm, her voice lost in the shadow of grief.

For most of her life, Yianna reflected, she had been surrounded by old Greek men who had no time and little aptitude for traditions Greek women kept alive decade after decade. If not for Olympia, she would know nothing of sewing, weaving and crocheting, the traditional songs, the home remedies passed from mother to daughter. But now, bumping down the highway in their battered pickup truck, Lula and Eleni filled Yianna with waves of quiet contentment. The age-old traditions of Greek women washed over her.

As she climbed out of the truck, almost two hours later, Yianna came face to face with two hearty-looking women who smiled their welcome. Lula spoke in her heavily accented English.

"Hello, sisters. This is Yianna who need your help. She look for someone. Her sister. Maybe she come here?"

Yianna had no photo of Olympia to show these women. *Damn Harry for the horrendous ride and for taking my knapsack!*

"My sister's name is Olympia. Olympia Diamantopoulos. She's in her late twenties, with long black hair, black eyes and she's absolutely beautiful. You would remember her. And she might be, probably is —" Yianna stammered, thinking these religious women might think badly of Olympia if she said the word.

Quickly, Lula pantomimed a swollen belly and looked up for recognition. The woman who seemed to be in charge nodded, motioned for them to follow her into the compound and enter a cabin.

Practically running up the steps, Yianna could hardly wait to learn any scrap of information. If Olympia had stayed in this wild place, surely these sisters would know where she'd gone and with whom. Yianna prayed this would be the last stop in her search, desperately hoping these women would produce a solid lead.

The cabin seemed to serve as the kitchen and dining room. The two religious women settled Yianna, Lula and Eleni at one side of a long picnic-style table and served up bowls of steaming vegetable soup and slices of dark rye bread. Taking their places across the table, the women bowed their heads in silent prayer. Everyone but Yianna began to eat.

The woman in charge wore her dark hair awkwardly short, as if cut by a razor. About forty-five, her sweet face was round and Yianna suspected her dark eyes soaked in everything. When standing, Yianna had looked her squarely in the eye which meant she, too, was about six feet tall. The other woman, perhaps the second in command, was older, frail, and wore a rough brown robe over blue jeans. Each women wore a silver cross on a long chain.

"So, yes, my sister might be pregnant." Yianna looked down at her bowl, avoiding any judgment. "Most likely. Can you tell me, did she stay here? Do you know where she might have gone?"

The tall sister put aside her spoon and rose from her seat. She brought out a slip of paper, old and crumpled from years of service and placed it in front of Yianna, who was sure she would find an address or name she could pounce on. Instead, the words stopped her cold.

We are in seclusion for two weeks. Our order will not speak during this time. We work and we pray. Thank you for respecting our devotion to the Lord.

Seclusion? Not speaking? Now? When she might finally get information, these sisters would not speak? Yianna wanted to respect their godly devotion but her own mission to find Olympia screamed for attention.

"You're not speaking? Won't you help me? I'm desperate!" Yianna's voice was loud in the silent room. "Surely you can talk for a moment, just to help me. Please, just to help my sister!" Hot frustration erupted. "Can't I write and you could write back? You wouldn't have to speak!"

The two sisters looked down at their folded hands as their mouths moved in prayer. Feeling more lost than ever, Yianna dropped her head on her arms and let out a wail. Lula rubbed her back and pulled her close for a hug.

"Give them time, Yianna. They will help you. They are servants of God." As usual, Lula's voice was strong and comforting.

An hour later, Yianna waited outside on the stairs, knowing Lula would have to return to Pete and the Garberville Café. Lula had lingered with the sisters a few more minutes at the table and she handed Yianna another note the sisters had given her. The note promised anyone in their care would eat well, sleep in safety and would be helped to their next destination.

"You want to come back with us?" Lula fidgeted with her keys. "If you no wanna stay, you come with us now." Eleni looked expectantly, but Yianna shook her head and hugged both women.

"Go home to Pete." Yianna cast off the thought of running back to the truck to the security of Lula's family. "You're right. I have to wait until they're ready to tell me what they know about Olympia. They must know something. They're all I've got."

Yianna watched as Lula and Eleni passed an outdoor chapel under a massive redwood tree. A miniature altar had been placed in a hollow of the tree trunk. Stopping briefly, they softly chanted their Greek Orthodox prayers and kissed the small gold crosses hanging around their necks.

Walking to the truck, Lula murmured in Yianna's ear, slipping her a five-dollar bill.

"If you need something, have them get you to Petrolia, a little town not so far away. They gotta pay phone at the general store. Call us at the Garberville Café and Eleni and I come. We will help our *kukla*, doll." She made the sign of the cross once again as Eleni, standing behind her, followed suit. "May God watch over you."

And with another goodbye hug, Yianna watched the two women drive away as the sun began to sink below the tree line. Standing in the shadows, Yianna shivered as the temperature dropped ten degrees.

In the flat gray light of late afternoon, the older religious sister showed Yianna to a small sleeping cabin. The matchbox of a room held a cot constructed from rough redwood slabs, and a small table. A stark iron cross over the bed was the only décor. Exhausted, Yianna fell asleep on the cot but was awakened by a deep clanging bell signaling a silent dinner of lentils and rye bread with the entire group of ten sisters. After the meal, Yianna was once again silently shown to the little cabin where the sister lit a small candle for light. She covered herself with coarse brown blankets that Yianna assumed were Army issue.

Lying on the thin mattress, Yianna decided that at first light she would beg these women for any information they kept behind their sealed lips. If the sisters were devoted to God, they certainly should be forthcoming with important information she so desperately needed.

Resting quietly in the dim candlelight, Yianna's thoughts drifted away from Olympia to her weekend in San Francisco and to Will, the happy surprise of her journey. Until that moment, Yianna had no time to reflect on this new person or her photography that now seemed to be entwined with Will and his work as a journalist. When she was with Will, Yianna felt her photography was important, that she, too, was telling a story. She smiled remembering when he described them as "a good team." Yianna was unsure of what to make of Will. At least she knew he worked at the *San Francisco Examiner*. Maybe someday, if she attended the California School of Fine Arts ..."

Yianna snapped herself back to reality. Here she was, in a forlorn backwoods location, the Lost Coast of California. Her pregnant sister was still lost. Allowing her mind to selfishly drift to her own work and future shamed her. She forced herself to focus on the quagmire that finding her sister had become.

The handmade candle burning next to the bed was nearly a stub and Yianna decided to make use of the remaining light. She found a neatly folded wash cloth on the little table and began to polish the dirt from her camera, her only remaining possession, her lifeline to her past and future. Looking closely at the Leica, she noticed a few granules lodged around the lens and got to work. Her long fingers popped off the lens cap but she fumbled and the cap dropped with a clatter onto the redwood floor. On her hands and knees now, Yianna reached under the cot, her arm sweeping the floor.

Not locating the lens cap, she peeked under the cot. In the dusty corner, Yianna noticed a small rectangular object. Again, she shoved her arm under the cot but could not reach it. She sprawled spread-eagle on the floor and stretched out her arm. She found the lens cap and pulled it out but thrust her arm again under the cot, stretching more, then a little more, finally grasping something else.

Yianna sat, knees up, on the cold floor to exame the object — a small yet thick handmade book. The volume was bound by strips of woven yarn laced in two holes that punctured the paper. Assuming she would find religious prayers on the pages, Yianna slowly opened the cardboard cover which was the size of the paperback books she had seen at City Lights bookstore. As the candle burned lower and the light dimmed, Yianna squinted to read it. Her stomach flipped as the familiarity of the handwriting melted into recognition.

This was Olympia's book.

Looking at the candle to gauge how much light was left, she turned to the first page in the book. Yianna gasped.

I'm just an immigrant girl who dropped out of high school with the skills of a seamstress. I write my thoughts on these scraps of paper, hoping to quiet my fears.

Knowing only a minute or two of light remained, Yianna skipped to the last few pages:

I've whipped myself for letting it happen but there he was. Stronger than me. He would not stop. Now all I feel is shamed and wonder if Uncle Stavros would ever take me back, pregnant and unmarried."

Yianna's heart stopped as she frantically turned a few more pages glancing at the sputtering candle.

This place is dank, gloomy and always cold, but the silence suits me. I love working in the herb garden and somehow feel it soothes my raw nerves. I don't find it silent anymore. Nature fills the air with bird calls, insect hums and breezes. I could be at home here, away from judgment and heartache. Here I can breathe. Here I could live with no shame.

With only a few moments of light left from the shrinking candle, Yianna jumped to the final entry:

As the baby inside me twists and kicks and hiccups, my heart has thawed, softened and decided to love. Is it an innocent baby's fault she or he materialized from that horrible night?

At that moment the candle flickered and darkness softly descended. Yianna pulled the book closer to her eyes to hungrily take in Olympia's handwriting with the last seconds of light. All at once, the candle took its final breath and snuffed itself out.

Palms sweating, sitting in shadows, Yianna clasped Olympia's handmade diary to her chest. Olympia had revealed she was raped. Yianna's breath came quickly and she began to shiver. Her mind could not measure her sister's pain, her torment. Jolted by this new information she wondered where Olympia was now and how she managed to hold on.

Having no one to confer with, Yianna could only cling to the fact she had found Olympia, at least the parts that were left. But her sister was alive! Heart beating like hummingbird's wings, she hoped daybreak would come soon. Then she would beg the religious sisters for any bit of information they possessed.

Seated on the floor, Yianna's optimism surged like a fountain of possibilities. She *would* find her sister and she *would* find Olympia's child too. With Olympia's words now in her hands, she could feel her sister's brooding presence crying out for Yianna to find her.

FIFTY-FOUR

Yianna paced the grounds in the long, dark hours before the sisters rose for morning prayers, brain blazing with her discovery. Not having slept, she sorted through every possible outcome. Was Olympia still in the compound, hidden away? In a local hospital outside the woods? Had she left her diary as a clue in case someone was searching for her? Was it shoved under the bed because she had to leave abruptly? In the dark early morning, Yianna's fingers gripped Olympia's diary for safekeeping.

The sisters walked past Yianna in the shadows and sat shoulder to shoulder in the chapel cabin. Slipping behind them Yianna waited silently in the darkness. But soon her mind churned with questions and she wanted to scream from the back row.

Camera tucked at her side and Olympia's diary tight in her hand, she slid out the door. With no light to read the diary or even take photos with the last of her film, Yianna's mind drifted to where Olympia might be now. Why would someone take Olympia away from her family when she needed them most? And where would they take her? Was it safe for Olympia's baby to come into the world? Was Olympia still alive?

Yianna's attention shifted to a low branch of a nearby redwood. A black and sapphire Steller's Jay squawked its wakeup call as the first dawn cracked the darkness. At least someone was talking! As the sun began to paint soft colors on the black forest, she wished she had paid more attention when her sister interpreted bird movements. But those days were long past.

Yianna looked up to see the sister in charge signal to come to the kitchen-cabin. After consuming hearty bowls of oatmeal and more rye bread, most of the women silently hurried away to their work. The head sister sat across from her at the long table and offered Yianna a steaming cup of herbal tea. Yianna sipped, waiting. Finally, the last of the women in the kitchen left the cabin.

"I have prayed over this. I will speak to you about your sister Olympia."

Gratitude flooded Yianna's heart upon hearing the woman's soft but sure voice. The sister stirred her tea steaming in a thick ceramic mug.

"Yes, Olympia did stay with us for several months. Yes, she is – was – pregnant. But she left us in what she thought was her ninth month. From our experience, it seemed she would deliver her baby very soon. But, of course, we are not doctors."

"So where in the world *did* she go?" Yianna practically leaped over the table for the answers. "Did she tell you? Was she in good health while she was here? Where can I find her?"

"While your sister was with us, she was in good health. As her baby grew she was so energetic. She helped us with cooking and gardening. Your sister started an herb garden for us!"

Yianna held back her tears, feeling Olympia so close. Of course she started an herb garden! She had to ask again.

"But where did she go? How can I find her?" Yianna's eyes locked onto the head sister who did not lower her gaze.

"We respect the privacy of anyone we harbor. We are sworn not to divulge her whereabouts." The sister seemed to be wrapping up the conversation. "But your sister left in good health. Still pregnant. About four weeks ago."

Yianna buried her face into her hands. She was so close to a link to Olympia but just as distant as before. She looked up again.

"How did she leave? Who took her?" Yianna's tone was demanding but she held herself in check. "What I mean is, thank you for helping me. But how can I locate her?"

"We have a friend, a former lumberjack from around here who comes by in his truck every Wednesday. He gives rides and drives us to town. Your sister said she needed to be in town by a certain date. We don't ask why." The sister began collecting the tea mugs concluding their conversation with one more bit of information.

"My guess is Jack took her to the bus stop at Fortuna on U.S. 101. That's the only way out of here. The Greyhound passes through every day, he knows the schedule. Jack is coming tomorrow and he can take you to the stop. Or you're welcome to stay here as long as you like. That is all I can say now. Please remember, we respect the privacy of everyone who stays with us. We ask no questions. We only help. And we pray for them all. Remember you are welcome to stay. God bless you, my child."

With a deep sigh of frustration, Yianna sat alone in the dining cabin, once again in silence. Yianna felt a flash of anger. Did these religious women learn nothing more about Olympia? Did they provide her food and shelter but allow her pregnant sister to simply drift away? Yianna's fierce desire to find Olympia nearly overwhelmed her as she sat in the empty cabin. The forward motion to find her sister was thwarted again. Yianna could not stomach another promising path that only offered a blockade at the end of the road. If only she could conjure up one useful shred of information.

Needing to keep occupied until the next day when she could catch a ride with the lumberjack, Yianna walked outside the cabin, carrying the diary with her camera over her shoulder. She planted herself under the redwoods, ready to read Olympia's writings. Yianna hoped to discover a phrase or a word that would spin her in the right direction.

Just before she read a new entry in the diary, the noisy Steller's Jay returned and bobbed in front of her, hopping from twig to log. Yianna slowly pulled her camera from her side. She snapped a photo of its indigo body, jet-black head and tufted crown. The magnificent bird again began his rant, shrieking at Yianna who remained silent and still. With one last cry the jay flew to a nearby branch and watched Yianna.

Suddenly she felt renewed. She understood the message of the jay: *Keep pushing, keep going, don't give up.* If she didn't find Olympia, who would? Her sister's future was in her hands and always had been. And Yianna would not let Olympia perish in the murky tunnel of the missing.

FIFTY-FIVE

Olympia's Diary

Months ago, after it happened, I didn't know how to tell Yianna, or anyone, the unspeakable news. How could I share a secret with my sister knowing it would forever change her opinion of me?

Yianna doesn't realize I have always considered her my baby. After all, at thirteen, I became a mother when my parents died and left her in my care. I sewed her dresses from fabric scraps and sang the lullabies our mother hummed at bedtime. Of course, rice pudding was Yianna's favorite so I was sure to make a constant supply. And when it was time for her to attend kindergarten, I walked her to her classroom door and asked to be excused early from my school to walk her back home. I hoped Yianna would become victorious over her orphan circumstances, something I lacked the strength to do. If I could fill the hole in Yianna's heart to brimming, perhaps she would not remember it had been empty at all.

To my amazement, I watched as Yianna cast off her sorrow with every month or new discovery. At age five, she bounded into school and, because she learned English so early in life, had no accent when speaking as I did. Making friends with boys, something I avoided, was not difficult for her and Yianna migrated to Frankie Chen,

Kenny's brother, who began to walk her home from school. At a young age Yianna blossomed into a stubborn survivor and an American girl, everything I was not.

Living not far from our bakery at his family's laundry, Kenny stumbled upon my small herb garden after school and told me how to pronounce the plant names in English and Chinese. Somehow Kenny understood my pain of being a foreigner in a small town. He soothed my wounds simply by his quiet presence. As he brought me clippings from his mother's Chinese herb garden, our friendship grew. Kenny was the only good thing during those first few years in Woodland, and all the rest, if I'm honest.

My parents would have been humiliated by what has become of me. I feel I've now stepped into this new sinkhole of trouble with no hope of pulling out my feet to walk the path of the blissful American life my father promised so long ago.

FIFTY-SIX

The next morning, Yianna was rolling in another truck on another bumpy northern California highway. This time the driver was Jack, a weedy, white-haired man who looked to be in his mid-seventies. Keeping her distance from him on the front seat, Yianna glued her hand to the passenger door handle, just in case. If the religious sisters approved of Jack, Yianna wanted to believe she should too. But Harry had left her suspicious of everyone.

Yianna's departure from the religious compound held little fanfare. The sisters had calculated the money she needed for a bus ticket from Fortuna to Santa Rosa on U.S. 101, then to Napa and then on to Woodland. The head sister handed her cash for the ticket before she left, silently blessing Yianna with the sign of the cross. The older sister handed Yianna a woven bag. Peeking inside, Yianna smiled to see muffins, slices of rye bread, berries and hard cheese, much like the hearty provisions Timoleon had prepared for her.

As they rumbled through the redwoods towards the outback stretch of U.S. 101, Jack had few words for her. He offered her a cup of water from his canteen, but Yianna shook her head, fearful of what he might have added to it. Then it occurred to her that hostility was not the card she should play. Jack had been the last to see Olympia, and Jack was not under a religious code of silence.

"So, Jack, the sisters back at the compound say you drove my sister along this route a few weeks ago. Olympia Diamantopoulos."

Lips tight in contemplation, Jack looked ahead through the windshield. "I take a lotta people for the sisters. Lotta girls. What she look like?"

"Long black hair, black eyes, beautiful smile, not as tall as me. And, well, pregnant."

"She's not the only one." Jack kept his eyes on the road and drove precisely the speed limit. "People around here know the sisters' camp is where you take girls in trouble. They rest up there until they are ready to deliver. They go there when no one else wants 'em. Gets them out of sight. Lotta times, I take 'em to the bus stop at Fortuna. The sisters give them money and they use it for bus fare. Then the girls go on their way."

"So do you remember Olympia?"

"Matter of fact, I do. I took her to the bus stop alright. About a month ago. Nice girl. Kinda quiet."

Jack easily took a hairpin turn, his hands light on the steering wheel. The tires of the truck bounced in and out of a large pothole and Yianna clung to the dashboard to steady herself.

"I usually take the girls to the bus stop and I stick around town awhile. I do a little shopping for me and 'course, the sisters. But I wait around to make sure the girls get safely on the bus. Anything can happen to pregnant girls, you know."

Yianna nodded, waiting for more.

"But your sister's trip to the bus stop was odd. I drive her to the stop, she gets out and sits on the bench. I ask does she need anything and she says no. Your sister looked like she was gonna have that baby any minute so I park my truck up the street and take a look back. She's doubled right over like she's hurt or maybe having labor pains. But before I get back to help her I see a car idling down the street.

As if someone was waiting for her. Some man helps your sister into the car and they drive away. No bus for her. South, they went. Down the highway."

Yianna grabbed the dashboard before they took the next curve in the road.

"And that's it. Off they went."

"What kind of car?"

"Hmmm, a four door. He put her coat in the back seat, now that I remember.

"You remember the color?"

"A dark color. Black. A black sedan, I think."

Yianna's pulse raced.

"What about this man? Can you tell me anything about him?"

"Seemed to be a youngish man, with dark hair."

Her hopes crashed with the vague description. A silence fell between them and a few miles passed before she spoke again.

"If you could picture it again, right now, do you remember anything else?" Yianna fidgeted waiting for Jack's answer.

"Now that you mention it, that car had Oregon license plates. White with black letters and numbers, not like our California plates. Yes, it did. Surprised to see 'em, myself. Yup, Oregon!"

"Anything else?" Yianna fished for more, holding her breath. Jack shot her a sympathetic glance.

"Nuthin' else, miss. Don't think anyone saw them two but me. He was waiting, got her in the car real quick and drove straight outta there. He didn't push her or nothin'. She just went with him, holding her stomach."

Yianna rode along silently while shuffling the new information in her mind. The young man could have been anyone. And from Jack's perspective, the man could have been in his 20s, 30s or 40s to be called "young." But the Oregon plates—that was a gem to hang on to.

FIFTY-SEVEN

The day after watching Marika dance at the Greek *glendi*, Stavros worked with Agamemnon to turn out the morning pastry and fresh loaves. Never able to keep quiet about his thoughts, Stavros had a plan for the future and couldn't wait to tell it.

"Agamemnon, I decide! I give up my dreams for Greece." Stavros shut the oven door on a dozen loaves and set the timer. "I stay here and make myself into the man Marika want. A man to love her. A man to depend for. I propose marriage to Marika tomorrow."

Stavros tapped his chest with a wooden spoon. "She is my woman, I know this in my heart."

"Good for you." Agamemnon shot him an angry look. "And when you have time to find Olympia?"

"Marika and I, we a good team. Together we find her." He began to dip old-fashioned donuts in chocolate icing.

"So after your wedding, exactly where you live?" Agamemnon asked the obvious question not allowing Stavros to float into fantasy. "You think she wanna live here with a bunch of old mens in a bakery and a card room?"

Stavros waved off the question with his hand in an oven mitt. "We figure it out. Maybe her place or we buy new. I work harder and make more money." He moved close to Agamemnon. "She is everything for me. We are a match. I feel this!"

"You better have a plan." Agamemnon warned as he washed his hands before starting the day's batch of Snowball cookies. "Marika, she smart and she no gonna marry a man with debt. And she no like the booze business from the basement. Big things gotta change, Stavros."

A worried look crossed Stavros' face but it instantly faded. His voice became louder now. "It's all gonna be OK. I work harder and make her want me. You watch, Agamemnon. I take care of her good."

Agamemnon nodded, pulling sugar cookies from the oven and sliding them on a wire rack with a spatula.

"You hear from Yianna yet?" he asked quietly. "We no forget her or Olympia while you chase Marika."

Stavros shook his head.

"I hear nothing. Now I lose sleep for Yianna. I worry for both girls." Stavros answered solemnly. "She so young and gone long time too."

"And brave." Agamemnon added throwing up his hands. "Who know where she at?"

"Marika take the list of people they interview from the sheriff. He say he talk with all the people on the list but I'm gonna visit them all again. Did he really talk to everyone? Maybe he make a mistake. But first I ask Marika to marry me. After we find Olympia and when Yianna come back, then we have wedding."

Agamemnon raised his eyebrows in doubt but said nothing.

Later that afternoon Stavros hurried downtown straight to Stan's clothing store. Trying on several suits, he nearly bought a gray double-breasted wool but looked at the price tag. Thirty-five dollars! Remembering Agamemnon's warning to save money for Marika's sake, he hastily walked to the secondhand store and found a brown corduroy suit in his size. Slightly out of date and too heavy for the late summer, Stavros bought it anyway. When he tried it on, he knew it looked as sincere as he felt.

Now, on to purchase a gift to finalize his proposal. Stavros was aware that Marika loved jewelry and wore plenty of it. Passing by Woody's Jewelry store on Main Street, Stavros cringed to see the high price of the bracelets and earrings in the window. He had never purchased jewelry for his previous amours as they were only spirits floating through his bedroom. As he debated the purchase, a gust of enthusiasm pushed him to the finish line: he would buy an engagement ring for Marika — the only piece of jewelry she had never worn.

The pawn shop was a half-block south of the jewelry store and Stavros knew this would be his stop. After examining diamond rings, a small dazzling ruby set on a thin gold band caught his eye. Perfect for a fiery, spirited woman. Thanks to a few scratches on the gold band, he could afford it.

With suit in a bag and ring in his pocket, Stavros had one more preparation. That evening, when the Greek boarders retired to their rooms, Stavros crept into the kitchen where he pulled out bowls, the double boiler and the candy-making cookbook he brought from Greece. After an hour of melting chocolate and pouring it into heart-shaped molds, Stavros had created perfect chocolate bon bons with brandy-cream filling. He would add a dozen handmade candies to his arsenal of love.

The night after Marika returned from her business trip, Stavros waited until a little before eight o'clock. He walked swiftly to her house in his corduroy suit, flowers and candy box in hand, ring polished and ready. Before leaving, he looked in the mirror and took stock. He was a mediocre businessman, a handsome-enough specimen, a superb lover. More than this, he was a changed man. If he was permanently paired with Marika, he would forever treat her with kindness and respect. His nieces too. He realized his selfish desire to return to

Greece did not honor Olympia and Yianna's lives in America. They required emotional security which he had not always provided.

But now, swearing on Christos' memory, he had changed. Uniting his good intentions with Marika's powerful spirit, he planned to achieve a full life in America, no longer yearning for Greece. Together they would be sure to find Olympia and he hoped Yianna would return soon. All together, they could become what Stavros had craved since he was thirteen: a family. He could taste it. And Marika stood at the center of his future plans.

At eight sharp, Stavros stood on Marika's step and rang the bell. Opening the door, Marika did not appear ready for a romantic evening or a night on the town. She wore her turquoise robe, but not seductively. Her belt was tight around her waist and she had wiped off most of her makeup.

"Come in, Stavros!" Kissing him sweetly on the cheek she led him to a chair at the kitchen table.

"Sit down. I got news." Marika turned her back to Stavros and poured Retsina in two short glasses. "And it's big." She offered the wine to Stavros.

"I have news too!" Stavros accepted the wine, patting the ring in his pocket. His eyes sparkled with delight and his mouth couldn't help but curl into a smile. Marika would soon understand how much he would give, how much he loved her.

"You looking nice, Stavros." Marika's eyes flickered over the suit, flowers and candy box. "Well, I tell you now."

Marika held her glass with two hands and did not sit down, as if formally announcing.

"No day goes by without me crying for my son. My Costas. I decide I must be bold. I must have courage."

Stavros couldn't think of a time when Marika hadn't been bold or shown courage. But he remained silent, waiting for her news. She tossed back her Retsina in one gulp as if it were a shot of whiskey.

"I check my bank account. I have enough to live in Greece for a couple of years. I go back and find Costas. I must find my son. My grandmother, she die last year. So no one sitting at our old home in case he come back." Marika slowly sat down as if picturing her son wandering through her former village. Her lip trembled.

Marika's face was flushed from the wine, tears filled her eyes. But then her old resolve returned. "I cannot live without my boy. I only pretend to be happy. So my life will be in Greece, or wherever he live now. America cannot hold me here. I leave soon."

Stavros slugged his wine in two swallows. Marika's words washed over him but the only ones that stuck were *America cannot hold me here*. He wished he could make the flowers and candy instantly disappear. His corduroy suit now seemed ridiculous.

"What you think, Stavros? You think I am crazy to go looking for a boy who probably is in Albania or somewhere I don't know?" Marika stared intently into Stavros' eyes.

Sucking in a long, deep breath, Stavros wanted to hold her, to protect her, to love her, to blot her pain. Having suffered Olympia's disappearance and now Yianna's, Stavros was without words. He wanted Marika badly but could not compete with her fierce intention to find her missing son.

"Uh, I –" Stavros stammered, searching for the right words. "I think you must find your love, your son. As I must find my Olympia." Looking down at his empty glass, he shoved the box containing the ring deeper into his pocket. "You must find your Costas. Marika, a woman like you – a mother like you – can never rest until you find him. And you will. I am sure of it."

Rushing around the table Marika hugged Stavros tightly.

"Of all the people, I know you understand." She broke away to stare into Stavros' face. "You know how it is, to lose your people."

Stavros could only clasp Marika to him again, never wanting to let go. Yes, he had lost his people and now he was losing her, even before he declared his love. Stavros' unspoken thought of marriage swirled in his head with no home. His proposal plan seemed pale and limp compared to her determination to find her son somewhere in the mountainous land north of Greece.

"I leave in four days, Stavros. In Greece I will look for mine. And here, you will look for yours. May we both find our loves. We will know no peace until we do." Marika's voice was low, solemn.

"But now, be with me. *Ella*, come!"

Stavros allowed Marika to lead him to her bedroom, leaving his flowers and candy untouched on the kitchen table, the ring still a secret in his pocket. He would soak up the heart of this woman, this mother. He would be hers forever. But at that moment, Stavros did not know where to deposit the lifetime of love and devotion he was prepared to promise her. Following Marika to her bed, Stavros decided he would worry about that later, after she had gone to travel six-thousand miles to find her missing son.

FIFTY-EIGHT

Olympia's Diary

This place where I write these pages is cold but the sisters are kind. And I have nowhere else to go. Who would take me anyway? I cannot live where people know me. They would say I was a fallen girl, a wild young woman who grew up without a mother's influence. I could never attend church with a bulging stomach and no wedding band on my finger. My life has become a landslide of problems with no escape from the rubble. Yet I continue to grow a baby inside me and cannot picture a shred of happiness in my future.

I'm grateful for the care I've received in this secluded place. These Catholic nuns explained to me they originally lived in a convent in northern Europe but wanted to live on the land, live simply. More than a decade ago, they arrived here in America and built cabins by hand, declaring their self-sufficiency kept them closer to God.

The sisters do not look down on me and they treat me without judgment. They help soothe my upset stomach with chamomile tea and have rubbed olive oil on my belly when my skin stretches beyond its limit. I have not asked, but they must often welcome pregnant girls here as they are practiced in just how to help. I continue to write my thoughts on this paper the sisters supply and have fashioned it into a little book all my own.

That brings me to him. Too busy to do the dirty work himself, that man's lackey dumped me and my pregnancy here in these remote mountains located who-knows-where. I fled from Eddy Street, to save my baby from what he ordered me to do. After that man's lackey found me outside the Apollo Hotel, we drove for hours. He told me this was my holding place until I entered the terrifying land of childbirth and delivery. I would write those men's name in this diary but cannot. I've been threatened.

Some people would question why I don't simply leave this compound. Why don't I find the strength to walk away to safety? It's simple. I have no money, no car, no way to leave. I am pregnant and would have to walk to some unknown destination through an unfamiliar forest. And if I found a road, I would not know which way to go.

I made the mistake of seeking that man's help once I was sure I was pregnant. On the December night when he took me away, he announced I could never name him as father of this child or he would harm us — my baby, me and my bakery family. Besides, who would believe me, a pregnant unmarried whore? That's exactly what he had called me before he dragged me away. My evil-eye bracelet should have protected me, but his wicked spirit had greater power.

If only I could spend one early morning in the cozy bakery, working with my uncle, neither of us speaking, hands automatically following the recipes. If only I could stand in the warm, familiar kitchen I would have a purpose and then perhaps look to my future without fear. But no one can help me now.

FIFTY-NINE

Four weeks after she left Woodland, Yianna stepped out of the bus at the Greyhound station and looked around her hometown. The streets seemed a bit narrower, the stores out of date, everything wilted. The late summer afternoon was broiling and Yianna braced herself for a walk to the bakery in the ninety-five-degree heat.

She was emotionally wrung out after discovering Olympia was alive, pregnant and probably in labor when Jack last saw her. Yianna now had the additional clue of the dark-haired man with the Oregon plates driving her away. But what was her next step?

With her Leica over her shoulder and Olympia's handmade diary in hand, she walked home in Pete's work shoes looking even more masculine than when she left. Riding the bus from Fortuna, she had time to scour each page of the diary for any name or location that could lead to her sister. But Olympia's words revealed no names, no specific clues. She had written she was terrified someone might read her diary and inflict additional pain upon her or her baby. She trusted no one.

On the bus, Yianna tried to imagine the emotional and physical pain during the violence Olympia endured but her mind switched off. Yianna couldn't forget her own desperate battle against Harry in the truck, attempting to break free from his attack. But Olympia had suffered far worse.

And then there was something else. Yianna churned with the discomfort that Olympia never expressed to her the deep feelings she had for Kenny. What else had Olympia not told her? Did she know the dark-haired man Jack saw in Fortuna driving the black sedan? For Yianna, too many mysteries were woven through the diary with no solid leads.

With the thought of Kenny foremost in mind, Yianna slipped into the Good Day Laundry. Although she was dressed like a man, she knew her appearance would not be held against her with the Chen family. As predicted, Mrs. Chen embraced her and handed her a bowl of warm slippery noodles. Ellie rushed out to greet Yianna, wrapping arms around her friend.

"We haven't seen you in so long!" Ellie was joyful and excited. "Look! My engagement ring! A replacement for the promise ring!" She flashed a small sparkling diamond towards Yianna. "I went to your bakery to show you but they said you were gone!"

Yianna hugged Ellie and then reached for her hand to observe her ring, nodding with approval.

"I've been away for weeks now. Today's my first day home." Yianna set her Leica next to a stack of perfectly folded starched shirts. "Has Kenny come home? I need to talk to him."

The cheerful expression drained from Ellie's face. She glanced towards the door and then back to Yianna.

"Look, Yianna. Our family is not talking about this outside our house, but Kenny is gone. Kenny told us the sheriff would not leave him alone about Olympia's disappearance. That he needed to get away. And when Frankie moved to Berkeley to start school, he went to Kenny's apartment but all his things were gone. His landlady had no forwarding address."

Yianna gripped the counter to keep her balance. Kenny gone too? She gathered her camera and turned to leave.

"Yianna," Ellie placed a hand on Yianna's shoulder. "Don't mention this to the sheriff. You know how he is."

Yianna knew exactly how the sheriff was.

Minutes later, Yianna cracked open the door to Angel's Bakery, the little bell chiming her entry. The bakery was in the mid-day slump between lunchtime and the late afternoon bustle. Agamemnon spotted Yianna and rushed around the counter to embrace her.

"Yianna! We wait for you! You are home!" Agamemnon pulled out a chair for Yianna to rest. "You hungry? You want to eat? Stavros! She has come!"

Stavros stumbled out of the kitchen. Seeing Yianna he brightened, his emotions spilling over. Stavros wrapped a bear hug around her and simply stared at his niece.

"Yianna! You are home! How you feel? You hungry?"

Yianna smiled at her uncles who were first concerned about her empty stomach.

"Thanks, Uncle Stavros, Agamemnon." She placed her camera on the café table and slouched into a chair. She could feel their eyes taking in her man-like clothes but they said nothing. Agamemnon scurried to the kitchen and brought a Coke and two *koulourakia* cookies. Reaching for the cold drink, Yianna chugged nearly half of the bottle before looking up.

"So good to be home. I missed you all. I have lots to tell but first I need to rest. So please tell me, what have *you* found out about Olympia?" Yianna searched Uncle Stavros' face. "You must know something more. I've been gone for a long time!"

Stavros inhaled a deep breath. "It go slow. We learn a little more and we keep working. But today we celebrate you are home, Yianna. We worry too much for you. We miss you!"

Yianna was unaccustomed to this emotional outpouring from her uncle but allowed his love to soak into her depleted body.

Agamemnon rose and clattered pans in the kitchen in preparation for the evening meal. Across the table Stavros grasped Yianna's hand.

"While you gone, I think I might lose you too. But now you home. And the time is now. We find our Olympia. Together."

SIXTY

Olympia's Diary

As a girl, I dreamt of creating a cheerful family, baby in my arms and toddlers gleefully weaving through my legs. But now instead of joy a fear grows inside me as my belly swells.

That man promised if I named him as the father, he would place the blame solely on me—that I tempted him beyond all reason. He said I lured him like many of the Mexican, Filipina and Negro girls did, those of us with darker skin and foreign looks. Girls like us would not tell anyway because, if we did, no one would believe us outsiders. He would not be shamed in our town. His reputation depended on it. Apparently, mine did not.

With the planting of this seed inside me, I wrestle with how I will make peace with it. Can I dig deep enough to discover a lifetime of love for this baby? Can this blameless baby evolve from an unwanted soul to an adored child, as all children should be? I had no choice but to become a mother, a victim of violent circumstances. I cannot inflict more cruelty on this innocent child.

That night, Despo, Alethea and Tasia had left the shop early for a church dinner in Sacramento and I was to handle the last customer, as I had done for years. After she left, I put the key in the lock, ready to walk home.

Then he appeared from nowhere, stepping out of the darkness. I jumped back and dropped the key in the dirt outside the shop. But when I saw who stood in the shadows, I relaxed as I knew him well, he was a regular customer. He explained he needed a suit jacket to be tailored quickly. Of course, I would accommodate a customer so I opened the front door again. But once inside the shop, he wasted no time. Before I could turn on the big light, he kissed me hard on the lips and he held back my arms. I broke away, not understanding what he was doing, why he was doing it.

"You notice me." He pulled me hard by my thick braid and pushed my back against the wall. "I see it in your eyes."

I was shocked and attempted to slide away, but his other hand yanked open my blouse. The tiny pearl buttons popped and clattered to the floor.

"You want me. Always have — I know it." Then, the last words his voice growled out. "Move and I'll kill you."

After this I can hardly remember the details, although some days I remember them all in one hellish dream. I froze in fear. I did not make a noise. My instinct was to live through it. I just wanted to live. And then it was done. He cinched his belt and turned back, barking his warning.

"You'll shut your mouth about this," he snarled. "No one will believe you anyway."

I am ashamed to admit that a stronger woman would have fought him off, wrestled against his surprising force, screamed to the rafters, somehow pushing him away. I hadn't been powerful enough, fierce enough. When I relive that moment Yianna's face always appears to me. I whip myself thinking I should have been more like Yianna who would have kicked, screamed and clawed his eyes out before giving up. But I wasn't Yianna. I kept silent so I would not make a scene somehow causing shame to Despo and her business.

Now that I have time to think in these woods, I wonder what would Kenny think of me now? He offered his ring to me and wanted us to be together forever. He said he loved me and we would be a family. I could only stand and sob, looking into his perfect face. He believed I was rejecting him. In truth, I was pushing him away so he did not inherit my bundle of problems. How could he bring me home to his parents? I was not Chinese and was pregnant with someone else's child. I had to save him before he attempted to save me. But he was so angry with me. I've never seen him so desperate and frustrated.

Each day I tend my herbs and cook for these open-hearted, religious women or else I would slowly unravel into madness. And who would raise a baby whose mother was unmarried and mad? No one, that's who. So, I continue to follow that man's malicious direction to keep silent. I suppose my baby and I will live on the outskirts of society forever.

But to my surprise, my heart which perches directly above the baby floating in my belly, has slowly done the work for my brain. As the baby inside me twists and kicks and hiccups, my heart has thawed, softened and decided to love. Is it an innocent baby's fault she or he materialized from that horrible night? I realize this tiny individual is part of me too, which means my parents would live through her or him. The thought of presenting to the world a new little Angeliki or Christos sparks joy in me for the first time in months. The silence of this place has helped me surrender myself to love this little baby. After all, my horrible attacker told me it was my problem now.

All right then. My problem. And my baby it will be.

SIXTY-ONE

The next morning Stavros gently closed the door to Yianna's room and tiptoed to the kitchen where Agamemnon was hard at work stretching and folding a batch of sourdough.

"We let Yianna sleep." Stavros grabbed a bowl and began whipping butter for the Snowball cookies he would bake later that day.

"Yianna she work hard. She no need to know about my heart breaking for Marika. No place for that now. Last night I see Marika and tell her goodbye. I tell her she do the right thing to find her boy. And that I wait for when she come home. I say nothing about marriage so she can think only about her son. Now, we do everything to find Olympia."

From his pocket Stavros placed keys on the counter. "These for Marika's car. She say drive it while she gone. Only for emergency. And no drinking before I drive." He smiled remembering her gentle scolding.

At that moment the tinkling of the front door announced bad news. A middle-aged man wearing a short sleeve white shirt, black pants and black tie stepped into the bakery.

"Stavros Diamond-oh-police?" His voice trailed off mangling the last name. Nodding, Stavros drew near.

The man handed Stavros an envelope.

"You've been served."

The man flew out the door and Stavros instantly handed the envelope to Agamemnon, the better reader of the two.

"It say here the sheriff say you sell illegal booze. You gotta pay five hundred dollars or go to jail." Agamemnon threw down the papers.

Stavros crashed down in a chair. "That jackass! Sheriff Lewin get even with me. He no like Marika and me, when we come to his office. So he no look for Olympia." Stavros lurched to his feet and returned to the kitchen, beating the butter faster knowing he needed the income from each cookie to pay the hefty fine for his mistake in judgment.

"Gotta work harder," he mumbled to himself. "Gotta work faster."

SIXTY-TWO

Hours later, after Angel's Bakery had closed for the day, the card room was again full but not with players. At the center table, Yianna, Stavros, Agamemnon and Lucky finished their plates of *stifado*, beef stew with tomatoes and onion. Timoleon was absent, as an early shipment of Gravenstein apples had arrived at his fruit stand that day. Yianna relaxed into the warmth of her uncles surrounding her.

Agamemnon spoke quietly into her ear.

"I find the film you shoot on your trip." Agamemnon filled her glass with water while Stavros slid another spoonful of fragrant stew onto her plate. "I will develop for you. And I leave new film in your room. No matter what happen, Yianna, you gotta save room for your art."

Yianna smiled and pushed away her plate. At least someone had remembered she wanted to shoot photos, even if she'd almost forgotten herself.

"Thank you, Agamemnon. But now I've got to focus on Olympia. We all do." Yianna looked at the three old men who seemed to be waiting for someone to lead them. She stood up to speak.

"Tonight we compare the information we each collected about Olympia," she told them. "Then, we make a plan. And each person will have a responsibility."

The men nodded in agreement, willingly accepting Yianna's leadership. She summarized what she had learned on her travels and the information she found in Olympia's diary. Then she came to the most difficult part.

"Olympia was hurt." She took a deep breath. "She was molested."

Lucky looked to Agamemnon, needing a translation.

"Hurt!" Yianna repeated. She could feel her veins surging with anger at Olympia's attacker. Finally her rage boiled over and she spat out the words.

"Someone raped our Olympia! And left her with a baby that she probably delivered by now!" Yianna realized she was yelling, standing at her place at the table. "We must find him! He has to tell us where she is!"

Shaking violently, she collapsed into her seat, exhausted. She had said the word that proper women rarely spoke out loud. Rape. Not "rip," "bother," "hurt" or "spoil." Yianna had never heard the word uttered by anyone her age, or any female adult for that matter.

The air around her immediately cooled and a chill rushed up her back. The faces of the old men appeared pained that Olympia had endured this unspeakable act.

But there was no time for sorrow. She had to push on with her summary.

The diary said the kidnapper was trusted in the community. Olympia was kidnapped to force her to abort the baby as the offender wanted, but Olympia ran away from the place where the procedure was to be performed. Then a dark-haired young man found her and drove her to the Catholic sisters' compound in the Mendocino forest. She stayed there until her baby was due. She was most likely in labor as a dark-haired young man drove her away in a car with Oregon license plates. After Yianna finished spilling her cascade of facts, the men again fell silent.

Uncle Stavros' mouth hung open, in shock. He took a long breath as if trying to digest the news. He poured another drink and slugged it back. Yianna cleared her throat.

"Uncle Stavros, your turn."

After a few seconds he cleared his throat and spoke in a low voice.

"Marika and I visit Sheriff Lewin. She take the list of people the sheriff talk to. And the customers at Mira's. But they find nothing. They no do nothing with it. Now we gotta do the work." Again the old men were silent, unsure of the next step.

Stavros paused then rose from his chair and walked to the painted chalkboard listing the bakery daily specials. He pulled it off the wall and flipped the board to the reverse side. With a piece of chalk in his hand, Stavros struggled to write SUSPEKTS at the top of the board. He handed the chalk to Agamemnon who simply corrected it to SUSPECTS.

"The sheriff has a list," Stavros observed. "Now, we make our own."

In choppy letters, Agamemnon wrote the name "Deputy Robbie" on the board.

"Young, got dark hair and people trust him," he explained. "He on list at Mira's Tailor Shop. Olympia trust him when he drive her home. He ask Olympia to marry, and she say no. Maybe he angry for that." Agamemnon frowned. "I no like that man. For the sheriff he work like a little *skilohs*, dog."

Yianna gasped. "Deputy Robbie asked Olympia to marry him?"

Around the table, heads nodded.

"And the deputy know when she walk home from work. *Nah!* There! That's our man!" Agamemnon sat back in his chair, arms folded across him, case proven.

"The Reynolds man! Councilman Reynolds." When Lucky spoke it was a rarity. "He always asking for Olympia. For years he ask. I no like *him*."

"Yes! Dark hair. Kind of young, very slim," Yianna nodded. "That fits."

"A few years back he ask if Olympia go on dates," Stavros remembered. "I tell him no, she no date nobody. But he always look at the girls in a bad way. Like a wolf!"

"Agamemnon, add his name." Yianna instructed and he wrote Reynolds' name, the second on the list.

"I no like that jackass Sheriff Lewin," Stavros growled. "Deputy Robbie maybe he just move Olympia place to place for the sheriff. But I think that sheriff hurt her and keep her from us. Why else he no help us? He cover up his own mess. *He* do this to Olympia. He think he own this town."

Sheriff Lewin became number three on the list.

"Agamemnon, add Congressman Harrison!" Yianna raised her voice. "Maybe it's because I don't like his wife, Porter's mother. But he is a trusted man in the community. And he has dark hair. So that could fit!"

"But he is a *yeros*, old man, Yianna," Stavros added shaking his head. "The sheriff, his notes say his wife just bring his suits to the shop. He no go there. And he have family dinner the night Olympia go missing. His wife and boy say he was home the night Olympia disappear."

"Just because his horrible wife don't want her boy to mix with Greeks in a bakery don't mean he do something bad." Agamemnon offered. "But add his name just the same."

The front door slammed open and Timoleon stood there wheezing for air.

"I hear it all!" Timoleon panted and sputtered out his words. "The principal at the high school. Sullivan, Principal Sullivan. They find him with a girl. A young girl. Sixteen she is. He do bad things to her!"

Timoleon steadied himself by clutching the card table and he used a napkin to mop his brow.

"Gonna be in the paper tomorrow. More girls telling he hurt them too. All day everybody talk about this!"

Yianna bolted from her seat and began to pace around the table.

"Principal Sullivan always asked about Olympia when he saw me in the hallway years after she graduated," she remembered. She turned to the old men and asked, "What do you think?"

"Sullivan, he is trusted." Agamemnon agreed. "And young enough, with dark hair."

"And he on the customers list at Mira's." Stavros announced. "Tomorrow I go see Sullivan in jail or wherever they take him, if they let me."

Agamemnon circled Principal Sullivan's name on the board. The old men began to break up their gathering, each shuffling to his room. As they were leaving, Yianna took the chalk from Agamemnon's hand.

"There is one more name." Yianna's voice was flat and she walked slowly to the chalkboard. "They had a fight the night before she left. He was angry! He shook her! We can't ignore that. Young, dark hair. Now I hear he's disappeared."

Yianna slowly added a single name to the list.

Kenny.

Agamemnon read the name out loud. The men looked up and slowly turned away, shutting off the light behind them, while Yianna stood holding the chalk. They did not want to see Kenny's name on the board of suspects who might have harmed their Olympia.

SIXTY-THREE

The next afternoon Stavros took the long route back to Angel's Bakery, around the dusty outskirts of town. He moved slowly, unsettled, brow furrowed in contemplation. He was returning from the Yolo County Jail where he was allowed to see Principal Sullivan as a visitor. He had brought a pastry box of cookies, as if he were a concerned friend. Allowed ten minutes, Stavros met with the prisoner across a heavy metal table in the center of a large empty room.

When Sullivan entered the visiting room he seemed confused at seeing Stavros, a man he hardly knew.

"I am Diamantopoulos. Stavros Diamantopoulos. From Angel's Bakery." Sullivan looked suspiciously at the pastry box. Stavros shoved it toward him nodding his head as if giving Sullivan permission to open it.

"I come to ask, why you hurt my niece, Olympia Diamantopoulos?"

"What are you talking about, man?" Sullivan opened the box, shoved a sugar cookie in his mouth and began crunching. "I hardly knew her. And that girl was a high school dropout, anyway. Right?"

Stavros stiffened at his harsh assessment of Olympia.

"But you know Olympia when she at the high school. Ten, maybe twelve years ago?"

"From afar," Sullivan rummaged through the pastry box, pulling out a Snowball cookie. "A pretty one! Lovely!" He took a bite. "If I'm remembering correctly."

"You *do* know her!" Stavros kept his voice low, rumbling. "You hurt Olympia? Like you hurt the other girls? You tell me now!"

Principal Sullivan closed the pastry box with a smash. He leaned toward Stavros, as much as the metal table between them would allow. The guard standing nearby took a half-step closer in anticipation.

"You accusing me of being with Olympia? Is that what you're saying?"

Stavros nodded curtly, never taking his eyes off Sullivan's face, attempting to read a flinch or nervous tick.

"Listen, pal," the principal whispered quietly. "I've got enough problems here. Don't know if you've read the papers, or if you can even read. But frankly I don't give a damn about that girl. Yes, she was pretty. But so what? There are millions of those out there."

Stavros leaned in closer to hear Sullivan's words.

"That niece of yours. She must be pushing thirty by now. Over the hill. Not my type." Sullivan cracked a sly smile. "Besides, she was a drop out."

Stavros yanked away the pastry box and nodded to the guard. His visit was concluded.

Principal Sullivan's insulting words about Olympia fueled his brisk walk home. A drop out? Pushing thirty? Over the hill? Stavros' fury flamed as he marched on the outskirts of town.

But as the cool evening breeze drifted in from the Sacramento delta and pushed the warm afternoon air from the valley, his temper began to cool as well. Stavros dredged up his past experience with the men he had encountered in his youth — the cheaters, the thieves, the swindlers, the drunks and the unfaithful. Stavros could always immediately spot a shady character and smell a liar in his midst. After all, without his brother Christos, he could easily be one of them. As much as Stavros despised Principal Sullivan, his truth sensor screamed the principal had no interest in Olympia. Sullivan preferred underage girls, the type Stavros had avoided at all costs.

As he pounded the pavement near the tomato processing plant, Stavros turned the corner in the direction of the bakery. He could not help but reflect on Sheriff Lewin. From Stavros' view, the sheriff's pompous attitude was definitely a cover. Lewin was a lawman who could break the law with no one to examine his actions. It made perfect sense. He could have easily ordered Deputy Robbie to transport Olympia from place to place – a young man with dark hair. And Robbie's marriage proposal was simply the sheriff's own cover for lusting after Olympia himself. Stavros concluded the sheriff's guilt was the reason his efforts to investigate Olympia's disappearance were lukewarm at best. Stavros was sure the sheriff was the man to follow and his hateful words rang in Stavros' ears. *With these missing girls, the family doesn't know they have a boyfriend. Then the girl runs away with him while no one is looking. It always comes down to the girl leaving with a man.*

But what if the investigating officer *was* the boyfriend – the criminal? And how could he, Stavros, a simple immigrant baker, pin the deed on the number one lawman in the county?

As he trudged toward the bakery, Stavros began to cook up a foolproof scheme. He would expose the sheriff and the harm he caused Olympia. All his senses told him to lay out a plan to snare the devious sheriff. He would start tonight.

SIXTY-FOUR

Two days after the chalkboard meeting in the card room, Yianna woke up late, past ten o'clock. It embarrassed her that Uncle Stavros allowed her to sleep so late. She was ready to take her shift at the front counter now that she had no school to attend.

Wrapping a fresh apron around her waist, Yianna brushed her uneven hair. Aware she needed a proper haircut, she ambled to the front of the bakery to find Lucky behind the counter waiting for a customer in the empty bakery. He smiled his greeting as the bright mid-morning sunshine streamed into the bakery.

She looked up to see a poster above Lucky's head that read *MISSING!* The small poster featured Yianna's photo of Olympia looking into the camera lens, her copper cross tight around her neck. Below the photo was a description of Olympia and when she was last seen at Mira's Tailor Shop. A small stack of flyers had been placed near the cash register. Lucky pointed outside the bakery and Yianna walked out to the glaring sun. Every telephone pole and shop window displayed a *MISSING!* poster. She slipped back into the bakery.

"Did Uncle Stavros and Agamemnon do this?" Lucky grinned, nodding yes.

Yianna walked outside again, viewing the photo of her sister plastered everywhere. With Olympia's face looking down from all angles,

Yianna realized that her uncles had switched into high gear to find Olympia. They were contributing what they could. Just maybe this flurry of posters might bring Olympia to mind for someone, somewhere.

As she walked back to the bakery, a sudden breeze loosened one of the posters and it floated down the alley where Olympia's herb garden had once grown. Yianna chased after the poster and leaned over to pick up her sister's image from the dirt.

She heard a voice.

"You still looking for the bakery girl? Your sister?"

Yianna looked up to the second floor of the building next door to see their Italian neighbor, Mrs. Parisi leaning out the window, a printed scarf tied around her hair as if she had been cleaning.

Shielding her eyes from the sun, Yianna stared up to the light streaming between Angel's Bakery and Mrs. Parisi's apartment building.

"Yes, we're still looking."

"So you no find her?" Mrs. Parisi wiped her hands on a rag and leaned out the window sill. She planted her jaw on her fist in contemplation. "Too bad. Such a beautiful girl. And she love that Chinese boy."

Yianna forced herself to ask.

"So, you saw them together?"

"Lotsa times. But they fight bad last time I see. He yell. She cry."

"Did you tell anyone about it?"

"A while ago, the sheriff talk to me. He ask if Olympia know the Chinese boy. He ask me no more questions."

Heart beating faster now, Yianna smoothed out the flyer that landed in the tangled brown weeds which had overtaken the garden.

"I see it all. The Chinese boy very mad. Your sister cry. He shake her shoulders. She runs away from him. Then he chase her around the corner and yell for her. He so angry!"

Mrs. Parisi waved her hands in the air. "Then nothing!"

Yianna looked from the poster to the older woman. There was nothing left to say.

"Thanks so much, Mrs. Parisi. I'm at the bakery if you remember anything else."

Yianna gave the older woman a polite nod and turned to walk away.

"And that other man? The one your sister no like?"

Yianna spun around and looked up, squinting. "Other man? What other man?"

Mrs. Parisi had disappeared from the window and in an instant stood near Yianna in the alley.

"Yes, for about a year before your sister gone, a man come on Thursday night. Every Thursday. Olympia she gives him a white envelope. He not a happy man. And he always drive away fast."

Mrs. Parisi's voice hushed to a whisper. "And one time she get in the car with him!"

Yianna could not speak. Why hadn't this come to light sooner? What else was Mrs. Parisi hiding? Yianna steadied her breathing, trying to focus.

"Did you tell the sheriff this?"

"I no like that sheriff and his deputy. He ask me only few things. So I tell him only few things. Then he tell that deputy I don't know nothing. Just another old lady Dago, he say. He think I no understand English so good. So he no ask more questions." Mrs. Parisi lodged a hand on her hip. "He no ask. I no tell."

Yianna was silent, understanding the older lady's reasoning.

Then Mrs. Parisi brightened a little. "But I like you and your uncle's Snowball cookies. He always give me one free when I buy a dozen. So I tell you what I know."

"What did he look like? What car did that man drive?"

"Always at night he come, so I no see so much. Dark hair. Dark car. White shirt, tie. Suit always wrinkled. Just a regular car."

Mrs. Parisi took a few steps toward the building but suddenly turned around.

"One more thing happen. *Strano*, strange it was."

Mrs. Parisi's words drew Yianna closer.

"One night this man he get mad because Olympia no want to give the envelope. Then Olympia shove a big box at him—but he drop it. And guess what come out? Bottles! Red wine! What a mess it make. Broke glass and red wine all over the alley! Strange! *Strano! Strano!*"

Mrs. Parisi shuffled back up the stairs and Yianna's feet sprinted to the bakery and Uncle Stavros. Yianna was now aware her uncle's backroom wine business had gone completely off the tracks and had endangered her sister's life for a few extra dollars.

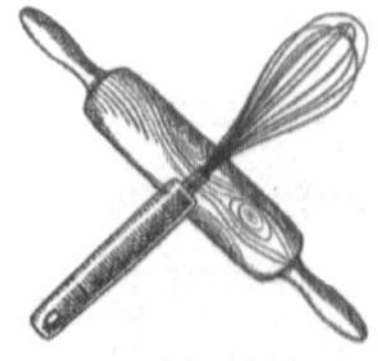

SIXTY-FIVE

Stavros' sweaty hands gripped the wheel of the bakery truck and his teeth clenched in anxiety. Although he was driving toward Sacramento, his mind stayed behind in the bakery, the cellar to be exact. He wished he could turn back time and take Agamemnon's advice: don't sell homemade wine to strangers.

Stavros lamented that his ego had swelled when he believed he could sidestep California law with his weekly exchange of dollars for wine with Johnny the insurance man. He seemed like a nice enough fellow, although Stavros never really believed this Johnny worked for an insurance company. The extra dollars had helped with the rent and no one was the wiser. What could be wrong with that arrangement? Apparently everything.

Earlier that day, Yianna had stormed into the bakery and found Stavros in the corner of his room struggling to pay bills. She relayed Mrs. Parisi's story of Olympia's money exchange, the description of the man and the crash of the wine bottles in the alley. Yianna demanded to learn the identity of this man to whom Stavros sold wine.

The description of the man's appearance hit Stavros with a gut punch. How could he have been so naïve? So greedy? He now realized what he should have sensed months ago: Johnny, who was so quick to make friends and receive backdoor wine, had blackmailed Olympia for extra cash each week. How had Stavros not spotted that he dressed like a government man, acted like a government man? He realized Johnny undoubtedly worked for the Alcohol Beverage Control. Who else would know or care about those regulations?

Stavros felt a tight grip around his heart. What had he done? Had Olympia truly paid off this man to cover his own sloppy business practices? Stavros stepped on the gas and hurried to the Alcohol Beverage Control office in Sacramento, hoping to encounter Johnny the "insurance man" getting off of work. If he could take a payoff, what else was he capable of? Had he hurt Olympia and left her with a baby?

An hour later, Stavros parked the truck across the street from where he suspected Johnny's office was located in downtown Sacramento. Flipping the visor down to hide his face, he inspected each employee trickling out of the windowless government building that looked like a prison. He would find Johnny and rip him apart.

The workers, mostly men and a few women, were released from work at exactly five o'clock. The crowd broke into groups to wait at the bus stop, stroll to their cars or simply walk home. After most of the employees had exited the building, he saw one lone man out of the corner of his eye. Stavros squinted to be sure. White shirt, black tie, black pants, wrinkled jacket. Yes, Stavros had his man. Time to avenge his own stupidity and shake the truth from Johnny or whatever his name was. Leaping out of the bakery truck Stavros swiftly paced behind him.

"Stop right there!" Stavros commanded, but the man kept walking. "You! There! Stop and turn around."

Johnny slowly turned to face him with hands up as if Stavros were a thief, holding him up for cash.

"Here! Take the two bucks!" The man tossed his wallet at Stavros feet. "That's all I got!"

Stavros kicked it aside and watched as Johnny slowly recognized him.

"What are *you* doing here?" He lowered his hands. "What do *you* want?"

With a shake of his head, Stavros silently motioned to move behind a row of camellia bushes.

"You tell me what you do with Olympia! My niece!" Stavros' words cut like a sharp kitchen knife. "What you do at night with her in the alley? Where you take her?"

"Whoa, whoa there buddy!" Stavros watched Johnny's eyes scour his body for a weapon. He was sweating at his temples. "You're that bakery guy. The one with the wine, right? I didn't do anything to your girl. She was protecting your ass, y'know."

"You break the law! You take her money!" Stavros was almost shouting.

"Shut up, will you, man? You're the one who broke the law! Selling illegal booze and wanting too much for it. One day I came to arrest you and that niece of yours said she'd offer a little 'stipend.' If I didn't press charges, that is. We had an arrangement! You can ask her! Your price tag was too high but I bought anyway. Because she paid me, I did not arrest you. Period. We both made out OK."

Stavros stepped close and grabbed Johnny's shirt pulling him close. "What about Olympia? They say you mad with her when you meet! Where is she?"

To Stavros' surprise, Johnny pushed him away and took a step back.

"I didn't touch that girl of yours. She was always complaining I asked for too much. I reminded her I could arrest you for illegal sales. One night she tried to pay me off with more booze. I dropped the whole lousy case. And once we went to the liquor store up the street so she could break a twenty into smaller bills. That's it pal. Don't be pinning anything on me. I haven't seen her in months."

Stavros took a step back and attempted to quiet his ragged breathing. Johnny stepped forward angrily wiping his wet brow.

"So when your girl didn't show up, I figured she didn't want to protect you anymore. Once the sheriff complained, I had to follow through. No reason not to. Your girl, guess she got sick of covering for your lowlife ways."

Minutes later, back in the bakery truck, Stavros crashed his forehead on the steering wheel. Johnny's words echoed in his head:

She got sick of covering for your lowlife ways.

Stavros sobbed in the front seat, using his sleeve for a handkerchief to wipe his face. Johnny was on target. Olympia had protected him when Stavros had completely failed her. He had exposed his whole family to the dangers of the outside world. His stupid wine sales had exploded in his face.

He and Johnny had parted ways with a man-to-man agreement: Stavros would not squeal about Johnny's kickbacks. And Johnny would find a way to drop the illegal wine sales charge with the sheriff. Honor between thieves.

Stavros collected himself the best he could and chugged the truck through the crowded streets of downtown Sacramento. He dreaded walking into the bakery to face Yianna and Agamemnon but he vowed to work harder, not only to find Olympia but also to possibly resurrect his shattered reputation.

SIXTY-SIX

Yianna sat on the curb outside the bakery, waiting for inspiration. She hoped that Olympia's spirit might somehow float along with the early autumn breeze and infuse her with a new direction. She toyed with her camera, which had sat idle too long. Only yesterday Uncle Stavros had returned from investigating the man from the Alcoholic Beverage Control Board. He could only spit out a brief explanation that the man was not Olympia's abductor but immediately vanished into his room. He refused to come out, no help to anyone.

Yianna knew one thing for sure. Olympia had covered for her uncle's bad judgment, paying out her own earnings from her tailoring work. With her uncle now secluded behind his door, Yianna was alone, again contemplating the next step of the search.

Sitting on the curb, she examined her own dismal situation: she was a high school graduate, working in the bakery with old Greek men, having produced no missing sister. Since she returned, Agamemnon quietly urged her to take more photos. Her memory of shooting photos with Will's encouragement began to fade as if it were only a hazy fantasy. Yianna could not go forward with her own future plans until she found Olympia, with or without Uncle Stavros' help.

Wiping her forehead with her sleeve, Yianna anticipated a busy afternoon shift when she heard the quick tap-tap-tap of high heels. She looked up to see Trina Harrison marching toward her. Stomach immediately clenching and breath caught in her throat, Yianna braced herself for trouble. Hands on her hips, looking down, Trina stopped in the street in front of Yianna.

"Why can't you leave him alone?" Trina's voice was jagged and she ground the heel of her black patent leather pump into the pavement.

"Who?" Yianna swallowed hard.

"What do you mean *who*?" Trina's eyes glittered, outraged. "My son, that's who! Porter!"

Yianna shot up from the curb to glare at Trina face to face.

"I haven't seen Porter in weeks!" She didn't care who might hear her shouting in the street. "I've been out of this town for over a month! Whatever you're thinking, you got it wrong!"

Trina exhaled a stiff breath of exasperation.

"Then what about this?" Yianna looked down at her outstretched hand. Something metallic glinted in the sun. Yianna focused more closely on it.

"I found this! And who else could it belong to?" Trina held her open hand closer to Yianna, nearly shoving it in her face. "It has your last name all over it!"

Yianna froze but her heart leaped to her throat. There in Trina's hand was Olympia's cross—the copper cross Olympia wore in the photo she had taken. The photo on posters plastered all over town and on the telephone pole directly behind Trina.

Yianna's words were halting and unsure. "Where—where did you find this?"

"Like you don't know! In our car! And it has your last name engraved on it!" Trina looked down to read it.

"'Diamond-oh-polis!' Or however you say it."

Yianna grabbed the cross from Trina's hand. Olympia's cross! The one Olympia had received as a baby at her baptism. Their father had engraved their family name on the back. While Yianna's thoughts ran wild, Trina renewed her grating tirade.

"Why does your kind keep coming back? You think you'll end up with my son?" Trina's eyes blazed. "That will never happen! In ten years, he'll be the youngest congressman in California history and take over our lumber industry. He can't be involved with some immigrant bakery girl."

Trina seized Yianna by the shoulders and shook her. "Just leave him alone, do you hear? Or there *will* be trouble!"

Not waiting for an answer, Trina spun around and marched away leaving her wrath in the space she had occupied.

Yianna's mind was a thousand miles from Trina and her threats. Olympia's cross! Trina found it in the car. Of course! Porter!

The mosaic pieces of Olympia's disappearance began to form a recognizable picture. Yianna realized who she should have been looking for all along. Porter, a young man with dark hair. Porter had somehow abducted Olympia and must be the father of her child. He had only pretended to love Yianna, to distract her from finding out the truth. He was the horrible perpetrator of the crimes against her own sister.

Porter had played her for a fool. Weeks ago she had actually mourned Trina's demand that she cut off any connection with her son. Now she realized Porter was a carbon copy of his mother: rich, wanting everything, doing nothing to earn it. A person using others for his own desires. How had she missed those signs?

Yianna pulled off her apron, tossing it on a chair inside the bakery and slung her camera over her shoulder. She nodded to Lucky that she'd be back later. In seconds Yianna found herself running down Main Street towards Porter's house, Leica bouncing against her body with Olympia's cross in her hand.

Yianna banged on the engraved front door glass which months ago she had admired. Now it was simply a barrier to the truth about her sister.

A plump maid in a grey uniform and starched white apron answered the door.

"Porter!" Yianna gasped, trying to catch her breath. "I need to see Porter!"

Before the maid could answer, Porter appeared and seeing Yianna, a giant grin spread across his face. The maid scuttled away into the living room.

"Yianna!" Porter seemed genuinely pleased but she would not be fooled. "Come in! So great to see you!" Yianna listened for a tone of insincerity in his voice but found none. "Want something to drink?"

Porter stepped back allowing Yianna to enter. She felt his eyes take in her ragged haircut and her camera. "Still shooting photos? That's great! Really miss you, you know."

Porter sat down on the sofa expecting Yianna to do the same. Instead she stood directly in front of him, unleashing her desperate words.

"Where is my sister?

Porter's face hemorrhaged from rosy to white.

"Heck if I know!" He looked away, his focus out the window, down the street.

"You do know!" At the far side of the room the maid instantly vanished closing the French doors behind her. Porter was suddenly breathing rapidly and beads of sweat popped out on his upper lip.

"Your mother returned this to me." Yianna held out the cross in Porter's face.

"What is it? I don't know who that belongs to!"

"It's Olympia's cross. Your mother found it in your car!"

"*My car?*" Porter bolted up as if insulted, his eyebrows pulled together in worry. "I haven't driven my car in ages. Come on! I'll show you!"

Yianna followed him to the side entrance and to a free standing garage. He pulled open the sliding door to reveal his dark Chevrolet sedan covered in a thick coat of dust and dirt in the dark, unlit garage. Yianna twinged as that was the vehicle in which she and

Porter kissed. One of the tires was nearly flat. The front bumper was crumpled like an accordion.

"I'm not allowed to drive it anymore. I got drunk on graduation night and crashed the car. My mother took the keys. She didn't want me having a police record before I go to Stanford. There is no way I drove this car after that. No one has!" But Porter's voice had hitched up a notch higher than when he first answered the door. "I don't even have the keys!"

He walked to the garage door to leave, waiting for her to follow. She moved closer, snapping a few photos of the dusty car. She stepped deeper into the garage to shoot another angle. Blinking in the low light, Yianna made out a form behind Porter's car in the deepest part of the garage. Another car. A dark sedan.

Her gaze drifted down to the rear of the car to see a sight that nearly knocked her off balance.

An Oregon license plate.

Yianna whirled around.

"Whose car is that?"

Porter began to stammer, no words forming.

Yianna rushed up to him, her hot breath in his face.

"Where is she?"

"The groundskeepers drive it around town. When they have to fix stuff. It's my family's but it's hardly used." He dropped his eyes to the ground.

Yianna spun around, turning her back on Porter. She moved closer to the car, snapped a few frames of the Oregon plates with the shutter wide open. Camera strapped across her body, Yianna darted from the garage, away from the criminal Porter and his loathsome family.

Two hours later, she stumbled home to the bakery, stinging from her visit to the sheriff's department. She had no alternative than to report Porter's actions to the sheriff. The secretary had reluctantly led her to Sheriff Lewin's office. Yianna hastily spilled everything she learned during her travels including the sedan, the young man with dark hair, the Oregon plates and her visit to Porter's home.

"Porter Harrison is responsible for my sister's disappearance. You've got to investigate! I've done all the work for you. The facts add up!"

Sheriff Lewin smiled at Yianna who was seated in the visitor's chair across from him. His casual pose seated on his desktop told Yianna he would do nothing.

"You gotta understand something, honey. You are mistaken." He looked down at Yianna from his perch. "Your sister must have been like the rest of you. You think you're better than the congressman's family."

Yianna squinted at the sheriff not understanding where his tirade was leading, waiting for an inkling of how he would help.

"You're forgetting Congressman Harrison owns Woodland. He is practically the sole supporter of the county orphanage and the two churches in town. He donates to every cause in this county and his wife heads most committees. He's a real upstanding philanthropist, especially to our Sheriff's Fund for Justice."

He stopped smiling and returned to sit in his chair and threw his pencil on the desk as if to wrap up the meeting. Deputy Robbie popped his head into the office but seeing Yianna, he hurried out the front door.

"That family is golden. The congressman could buy this town ten times over. Including your bakery and everything in it. His kid had nothing to do with your sister's absence. You can forget about it!"

The sheriff's words rang in Yianna's ears as she slowly walked to the bakery resentful and exhausted. *Nothing to do with your sister's absence. You can forget about it.*

The vision of the Oregon license plates rolled over in her mind. And then Yianna considered the Sheriff's Fund for Justice. She was sure there was no justice in Sheriff Lewin's territory—at least for an immigrant woman.

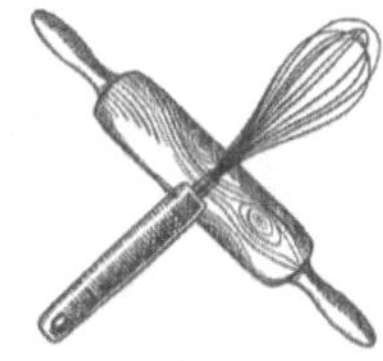

SIXTY-SEVEN

Slamming into the bakery, Yianna yelled to her uncle the story of Olympia's cross through his bedroom door. Stavros swung open the door to find Yianna in mid-sentence, explaining the facts about Porter's involvement.

"We go!" Stavros grabbed his keys.

Once again he steered the rickety bakery truck down the streets of Woodland, Yianna by his side. Yianna's story left him no doubt that Porter committed the crime. Although Yianna seemed bitterly disappointed the sheriff refused to help, Stavros was not. Years ago he learned that when in trouble, the rich and prominent were always allowed latitude by the law. They skirted sticky situations simply with a signature on a check.

Bounding up the front stairs two at a time, Stavros pummeled the door of Porter's mansion with his fist. The maid slowly opened the heavy door and Stavros pushed past her with Yianna close behind. As if he owned the home, Stavros lumbered into the Harrison's dining room where the congressman, Trina and Porter sat quietly at the dinner table.

With the maid running behind them gurgling excuses, Stavros rooted himself in front of the family. The trio looked up from their meal, confused by the old man in rumpled clothes and work boots invading their home. Yianna glued herself to Stavros, her camera over her shoulder.

"Give me my niece!" Stavros roared like a lion. "Olympia Diamantopoulos!" He gave the last name the full benefit of his Greek accent.

"Yianna say Porter take her! GIVE ME MY OLYMPIA!" Stavros' commanding voice bounced off the walnut paneling leaving the family speechless.

Yianna pushed forward speaking directly to Porter.

"Where *is* Olympia? What happened to her after she had her baby? Tell me!"

Porter said nothing and simply stared down at his plate.

Congressman Harrison vaulted from his chair, Trina scurrying behind him shielding herself from the intruders. Stavros watched as the congressman inched almost imperceptibly towards the phone. "I'm calling the sheriff! You must leave! Immediately!"

"Stop there! You no move!" Stavros' words had enough force to nearly shatter the crystal on the table. *"TELL ME! WHERE IS MY OLYMPIA?"*

"I don't know anything about that girl!" The congressman snapped, his eyes darting between Stavros and Porter.

Porter had slumped in his chair, looking up at his father, tears streaming down his cheeks. Stavros whipped his body toward the congressman. The switch had flipped. Stavros smelled guilt.

"Tell them Dad." Porter sounded drained, shattered. He laid his forehead on the dining room table.

All eyes flashed back to the congressman. Trina took a step apart from him, watching, waiting.

The congressman said nothing. Then a voice floated from Porter, his face still buried on the table.

"I just drove Olympia a few places to keep her safe, just like my dad told me. I drove her when she was pregnant and when she was in labor. Dad said she really needed our help." Porter's voice was small and shaky. "That's all I know. He told me we were helping her."

Suddenly Porter shot up from his chair pointing at his father. "*He told me to do it!*"

Porter was bellowing now between sobs.

"Dad said Olympia came to him 'in trouble.' He said your sister didn't want to shame her family and came to him for help. I thought I was helping your sister! Helping *you*, Yianna!" Porter's finger jabbed toward his father. "He knows what happened!"

Porter collapsed in his chair. Stavros watched Congressman Harrison slowly take a step forward as if making an announcement to the press.

"What Porter says is true. But I hardly knew your girl. She came to my office begging for help. She got in trouble. Pregnant — I don't know where. Probably with that Chinese boy I heard rumors about months ago. She didn't want that baby. Wanted to get rid of it. But I advised her to keep it. I was just trying to protect her. She asked me to help!"

Instantly Stavros jumped toward the congressman pushing him against the wall. His fingers wrapped around the handle of a knife dangling from his belt, fist clenched around his weapon. Spotting the knife, Yianna swept in front of her uncle firmly swatting his hand with one stroke to stop him. For a moment, Stavros hesitated, then unclenched his grip on the knife. He swiftly moved behind the congressman pulling his arms behind his back with the fierceness he learned on the dangerous backstreets of Athens.

"You lie. She never come to you!" Stavros leaned toward the congressman's ear and barked his words. "It's your baby! You do this to her! It is *you*!"

Yianna stared at Stavros in awe of his raw power.

Trina was a silent, frozen figure standing against the wall, eyes locked onto her husband.

Stavros yanked the congressman's arms farther back until he howled with pain. "You tell me now! Where is my Olympia?"

Stavros pulled the congressman's arms even harder causing his face to inflame like a ripe tomato. Rage unleashed, Stavros pushed him onto the floor planting his large work boot on the congressman's back.

"Olympia not want her baby? You a liar!"

Stavros pulled his boot off the congressman and readied to kick him in the ribs. No one dared to move.

CLICK!

All focus was on Yianna. She had used her weapon. Her Leica captured the congressman on the floor, fear paralyzing his face.

CLICK!

Yianna moved closer to the congressman's face, dripping in sweat, his eyes cruel and cold.

CLICK!

Yianna's camera framed Trina in shock, observing the violent scene, fearful of the outcome.

CLICK!

She caught Porter, face down on the table, hopelessly whimpering.

Suddenly the congressman broke free and the men were rolling on the floor, fists and blows everywhere. Then Stavros managed to slide his hands around the congressman's throat, ready to press down for the kill.

CRASH!

Trina had heaved a crystal wine decanter across the room. Red wine sluiced down the textured wallpaper. Silence hushed the room.

She slammed down her fist on the polished dining table.

"Where *is* that damn girl, Cole?" Trina hissed.

Stavros slowly released his hold on the congressman.

She, I, uh, well—" The congressman babbled as he crawled to a chair with Stavros poised to pounce. Completely motionless, Trina radiated piercing energy, not blinking, barely breathing. She then purposefully strode to the pile of glass shards on the floor, picked up a sharp piece and held it near her husband's throat. Her voice was low and mean.

"Tell me! *Now!*"

"San Pablo! San Pablo Valley State Hospital." The congressman's voice was hollow and his color was suddenly pale. "But that's the last I heard. I had nothing to do with it! I'm innocent!"

As Stavros and Yianna slowly backed away, she snapped one more photo: the congressman struggling to stand, Trina with the glass at his throat and Porter continuing to weep, head down on the table.

Turning away from the family, Stavros and Yianna sprinted out the front door.

SIXTY-EIGHT

Yianna sat next to Uncle Stavros on the hour and a half drive through the countryside past of the town of Sonoma to San Pablo Valley State Hospital. At the nurses' desk, Yianna took the lead and simply asked for Olympia Diamantopoulos. The pleasant nurse wearing a starched white cap looked through her files, finger scrolling down the page, reading glasses on her nose. She shook her head.

"No one by that name." Closing the book she looked up at Yianna. Not knowing her next move, Yianna retreated to the hallway where Stavros waited but she reversed her steps and marched back to the desk.

"Try again. Probably came in about a month ago. Dark hair. Very pretty. Olympia Diamantopoulos." Yianna's voice trailed off to a whisper. "Please, look again."

The nurse perused the list of patients and shook her head no. Realizing the congressman had lied to their faces, Yianna sat down opposite the nursing station, the exhaustion of the last few months seeped out of her pores. Beyond tears, Yianna began to shudder with desperation. She was disappointed, dog-tired and had come so close yet—

"Maybe we can look in another place." The nurse stood up and opened a large file cabinet. "I have a different list but she's probably not on it."

Yianna approached the desk. Pulling a large black ledger from the cabinet, the nurse flipped through it.

"These are the unidentified indigent patients. We have no background information on them. Some are mental patients, some not. Others were just dropped off for us to deal with. We list approximate ages, their sex and anything else that can possibly identify them."

The nurse turned the large ledger toward Yianna who scanned the list, holding her breath. Very few ages matched. But in the comments section one entry was listed as "female, mid-twenties, Mexican." Yianna asked to visit that patient's room.

While Uncle Stavros stayed behind in the waiting area, Yianna was escorted to a tiny room painted a grayish-yellow where two beds were separated by a cotton screen. The first was occupied by a woman with flowing black hair. With a flicker of hope, Yianna stepped around her to see a female about forty, chubby, definitely not her sister. Peeking around the curtain, the second bed was empty with only rumpled sheets strewn across it. Yianna's expectations instantly plummeted with nobody lying in the bed, no sister, no hope.

From the open window with bars across the panes, a soft wind blew the curtains into the room. Along with the breeze, a slight figure, almost a ghost, unwound herself from the curtains and stepped into the room. There, floating toward her bed was a gaunt, pale phantom. Yianna was jolted by the beautiful dark eyes that lay deep in their sockets, listless and heavy-lidded. The phantom's figure had winnowed to war-time thin, her arms willow branches at her side, hair matted and dull. But there! Yianna's eyes lit on the delicate Evil Eye bracelet, matching Yianna's, dangling around her wrist. It was Olympia! Her figure wafted toward the bed, eyes unseeing, then lay down, face toward the wall.

SIXTY-NINE

Three weeks later, waiting for a sign from Olympia, Yianna had hoped for more. During the many months her sister was missing, Yianna had pictured the glorious day she and Olympia would be reunited. She imagined their laughter and embraces would soon erase whatever horrors Olympia had endured. But those joyful dreams faded the day after Olympia arrived.

At first Olympia seemed to barely recognize Yianna and Stavros but had not objected to going home with them. Once at Angel's Bakery, Stavros took her arm and led her into her old, shared bedroom. Olympia climbed in bed and again turned her face to the wall, mumbling *drepomai*, I am ashamed.

Stavros and other uncles sat vigil outside the room, clacking their wooden worry beads, the cards sitting unused in a stack. Occasionally, a few bakery customers asked about Olympia as word had spread she was home. Yianna paced, sat and paced again, camera idle. Everyone at the bakery waited for Olympia to step out from the shadows and reach for a helping hand.

Yianna soon realized she had no right to expect Olympia to revive her previous spirit, just because her body had been escorted home. She had to assume that the previous version of her sister was in hibernation. What would be left inside? She doubted she herself, a devoted sister with a heart full of love, was enough to heal Olympia's wounds.

As Yianna shuffled out of their shared bedroom with another plate of untouched food, she felt inadequate, unsure how to help her sister heal. Again, her Olympia was out of reach.

Yianna walked to the card room and sat down to read a letter from Will. She yearned to be connected with someone who craved a world alive with art, current events and travel outside of northern California. Yianna simply missed Will and his adventuresome, optimistic outlook.

Agamemnon ambled into the card room and sat down next to Yianna with a colander of green beans. Pulling out a sharp knife he began cutting off the tips.

"So what you do now, Yianna?" He always had a way of reading Yianna's thoughts.

"Just waiting for Olympia." Yianna folded Will's letter and shoved it into the envelope. "She's not really back. I guess we wait some more."

"You can watch and wait and be busy too." Agamemnon pushed four rolls of film toward her. "You must keep working and not just sell Snowball cookies."

"You know I can't leave Olympia –" Yianna's voice trailed off.

"Why to leave?" Agamemnon sat back in his chair, arms folded. "You need to look around you, like your Dorothea Lange. She look close at people and where they live. It's all here for you."

Agamemnon produced the Leica she had abandoned and pushed it across the table with the film.

"While Olympia heal, you look through your camera. This you must do with the heart of an artist. You no have to wait. You work with what you have. I do this every day."

Wondering how this man, a simple shepherd and cook, had acquired such wisdom, Yianna watched Agamemnon closely as he moved toward the kitchen. Knowing Olympia was napping now, Yianna began loading film into the camera for the first time in weeks.

SEVENTY

Once again Yianna became best friends with the camera that accompanied her everywhere. She draped it on her back as she worked the bakery counter, often taking photos of willing customers as they crunched into their bakery treats.

Before Angel's Bakery opened for the day, she photographed the whisk, the pastry cutter, pie pans gleaming in early morning light. She captured Timoleon napping in the sun outside the bakery, hat tilted forward covering his eyes. Yianna focused on closeups of steaming French bread loaves piled on stainless steel racks. She captured the empty card room, wooden chairs around the table waiting for the next game to begin.

As Agamemnon kept a steady stream of film coming her way, Yianna trained her eyes to see the story inside ordinary people and the delicate beauty in everyday objects. In the evening, Agamemnon taught her how to develop her own film in a tiny storage room he had refurbished to become a photo lab. Encouraged to shoot every day, Yianna felt her heart begin to flutter open like a newly formed butterfly.

When Olympia was awake, Yianna rarely strayed far from the bakery in case her sister needed to talk or wanted something special to eat. But Olympia only nibbled on toast and sipped chamomile tea. Yianna brushed Olympia's hair and bought her a few new dresses for her thin frame. Occasionally Olympia smiled and quietly thanked Yianna for her help. It occurred to Yianna that Olympia might not know how to fit into the family. Was she a victim? A niece? A mother? And then there was the question Yianna could not bring herself to ask. What happened to the baby?

Three months after her sister's return, Yianna sorted through a stack of her photos in the card room. She lingered on the photo of Olympia when she was healthy and happy, the photo used on the poster plastered all over town. She had aged ten years since Yianna snapped that photo, black eyes sunken in their sockets, olive skin without luster, waist whisper thin.

Yianna stared at the cross Olympia wore in the photo. Maybe it could help again. Locating the cross from a small jewelry box, she simply placed the cross into Olympia's hands, curled her sister's fingers around it and took a step back.

Olympia silently stared at the cross. She took a breath and became animated for the first time.

"Where is he?" Olympia stood up with the cross in her fist. She spoke louder now. "Where did he go?" Energy seemed to flow through her body now.

Yianna rushed to her sister's side, amazed that the cross so easily broke the glass of separation between Olympia and the real world.

"Do you mean that Congressman Harrison? The man who hurt you?"

Olympia clutched the cross to her chest.

"No! My baby! He should be wearing this cross! I heard them say my baby was a boy!"

Yianna stared at Olympia face to face. This was the first time she heard Olympia speak more than a few words.

"The place I had the baby—wherever that was—I asked to see him, of course. They told me he was dead at birth. But I heard him cry after I delivered him. I know he is alive! I heard a baby cry down the hall when no other mother was due! He was calling for me! They told me he died!"

Completely unprepared for this revelation, Yianna attempted to hug Olympia, but her sister backed away, her eyes distant.

"My baby! I want my baby! I know he is alive!" A crackling life force returned to Olympia's black eyes. Then, suddenly she grabbed Yianna's shoulders, her face flushed with intensity, the first time since her return.

"I have to find my baby! I can't lose him! I know he is alive!"

In the hours that followed, Yianna listened as Olympia poured out the story she had choked back since her return. Yianna learned the place Olympia had delivered the baby was reserved for unmarried pregnant women, most much younger than Olympia. She heard the staff refer to the young mothers-to-be as "bad girls." She reported she barely arrived there before her delivery and stayed there for two weeks after. During that time she saw no mother leaving with a baby. Every young woman left without her child.

Olympia made friends with two other mothers, both teenagers. Their babies had been taken to a "good home," the head nurse had explained. And as a bonus, their entire hospital stay was paid for. The mothers and their families, mostly poor, paid nothing. The teenage mothers would be free from the burden of raising their child. When they returned home, their reputations could be restored. No baby. No problem.

"The nurse told me, 'Accept the fact that your baby is dead. In a few weeks you will forget about him.'" Olympia spoke in the dark as she and Yianna lay in their beds later that evening. "I begged for my baby's body for an Orthodox funeral. 'He's already cremated,' the nurse said. Imagine — so fast — cremated! They had no ashes for me."

Olympia heaved a sigh and looked away. Yianna was silent, listening to the cruel story of Olympia's delivery and a baby that was supposedly dead. That was enough anguish for a lifetime. But there was one more blow Yianna had to deliver herself. She had not wanted to brutalize her sister with the truth, now that she was just beginning to speak.

But the time was now.

"On your discharge papers, I saw something, Oly." Yianna moved over to Olympia's bed and squeezed herself next to her sister. "I'm just going to say it. I'm so sorry. You can't have any more babies. They sterilized you after you delivered your son."

The darkness inside the room became blacker, bleaker. Yianna could not hear Olympia breathe, she made no sound. Yianna wondered if her sister ever would.

SEVENTY-ONE

The next day, Yianna expected Olympia would become lost and silent again. Her sister had been robbed of a baby and now she knew her ability to have another was forever severed. How could all this happen to Olympia, a young immigrant woman, with no status in society?

Yianna realized Olympia had been raped, sterilized and her baby was missing because she *was-* a young immigrant woman who did not belong—an insignificant undesirable living on the fringes of society. Under brutal force she became pregnant and then permanently punished, forever reminded that society did not want her to bear any more children like her.

After the morning flurry subsided, Yianna restocked the Snowball cookies for the lunch crowd. She was surprised to see Olympia's figure suddenly standing in front of her. Her sister had brushed her hair, changed into a clean dress and stood with purpose on the other side of the counter.

"I will cry for myself later." Olympia's voice was strong. "But now we have no time to waste! Yianna, you must help me find him. The only one I will ever have. I need your help. Again. *NOW!*" Olympia's hand reached out to Yianna's and gripped it tight.

Yianna dropped the cookies and bolted out the door. For the first time in months she knew exactly what to do.

Minutes later, Yianna pounded with her fist on Porter's door the way Uncle Stavros had. Within moments Trina herself answered and motioned for Yianna to come around the back of the house, as if she were a servant. Yianna rushed to the back door and stood on the stairs, looking down at Trina.

"My husband is away, on business." Trina answered without being asked a question. "I have no idea when he will be back."

She swiftly tried to close the back door when Yianna pushed her black boot into the doorway. Pulling her Leica from her side, Yianna looked through the viewfinder prepared to snap the shutter.

"Put that thing away or I'll call the police! Don't you have enough pictures of us?" Trina's face was contorted but the door not completely shut.

"Where is Olympia's baby? I found my sister at San Pablo State Hospital like your husband said. So he must know where the baby was sent – Olympia's baby!"

"I know nothing about that bastard child!" Trina spat out. "Cole has been gone on business for weeks now. He left after you people invaded our house."

Then for a moment Trina allowed her voice to sound normal, human, almost one woman to another.

"I need to know where that baby is too." Trina looked at her feet. Was she ashamed of her vile husband?

Suddenly Porter was standing behind his mother.

"Yianna, try this place." Porter's voice was despondent, miserable. "I heard my father talking on the phone. It's where they sent your sister's baby." He handed her a scrap of paper with an address.

Within minutes of arriving back at the bakery, Yianna pushed Uncle Stavros into the driver's side of Marika's car, with no explanation. The address on the slip of paper was for an adoption agency in Lodi, California. With Stavros at the wheel speeding on Highway 12,

Yianna hung the camera out the window, shooting the passing landscape and tiny towns they passed.

They found the agency on the deserted outskirts of Lodi on the road to Stockton. Yianna photographed the shabby entrance and the deserted run-down waiting room. Stavros pressed his finger on a buzzer and a neatly-dressed woman in her late fifties answered and led them to sit at a desk.

"We want to ask about a baby we believe was brought here." Yianna immediately burst out talking before the agency woman said a word. "A boy. A baby boy born around August of this year. The mother delivered at San Pablo Bay Hospital."

"I'll look to see what information I have." The woman flipped through files in a cabinet behind her desk. Locating a thin file and she opened it and shuffled a few forms. "I seem to recall a baby boy from that area about that time."

"Hmmm. Birthday August third, father unknown. Mother "Olympia Diamond — something foreign. The mother signed off right here. The boy was adopted. A closed adoption. Let me ask my supervisor if there is anything else I can tell you."

Leaving the file open, she stepped into a small adjoining office. Jumping from her seat, Yianna darted to the desk and snapped a photo of the birth certificate. One glance told her Olympia's signature had been forged. The woman returned, shut the file, clasped her hands on top of it and smiled.

"Like I said before, the adoption is legal and sealed. After the child is eighteen he can look for his mother. I'm sorry. These files will never be made public."

On the ride home, Yianna and Uncle Stavros were silent. A live birth. Male. 8 lb. 3 oz. Father unknown. Olympia's signature. Forged. Someone would have to tell her. Looking over at Uncle Stavros whose gray face was drained of emotion, Yianna knew she would have to deliver the bad news — again.

SEVENTY-TWO

In the cool of the next morning, Yianna hurried to the Good Day Laundry, hoping no inquisitive eyes watched her leave the bakery. She had a plan and needed to put it into action.

Frankie, home from college, approached the counter with a smile. Yianna sighed with relief.

"Yianna! How's life treating you?"

As usual, Yianna calmed when she was near Frankie's warm friendship. She decided not to mention the gruesome facts that surrounded Olympia. Most people who cared about her sister were well aware she was home. That was enough news for now.

"Frankie, please help me find Kenny. Olympia needs his help. She needs to talk with someone who cares about her. We have done everything we can at the bakery." She looked deeply into Frankie's brown eyes. "She needs Kenny. She trusts him. You have to bring Kenny home to my sister."

Frankie pulled her aside speaking quietly.

"He's not that far away. Still laying low, just in case. He's been in touch with my father but us kids weren't allowed to talk about it with anyone. But don't worry, I'll let him know."

Nodding her thanks she spun out of the Good Day Laundry onto the street, face burning with shame. She, herself, had written Kenny's name on the chalkboard of suspects. Now she was begging for his help.

Weeks of silence passed, casting a sorrowful pallor over Angel's Bakery. From the outside, little had changed. But in truth, everything had calcified inside. The tension of Olympia's fragile emotional and physical health caused the bakery crew to eat dinner separately, grabbing a meal when they could, soon returning to work. No more cordial family dinners, no card games in the sala with the shepherds and friends. Timoleon's heart had weakened considerably and he spent much of his time in bed, away from his fruit stand and his vital vein of gossip. Lucky had taken many of Timoleon's shifts. Now Yianna worked the bakery counter alone while Uncle Stavros and Agamemnon turned out pastries in the kitchen.

When Olympia was missing, their world was kept intact by a slender thread. Now she had returned and lived like a planet fallen from their galaxy. The universe at the bakery was unbalanced, on the verge of disaster. Yianna's only lifeline was writing letters to Will, which described day-to-day life and her recent visit to the illegal adoption agency in search of Olympia's missing baby. Occasionally Yianna sent a few of her photos, hoping Will might continue to think of her as a photographer, not a bakery girl wasting away in Woodland.

Working behind the counter on a busy November morning before Thanksgiving, Yianna mused that although she was ten years younger than Olympia, she had reversed roles to become the big sister. Her hopes were glued to Kenny's presence in Olympia's life.

A week after Yianna's visit to the Good Day Laundry, Kenny appeared quietly at Olympia's window. Yianna had observed their silent meeting from a crack in the bedroom door and let out a sigh of relief.

Just maybe Kenny's love for Olympia might be the soothing balm that would allow her to live with the heartache of a missing son and the knowledge she would have no more children. Yianna watched them begin to walk together again and sit in Olympia's garden which Kenny cleared and replanted with winter herbs and bulbs for spring. Yianna could see Olympia's dead eyes occasionally flickering with interest.

SEVENTY-THREE

On a late November morning, Agamemnon finished his kitchen work and strolled behind the counter, wiping his hands on a clean towel.

"I show you something, Yianna."

Yianna watched him enter the darkroom and emerge with a large black leather book. Walking to the card room, he sat at a table and presented it to Yianna. She opened the book and was astonished to see Agamemnon had collected dozens of her photos capturing her surroundings: Timoleon at his fruit stand stacking melons; Lucky grinning behind a winning hand of cards; Marika wearing a silk white blouse and too much lipstick with a cigarette hanging from her mouth; Agamemnon in the makeshift darkroom with prints hanging behind him on a clothesline; Uncle Stavros with a swipe of flour on his brow, fingers deep in dough; the much-viewed close up of Olympia with the copper cross at her throat.

"Now you have pictures to show your San Francisco art school. I read the booklet. You got until March to apply for school. And then you go in September. Now you got something to show them!"

Agamemnon sat down next to Yianna as she leafed through pages of her own photos. Overwhelmed, Yianna held in her hands a portfolio of her photos capturing her Greek-immigrant world the way Dorothea Lange might have as a young photographer.

Yianna's words caught in her throat.

"Agamemnon, I can't thank you enough."

Agamemnon plunked down a stack of cash in front of her.

"Us mens play cards Saturday night. Everyone who win give money to start your school. This is your Uncle Stavros' idea. Time to help you too."

Yianna hugged Agamemnon with the portfolio smashed between them. She made a silent promise to use her collection of photos the way Agamemnon intended. Yet she continued to feel the long reach of Olympia's darkness and pain holding her back. She could not leave any time soon.

A month later, as Christmas loomed closer and daylight became scarce, Yianna cleaned the bakery case until it sparkled. In the glass she saw a familiar reflection and turned to see Porter in the doorway.

"Just thought I'd say goodbye, Yianna." Porter gripped a suitcase and looked down, not meeting Yianna's eyes.

"I want to say I'm sorry for what I did, how I helped my father."

Yianna was stunned to silence.

"I actually believed my father. I thought I was really helping Olympia because she didn't want her family to know about the baby. She said nothing when she was in my car. I just thought I was helping your sister."

Porter shifted his weight and switched his suitcase to his other hand. His voice broke but he continued.

"I'm leaving. Leaving my family. I let Stanford go. That was my father's university and I don't want part of anything he touched. I never thought he could hurt someone. But what he did." Porter shook his head. "And no one will ever make him account for it."

He patted his pocket. "So I took a hundred bucks from the cookie jar and I'll see where that takes me." He directed his thumb toward his mansion home and parents.

"To them, I'm just gone. Didn't even leave a note. Didn't want to."

He set down his suitcase and gently touched Yianna's shoulder.

"It seems so long ago. But I really loved you. I just want you to know I'm sorry. For everything."

Yianna watched as Porter turned and walked down Main Street toward the bus stop, not looking back to wave. She watched him with new respect. The person she believed to be a privileged rich boy had become his own man, determining his own future without the shackles of his family lies.

SEVENTY-FOUR

The winter dragged on as Yianna waited for Olympia to break out of her darkness. Yianna reminded herself to have patience knowing grief kept its own schedule.

Adding to the melancholy at the bakery, a few days after Christmas, Yianna opened Timoleon's door to wake him, but he did not move. He died of what the doctor believed was a silent heart attack. At his funeral luncheon at the Knight's Landing farmhouse, the four uncles were winnowed to three. Yianna flashed on vague memories of her father's funeral, at the same place so long ago, when Olympia had become her only parent.

Lucky had already taken over many hours at the fruit stand and seemed to enjoy the outdoor work. Deciding to take over Timoleon's business, he was away from the bakery most of the time.

Meanwhile, with no rollicking card games, the once-cozy card room echoed with emptiness, drained of cheer. Yianna's large photo of Timoleon mischievously peering from behind a handful of cards was hung in his memory.

On a dreary January afternoon, Yianna quietly worked in the tiny darkroom, developing the rolls of film she had shoved aside since returning from her journey in the Mendocino forest. Content in her work, she developed photos of the monied ceiling at the Washoe House and the giant redwoods near the Lost Coast. She also developed photos of Pete, Lula and Eleni in Garberville and the religious sisters in their secluded compound.

As she hung the photos to dry on the wire strung across the room, the door to the darkroom cracked open.

She turned to see Olympia creep into the dim space, stepping carefully as if she were entering a holy sanctum.

"Didn't want to disturb you."

Yianna held her breath. Olympia had not only left the bedroom but also ventured into the dark room, a place she had not yet braved.

"This is where you've been these afternoons after your shift." Olympia carefully observed one photo and then another, leaning in close.

Yianna looked up as Olympia examined the photo of the small cabin room she occupied at the religious compound; the photo of the kind Catholic sisters who looked after them; the bus stop at Fortuna; Jack behind the wheel driving his truck in the Mendocino forest.

Yianna quietly watched Olympia absorb the images of her own nightmare journey. "You did all this for me." Olympia posed a statement, not a question.

"I overheard stories Agamemnon tells of how you tracked me down. I know what you did, Yianna." She used the back of her hand to wipe away a tear. "You risked everything for me. And you still are, Yianna. You are standing still, waiting for me."

"I know you need time." Yianna quietly returned to hanging her wet prints.

Olympia walked among the forest of black and white photos hanging from the wires above: Lula and Eleni riding in the truck, Pete in a cook's apron leaving for work at the diner. Olympia's eyes widened as she observed the photo of Will, satchel on his shoulder, waiting patiently at the Civic Center Diner. She noticed a photo of herself sitting at her bedroom window as a mockingbird perched on a fence outside. Finally she squinted at the exterior of the San Pablo State Hospital and the interior of her room there. She quickly turned away.

"And look what you can do, *atherfi-mou*, my sister. Just look!" Olympia's words were filled with wonder and respect.

Yianna smiled and continued hanging photos, satisfied that Olympia had entered her darkroom. She expected nothing more but felt Olympia's arms sliding around her shoulders in an embrace.

"I can never thank you enough, Yianna. But you need to live your life now."

Yianna turned around to face her sister who seemed a trace healthier, the gold flecks in her dark eyes shimmering a bit more.

"I see what you can do, Yianna. Now it's time to show everyone else."

Olympia continued to examine the flurry of photos hanging from above.

"You know I'll be here as long as you need me." Yianna replied.

"You have been here. But it's time to live your life, learn everything you can. I have to heal on my own. Might take a long time, but you've given me all you can. Now it's your time."

Yianna felt another tight embrace and Olympia released her with a little push forward. For a moment, Yianna sensed Olympia slide into the big sister role. Yianna hoped it would stick.

"Go now! Show the world!"

SEVENTY-FIVE

About eight o'clock, when Angel's Bakery should have been closed for the night, Yianna lugged her feet to the kitchen. She clattered the tower of baking pans she should have washed hours ago. Timoleon's passing had unbalanced the bakery workforce, leaving Stavros, Agamemnon and Yianna to shoulder the work without Lucky. But in the last few days Olympia had occasionally been slipping into the kitchen to wash dishes or help lock up for the night. She said nothing but kept her hands busy.

Hearing Yianna run water and bang pans, Stavros and Agamemnon trickled into the kitchen and took their places. Soon a worn out Lucky shuffled in from the fruit stand to sweep the floor and polish the glass cases. After an hour, the kitchen was clean and they hung up their aprons for the night. Agamemnon and Lucky laid out ingredients for the early morning baking.

At that moment, Olympia quietly walked into the kitchen and waited for the bakery crew to become noiseless, motionless, like a conductor ready to begin a concert.

"I have news," Olympia spoke quietly but steadily. Yianna immediately ushered the group into the card room and everyone found a seat around a table.

"What news do you have?" Stavros poured small glasses of wine and slid one to each person. Olympia was talking! She had news!

"Kenny has asked me to marry him. He asked me a year ago, before I was taken away. But I would have only shamed him. And his family." Olympia sipped her wine like a hummingbird. Her cheeks flushed with color.

Yianna felt dizzy with happiness. She wanted to hug Olympia but dared not interrupt her.

"He asked me again when he returned two months ago, but I didn't want him to ask from pity. He wants to move to Berkeley. I want to go with him."

Yianna could not contain herself and rushed to hug her sister. Stavros used his handkerchief to dab away the tears welling in his eyes. Agamemnon and Lucky quietly smiled, waiting to hear more from Olympia.

"I love Kenny. I trust him. I always have."

Stavros stood and raised his glass. "I am very happy for you, Olympia. You and Kenny have my blessing!" Yianna smiled noting Olympia had not asked for his permission.

"A good man is Kenny. And a good family." Agamemnon raised his glass and everyone took another sip of wine.

"But after all you go through. You ready for people talking?" Uncle Stavros burst out. "A Chinese man? A Greek woman? Life gonna be hard – again."

Olympia's eyes were full as she considered her next words.

"Kenny is my strength. And you always say, Uncle Stavros, love is love." Olympia looked down at her wine glass, not meeting anyone's eyes. "I know none of this will be easy. I fight every day not to fall into sadness and stay there. Kenny makes it easier. With Kenny I can try."

Yianna embraced Olympia again with Stavros, Agamemnon and Lucky close behind.

Stavros looked up and turned to Olympia.

"So what Mr. Chen have to say for this?"

"He already approved our marriage. Kenny's sister Ellie eloped with a Caucasian man a while ago, so Mr. Chen was broken in. He's just happy he knows me and our family. And yes, he gave his blessing too. He says you two will be fathers-in-law!"

"Do we plan a wedding?" Yianna pulled up her camera and snapped Olympia whose eyes shone with a soft glow of contentment. Agamemnon and Lucky poured themselves more wine and drank it down.

Olympia cleared her throat and again patiently waited for the bakery crew to settle.

"Things are moving so very fast, I can hardly keep up." She steadied herself and continued. "I have more news. Next week, Kenny and I will marry at the Greek church in Sacramento. A very small ceremony. His immediate family and you. No party, no celebration because we leave soon for Taiwan. Kenny's cousin and her husband were killed in a political uprising and their three-year-old daughter is now an orphan. Kenny's cousin's daughter, he calls her his niece, has no one. No family. We will bring her home, here, and raise her as our own."

Yianna instantly felt deep admiration for her sister who had done the same for her.

"Now she will have us." Olympia looked at Yianna, Uncle Stavros, Agamemnon and Lucky. "All of us."

The group suddenly became quiet, content to enjoy a moment of joy after their year of despair. Yianna reached out to take Olympia's hand. Then each person around the table held the hand of the next in an unbroken chain of love with Olympia at the center.

"One more thing you should all know." Olympia's voice took on a somber tone. Turning to Yianna she squeezed her sister's hand tighter.

"I will never quit looking for my Christos. I have your photo of his birth certificate. I will never stop looking. And I will find him."

SEVENTY-SIX

Sitting at a table in the café at Angel's Bakery, Yianna was hidden behind the front section of the *San Francisco Examiner*. A fat letter from Will lay open on the table, contents spilled everywhere.

Agamemnon wiped down the counters while Stavros frosted cakes in the kitchen. Yianna let out a whoop and ran to find them with the newspaper in her hand.

"This article says Dorothea Lange will be in our area photographing the town of Monticello. Only about twenty miles away! The town will soon disappear because the government will build a dam and everything will be underwater. She'll photograph the changes to the land and the people who live there."

Yianna circled the kitchen waving the paper. "Uncle Stavros, I need to borrow the bakery truck! I need to drive to Monticello and meet Dorothea Lange. I want to work for her, even if it's for free! I've got to get there!"

Uncle Stavros nodded. "You know where the keys are. But maybe the truck not good enough. Lotta hills. You take Marika's car."

Yianna looked up concerned. "You think she'd mind?"

"She say it for emergencies." Agamemnon spoke for Uncle Stavros with a smile.

"And this is emergency!" Uncle Stavros completed Agamemnon's thought. "You need to show you reliable, a dedicated business-lady like Marika! You gotta go, Yianna!"

"You know I'm applying to the California School of Fine Arts, where Dorothea Lange teaches. Photography is my work, Uncle Stavros. My future."

A wash of confusion spilled over Uncle Stavros' face.

"Hmmm... A woman can do that? And make money?"

Yianna moved closer to Uncle Stavros and Agamemnon and slid from Will's envelope a *San Francisco Examiner* newspaper article.

Yianna read aloud the headline, *Illegal Lodi Adoption Ring Exposed by Will Stafford, Photos by Yianna Diamantopoulos* and she waved a check in her hand.

SEVENTY-SEVEN

Olympia's Diary

This chapter in my diary may feel like the end of my story, but I have come to realize it's just the beginning. I always lived in a shell, afraid of attention, fearful of men, terrified of losing someone I love. Now I've lived through all that — and I'm still here.

I am nearly thirty-years-old but I feel like I could be fifty. I am a mother of a son who is lost to me in America. And soon I will become a mother of a girl the same age as Yianna when I became her mother. Another orphan, another war, another soul scarred. My simple life was butchered by an evil man who tried to carve away my dignity and left my body and spirit in a heap of wreckage. Yet I am still here.

I never believed I was a strong person but I survived my parents' deaths and became uprooted and discarded in America. I survived the never ending taunting by men that drove me out of school only to hide my face and body. But strength comes in odd pieces and fragments, as do families. I've learned that now. Sometimes strength is a sister who never quits searching for you — no matter the cost.

I've learned sometimes you must simply create a family or just keep one together like Uncle Stavros who suddenly became a shepherd of two nieces. Maybe it's Marika who now searches for a son who was ripped from her arms. Maybe it's three old Greek bachelors who delighted in watching Yianna and me grow up. Now, I will piece together a family of my own with Kenny, his niece and maybe more lost souls. And I will look for my son, my Christos. I learned this from Yianna and Marika. Never quit looking for your family, as they are probably looking for you. The chain is never broken. I will use my strength and love to build the family I have — or the one I will find.

For years, I believed I was an outsider, caught between two worlds, never comfortable in either. Now I am certain — I belong to this world and this world belongs to me.

THE END

ACKNOWLEDGEMENTS

**I am deeply grateful to my family for their support
and patience throughout this writing journey.**
Love and thanks to my husband Daniel and
children Jessica and Thomas

**A sincere thank you for the countless hours poring
over my manuscript with your outstanding edits and ideas,
from grammar to logic to emotional content.
You are my safety net. THANK YOU!**
Lissa McLaughlin • Avery Econome
Mindy Anderson • Janet Econome
Dave Collins • Gia Plesha • Lori Tsukiji
Thomas Gutierrez • Daniel Gutierrez • Georgia Econome

**Much appreciation and thanks for your careful reading of this
book and your back cover commentary.**
Andonia Cakouros • Maria A. Karamitsos • Rich Moreno

**Your historical background information about
Woodland brought this book to life.
Thanks for the colorful details!**
Greg Kareofelas • Sue Russell • Jean Kareofelas • Nita Keehn
Tim Manolis • Annette Manolis • Frank Din
Diedre Din • Jack Din • John Din
Yolo County Archives and Records Center,
Rachel Poutasse, Library Assistant
Father Timothy Robinson

**Thank you for your graphic assistance on
the cover and for years of moral support.**
Allyson Pirenian

**Thank you for your encouragement,
knowledge about specific details and for always asking,
"How's the book coming along?"**
Claudia Stetler • Gege Manolis • Carrie Hamilton
Julia Gluesing • Angie Minkin
Irene Moosen • Christine Walwyn
Bill Sorensen • Stella Kwiecinski
Pauline Cazanis • Terry Kastanis
Rick Dower • Jackie Werth
Chef Timothy Garrow

**Your printing expertise was extremely
helpful on the cover design.**
Dennise Pennewell • Mike Craig

**Special thanks for your continuing expert tech
support on nancyeconome.com**
Bill Walters